That'll be the day when I die . . .

The second bell rang. Hope Hubbard realized she was late. With a sigh, she turned to open her locker. Her combination was 35–23–35, about which she was frequently heckled. It was a "famous" locker, since the numbers matched Lacey Pinkerton's measurements—or so the boys claimed. Hope dialed the combination, thinking lockers were pretty useless in a school as small as Paradiso High, where everybody knew every . . .

She started to pull open her locker door.

That was when she saw the hand—a girl's hand with pink-polished fingernails and a silver bracelet twinkling on its wrist. It had popped out at her, and was now dangling from the bluish-white arm that protruded from Hope's half-open locker.

Hope felt something heavy pressing against the metal door, and before she could unlock her frozen throat to scream, the door swung all the way open, and a body tumbled out.

Pretty Peggy Sue stared up at Hope with sightless eyes.

Her hair was tangled and her mouth was open, its bluish tongue lolling out. Around her neck was a tightly knotted cord.

Who Killed Peggy Sue?

Dying To Win

Created by Eileen Goudge

PUFFIN BOOKS

PUFFIN BOOKS
Published by the Penguin Group
Viking Penguin, a division of Penguin Books USA Inc.,
375 Hudson Street, New York, New York 10014, U.S.A.
Penguin Books Ltd, 27 Wrights Lane, London W8 5TZ, England
Penguin Books Australia Ltd, Ringwood, Victoria, Australia
Penguin Books Canada Ltd, 10 Alcorn Avenue, Toronto, Ontario,
Canada M4V 3B2
Penguin Books (N.Z.) Ltd, 182–190 Wairau Road, Auckland 10, New Zealand

Penguin Books Ltd, Registered Offices: Harmondsworth, Middlesex, England

First published in 1991 by Viking Penguin, a division of Penguin Books USA Inc.
3 5 7 9 10 8 6 4 2
Produced by Daniel Weiss Associates, Inc.
33 West 17th Street, New York, New York 10011
Copyright © 1991 Eileen Zuckerman and Daniel Weiss Associates, Inc.
Cover illustration copyright © 1991 Daniel Weiss Associates, Inc.
All rights reserved

Library of Congress Catalog Card Number: 91-52894
ISBN 0-14-034887-5
Printed in the United States of America
Set in Avanta

Dying To Win

Friday, May 26

CHAPTER 1

A shrill, metallic wail split the air. Hope Hubbard bolted upright in her bed. Her arm shot out to silence the sound, and she gave her alarm clock a vicious smack.

Better. Much better. Calm returned to the room. The clear, bright California sun streamed in under the shades, throwing stripes of daylight on Hope's lavender rug. Birds chirped outside. In the distance, a lawn mower whirred softly. Another perfect morning in Paradiso.

Mmm. Hope nestled her head under her pillow and closed her eyes again. Just five more minutes. Maybe ten. Then she'd get up. But as she realized what day it was, she was suddenly wide awake. Today the suspense was over. Today, one of the four finalists would be chosen Queen of Saturday's Peach Blossom Festival.

1

Hope got right out of bed and headed for the shower, giving her computer a "Good Morning" pat. Did her cousin April stand a chance of winning? Everyone knew April was the best artist at Paradiso High, but the race for Peach Blossom Queen was more than a talent contest. Hope got into the shower and turned her face up to the spray of cool water. Besides, April's competition was pretty stiff. But wouldn't it be incredible if she won? She really deserved it. As far as Hope was concerned.

Hope dressed quickly, pulling on her baggy blue jeans and gray sweatshirt. She went down to the kitchen and switched on the radio.

All a' my love, all a' my kissin',
You don't know what you been a' missin',
Oh boy!

KPOP, Paradiso's only radio station, was playing yet another Buddy Holly hit. As if a whole week of Buddy weren't enough.

But the theme for this year's Peach Blossom Festival was the Fifties. The Queen—whoever she would be—had already been nicknamed Pretty Peggy Sue by all the kids at Paradiso High School, and KPOP was playing every note Buddy Holly had ever recorded.

2

Stars appear, and the shadows a' fallin' . . .

sang Buddy now. Hope began preparing her usual breakfast: six strips of bacon, two scrambled eggs, and three dinner-plate-size pancakes, all of which—bacon, too—she would drench with Sacramento Valley honey. BEST HONEY EAST OF EDEN, proclaimed the label on the plastic dispenser.

She poured two glasses of orange juice from the gallon-size jug in the fridge and put a single slice of low-cal wheat bread into the toaster. The toast was for her mother, who always said that Hope got her tall, reed-thin frame from her father. "That's lucky for you, but thank goodness you got everything else from me," Leanne Hubbard would add. Hope's father had left when she was a baby. She didn't even remember him.

The toast popped. Hope spread it with margarine, cut it diagonally, and placed it on the kitchen counter next to her mother's orange juice.

You were meant for me. . . .

concluded Buddy Holly and his Crickets. Then KPOP's own T. J. the D. J. came on, babbling smoothly: "Well, hey and yo! That was the LEGEND of LUBBOCK himself with 'Oh, Boy!' And, oh, BOY, it's a gorgeous day here in POP-land! The shadows may not be a' fallin' anymore, not at seven-fifteen on an AWESOME May a.m. Mr. Sun's been up a long time. The peach orchards are a' bloomin', the little birds are a' singin', and the whole valley's a' buzzin' about Pretty Peggy Sue. Who will it be, guys and gals? Who will wear that GORGEOUS crown? Who will win the FULL COLLEGE SCHOLARSHIP and the HOLLYWOOD SCREEN TEST? Will it be Lacey Pinkerton? Raven Cruz? Kiki De Santis? Or April Lovewell?"

April! Hope wished. *Please be April.* But it was going to be close. Hope had grown up with all the contestants, and each one had plenty of reason to win. Even Lacey, who Hope thought might have been a rattlesnake in a past life. Lacey *did* know how to have fun, though—and she was beautiful and the most popular girl in the senior class. Raven and Kiki were no slouches either. But April was really special. She was Hope's best friend, and her cousin, too.

Ever since Hope could remember, her mother had been telling her to stay away from Uncle Ward and Aunt Sara, who were probably the strictest and most uptight people in Paradiso. "And stay away from April, too," she always added. "If you're not good enough for my brother and his wife, then *his* daughter isn't good enough for *you.*" But in spite of all this adult bad-mouthing—or maybe because of it—the two girls were friends. Hope knew she would be the first to cheer if her cousin won the crown. Leanne, Hope's mother, wouldn't be too happy about it, though.

Leanne Hubbard came rushing into the kitchen then, in a hurry as usual, pinning a plastic nametag onto her nurse's whites.

Lunging abruptly, Hope clicked off the radio, ending T. J. in mid-babble.

Too late.

"Did I hear him say 'Lovewell?' " demanded Leanne Hubbard, sitting down to her juice and toast.

Pretending not to have heard her mom's question, Hope made a great racket and clatter with skillet and spatula, plate and fork, as she dished up her own food.

"Hope!" said her mother. "I asked you a question!"

"I can't help what comes over the radio, Mom," Hope said. Wasn't her mom *ever* going to lighten up?

"Don't talk with your mouth full! It's so . . ."

"Gross?" mumbled Hope, chewing.

". . . un*lady*like. And how can you eat that—that mess? All that honey!"

Hope speared another humongous forkful of breakfast, which not only tasted great but had also gotten her mother off the subject of . . .

Sorry, no such luck.

"My brother," declared Leanne Hubbard, with that sour voice and pinched expression Hope hated, "Ward Lovewell, may be a minister of the church, and all kinds of people here in town may think he's a champion of charity and good works, but . . ."

Hope stopped listening after that first deadly *but*. After all these years, she knew the story by heart. How Hope's father had taken off—*for good, for keeps,* and *forever,* leaving Leanne Lovewell Hubbard and tiny Hope in a rented mobile home from which they were soon evicted. Leanne hadn't even considered going to her parents for help, since they'd branded Louie Hubbard a "greasy-haired Elvis-Presley hood" as soon as they'd laid eyes on him.

"I actually expected my brother to *help* me!" Leanne said now, sitting across the kitchen table from Hope, tearing the crust of her toast into nearly microscopic particles.

"I carried you all the way over to the Church of Christ, lugging our single suitcase. We had just seventy-seven cents to our name, and that's only because I checked under the couch cushions before Calvin Pinkerton's thug kicked us out."

Hope's mom went on, imitating Ward Lovewell's flowery pulpit voice: "Leanne, there's truly nothing I'd like more than to ask you in, but

6

that would be the wrong thing to do. It would make you weak and dependent. Worse, it would reward your willfulness."

Hope watched as her mother took a swallow of orange juice, grimacing as if it were sour. "He hasn't changed a bit," Leanne continued in a tiny voice. "Neither has Sara. They're both bad people, mean and hard, and that's all they'll ever be."

"Yeah, Mom," said Hope, feeling close to tears. All that stuff had happened so long ago. Couldn't it be laid to rest? Hope had no doubt that her mother had been badly treated. But what did it have to do with *now*, with April and her?

April was nothing like her parents. Uncle Ward and Aunt Sara were just as judgmental, cold, and uptight as Hope's mother said, but April somehow had managed to escape that. If anything, where Ward and Sara were completely sure of themselves and their superiority over ordinary mortals, April had a small self-confidence problem. In fact, it probably came from the sheer impossibility of living up to her parents' standards of behavior—that and the way Lacey Pinkerton, whom April worshipped, took advantage of April's kindness and generosity to treat her like some sort of personal handmaiden.

But the people who really knew April—Spike Navarrone; her art teacher, Mr. Woolery; Hope—and even some people who didn't know her so well, admired April. For starters, she could paint anything—landscapes, portraits, still lifes. And each one of her paintings was like a window into her soul, which was as warm and rich as the thick, curly, red hair that cascaded around her round, open, welcoming face. Hope smiled to herself. Ward and Sara didn't allow April to cut her hair, because it was her "crown of glory." They might have thought twice about that prohibition, if they'd had any inkling of the effect of that hair, combined with April's fabulously healthy body (nourished by a diet of wholesome foods—no junk and no caffeine to defile the Lord's temple) and her friendly, eager-to-please personality on the male population of Paradiso.

"When my brother closed the door on us that night," said Hope's mother, finally ending her story as she always did, "you and April both broke into tears. Neither of you could possibly have understood what was happening."

"Probably the reason April and I were crying that day," said Hope gently, desperate to make her mother understand, "was because we *did* know what was happening. You and Uncle Ward and Aunt Sara were tearing us apart. We're first cousins. We're meant to be close."

Leanne swallowed some orange juice, saying nothing.

8

Well, thought Hope, April and I *are* close. So there. They had to hide their friendship from Leanne, Ward, and Sara, but they shared confidences all the time, especially about April's boyfriend, Spike. His name was actually Carlos, but everybody called him Spike. He was gorgeous, and he rode a Harley Davidson motorcycle. If Ward and Sara Lovewell hadn't approved of Louie Hubbard, they would go totally ballistic to learn that their daughter was dating a biker.

But Hope had the feeling that something was up between April and Spike—something bad. Yesterday afternoon, in Mrs. Tugwell's sixth-period English class, while Mrs. Tugwell was chalking "Hamlet: indecisive; Ophelia: neurotic" on the blackboard, April leaned across the aisle between the desks and whispered to Hope: "Can I see you after school? There's something important I have to talk to you about."

Hope could guess what: since last week, April had been worried because Spike didn't want to "sneak around" in order to date her. And Hope wanted the chance to talk to April about Jess Gardner. But she hadn't been able to find her cousin after the final bell at three-fifteen.

"Want a lift to school, honey?" Leanne asked, pausing at the front door. She was trying to be nice,

9

Hope knew from the tone of her voice, trying to make up for the way she'd acted with April.

Hope *wanted* her mother to be happy, and for the two of them to get along. But she *didn't* want to be seen in Leanne's decrepit, powder blue 1981 Ford, which had over 130,000 miles to its credit, and looked like the loser in a demolition derby. It would be death even to *think* of being caught in the Ford by Lacey Pinkerton and Kiki De Santis.

Leanne lingered at the door, straightening her uniform, fiddling with her car keys. Hope knew her mother was trying to apologize somehow. Finally, in a ragged, almost tearful-sounding voice, Leanne said, "I love you, honey. Have a wonderful day."

Hope swallowed the lump in her throat, then replied, "You too, Mom."

Later that day, when Hope remembered the exchange, it seemed not like the apology her mother had intended, but like an awful, accidental curse.

CHAPTER 2

Hope licked her fork clean of honey, put her dishes in the sink, and picked up her red backpack. It held a textbook in advanced calculus, a thick paperback copy of Gibbon's *Decline and Fall of the Roman Empire,* Flaubert's *Madame Bovary* in French, four books on computer science from the school library, and the May issues of *Sassy, Sports Illustrated,* and *Motor Trend.* In her sophomore year, while fretting with a tampon in a girls' room stall, Hope had heard potentially disastrous chatter about the "class brain" who "studies all the time" and "even reads stuff she doesn't have to." It didn't take long for Hope to figure out who the "class brain" was. She had asked April how to combat— or at least control—the social damage. April had advised, "Why don't you have a magazine or two sticking out of your junk? It won't make you dumber, it might help your image, and you might learn something new."

Now, locking the door and leaving the house, Hope made sure the top of the magazines protruded from her backpack. Maybe Jess Gardner would notice and say something, stop a minute and talk to her. Hope knew he liked *Sports Illustrated*, *Motor Trend*, and *National Lampoon*. Hope knew just about all there was to know about Jess Gardner, in fact, except what it would be like to date him. And, now that Lacey Pinkerton had dropped Jess . . .

Nope, never happen, mourned Hope. Swimming champ Jess, with his thick reddish-blond hair and denim-blue eyes, was way out of reach. Even if April *had* said she'd heard he didn't have a date for the Peach Blossom Ball yet. Still, Hope could always make him smile. She remembered the other day in the cafeteria, when she'd joked about the "mystery-meat" loaf, saying the only mystery was why anyone would want to eat it, and Jess had laughed, throwing back his head, his eyes sparkling. She'd felt so great right then, as if she really might stand a chance.

But now, walking up DeSoto Drive toward Old Town Road, Hope gloomily pondered the subtle distinctions between being "well-liked," "popular," and "date bait." Did you just get *born* into one of those categories and stay there all your life? Or was it possible, with a little plotting and effort, to move from one plateau to another? She'd heard a thousand times how "intelligent" she was, how "well adjusted," how "easy to get along with." Certainly, those weren't bad qualities, although not as socially valuable as "pretty" or "beautiful" or "hot." Kiki De Santis was pretty, Raven Cruz was beautiful, and Lacey Pinkerton was definitely hot. Hope Hubbard was . . . well, Hope Hubbard.

Something else, too. "She's a computer whiz," Hope had overheard Principal Appleby telling Mr. Woolery, the hunky art teacher. "I wouldn't be at all surprised to read about Hope someday in the business pages of the Sacramento *Bee.*"

Hope used to consider her computer skills maybe just a little above average. She'd enjoyed using the Commodore in her room at home, as well as playing with the more sophisticated Macintoshes at school. But now things were beginning to get really interesting. Remembering her new computer "game," Hope felt her spirits rise. All week long she had been using her skills to track bets on the Peach Blossom Queen competition. She kept a record of all bets and calculated the changing odds on her Commodore. In her locker at school, tightly rolled inside a tennis-ball container, was a computer printout with all the final data on it. Her mother wasn't a snooper, but Hope didn't want that stuff lying around the house. Hope began to wonder if she might not have some criminal tendencies: after all, she was a bookie!

This morning the sky was cloudless and brilliantly blue, and the May sun was comfortably warm. The air was perfumed with the blossoms of a hundred thousand peach trees in the orchards all around town and the faint, acrid tang of the native scrublands west of town—land untouched since the last glaciers had receded. Hope frowned as she remembered that if Lacey's father, Calvin Pinkerton, got his way there would soon be a huge shopping mall on the scrublands. Cal Pinkerton owned Pinkerton Canneries—Paradiso's only industry—and he owned half the town as well, it sometimes seemed. Now he was after the scrublands. All that natural beauty, not to mention quite a few animals, would be gone forever. Hope felt herself getting angry. And she knew she wasn't the only one. There was a lot of controversy about the mall, and Raven Cruz, one of the four prospective Pretty Peggy Sues, had organized the local opposition. All right, Raven! Hope thought.

Hope really admired Raven's fiery, fighting spirit, but the odds against her winning the Peach Blossom crown were three to one. There was very little that any of the contestants could do to improve their chances. The four finalists had been chosen through an official ballot of students, printed in the *Grapevine*, Paradiso High's student newspaper. But the final choice would be made by a committee composed of the four senior class officers, three teachers—including Mr. Woolery, the dreamboat art instructor—two ancient fuddy-duddies from the school board, and Principal Appleby. What made everything so dicey, including Hope's computer calculations, was that the committee didn't have to choose the prettiest girl (Lacey), or the most intelligent (Raven), or the nicest (Kiki), or the most talented (which everybody agreed was April). The committee could choose any one of the four girls, depending on how they felt when they met to decide.

Hope turned onto Old Town Road and shifted her backpack to her other shoulder. She'd heard a rumor yesterday afternoon, while looking around school for April, that the selection committee was going to meet at Principal Appleby's house last night. If it was true, there were at least ten people in Paradiso this morning who knew the identity of Pretty Peggy Sue. Formal announcement of the Peach Blossom Queen selection was always made at an all-school assembly, just before Friday's classes ended. Hope had decided that she wasn't going to wait until three o'clock to find out who had won. Curiosity nibbled at her insides. There had to be a way to get the jump on everyone else. Who among the selection committee members would be most likely to blab?

Sheriff Rodriguez cruised past Hope in his black and white Plymouth. He was always out on Old Town Road in the morning, ready to ticket kids speeding on their way to school. Hardly a day went by without the sheriff's nailing at least one perpetrator, and at least once every two or three weeks he hauled Lacey Pinkerton and her red Ferrari over to the side of the road.

Hope was not surprised to see that Carter's Drugstore was already open at twenty minutes to eight. It had probably been open since six, because old Mr. Carter suffered from galloping insomnia. Also, he'd been very busy this week, having ordered a huge shipment of Brylcreem, which was selling in quantity. All the guys wanted to look "Fifties" at the Peach Blossom Ball on Saturday night, and Brylcreem was just the thing. The girls, in the meantime, had been hunting through closets and basements, attics and garages, in search of old saddle shoes and poodle skirts.

Hope pictured herself in a swirly skirt and tight

16

sweater, her hair pulled back in a bouncy ponytail. And beside her, Jess, in a motorcycle jacket, his hair slicked back, whispering in her ear, "Show me your stuff, baby." No, wait. Jess would never say that. Nor could he ever look like a greasy biker. There were those blue eyes of his, for one thing, open and warm as the sky overhead. And the way his reddish-blond hair curled down around his ears. And that adorable hole in his jeans, just above his left knee. What she *could* imagine him saying to her was something incredibly cool, but incredibly romantic, like . . .

"Hi, Hopey!"

Hope was rudely jerked from her fantasy. *Oh. God. No.* It was Winston Purdy III, the loony son of Paradiso's one psychiatrist, pedaling past Hope on his three-speed Schwinn. Hope was terrified that Winston would ask her to the ball.

Please don't stop! prayed Hope. She glanced around and saw a school bus coming up the road.

Winston geared down, matching Hope's pace. It didn't bother Hope that he was skinny and gangly and goofy-looking. But Winston might have purchased a comb, brushed his teeth, changed his clothes at least every other week, and found an inconspicuous place to stow the seventeen Bics, the scientific calculator, the protractor, and the tape measure that bulged in the front pocket of his once-white short-sleeved sport shirt.

"Hi, Winston," Hope said dutifully, wondering how to get him on the move before the bus came closer.

"I see you like *Motor Trend*," observed Winston Purdy III, coasting unsteadily alongside the curb. Before Hope had a chance to respond, Winston, still wobbling on his Schwinn, added, "Uh, Hope, about the Peach Blossom . . ."

Hope closed her eyes and prayed, *No, please, please, don't ask me to the ball . . .*

". . . Queen," she heard Winston say, and relaxed a bit. "I'd like to place my bet on your cousin April. Say, uh, ten dollars."

"Sure," she said, then lowered her voice and added, "Just don't let it get back to Mr. Appleby. He'd have a fit if he knew about this." She could hear the bus very clearly now: fat tires hissing, old engine growling, kids yelling. "Why April?" Since she'd begun taking bets, Hope had been fascinated by people's choices. She would have figured Winston for a fan of the more exotic sort of Queen, like Raven Cruz.

Winston blinked at her and fiddled with his Bics. "You don't know? There's lots of things around here that people don't understand. But maybe they will, sooner than you think." He cast

18

her a dark look that sent a dart of unease through her. Did Winston really know something, or was he just being weird, as usual?

The bus rolled by, all windows open to the nice day, everybody looking and yelling. "I'll save you, Hope!" yelled some boy, in a falsetto voice. A girl cried, "True love! True love!" There were a lot of loud, elongated *"Naaaaays!"* too, because if Winston Purdy III had a nickname, it would have sounded like the call of a horse.

Finally the bus moved out of range and Winston wavered after it, not looking back. Hope noticed a cord or thin rope of some kind sticking up from the right rear pocket of his high-belted polyester pants. A Bic pen fell out of his shirt pocket and bounced onto the street, where it was immediately flattened by the thick black tire of Spike Navarrone's "Hog." Spike whipped past, leaving Winston Purdy III in a cloud of dust and exhaust fumes.

Sometimes Spike stopped and offered Hope a ride to school. Not today, though. And what on earth was *with* nerdy Winston? There's been a kind of taunt in his words that Hope didn't like at all.

Was something going on here in town? Something that she didn't know about?

Hope reached the intersection where Winding Hill Road dead-ended into Paradiso's main drag. The Cutter State Savings and Loan, a windowless pile of white brick, squatted next to the new glass-and-steel Pinkerton Building. Between the Pinkerton Building and the almost as impressive Paradiso Clinic and Counseling Center was Huck Spector's barber shop. It was a real eyesore, hardly more than a shack. All the guys at school went there to get their hair cut . . . and to riffle through the pages of Huck's collection of "adult" magazines. Cal Pinkerton and Lars Cutter, who was Pinkerton's partner in the Greenway Mall plan, had tried several times to have the barbershop condemned. But Huck was still in business, and his example had encouraged opponents of the Greenway Mall. If eccentric, brandy-nipping old Huck could stand up to Cal Pinkerton, well, maybe they could too.

Hope paused, waiting for the green light, and glanced up Winding Hill Road. No sign of Lacey or her Ferrari, nor of Kiki De Santis in her dad's Isuzu Trooper II. Were they late this morning, or were they already at school? As Queen contestants, they'd be even more curious than everyone else to find out who'd won the Peach Blossom crown.

Hope walked past the Church of Christ, a gleaming white clapboard building with a thin white steeple. REV. WARD N. LOVEWELL, read the black and white sign in front of the church. The theme for Sunday's sermon was also on the sign:

Would Uncle Ward ever learn to start practicing what he was obviously preaching?

Again, Hope got that deep-down feeling that something bad was bound to come out of this feud —something even worse than what had already happened. Remembering yesterday, her cousin's white, tense-looking face when she'd whispered to Hope that she had "something important" to tell her, Hope wondered now if April was in some kind of trouble with her parents. Had her aunt and uncle found out about them sneaking off to the movies together last Saturday? Or worse, had they found out about April and Spike?

Hope shuddered, not wanting even to *imagine* how angry they would be, and how self-righteous. Poor April!

Hope was halfway up the hill by now. The high school, a two-story Mission-style building with lime-washed stucco walls and a terra-cotta roof, was surrounded by lush green lawns. If the building had been larger, Paradiso High might have looked like the campus of a small college. Hope walked past an ancient bell set in concrete, the only surviving piece of the historic one-room school that had once been on this site. There was a truck garden in back of the school, worked by the kids in the ag' classes who wanted to be farmers, but the vast lawns out front served as the center of student life.

Raven. April. Lacey and Kiki. Where was everybody this morning, anyway?

CHAPTER 3

All was not out of whack in Paradiso that morning, Hope saw with some relief. Principal Dwight Appleby, as usual, stood outside the main entrance, next to the tall silver flagpole. "Dwight the Dweeb," as everybody called him, was a total embarrassment to Paradiso kids: a scrawny, loose-jointed guy in his mid-fifties pretending to be cool. Or maybe he believed he really *was* cool. "I understand kids," he said at least twenty times a day. "I know how to groove with them." One entire wall in Appleby's office was covered with the stick-on signs kids had applied to the back of the tacky plaid sports coat he always wore. The signs bore messages such as: KICK ME, I'M STUPID and HEADS UP! with an arrow pointing down. "I saved these signs 'cause the kids love me," he explained to teachers and

23

parents. "It's their way of showing me I'm one of them."

Hope noticed that Winston Purdy III's Schwinn was chained, as always, to the flagpole. Penny Bolton—the school gossip and a Lacey-wanna-be—joked—or was she joking? With Penny you never knew for sure—that Winston was really the illegitimate son of Dwight the Dweeb.

"Good morning, Mr. Appleby," said Hope. "Nice day."

"I can dig it," replied the principal, laughing through his nose and arranging thin strands of once-black hair sideways across his shining pink dome.

"Mind if I ask you something?" said Hope, setting her backpack down on the flagstones and sidling up to him. Hope knew that if anyone on the selection committee would spill the beans, it was hang-loose Dwight Appleby. Maybe if she acted real buddy-buddy with him, he'd tell her. She leaned close to him and asked, "Who got chosen as Pretty Peggy Sue?"

"You don't know?" he said, looking uncomfortable.

"Me? How would I know?"

The dome beneath his thinning hair turned bright red. He looked away. "Perhaps I should explain. The committee met at my house last night and chose a winner. Shortly after that, I got a phone call from Willa Flicker. She really wanted to know who'd won . . ."

Hope knew Willa Flicker, editor of the Paradiso *Record* and the biggest gossip in town.

". . . and I was so excited that I let it slip out somehow," Mr. Appleby said guiltily. "I know we were all sworn to secrecy, but . . ."

Hope felt her pulse begin to race. Now he would tell her! He *had* to. She was absolutely *dying* to know. "So it's not a secret anymore," prodded Hope. "So you can tell me." She gave him what she hoped was the fetching smile she'd been practicing in her bedroom mirror.

"Well, I don't know . . ."

"Please! Half the town must know already."

"Well, okay. But promise you'll keep a lid on this so the *rest* of the town doesn't hear the news until I announce it at the assembly."

"I promise," said Hope.

Dwight Appleby whispered in Hope's ear, as if they were best friends sharing some juicy secret.

She just stood there for a moment, registering the news. *Well!* was her only thought.

"Thanks, Mr. Appleby," Hope said. "I promise I won't tell." She felt sorry for him now; he looked so sheepish. But thoughts of her principal faded as she digested the news he'd given her, which Hope had no intention of keeping secret. Wait until she told—

The second bell rang. Hope realized she was late. The principal winked at Hope, reached into his shirt pocket for a pad of hall passes, scribbled his name on one of them and handed it to her. Hope dashed into the building. Before her first-period class she had to get to her locker, check her computer betting figures, and do some calculations.

Buddy Holly was singing over the school P.A. system as Hope hurried down the corridor toward her locker. Dwight, ever "with it," wanted to put everybody in a real Fifties mood. Most of the kids were in class already, but Hope saw Eddie Hagenspitzel lumbering toward her from one end of the hallway. Eddie, a huge bear of a kid, had been chosen "Most Likely To Cause Principal Appleby's First Coronary" in the election for Senior Mosts. "Yo! Hope!" he bellowed cheerfully. "Still takin' bets?"

From the other direction she saw sprinting toward her . . . Jess Gardner! Hope, her heart pounding, pulled *Sports Illustrated* a little bit further out of the top of her backpack and tried to think of something to say that would make him notice her, but he jogged easily past her on his way to class. "Hope!" he called. "Catch you later."

Her heart sank, and she felt her hopes dwindling.

It didn't seem he was going to ask her to the Peach Blossom Ball after all. Yet his smile had been warm, hadn't it?

Then she remembered: Jess Gardner's smile was *always* warm.

With a dejected sigh, Hope turned to open her locker. Her combination was 35-23-35, about which she was frequently heckled. It was a "famous" locker, since the numbers matched Lacey Pinkerton's measurements—or so the boys claimed. Hope dialed the combination, thinking lockers were pretty useless in a school as small as Paradiso, where everybody knew every . . .

She started to pull open her locker door.

That was when she saw the hand—a girl's hand with pink-polished fingernails and a silver bracelet twinkling on its wrist. It had popped out at her, and was now dangling from the bluish-white arm that protruded from Hope's half-open locker.

Hope felt something heavy pressing against the metal door, and before she could unlock her frozen throat to scream, the door swung all the way open, and a body tumbled out.

Pretty Peggy Sue stared up at Hope with sightless eyes.

Her hair was tangled and her mouth was open, its bluish tongue lolling out. Around her neck was a tightly knotted cord.

Time froze. Hope heard the *slap* of Jess Gardner's sneakers far up the hallway and the lumbering *thud-thud-thud* of big Eddie Hagenspitzel's clodhoppers on the linoleum. She heard Buddy Holly, smelled floor wax, and saw the dull, dead, wide-open startled eyes of Pretty Peggy Sue.

Hope tried to scream. Nothing happened. A great gray veil was coming down on her, falling over her eyes, and she was falling too. I'm fainting, Hope realized. She tried to scream again, but heard nothing, nothing at all except Buddy Holly:

That'll be the daaa . . . a . . . aaay
When I die!

Monday, May 22

CHAPTER 4

Nobody knew, the previous Monday morning, that the girl crowned Peach Blossom Queen would be found dead in Hope Hubbard's locker four days later. Certainly Lacey Pinkerton did not know that the odds she'd be dead by Friday morning were one in four. As she lay in bed, rising slowly out of sleep, Lacey was aware of only one concrete piece of knowledge: she really really *really* did not want to wake up that morning. Waking up meant pain. But the terrible pain that shot through her aching body was nothing compared to the pain inside.

"Oh, Daddy. Why?" Lacey whispered, her voice tight from the effort of holding back tears.

Lacey's room, in what had once been a vast attic in the Pinkertons' fifteen-room Victorian mansion atop Winding Hill, was white and blue. The thick shag carpeting, so soft beneath the feet, was blue, as were the canopy and the downy coverlet on Lacey's queen-size bed. The draperies on the four dormer windows that looked out over the valley were blue as well. Everything else was white: couch, dressing table, armoire, and walls. Except that most of the wall space was covered with glossy posters and with framed pictures of Lacey and her group, the Pinks: Kiki De Santis, Janice Campbell, Renée Henderson, Penny Bolton, and sometimes—when Lacey was in an especially good mood or just wanted someone around to remind her of how all the common kids at Paradiso looked up to her—April Lovewell. (Besides, everyone else seemed to be so *fond* of April, it would make Lacey look bad to mention how much April truly *annoyed* her.)

The white clock radio beneath the white lamp on Lacey's white night table clicked on at six-thirty.

". . . said Governor Wilson in Sacramento. That's it on local news, KPOP listeners, and now here's T. J. the D. J. . . ."

More asleep than awake, Lacey reached out and snuffed T. J. the D. J.

Forcing herself to push aside the recollection of last night, Lacey glanced about her huge room, so high up in the house it seemed to be floating in brilliant blue air. Morning sunshine turned the shining walls into a color that was almost gold. Sunlight glinted off the silver picture frames. Peering

32

out from under her sheets, Lacey saw her feet poking up—big and bare. Her only flaw perhaps, but a gigantic, obvious, humiliating one.

The intercom on Lacey's night table chimed, a tingling little *ding-dong-ding*. *"Buenos días*, Señorita Lacey," said Paulita. "You wish something to eat?"

Paulita was the Pinkertons' live-in cook, a Mexican woman Daddy had hired last month after Lacey's mother fired Teresa. Paulita was the third family cook this year, and it was only May.

"No, thanks," said Lacey into the speaker. She knew, of course, how to say *"No, gracias,"* but Daddy believed the "help" should speak English, not the other way around. Besides, the Spanish language only reminded Lacey of Raven Cruz. Whenever Raven spoke Spanish in Lacey's presence, hands moving, bracelets jingling, dark eyes flashing, Lacey was sure Raven was ridiculing her. She had no definite reason for believing this, because if Raven wanted to tell you something, she told you straight out. It was probably one of the reasons Raven bothered Lacey so much. Raven Cruz was definitely her own person. Besides, Lacey had a feeling that maybe a girl who sewed her own clothes shouldn't be trusted.

Especially when she sewed them so well.

Clothes. I have to decide what to wear, thought

Lacey. Moving slowly, wincing as she slid out of bed, Lacey walked across the room to the full-length mirror that hung on the back of the closet door. Slowly she slipped off her nightgown of pale blue silk, and checked for damage. "Oh . . ." her heart sank. It was worse than she'd feared. Angry red welts covered the tender skin on the backs of her legs.

What excuse can I use to get out of gym class *this* time? Lacey wondered, as feelings of helplessness and shame swept over her. No way could she wear a gym outfit looking like this. Everybody would see. It wouldn't be hard to figure out, and then they'd begin to *talk*. No one could ever know. None of the Pinks knew, not even after all these years, although Lacey was sure some of the girls wondered why they always had their parties at Kiki's house and not at the Pinkertons'.

How could she tell Coach Monfort that she wanted to sit on the sidelines *again?* She'd asked to be excused only two weeks ago, also on a Monday, using the "cramps" complaint.

Turning away from her bruised reflection in the mirror, Lacey crossed to her white marble, blue tile bathroom, custom-designed by a Beverly Hills contractor her father had hired. "Only the best for my princess," Lacey had heard her father tell the man.

Her father's latest gift was two third-row tickets

to the Madonna concert next weekend in Sacramento. Maybe he was hoping Lacey would pick up some pointers. Cal Pinkerton hadn't said a word, but Lacey knew he'd been very disappointed last year when she'd lost the All-School talent competition to drippy little Emily Gilman. A stripper's daughter; no wonder! Well, maybe not an actual stripper, but modern dancing was just as sleazy, wasn't it? If people at school thought so, it certainly wasn't Lacey's problem. And she wasn't actually responsible for the rumor about Emily. She herself had sworn Penny Bolton to secrecy.

Losing to Emily won't mean a thing anymore, Lacey decided, stepping into the shower and almost crying out when the cascading water struck her skin. I'll be Peach Blossom Queen, take the screen test, and use it as a springboard into music. I'll follow in Mother's footsteps, except I'll go further —a *lot* further.

Lacey was almost done showering when she heard the Pink phone ringing. Turning off the water, draping a huge fluffy blue towel around her shoulders, she dripped her way out of the bathroom to the phone on her night table. The Pink phone was actually blue, because Lacey hadn't wanted to depart from the color scheme in her room. But only members of the Pinks had this number.

Lacey picked up the handset in the middle of the

third ring. She knew who was calling. Kiki De Santis. Kiki called every morning just to say, "Give me a ride?" To which Lacey always responded, "Yeah, sure" or "You got it, babe."

Lowering her voice, as she always did when answering the phone, Lacey murmured a husky "Hello?"

"Lace! Lace! Did you hear T. J. on KPOP just now?"

It wasn't Kiki calling. Lacey recognized Penny Bolton's exuberant chirp. "No," she replied. "I was in the shower. Why?"

"T. J. just announced the four finalists for Peach Blossom Queen . . ."

Lacey tensed slightly. She had no doubt that she was one of the four, but she'd been worrying all weekend about who her three competitors would be.

"Wanna guess who?" Penny Bolton asked.

Sometimes, Penny was simply too bubbly and perky for her own good. Becoming Queen, for Lacey, was serious business. She didn't have it in her heart to upbraid Penny for her effervescence, though. The girl's six-month-old sister had recently died. Crib death. Penny had been devastated, and beneath her chirpy cheer, she still was. Besides, no Pink was more loyal to Lacey than Penny Bolton.

"I'd rather not guess," said Lacey, keeping her

tone light and even, as if she were interested but not *that* interested. "Tell me who."

"You, of course," said Penny. "Kiki and Raven. And—get this—April Lovewell!"

Yesssss! Lacey pumped her arm like a tennis star who'd just served a crucial ace. Her "campaign" on April's behalf had worked! No way would the festival committee select April as Queen, which meant that Kiki and Raven were Lacey's only real competitors.

"It's nice that April got chosen," Lacey commented innocently. She was already wondering how to improve her chances against the other two girls. "Did T. J. say anything about the vote totals?"

"No. He didn't, but Denise Guthrie at the *Grapevine* told Vaughn Cutter who told me that you came in first with a hundred and thirty-two votes. Kiki got a hundred and nine, Raven a hundred and seven. April had eighty-eight."

Lacey's heart sank. According to her calculations, her actual vote tally was a disaster. She'd gone through the *Bell*, Paradiso High's yearbook, picture by picture. Two hundred and seven kids would definitely vote for her, she'd figured, with from forty-three to fifty-nine "maybes." Raven and Kiki had done much better than she had expected. And April Lovewell had actually received eighty-eight votes! That was double what Lacey had calculated. I made a mistake telling kids to vote for her, thought Lacey. Unless . . .

Unless the selection committee would consider her selfless effort on April's behalf.

Poor April. Lacey knew how she had to sneak around with Spike Navarrone to keep her mom and dad from finding out. Lacey knew, and the information just might come in handy . . . if, during the week, April appeared to have a real chance at becoming Queen.

"You came in first, Lace," Penny Bolton chirped over the phone. "Isn't it great?"

"I guess so," Lacey said modestly. First, yes, but not that far ahead of Kiki and Raven. The selection committee didn't make its choice on the basis of who received the most votes. But if one girl was way out ahead of everybody else, well, committee members might be influenced. I'm not anywhere near being way out ahead, Lacey concluded grimly as a feeling of uneasiness swept over her. I've got to do something to improve my chances.

It wouldn't do to let Penny think she was worried, though. "You heard the vote tallies from Vaughn?" she asked, changing the subject. "When?"

"Last night at Rosa's Café."

"Daddy and I were in San Francisco this weekend," said Lacey, explaining why she hadn't been

with Vaughn, her boyfriend-of-the-month. Naturally, he was also her date for Saturday's Peach Blossom Ball. "Was Vaughn . . . with anyone?" she
asked, as casually as she could.

"Just Jess Gardner," said Penny. "They must
have eaten at least ten tacos each."

Lacey forced a laugh. Jess Gardner had been her
boyfriend prior to Vaughn. She liked Vaughn a lot,
but she still liked Jess, too. She felt a twinge of
regret when she recalled why she'd had to dump
him. He'd broken a date with her—an emergency,
he'd claimed. Some emergency! Renée Henderson,
a Pink, had seen Jess that same night on Old Town
Road. Michelle Wheeler was with Jess in his vintage 1967 Pontiac GTO. Michelle Wheeler, who
wasn't a Pink or a cheerleader, or even a pom-pom
girl like Renée! When Jess offered no explanation
for being with Michelle, Lacey had no choice but
to break up with him.

"I bet Hope Hubbard's gearing up her computer
already," Penny Bolton was saying. "Our local
bookie."

"Good old Hope," responded Lacey. But something about Hope had always bothered her. Hope
wasn't "in," or even close, yet everybody seemed to
like her. And she didn't even *try* to get herself liked.
Even weirder, Hope never seemed to be very much

impressed by the more popular kids who were really *in*, like, for example, Lacey herself.

"I'm gonna find out Hope's odds as soon as I can," Penny said.

"Good idea." Lacey realized that it was. By keeping track of betting odds throughout the week, she would be able to judge how well she was doing in what Daddy called "the old P.O." Public opinion, that is. Except for Principal Appleby, the ten people on the selection committee were only human. If they heard lots of good things about a prospective Peggy Sue, they'd have to choose her.

If, on the other hand, they heard *bad* things . . .

Plans were beginning to take shape in Lacey's mind. "Gotta go," she said to Penny. "Not even dressed yet. See ya at school."

There was a kind of disappointed silence from Penny's end of the wire. Poor Penny, so ceaselessly devoted, determinedly cheerful in spite of her dead sister. Lacey realized she shouldn't end the call this abruptly. "Oh, by the way," she said, "I've gotten my little hands on a couple of tickets for Madonna. In the capital on Sunday."

"Oh! Wow!" Penny said.

"I don't know if you'll be free . . ."

"I'll be free, I'll be free."

"Well, let's talk about it later. We've got to get through the week, and there's the ball too. See ya."

"Later," Penny said.

Lacey hung up and began toweling off, thinking about Hope Hubbard and her computer. Lacey didn't want her odds to diminish by one single point during the week. If her odds dropped and Hope blabbed about it, Lacey would begin to look bad during a week in which she needed, above all else, to look good. No, better than good.

There was no way to keep Hope from running her betting business, but maybe there was a way to prevent her from yakking all the time about "the odds." Maybe I'll send Hope a case of canned peach halves with a sweet little note, thought Lacey. She smiled at the idea, but knew she'd never do it. My odds aren't going to sink anyway, she decided as newfound determination shot through her. They're going to rise and keep on rising all week long. *If* I figure out how to handle Raven and Kiki.

Lacey blow-dried her tawny-golden mane of hair, brushed it out until it glowed, and walked to her closet. It was larger than most of her friends' bedrooms. Her Peggy Sue dress, a blooming wonder of pink chiffon, hung just inside the door. Lacey's mother had worn it an age ago, when she'd been chosen Peach Blossom Queen. It amazed Lacey to think back across all those years, to imagine beautiful young Darla Jennings and handsome, dashing Cal Pinkerton jitterbugging the night away. Their whole lives had been ahead of them then, and it must have seemed that nothing bad could ever happen. How could it? They'd been so much in love.

Lacey tried to picture her mom and dad back then, all young and hot and bothered. She understood, intellectually, that they must have been passionate once. After all, she was living proof. And yet . . . and yet now, all these years later, they were somewhere downstairs in separate bedrooms. But once upon a time, Daddy had held Mother and they had slow-danced at the Peach Blossom Ball and she had worn the pink dress.

Lacey was amazed by how well the pink dress fit her. She hoped it wasn't some kind of an omen. She wanted more, more than her mother could have ever hoped for when she wore the dress so many years ago. My life is going to be different, she thought. I'm *not* going to end up like my mother. I'm not going to let my future slip away like she did. I'm going to be somebody. I'm going to get out of Paradiso.

CHAPTER 5

Winston Purdy better get that picture, thought Raven as she walked to the hen yard to give the four dozen Leghorns their morning water, mash, and oyster shells. Raven hated the chickens, but there were seven Cruz kids and everybody had to help out. Even little Orlando, a kindergartner, had a job. He kept the café's napkin dispensers filled.

Raven filled a bucket of water from a spigot outside the wire-mesh chicken enclosure, feeling the morning sun on her bare arms and the top of her shoulders. She wore a sleeveless white blouse and a long white skirt, both of which she'd made herself. Her long black hair was tied back. She would comb it out before going to school. She would also slip on two—or three, or four, or five—of the bracelets she loved to wear and change out of the old sneakers she wore to feed the chickens.

43

Raven turned off the spigot and stood upright. A hint of breeze touched her face, bearing the keen, dry scent of the scrublands west of Paradiso and momentarily erasing the pervasive scent of peach blossoms. Raven looked out toward the scrublands, hoping that Winston was having good luck getting the photo. *If he doesn't . . .*

Raven didn't want to think what would happen if Winston didn't get the shot. It was absolutely crucial that he succeed. The future of the scrublands depended on it. "Don't worry, Raven," he'd assured her a half hour earlier before pedaling off to the scrublands on his Schwinn. "I know almost everybody in school considers me an incompetent dork, but they're wrong. We're going to show them just how wrong, and stop Pinkerton from building Greenway Mall, too."

Raven hoped he was right. She'd written State Senator Humphrey T. Miller at the capitol in Sacramento about her desire to save the scrublands, and he'd responded immediately. He was a champion of the environment—but he'd also been discouragingly realistic. "The money and momentum behind Greenway are considerable," he'd written, "and in order to halt development we need positive proof of negative environmental impact."

Positive proof, Raven hoped, could be provided by Winston Purdy and his camera. Well, she thought, trying to see the best side of things, at least I'm learning a little something about politics. That'll help me in the future, *if* I ever get out of Paradiso. A few minutes earlier, while dressing in the tiny bedroom she shared with her sisters, Raven had heard T. J. the D. J. read her name on KPOP. She was a Peach Blossom finalist. Raven had no interest at all in the crown, or the convertible ride down Old Town Road, or even in the Hollywood screen test, although cameras were sure to love her bronze skin, high sculpted cheekbones, and black, flashing eyes. Raven wanted the scholarship. It was her ticket out of Paradiso, her only chance to go to college. She was determined to become a lawyer—an environmental lawyer, just like State Senator Miller—and after that . . .

Well, Congresswoman Cruz had a nice ring, didn't it?

Right now, though, she had to feed the chickens. They were restless, squawking, pecking at the dirt and at one another. If I don't win Pretty Peggy Sue, thought Raven, feeding the beady-eyed birds, I hope April Lovewell does. Or even Kiki De Santis, the ditz. *Anybody* but Lacey Pinkerton!

Raven glanced toward the parking area by the café. She wanted to get this job over with before Lacey and Kiki showed up for their morning iced tea. "With lemon, if you please." Raven knew how

45

much Lacey loved to see her out here in the hen yard. One morning last fall, Lacey and Kiki had spotted her there. They'd strolled over to the fence to watch. "I think it's *so-o* wonderful how you help your poor parents, Raven," Lacey had said, sort of smirking but not quite. "And you're so quick on your feet, too."

Raven, who knew from experience to be wary of Lacey's compliments, looked down to find that she'd planted her shoes in steaming-fresh chicken droppings. She'd worn different shoes to school, of course, but kids looked at her feet all day. Lacey had made sure to tell everyone about Raven's amusing misstep.

It hadn't been at all amusing to Raven, though. "I wouldn't talk about shoes or feet if I were Lacey Pinkerton!" Raven had grouched to her best friend, *Grapevine* editor Denise Guthrie. "She needs camouflage shoes for those landing pads of hers!"

Raven knew Lacey was overly sensitive about her exceptionally large feet, too. One day in social studies class, Mr. Goren had rambled into a digression about the Sasquatch, or "Bigfoot." Raven had watched, fascinated, as Lacey's face turned fire-hydrant red beneath her deep golden tan.

Nobody at school would be foolish enough to go around calling Lacey "Bigfoot," though. Lacey and her clique, the Pinks, could make life miserable for anyone witless enough to give them grief.

After spreading mash in an aluminum feeder, Raven stepped carefully out of the hen yard, closed the gate, and headed toward the café. She wanted to get the film from Winston Purdy here at the café, rather than later in school. Someone might see the exchange, wonder what was going on, and start asking questions. It was better, at this point, to be discreet. Basic politics. You didn't go around proclaiming success until you were sure you'd succeeded. "Counting chickens" came to Raven's mind too, but she didn't care for proverbs which involved chickens.

Far up the road, Raven saw the tiny wobbling figure of Winston on his bike, outlined against the low, rambling shamble of the Menendez Motor Lodge. The lodge bordered on the scrublands, several square miles of dunes and brush, wildflowers and wilder grass. When Raven hiked out into the scrublands—which she did during her rare hours of freedom from study or work—she felt a sense of being at one with the past. The scrublands were primitive, untouched by time or "progress," and Raven felt the souls of her Indian ancestors speaking to her there. "Do not let them take this, Raven," she could hear them telling her. "They have already destroyed all that they have touched.

But not this. You must not let them lay their greedy hands upon this land."

In the scrublands, alone and completely at peace, Raven listened to the wind voices of history and time. Wild birds sang to her there, deep within the sagebrush and the grass, and Raven listened.

Birds. *A* bird. And Winston Purdy III. One good, clean, *accurate* photo would do the job. *Positive proof.*

Raven thought back to last week, when Winston had volunteered to help her fight to save the scrublands. Winston could be a real dork, but the scrublands had become his "mission." For days he had been acting like a spy, winking his beady eyes at Raven whenever they passed in the hallways at school.

Raven waited by the roadside as Winston drew nearer. He was passed by an old car, which Raven didn't even think about until she realized it was the faded maroon beat-up Jaguar that Vaughn Cutter drove. Just what she needed—Vaughn Cutter wondering why Winston Purdy was slipping film to Raven Cruz so early in the morning. Vaughn was not only dating Lacey Pinkerton; he was also the son of Lars Cutter, Mr. Pinkerton's chief partner.

Vaughn slowly drove past, waving and smiling. Raven waved back, hoping he hadn't guessed that she was waiting for Winston, hoping he hadn't noticed the ratty old sneakers she wore to feed the chickens.

Then she retreated to the hen yard fence, away from the road. It would be safer if Winston gave her the film back there. She waited for him, feeling her chest tighten as she thought about Vaughn Cutter. Why was a guy like Vaughn wasting his time with a witch like Lacey Pinkerton? Sure, wrestling-champ Vaughn, a heavyweight and the catcher on the baseball team, was the athletic type Lacey tended to prefer. Even if he hadn't been a jock, he would have been a hunk anyway, with his taut, muscular build and those light blue eyes and wavy blond hair. But he wasn't at all like Lacey. He wasn't crafty, or calculating, or manipulative.

Maybe, because he was so strong, he could be nice without being considered weak. Or a pushover.

Yet he'd been a pushover for Lacey Pinkerton. No sooner had she dumped Jess Gardner than she had Vaughn Cutter dancing on the end of her string.

Raven herself seldom dated. She was always too busy studying or waitressing at the café. "You know what the guys say about you?" her friend Denise Guthrie had informed Raven once. "They say they'd love to ask you out, but they're afraid you'll turn them down, say you're too busy."

"I *am* too busy!" Raven had protested. Still, she

49

had been hoping that Vaughn would ask her to the movies in Springfield Hills last Valentine's Day. She'd heard from Bobby Deeter that Vaughn was just waiting for the right moment to ask her out. Then Lacey dumped Jess Gardner and wasted no time in finding his replacement. Vaughn didn't have a chance once Lacey set her sights on him. Lacey had invited him to the movies on Valentine's Day, and Raven never did find out if Vaughn was as warm and strong as she imagined him to be . . .

I haven't got time for the guys around here anyway! Raven told herself, watching as Winston Purdy, camera slung around his neck, turned into the parking area at Rosa's.

"I got it, Raven!" exclaimed Winston Purdy, so eager that he almost rammed his bicycle into the wire fence. Chickens squawked and scattered as he hopped off the Schwinn and let it fall. "I got it!" he repeated, fumbling with a camera that looked like a space weapon.

"I *think* I got it," he amended, opening the back of the camera and handing Raven a roll of film.

"I hope so," Raven said. She held the film in her hand. "What did it look like?"

"You'll see. I shot a whole roll, too. A lot of up-close shots. It wasn't shy at all. It didn't seem to mind me in the least."

"But what did it look like?"

"Red. Pretty much."

"All over red? Or just parts?"

"Just parts, I think. I was concentrating on getting the shots. Anyway, it's all on the film."

Just parts were red. That sounded right. "We'll know for sure when the pictures are developed," she said. "I'll drop the film off at Carter's Drugstore on my way to school."

"Okay," said Winston, picking his bike up off the ground.

He looked so pleased and happy to have done a good job, so excited to have helped her, that Raven leaned over and kissed him on the cheek. He seemed startled for an instant, then his innate niceness came through, the innocent quality he had to keep hidden in order to survive at school, and he blushed.

"You're a good guy, Winston."

He just sort of smiled and pedaled away, the camera still hanging from a strap around his neck.

Raven watched him waver onto Old Town Road, then started toward the café. Lacey Pinkerton and Kiki De Santis hadn't come for their before-school iced tea.

Raven wondered what was up.

CHAPTER 6

Kiki De Santis liked what she saw when she looked into her big bedroom mirror. She just wished there were more of it.

She'd gotten up a little earlier than usual, showered, and chosen her outfit for the day: seersucker mini, sky blue polo shirt, and sneakers. She always wore sneakers, except when she absolutely *had* to put on regular shoes, of which she had only three pairs. Church shoes in bone, dress shoes in black patent leather, and some old scuffed Docksiders. She had dozens of pairs of sneakers, though, from gleaming white to frayed and tattered gray. Kiki loved her sneakers. She couldn't bring herself to throw out even the rattiest old pair. They were special. They had *memories*. These old red-and-white Nikes, for example. She'd been wearing them when Bobby Deeter had asked her out for the first time two years ago. And those Reeboks on the floor in the far corner of her closet, fatally mud spattered and torn. She'd worn them the first time Bobby had kissed her, in his dad's Nissan Maxima after the Paradiso-Melrose football game sophomore year. She felt all warm and tingly inside just remembering that special night. They had both been so nervous that when the big moment came—*the* kiss—they accidentally knocked heads and practically gave each other a concussion. Kiki couldn't remember ever laughing so hard, and from that moment on she knew Bobby was the one for her. When they kissed she felt the heat rise inside her— almost as if her heart was on fire. And she could be herself with him, completely natural, unafraid, and appreciated—not worried or guarded or taken for granted, the way she sometimes was with Lacey, who was supposed to be her best friend. Funny— Kiki had never realized she felt like that around Lacey until Bobby came along.

Kiki stood before her mirror now, brushing out her long chocolate-brown hair. Kiki felt blessed with her hair and its natural golden highlights, and also for her long, long, black eyelashes and large hazel eyes.

She smiled.

The mirror showed a slightly slanted smile, formed out of long habit to compensate for Kiki's left canine tooth. It was shorter than the right canine by 1/32 of an inch. Kiki had measured her canines a million times, hoping the left one would grow.

Lacey Pinkerton's teeth were absolutely perfect, and her mouth was even and straight when she smiled. Also, Kiki was a half-inch shy of Lacey's five six, and her trim, slender body, which none of the guys had ever criticized, not even a bit, could not compare with Lacey's for fullness and curves.

"Kiki! Kiki!" her mom suddenly called from the kitchen. "It was just announced on KPOP! You're one of the finalists for Peggy Sue."

Kiki quickly switched on the radio in her room, just as the announcement was ending. Having her name announced on the radio—there was something so exciting and glamorous about it, almost as if she were a real celebrity. Still, she knew she had no chance of actually winning. "Of course you could be Pretty Peggy Sue," Bobby kept insisting. "You're nice and friendly and down-to-earth, *and* just as pretty as Lacey Pinkerton. Besides, people don't like Lacey, they're in awe of her." Kiki liked to imagine there was some truth in what Bobby said. But when she was done daydreaming, she knew Lacey Pinkerton would win. For Kiki, it was a thrill just to have been nominated. It meant a lot of kids at school liked her enough to have written her name on the *Grapevine* ballot.

I'm going to need a new dress, she thought. Win or lose, she had to look fantastic at the Peach Blossom Ball.

"You're going to need a new dress, honey," said her mom. She'd come upstairs and was standing in the doorway.

"Mom," Kiki said, with the most reasonable, the *nicest* smile she could muster . . .

"Don't smile crooked, honey," her mom said.

". . . Mom, I have an idea. I'm a senior now, right? And school is almost over?"

"Well, yes . . ."

"So how about if Lacey and I run up to Sacramento today and shop for a dress?"

"Oh, honey, I don't know. Your school-work . . ."

"We're hardly doing anything anymore in my classes. Really. I wouldn't miss a thing. If I did, I'd make it up right away. I really would. I promise."

"How do you know Lacey will be allowed to go with you?"

"Oh, she'll be allowed. Don't worry about that. Lacey's parents let her do anything she wants."

"Well, all right," said her mom. "I guess it'll be okay. But you be very careful in Sacramento." She started back downstairs, then called, "I'm fixing bacon and eggs for your dad. Want some?"

"No, thanks. Lace and I'll stop at Rosa's, like usual."

Her mother wondered how Kiki and her friend had time for *huevos rancheros* at Rosa's every morning. She didn't know that all they had was iced tea. "I've seen Raven feed those chickens," Lacey had said once. "I'll never have anything at Rosa's even remotely connected to a chicken." Well, that was a little mean to say, but funny, too. It was mean because the Cruzes were pretty poor, with all those kids. But it was also funny, because Lacey had said it.

Lacey could say, do, get away with anything. She had been born blessed with . . . something. Look at her dad, Calvin Pinkerton, the richest man in town, with his iron-gray hair slicked back so neatly, and his suits from someplace in England. Lacey's dad looked like that dead movie star—Cary Grant, or something. And then there was Lacey's mom, so cool and sexy, who looked like that dead princess Grace, also a movie star. Kiki always kept her eye out for Darla Pinkerton's Town Car, hoping to get a smile back for her wave, but it was rare if she got any response at all.

Kiki's own dad—Dominick, but everyone called him Dom—wore old blue jeans and flannel shirts to work, even though he owned his own company, De Santis Trucking. She loved her dad, but couldn't he say, "I'll look forward to seeing you again," like Mr. Pinkerton did, instead of "Yo, dudesky, see ya 'round" ? And Kiki's mom. Sue. Just *Sue*. Her real name was Susanna Alyce, which was even better than Darla. But did she want anyone to call her Susanna? She did not. It was, like, deliberately uncool.

Kiki had been aware, for a long time now, that Mr. and Mrs. Pinkerton really didn't approve of her, nor of the other Pinks. She didn't know why, not exactly, but the gang didn't hang out at Lacey's hilltop house. Mostly, they had their parties in Kiki's huge rec room downstairs, with the pool table, the pinball machine, and the old Wurlitzer organ her dad had "got for a song from a yo-yo who didn't know the sucker was a prize." Or, in the summer, the Pinks—and tons of other kids—hung out around the pool out back, rock music blasting from a dozen boxes at once. Her mother never complained when the kids tracked water on the kitchen floor, going for sodas in the fridge, or if they spilled chips at the poolside.

Yes, Kiki did know why Darla Jennings Pinkerton, once Peach Blossom Queen, did not approve of her and the other kids. It was because Mrs. Pinkerton did not think they quite "came up to standard."

Kiki De Santis examined the image of herself that she kept inside her mind. She was pretty, sure, but a lot of other girls were, too. Besides, you couldn't make a career, let alone a life, out of being pretty. You also needed some brains, some talent. Kiki had a good solid *B* average, but after four years of high school she could count her *A*'s on one hand. She was on the field hockey and volleyball teams, but she wasn't a starter. She had no special talents, not even enough to be a pom-pom girl. Which, except for spinning a baton, were among the lowest talent levels imaginable.

Even Kiki's boyfriend did not quite "measure up" to the guys her friends dated. Lacey was going with Vaughn Cutter; Renée Henderson with Doug Mattinsky, the football team's quarterback; Janice Campbell with Jason Edwards, the six foot six basketball center. Penny Bolton went out with Hal Bemis, who was an all-state tennis star being recruited by Stanford. But Kiki was dating Bobby Deeter, who was only editor of the *Bell* and captain of the debating team. Kiki loved him, she was sure he had a great future, but he wasn't really that "in" at Paradiso High. And Kiki knew that Lacey did not entirely approve of Bobby Deeter.

Still, Kiki felt that Bobby was worth holding

onto, no matter what Lacey thought. And she couldn't quite shake the notion that maybe there was something just a little bit less than perfect about Lacey's life.

Why was Lacey herself so on-again, off-again about the kids at school? Take the time that Lacey, out of the clear blue, had brought a University of California–Berkeley sweatshirt back from San Francisco and had given it to Hope Hubbard. It was weird, because Lacey barely knew Hope, and Kiki had noticed that although Hope was flattered by the gift, she had seemed almost suspicious of Lacey's generosity. A couple days later Hope had been wearing the sweatshirt at lunch in the caf' when Lacey had stopped at the table. Kiki had been with her. She'd seen and heard it all.

"What kind of stain did you slobber onto my sweatshirt?" Lacey had demanded of Hope. *My* sweatshirt, just like that, as if she still owned it.

Poor Hope. Startled and embarrassed, she glanced down at the sweatshirt to find a dark, tear-drop-shaped blotch at the top of the Berkeley *B*. While Lacey looked on in regal disdain, Hope wet a fingertip, touched the blotch, and tasted.

"Honey," she said, smiling bravely and trying to make the best of the situation. "I always have honey at breakfast, and—"

"A *lit-tle* sloppy, hmm?" said Lacey, her sarcasm

thick as the honey on Hope's sweatshirt. She seemed ready to cut Hope into pieces, but Kiki had spoken up then. It hadn't been right for Lacey to go off on Hope for no reason.

"Leave it alone, Lace!" Kiki had demanded.

The look on Lacey's face then had been incredulous. She was not accustomed to being challenged. "But, my God, *honey.* . . ."

"Leave it alone," Kiki repeated sternly.

That was all Kiki had said, but it had been enough to get Lacey away from Hope's lunch table and a possible fight. For three days afterward, Lacey hadn't spoken to Kiki or even acknowledged her existence. And Kiki had surprised herself; she didn't go to Lacey to apologize. Then, as suddenly as it had come, the storm ended. Lacey invited Kiki for a weekend trip to San Francisco aboard Mr. Pinkerton's Learjet. Lacey had never mentioned the sweatshirt again, although Hope Hubbard had. A couple of weeks after the confrontation, Kiki and Hope had been in adjacent library carrels.

"Thanks for that day in the caf'," Hope had said.

"Oh. Oh . . . just one of those things, I guess. Chalk it up to a bad day."

"Really?" Hope had said. "Well, whatever. But tell your friend I burned her damned shirt."

Now Kiki was just about to call Lacey for a ride

to school when the phone rang. "I got it, Mom!" she called.

"Hi, Peggy Sue," said Bobby Deeter. "Pretty Peggy Sue. Congratulations. You've heard?"

"Hi, Bobby. Yeah. Mom said it was on KPOP. But Lacey's sure to—"

"Win?" Bobby sounded faintly exasperated. "Don't be so certain. Your chances are one in four, although I think they're better. I'm placing ten bucks with Hope Hubbard to back up my word."

"You might lose your ten."

"Why so negative? This is a congratulatory call."

Now Kiki felt a little bit graceless. "You're right, Bobby," she said. Sometimes he seemed to know her better than she knew herself. "Whatever happens, we'll have a great time at the festival."

"You got that right. I'll be with the prettiest girl in Paradiso. See you at lunch?"

"Oh. I'm skipping today. I won't be there."

"You're skipping? Why?"

"I'm going shopping for a dress in Sacramento. With Lace. Except she doesn't know it yet. I've got to call her and—"

"What's Lacey Pinkerton got to do with your dress?" He sounded really exasperated now. "Can't you do *anything* without Lacey being involved?"

That's not fair, thought Kiki. I've been doing

62

lots of things without Lacey lately. "Lacey's good at picking out clothes," she said to Bobby.

"Why don't you choose your own this time?" He was just making a suggestion, but Kiki took his remark as a challenge. She would show him that she could think for herself.

"Maybe you're right, Bobby," she said. "Do *you* want to come with me to Sacramento?"

"Hey!" he replied, laughing. "When it comes to women's clothing, I'm completely useless. Besides, we have the final debate of the year after school, with those fast talkers from Fresno. Give me a call when you get back, okay?"

"Okay," Kiki said. "Bye."

I *don't* need Lacey to help me choose a dress for the Peach Blossom Ball, Kiki thought, hanging up the phone. I'll do it myself.

Since Kiki wasn't going to school at all, she didn't bother calling Lacey. I don't have to check with her on every little move, right? Kiki thought. After changing out of her seersucker mini and into a flowered sundress, Kiki left the house, climbed into the Trooper II, and set out toward Sacramento.

Her chances of living until Friday were one in four.

CHAPTER 7

Kiki still hadn't called for her ride. It was almost seven-thirty. Well, maybe she'd overslept. Maybe she was getting congratulatory calls. Lacey, considering her attire for the day, wondered who those calls might be from. Kiki had received only twenty-three fewer votes than Lacey had herself. All the Pinks were popular at school—it went without saying—but Lacey hadn't realized her best friend was almost as popular as she was.

Then, while deciding on soft gray leather pants and an ivory silk blouse, she had a great idea. Kiki would be no threat at all! It was so logical. Lacey wondered why she hadn't thought of it right away. She'd simply ask Kiki to withdraw.

Lacey was ready for school now, but Kiki still hadn't phoned. Lacey took a pair of powerful binoculars from her desk drawer, went to the window, and looked down at the De Santises' sprawling blue and white split level, which was built on a three-acre plot about two hundred yards down Winding Hill Road from the Pinkerton house. She saw Kiki's dad, Dom, come out the back door and swing up into the dirty Dodge pickup he drove to work. Lacey thought he was sort of rough and sensed that he thought she was spoiled, so she didn't like him. But, except for the fact that he refused to buy Kiki her own car, Kiki herself worshiped the ground he walked on.

Just as Lacey pretended to adore her own father.

Dom De Santis pulled onto Winding Hill Road, leaving the Isuzu Trooper II on the driveway outside the garage.

Why hadn't Kiki called yet? Lacey searched her memory, but found nothing to explain her friend's behavior. They'd had no disagreements lately, no quarrels. No matter how the Queen competition turned out, Lacey was sure that Kiki would remain her friend. Kiki had never won anything big—nor had she wanted to—in her whole life. How could she possibly expect to be Peach Blossom Queen?

And yet there was the possibility.

Lacey decided she would wait two more minutes. That was *it*! If Kiki didn't call, she could get to school on her own. It wouldn't hurt Kiki a bit to realize people weren't at her beck and call every morning!

Secretly hoping Kiki would call, Lacey swung the binoculars out over the town and the valley as she often did. From her peerless vantage point at the top of Winding Hill, she could see everything for miles. There, in the distance, stood the massive Pinkerton cannery complex, adjacent to the airstrip and the silver hangar for Daddy's plane, the *Darlacey*. A long column of cars was pulling into the cannery lot right now: the early shift arriving for work. Daddy employed all these people. He had such awesome responsibilities.

Maybe that was why he sometimes went, as he said, "off the deep end."

Lacey looked through the binoculars at the town below. She saw a school bus grinding uphill, a cloud of black smoke coming out its exhaust pipe. Spike Navarrone, on his motorcycle, shot past the bus as if it were standing still. Lacey suddenly had an image of Spike kissing April Lovewell, which gave her a strange, uneasy feeling. *Weird!* She'd never given Spike much thought before, except for his brooding, dark eyes and tense, soulful silences. What he saw in April Lovewell, Lacey would never know.

Hope Hubbard, lugging her backpack, had turned out of DeSoto Drive and onto Old Town Road. Right on time. Hope had on a gray sweatshirt today. Jeez, Hope and her sweatshirts. No wonder nobody'd asked her to the festival ball. She should put on a little makeup and buy some decent clothes.

Then Lacey lifted her binoculars to look out beyond the town to the scrublands, where Daddy and Mr. Cutter were going to build Greenway Mall. They *were* going to build it, too, as soon as they silenced all the irritating and vocal opposition in town. Like Raven Cruz, for example, always carrying around a briefcase full of environmental clippings, shooting her mouth off about conservation all the time. What did Raven know about conservation anyway, or land development, or shopping malls? Raven was "too big for her britches," Daddy said. Why, Raven's parents had once picked fruit in orchards owned by Pinkerton Canneries, Inc. And now they ran a *diner*. Where did Raven get off, champion of the scrublands!

The scrublands were very pretty, though, Lacey admitted as she studied them through her binoculars. Even the scrawniest bushes were abloom out there, and there were strange and beautiful flowers of yellow and violet and rusty red.

Kiki *still* hadn't called. Okay, be that way; see if I care, Lacey thought. She was just about to put down the powerful glasses when she caught a glimpse of something out among the bushes. An unusual movement. An unexpected glint of light.

A person? Kids went into the scrublands at night to make out in cars—Lacey had, many times, with Vaughn and Jess and other boys—but nobody went there in the morning. Except—she adjusted the glasses, focusing for clarity—except . . . Winston Purdy III! Now what on earth was *he* doing there? He'd dropped out of Cub Scouts when an ant had crawled on his shoe at a picnic. Winston Purdy was definitely not a scrubland type of person. What was he up to?

Lacey watched, fascinated, as Winston pedaled his raunchy old three-speed that nobody cool would be caught dead with, eastward on Old Town Road toward town. He swung waveringly into the lot at Rosa's Café, wobbled past the café, and halted at the hen yard out back. Where Raven Cruz seemed to have been waiting for him! Lacey was so utterly astounded by what she was witnessing that she forgot, for a moment, the pain in her legs.

Now Winston was handing something to Raven. Lacey tried to focus the binoculars more clearly, with no luck. She saw the nerd hand something to the Mex—Lacey privately thought of Raven as "the Mex"—and then she *kissed* him! Just on the cheek, but still, *yuk!*

Then Winston got on his bike and pedaled away toward school.

Bewildered, Lacey put the binoculars back into her desk drawer. Something was going on in town that she did not know about, and over which she had no control. Not having control made Lacey nervous.

Just then the intercom chimed, *ding-dong-ding*. Daddy's voice was hoarse. "Princess, there's a little something for you in the breakfast nook. Have a nice day."

"Daddy, wait—" she started to say, but he had already clicked off.

Lacey looked out the window again, checking Kiki's house for signs of life, giving her one last chance to call. The fact that she hadn't called was beginning to really bother Lacey. Kiki was so agreeable, so predictable, so . . . Pink. I could call *her*, Lacey thought. No. *She* calls *me*.

Then, suddenly, Kiki came out of her house, crossed from the back door to the Trooper II, and got behind the wheel. She was wearing a pretty, loose-fitting sundress and her walk was happy, jaunty. She looked slim and lovely, her long dark hair swinging and shining.

Kiki, without so much as a glance up toward the Pinkerton house, backed the Trooper out of her driveway and headed down Winding Hill Road.

A tidal wave of loneliness washed over Lacey, threatening to drown her. For just an instant, it seemed as if her world was beginning to crumble. But that was ridiculous, wasn't it? Kiki probably had an errand to run before school, no big deal.

Lacey flew downstairs to the breakfast nook where Paulita was busy preparing a tray for Lacey's mother, who took breakfast in her room. The meal consisted of strong coffee, black, and tomato juice. Lacey was glad that her mom hadn't come to the kitchen to say good morning. Had she heard all that ruckus last night? If she had, would she pretend ignorance? It was better for her mother to stay in her pleasant world of Junior League meetings and functions at the Paradiso-Walnut Hills Country Club. It would be good, too, for Darla Pinkerton to stop adding vodka to her morning tomato juice, but Lacey had long since given up hope that this would happen. Lacey grabbed the keys to her Ferrari, which were on a hook next to the back door. Beside the keys, Scotch-taped to the wall, was a small white envelope stuffed full of something soft and foldy. Lacey hesitated, feeling Paulita's eyes on her.

"Señor Pinkerton, before he go to work, say it is for you," Paulita said.

"I know that," Lacey snapped. She didn't care for the cook's inquisitive gaze.

She wanted to leave the envelope where it was,

knowing Daddy would feel bad if she didn't take it. But if she didn't take it, Paulita might think something was wrong. So she took the damn envelope, called a flippant *"Adios!,"* walked to her Ferrari in the four-car garage, and got in.

First, she opened the envelope. It contained five hundred dollars in fifties and twenties and tens. Guilt money. Lacey felt tears pushing behind her eyes. She tossed the envelope, with the money still inside, onto the passenger seat.

Then she reached down and removed her black shoes. The Ferrari was gorgeous, but Lacey found it difficult to work the clutch, the brake, and the accelerator efficiently when she had shoes on. *Damn bigfoot. Klutz!* She placed her shoes on top of the money envelope, started the engine, heard its growl, and shot backward out of the garage so recklessly that she almost crashed into her mother's Town Car, to which Manuel, the driver, was applying yet another coat of Turtle Wax.

"Caramba!" he shouted.

"No hablo," Lacey gave him her brightest smile and roared off down Winding Hill Road.

I have to win Peach Blossom Queen! And to do that, I have to beat Kiki and Raven and *April.* It had seemed a good plan only a little while ago, a stroke of genius, in fact, simply to ask Kiki to withdraw from the competition. But Kiki had behaved very oddly this morning, so it was best that Lacey tread lightly until she found out what was going on. Raven was an even bigger problem. She was—face it, Lace!—gorgeous, smart, and respected by everybody. The adults on the selection committee would naturally give Raven very serious consideration. Lacey didn't know what to think about April. Until that morning she wouldn't have given April any thought. But eighty-eight votes! Had Lacey's sympathy campaign worked too well? Was there something about April that Lacey had overlooked? Or didn't know?

"Know as much as you can about everybody," Daddy was always advising. "You never know when it'll come in handy."

Yes, but it was sometimes unpleasant to know too much about people. Lacey knew, for example, that her good friend Renée Henderson had spent time in a mental hospital in Sacramento before her family had moved here to Paradiso. Renée had told her about it, a kind of blurted confession. Renée's mom had disapproved of a certain Sacramento boy —Terry or Larry; Lacey couldn't recall—with whom Renée had been in love. So, after a picnic dinner one night, during yet another battle about Barry or Jerry, Renée had attacked her mom with a long, two-tined barbecue fork. Renée's older brother had prevented any injury, but Renée, unable to face what she'd almost done, had broken down. She'd spent six months at the hospital. "Please, never tell a soul," Renée had pleaded with Lacey. "I'm telling you this because you're my best friend in the world."

"Your secret is safe with me," Lacey had promised. And she meant it, too. It was just lucky that Renée wasn't a candidate for Peach Blossom Queen, Lacey thought. That would have changed everything.

CHAPTER 8

April Lovewell scrunched down as low as possible in the front seat of her father's black Chevrolet, poking her head up only after Lacey Pinkerton had roared by in her Ferrari.

"There goes the girl who ruined your reputation," said the Reverend Ward Lovewell, sitting up straight behind the steering wheel. "I'm not at all surprised that you're still embarrassed. What I can't understand is why *she's* not?"

For a saint, April thought, her father was remarkably unperceptive. "St. Ward" was April's private name for him. Her mother was "St. Sara." And that was exactly two saints more than any girl needed in her family.

"Thanks for driving me to school again, Father," April said, getting out of the car and slamming the door shut. "Who knows what terrible trouble I might've gotten into if I'd walked?"

April saw, briefly, a look of anguish break across her father's long, lean face, then turned away and walked toward school, carrying her backpack in her left hand, shielding her face from the sun with her right. April kept her face protected from sunlight as much as possible, knowing her capacity to grow ten new freckles per minute in direct light. Something to do with melanin. It was a scientific fact. There was nothing to be done about it, either. Sunblock didn't keep freckles from appearing, and freckle removers just seemed to discolor what little bits of actual skin still appeared between the freckles.

This fact, bleak as it was, didn't keep April from purchasing whatever new ointment or miracle cure old Jerry Carter, at the drugstore, managed to put on his shelves.

"It must have been something evil my parents did before I was born," April had once said to Spike. "I've got this *curse* on my face, my hair makes a carrot look dull, and my eyes are a sort of watery brown."

"You've been listening to Lacey Pinkerton too much," Spike said. "You're pretty, very pretty. You're beautiful. Your skin is like porcelain. And I love your wild hair," he said, laughing. "In the sun, it's like it's on fire—which is exactly how you make me feel."

April could hear her heart thudding as she looked into Spike's intensely dark eyes. "But almost everybody in school thinks I'm a slut," she protested.

"Nobody thinks that," Spike said. "You made a mistake, a long time ago. And besides, I respect you more than any other person I know." He brushed his fingers lightly across her face and gently pressed his hot lips to hers. April closed her eyes and floated weightlessly up into the spring sky on a cloud of pure love.

At the moment, though, April wasn't worried about her looks or reputation. She was desperately in need of a product, other than freckle remover. She'd gone to the drugstore on Saturday, but there'd been too many people around. She hadn't mustered the nerve to buy it.

April walked past Principal Appleby, standing at his usual flagpole spot beside Winston Purdy's decrepit three-speed.

"Well, if it isn't one of our Pretty Peggy Sues," he exuded. "How are you today?"

"Hi, Mr. Appleby. Fine, thanks."

"Mr. Woolery's looking for you," the principal said.

"Okay." Mark Woolery, the art instructor, was

April's favorite teacher. April was well aware that a lot of kids envied her relationship with "Mark Wonderful," who was as handsome as any movie star, young, *single*, and the owner of a new BMW. She'd heard a few semi-spiteful remarks about Mark's interest in her, but the people who said those mean things were wrong. Besides Spike and Hope, he was the only person who encouraged her artistic talent, and she relied on him for support when the going got tough at home.

St. Ward and St. Sara weren't aware of Mr. Woolery's influence on April. April kept it, like her relationship with Spike, from them. In fact, April had had to keep a *lot* of things from them, ever since they'd found out what happened at Lacey Pinkerton's birthday party freshman year.

April had been so excited to receive an invitation. But when she was actually at the party, she felt horrible. No one paid any attention to her, especially not Lacey, whom April respected and admired above anybody else.

April couldn't dance like the rest of the kids at Lacey's party, either. Dancing was forbidden by her parents, who believed it was pointless, if not downright sinful. She was thinking of sneaking off into the night and walking home, but Lacey's parents—they were so unbelievably cool—had said good night and gone upstairs. Shortly thereafter, Lacey liberated a bottle from a locked cabinet and poured quite a bit of clear liquid into the tepid fruit punch that the kids had been sipping.

The new, improved punch tasted great to April. It was amazing how easy it was to talk and laugh after two or three glasses.

April was more than willing when Lacey proposed a game of strip poker.

The punch did nothing for April's poker game, though. At midnight, when Cal Pinkerton descended the stairs in bathrobe and slippers to see if the party was over, he found giggling, glassy-eyed April sitting cross-legged on a red leather ottoman. Other than her bra, which she was trying clumsily to unhook, she had on only her panties. " 'Ere gossh NOTHIN'!" she shouted to Mr. Pinkerton, preparing to yank off the bra to the delighted laughter of the other partiers.

Only Lacey's quick thinking saved the day. She hastily grabbed hold of April's arms and began pulling a sweater over April's head.

April remembered the ride down the hill in the Chevy with her father, who'd been summoned by Mr. Pinkerton to collect his tipsy daughter. "It grieves me," St. Ward had said. "You have those negative family tendencies in the blood, just like your aunt Leanne and her daughter—"

"Buzz off, Dad!" April had replied. "I'm . . . it

wash a grrrr-ate parshy. I'm real . . . reeeee-al pop'lar now. . . ."

April sort of vaguely remembered her father carrying her into the house, her mother crying, and both of them putting her to bed. She remembered the next morning all too well—a pounding headache and nausea that emptied her stomach and still didn't subside—but that didn't matter. She couldn't wait to get to school Monday morning. The news of her social coup at the party would have gotten around. Everybody would be talking about it.

Everybody *was* talking about it, but not the way April had expected. Someone had started a rumor that, after stripping to the buff, April had gone out onto the Pinkertons' lawn with Bubba Dole, the guy everybody called "Psycho," who was the only seventeen-year-old freshman in Paradiso history. Bubba hadn't even been at the party, but that fact didn't matter to the rumor. Within a week, April had heard that she'd "partied on the lawn" not only with Bubba, but with a half-dozen other guys as well.

Overnight, April's social life had plummeted off the chart. Even the kids who might have asked her to their parties were forbidden to do so by their nervous parents. Only the understanding friendship of her cousin, Hope, had gotten April through that first awful year. April still couldn't understand why Hope sometimes hinted that Lacey Pinkerton might not be all she appeared, though.

By sophomore year, people were forgetting April's shame as new rumors cropped up to occupy their interest. This past year had been her best since she started high school.

Mr. Woolery had taken her under his wing.

She and Spike Navarrone had fallen in love.

And she'd just been chosen as a candidate for Pretty Peggy Sue.

Things had been going pretty well—until now. Maybe I should just run away, thought April, walking down the hall toward her locker.

Finally, just when her life seemed to be going somewhere, she felt as if she were just about to step off a cliff.

"April! There you are!"

It was Mr. Woolery, looking incredibly vigorous. He jogged around the track each morning before school began, working up a bit of a sweat but never even breathing hard. Just standing there, he *glowed.* And he was so confident. April knew he would've dated Lacey Pinkerton, had she been in his high school class.

"Why so glum?" Mr. Woolery said. "Got a problem?"

"Oh, no. No."

He smiled suspiciously. He knew her pretty well. "Fight with Spike, huh?"

She shook her head. Not yet, anyway.

"Mom and Dad won't let you go to the festival ball?"

"No, they were pretty calm when they heard about my nomination this morning. I won't be allowed to dance, though."

He grinned. "*I'll* ask you to dance. Your dad can't say no to a teacher. That takes care of that. Now, you've been wondering about your next art project, right? Well, I had an idea you might like. Want to try some sketches out in the scrublands? The lighting would be terrific early in the morning when the sun's coming up. How about it?"

"Sure," agreed April. It was a great idea. Her spirits rose a little.

"The next couple days are bad for me," he said. "But how about Thursday morning? I'll pick you up at your house at six. That too early?"

"No. That's fine."

"Excellent! Somebody better sketch the scrublands while there's still the chance," he added, before heading off to the gym showers. "If that Greenway Mall gets built, the whole area will be history."

"Don't we all know it," said April.

She walked to her locker. Kids said, "Good luck,

April," or "Way to go" or "I voted for you in the *Grapevine.*" It was nice, but just a little bit late. The very *last* thing on April Lovewell's mind at the moment was the Peach Blossom competition.

On days when Spike got to school early, which wasn't often because of his chores on the farm, he waited for April at her locker. She loved to see him standing there, looking strong, self-contained, and way more mature than the other kids. She also liked to see the way the girls looked him over, and to know they knew that he was her boyfriend. Sometimes she couldn't believe it herself. Having been trapped in the parsonage, April often still felt like a little kid. Spike had real problems, real family problems, food-on-the-table-for-little-kids problems. Spike's father was in jail, and his mother spent most of her waking hours—and some of her sleeping hours—at the Blue Hawaii Bar. Why had he chosen her?

"Because I love you," he'd said. They'd been out at their secret place in the cliffs above Old Smuggler's Road.

"Well, *why* do you love me?" she'd persisted.

He never spoke much. It wasn't that words came hard to him. They didn't. And it wasn't because, like a lot of other guys, he was uncomfortable expressing his emotions. It was simply that he didn't speak unless he had something to say.

"Why?" April had asked again, lying beside him in sweet grass, feeling his strong arms around her.

"Because," he'd finally said, after she'd almost given up hope of getting an answer, "you're different. You don't flirt or play stupid games like other girls. I can be myself with you. Besides, you're the only person I know who'll get out of here and make a mark in the world. You're so talented, April—a real artist. You see the world differently than everyone else."

"I'm so lucky to be with you," she said, moving in closer, feeling his warm breath against her cheek. Then he was kissing her slowly and softly, until April found herself responding to his deepening kisses in a way she would have never dreamed possible, losing herself to him joyfully. "We'll always be together," she murmured.

This morning, though, she was a little relieved to see that Spike wasn't waiting for her at her locker. Something had happened. It threatened to destroy those happy dreams they'd conjured on the grassy cliffs. April wasn't yet completely certain of disaster, but she had a pretty fair idea.

She had to get to Carter's Drugstore!

CHAPTER 9

The student parking lot behind school was almost full, so Lacey knew she was late. Slipping on her shoes, not bothering to lock the Ferrari, she walked to the rear entrance. It wouldn't do to hurry, wouldn't be cool . . . but then she saw Coach Monfort getting out of her dusty old Chevrolet Blazer 4×4. Coach lived out in the country. "Lives in the trees and eats raw meat," kids said. She was a rangy, muscular woman, sandy haired, broad faced, strong jawed, who could still run a seven-minute mile.

"Coach!" Lacey called, catching up with Mrs. Monfort at the rear entrance to the building. "Can I talk to you a sec?" She attempted to look *very* tired.

"Oh, hi. Of course, Lacey. What's on your mind?"

"I . . . I don't feel so well. Would it be all right if I sat out today?"

Coach looked sympathetic, but skeptical. "Why don't we wait and see how you feel fourth period?" Fourth period was Lacey's gym class.

"I really don't feel well at all."

Coach held open the door. Lacey entered, and Coach followed. "Have you had a checkup lately?" she asked. "It seems to me you've sat out quite a few classes recently. Maybe you ought to see Nurse Pritchard."

"Oh, I don't think . . ."

Coach put her hand on Lacey's shoulder. That was her no-nonsense gesture, known to all the kids in her classes and on her teams. Her hand on your shoulder meant, "Okay, not another word out of you. I am going to tell you what you are going to do, and you are going to do it."

"Nurse Pritchard will expect you fourth period," said Coach. "I'll tell her you'll be there."

She left Lacey standing disconsolately in the hall. Now what? Lacey thought. She couldn't go to gym because she'd have to undress and shower. Nurse Pritchard could be pretty intrusive too. And *nobody* should see the angry stripes on the backs of her legs. Unfortunately, she'd been wearing her jade green mini when Daddy had "gone off the deep end."

86

Maybe I'll just duck out of school, Lacey thought desperately, and forge a letter of excuse to bring in tomorrow. Once, last year, she'd been so angry with Daddy that she'd gone to Principal Appleby's office. She'd intended to tell him everything. But while waiting to see him, the horrible consequences had swarmed in her mind like a hive of killer bees. Daddy would be ruined. Mother would be left defenseless, since even Lacey knew how much of her father's fortune was already tied up in the Greenway project. Worst of all, if Lacey told, she would be the object of talk, of pity. Her whole world would turn to ashes overnight.

So she'd given Appleby a song and dance about college plans. Dwight the Dweeb had been so pleased. He loved to give advice.

Maybe, hoped Lacey, heading toward her locker, Daddy will finally keep his promise to change. When I win Peach Blossom Queen, he'll see at last that I deserve some respect.

In order to reach her locker, Lacey had to walk through half the lower level, past the boiler room and the custodians' equipment area, then climb a stairwell to the main floor. Usually, some of the Pinks and other kids waited for her arrival at the top of the stairwell. But not today. Instead, as she climbed the stairs she heard kids talking about the Peach Blossom Queen competition.

"I don't know why you're even bothering to take bets on this, Hope. Lacey's gonna win for sure."

Lacey recognized Penny Bolton's unmistakable tweet. She imagined a bunch of kids gathered in front of Hope's locker, which, if its combination accurately reflected Lacey's measurements, would have been 34-24-35. But let the guys guess and dream.

"You're gonna lose money, Hope," Penny was saying. Dear, loyal Penny. After her baby sister's crib death, when Lacey had attempted to be comforting, Penny had gone into a sobbing rage. "Never say anything about that to me again! Never! I can't stand to hear it! Nobody's pity can help."

Lacey, who understood the horror of unwanted pity, had never mentioned the crib death again. Nor, as far as she knew, had anyone else. Penny kept herself busy with school, the pom-pom squad, the Pinks, and a part-time job at Bolton's Hardware, her dad's store.

Lacey pressed close to the stairwell wall, listening. Eavesdropping, while not exactly up-and-up, was a good way to find out stuff.

"Oh, I don't know," Hope Hubbard said. "It's only Monday. Lacey's a way-ahead favorite now, but things could change. I'm not doing this for money anyway. I'll barely break even, if that. It's fun to see if the computer is smart enough to replicate the real world."

Replicate? wondered Lacey. She had no idea what that meant. Hope Hubbard was too smart for her own good, sometimes.

A guy spoke up then. "I think Raven and Kiki both have a good shot at winning," he said. Lacey recognized the voice of Jess Gardner. "What you have to keep in mind," Jess added, "is that being a Pink won't necessarily swing much weight with the selection committee. Being a Pink might even hurt. *Cliques* are sort of teenybopperish and juvenile."

Lacey was furious, shocked. Jess was talking sour grapes, just like the girls who'd never be cool enough to be Pinks. Then she was happy because she heard Renée Henderson say, "Oh, Jess, come off it. You know Lacey's gonna be Pretty Peggy Sue. You're just mad because Lacey dumped you."

That was what the Pinks were for! Loyalty. Support.

"Yeah, right," said Jess. "Think whatever you like, Renée. Anyway, Hope, I'm betting five bucks that Kiki De Santis wins."

Jess betting on Kiki? Lacey had always imagined that all of her former boyfriends still loved her. And would love her forever. But the shock of discovering that her romantic belief was unfounded did not prepare her for the truly startling blow that came

89

now. Another boy spoke up and said, "I don't think anybody's a sure bet for Peggy Sue. Even April Lovewell could win. . . ."

Lacey recognized Vaughn Cutter's voice, a strong, easy baritone. Jess was cute, but Vaughn was handsome, tall, and muscular. He wasn't skittish about anything physical. Bubba Dole had jumped Vaughn once. Bubba's claim to fame was an ability to split bricks with his head or his hands. But Vaughn had broken Bubba's head, sending him to the hospital with a concussion.

Lacey had secretly wanted Jess and Vaughn to have a big fight over her, but they got along just fine. Darn. And now Vaughn was hyping April Lovewell!

"Look at it this way," Lacey heard him explain. "April may not be as popular as Lacey or Kiki, but she doesn't have any enemies, either. And she's more of a serious student type than Raven. Her art teacher, Mr. Woolery, is on the selection committee, too. He's probably the most popular teacher in school, and the most respected teacher in the community. Committee members are going to listen to him. And everybody knows who Mr. Woolery's favorite art student is."

Lacey heard a momentary silence of assent from the other kids. They all knew April Lovewell was

Mr. Woolery's pet. "Pet" was Lacey's word. "Favorite" sounded too nice. She felt frustrated, peeved. After all, Lacey had gotten April nominated. She'd figured April Lovewell would be no competition whatever. Now she'd have to alter her thinking. April might not be as much of a threat as Raven or Kiki, but she had to be taken seriously as a challenger. What can I do about April? Lacey wondered. There must be *something*!

"Do you want to place a bet on April?" Hope Hubbard asked.

"I'm not in a position to do that right now," Vaughn replied.

Aware that he was dating Lacey, everybody laughed.

"Well, *I'll* place a bet! Ten dollars says Raven Cruz will be Peggy Sue."

Denise Guthrie, editor of the *Grapevine*. Lacey recognized the breathy expressiveness, as if she'd just that moment learned something tremendously exciting and had to tell you about it right away. Raven and Denise were best friends, so the wager came as no surprise to Lacey, but then Denise said, "After the anti-Greenway Mall rally tomorrow, people are going to be carrying Raven Cruz around on their shoulders."

"Yeah, right!" said Penny Bolton. "Dream on."

Good for you, Penny! Lacey thought. That's tellin' 'em.

The first bell rang then. Lockers started slamming. Lacey retreated quietly to the bottom of the stairwell and started singing, as if to herself, but loud enough to be heard up by the lockers.

"Lacey!"

"Hi, Lace. You're almost late."

"Congratulations! You're one of the four!"

Lacey tilted up to kiss Vaughn—disloyal, doubting Vaughn!—and he kissed her back. She'd wanted Jess Gardner to see the kiss, but he was going down the hall, talking to Denise Guthrie and paying no attention.

It occurred to Lacey, right in the middle of kissing Vaughn, that she might be able to get Jess Gardner back with hardly any effort at all. He'd been "protesting too much" when, moments earlier, he'd touted Raven's chances of winning. He *did* still love her. Lacey was sure of it.

"Break it up, you two!" said Dwight the Dweeb, shuffling down the corridor. "Come out of the clinch."

Vaughn obediently ended the kiss. He was so . . . so straight. That was one of the problems with most of the Paradiso guys. They were exciting to look at—the best ones, anyway—but after you got to know them, they were so . . . straight. No thrills. No danger. No mystery.

Except for one, Lacey thought as Spike Navarrone strode insolently past without so much as a glance in her direction.

CHAPTER 10

"What a day!" Lacey complained to Renée Henderson as the two girls left school and walked across the parking lot toward Lacey's car. It was 3:15 p.m. The sun, comfortably warm this morning, had turned almost fiercely hot. Millions of peach blossoms, having baked all day, smelled like the cheap perfume Spike Navarrone's mother trailed down Old Town Road on her way to the Blue Hawaii Bar.

Lacey got behind the wheel. Renée slid into the passenger seat, reached beneath her, and pulled out the white envelope. "What's this?"

"Oh!" Lacey had forgotten. "Daddy gave me a little something for being one of the final four."

"Really?" Renée glanced inside the envelope. Her eyes widened. "Wow! Geez, Lace, there must be a couple hundred bucks in here!"

"Oh, that's just Daddy," said Lacey, laughing

gaily. "You know how he is." She stuffed the envelope under her seat.

"Boy!" said Renée. "I wish I had your dad."

No, you don't, thought Lacey. She started the Ferrari, backed out of her parking space, and headed toward the exit.

For Lacey the day had been tiring in a frustrating, grinding kind of way. She had only managed to get excused from gym after practically faking a nervous breakdown for Nurse Pritchard. Excessive stress, Lacey claimed, brought on by Festival Week, upcoming senior exams, and the need to retake her SATs had left her too weak and discombobulated to run around the track. Then Kiki hadn't come to school *at all*, and nobody had any idea where she was. Lacey had contemplated phoning the De Santises during lunch period, but had decided against it. First, she hadn't wanted to appear concerned. Second, she hadn't wanted to get Kiki in trouble with her parents if she was doing something on her own that Dom and Sue De Santis didn't know about.

Lacey had been waiting all day to ask Kiki to withdraw from the Queen competition.

"Wheeeeee! God, I love this car!" Renée's head was out the window, her gold-flecked hair streaming, as Lacey flashed down Old Town Road toward the center of town. Her mind was working hard.

She'd decided what to do about Kiki, true. But what about April and Raven?

"Let's go over to Rosa's and have some tacos and a soda," Lacey suggested. She knew that Raven sometimes did waitress duty in the afternoons. This might be a good time to pump her about Winston Purdy III.

"I can't," replied Renée, instantly glum. "It's my . . . regular trip night."

Lacey knew about trip night. Every Monday, Renée and her mom drove up to Sacrmento for a joint therapy session. The psychologist's name was Dr. Toulouse. "Screwloose Toulouse," Renée called him. Lacey was the only one of Renée's friends who knew about these sessions, which were intended to resolve any lingering hostility between Renée and her mother. Not even Doug Mattinsky, Renée's longtime steady, knew the reason for these Monday night out-of-town treks. He thought Renée might have another guy somewhere, or something. Of course, Doug didn't know about the attempted barbecue-fork matricide either.

Lacey's lips were sealed.

"Oh, c'mon," prodded Lacey. "Just a Coke, then. How long can it take?"

"Sorry. I really have to get home."

"Oh, all right." Lacey felt irritated. She didn't

want to go home yet, and she couldn't think of anything to do. Now she was at loose ends . . .

. . . and then, right there in her rearview mirror, Lacey glimpsed Spike Navarrone coming up fast on his powerful Harley Davidson. No way was he going to pass her! "Oh-*kay*!" she shouted gleefully, slamming her foot down hard on the accelerator. The Ferrari leapt forward, all those hundreds and hundreds of horses suddenly free of the corral. Within seconds, Lacey and Renée were only part of a red blur rocketing down Old Town Road. Spike and his cycle dropped away, barely a speck in the rearview mirror now. The light at the big T intersection was turning red when Lacey shot through it. "*Yowwwwwwww!*" she was yelling, triumphant and excited. "*Yiiiiiiiiii!*" screamed Renée, frightened.

"Don't be a wuss!" Lacey chided. "Nothing's gonna happen . . . uh-oh."

She saw flashing red lights in the rearview mirror now, and a black and white Plymouth. Sheriff Rodriguez. Again. Lacey had just gotten a ticket for speeding two weeks ago. If there was one thing that made Daddy mad—really, normally mad, not "off the deep end"—it was Lacey's traffic tickets. "I can't fix them for you, Princess!" he'd yelled when she'd once asked him to. "How would it look? Have a little discretion, for God's sake!"

Lacey managed to slow the car down, having a little trouble with her big feet. She eased to a stop at the curb in front of Carter's Drugstore. A bunch of kids were going in or coming out. They all looked. Most of them grinned. "Go, Lace!" shouted some sophomore wiseass. "Indy five-hundred. Richard Petty's in big trouble."

Lacey also caught a glimpse of April Lovewell. April seemed preoccupied, even worried, as she ducked into Carter's. Probably buying the latest brand of freckle remover, Lacey thought wryly.

Then there was Sheriff Rodriguez, approaching the Ferrari. He already had his summons book poised, pencil too. Showboat cop—he hadn't switched off the flashing lights of his patrol car, which was parked right in front of her. Daddy could just glance out his office window and see this whole thing. I'm really in for it now, Lacey thought.

"I'm gonna be late getting home," whined Renée.

"Oh, stop bitching," Lacey snapped.

"License, please, Miss Pinkerton," said the sheriff. "Again," he added, but he was not amused.

Lacey pulled it out of her wallet and handed it up to the sheriff, who retreated to his patrol car to fill out the summons.

Spike Navarrone wheeled up then, stopping next

to Lacey's car. He throttled the Harley down to a low, rumbling purr and removed his black-visored helmet. There was a hint of a smile on his strong, finely shaped lips, and Lacey even caught a trace of amusement in his dark, broodingly intelligent eyes. He smoothed back his thick hair with a sweep of his hand and said, "Your car goes pretty fast, Lacey. Pretty fast. You want to take me on some night? Smuggler's Road, off the main highway? How about it?"

"I don't think I'd mind," replied Lacey, flirting with him, speaking in her telephone voice and trying for a sleepy, sultry look. "Taking you on. But what would April say?"

For just an instant, Spike Navarrone seemed to lose his slow, easy cool, the self-confident aura admired by kids and adults alike. Then it was back. "Maybe April doesn't have to know," he said.

"I won't tell her if you don't," Lacey shot back, batting her eyelashes, running the tip of her tongue across her upper lip. She knew boys liked that.

Spike didn't say anything. He just met her eyes and smiled. Lacey was about to tell him that April, right this minute, was inside Carter's Drugstore. But Sheriff Rodriguez returned bearing the summons and handed it to her. "Move it along, Carlos," he said. "You're blocking traffic."

Old Town Road was completely empty of traffic.

Lacey had the disconcerting feeling that the sheriff didn't want a nice Hispanic boy like Spike wasting his time with . . . with a gringo bimbo. It was an expression she'd once heard Raven use. It had infuriated her, too, mainly because Lacey had suspected that Raven was talking about *her.*

Spike replaced his helmet, throttled up, checked for traffic, and roared away.

"Better watch yourself, Miss Pinkerton," advised Sheriff Rodriguez. "I don't know how many points you've lost already, but keep it up and you'll be on the hoof for a long time to come."

"Yes, sir. I'm sorry. I really am."

"Right," he grunted, grinning in a way Lacey didn't like at all.

Lacey sat in her car, fuming and furious, until the sheriff drove away. "The nerve!" she sputtered.

"People vote for him, though," commented Renée, in a what-can-you-do-about-it? tone.

"Democracy has its drawbacks," said Lacey sourly. She was thinking about Daddy. He would be *so-o* mad. Even if he hadn't seen her being ticketed, he was sure to find out.

"You okay, Lace?" Renée was asking. "I got to get home."

"Oh. Sure."

The crowd in front of Carter's Drugstore had drifted away now that the show was over. The

101

drugstore windows were plastered with Jerry's painstakingly hand-lettered signs: BRYLCREEM— $2.98, 32 OZ.; SCOPE—48 OZ. FAMILY SIZE, $4.69; 48-HOUR PHOTO SERVICE . . .

Lacey moved her feet around, shifted into first, and roared away from Carter's Drugstore, almost colliding, in her haste, with a flatbed truck carrying several dozen migrant laborers. Something about their presence here in Paradiso troubled her. It was as if the world she had known since birth was shifting beneath her feet. This morning, in her room, she'd sensed her own little universe beginning to crumble. Vaughn, school, the Pinks: maybe they weren't forever. Inevitably, they would drop away into the past, just as Paradiso's past was dropping away.

I won't think about it now, she told herself. The most important thing today and for the rest of the week is to win the Peach Blossom crown. I'm *dying* to win, Lacey realized. I'll die if I don't.

Lacey turned at the T intersection and gunned up Winding Hill Road. "There's April," she said to Renée. The two girls got a fleeting look at April Lovewell, who was trudging home. April was carrying a huge yellow plastic shopping bag from Carter's Drugstore. "Must be a new brand of freckle remover on the market," Lacey wisecracked.

102

She cut a hard left onto Revere Road, Renée's street, and pulled into the Hendersons' driveway.

"Oh, Lace," said Renée, "don't make fun of April. She's really nice. And think what she has to put up with. A minister for a father. It'd be like living with God, sort of. He's got his eye on her all the time."

"Not quite *all* the time. She manages to see Spike Navarrone often enough."

Lacey smiled.

"I *saw* that little smirk, Lace. What are you planning now?"

Lacey was sure that Renée would be amused and appreciative. "You know the Mendola sisters?" she asked Renée. "That work at the Blue Belle Dairy? Well, I heard one of them saying that Spike is tired of sneaking around with April. He thinks it's cheap and dishonest, and he's getting sick of dodging Reverend Lovewell all the time."

"So?" Renée asked.

"So maybe I'll take up his invitation to race on Smuggler's Road, and see what happens after that."

"Oh, Lace!" Renée blurted. "You wouldn't. Would you? April would be crushed. Spike's her first real boyfriend—and she's real serious about him. And besides, what about Vaughn?"

"Oh, Vaughn," said Lacey dismissively. She was still mad at him for having suggested, this morning at Hope Hubbard's locker, that April had a chance of winning Pretty Peggy Sue.

Jeez, sometimes you had to explain *everything*.

"I can't just go tell Reverend and Mrs. Lovewell that April's sneaking around with Spike, can I? But if April finds out I've been spending a little time with Spike, she'll be upset. Her mom and dad will notice, the whole thing will come out, and the Rev might even make April drop out of the competition."

Lacey was very pleased with her scheme, which had the additional advantage of making Vaughn Cutter jealous. But Renée was aghast. "Oh, Lacey!" she cried. "How could you even *think* of such a thing? It's mean. April's never done anything to you, has she?"

Lacey, surprised by Renée's reaction, felt angry and guilty . . . and angry because she felt guilty. "Well, don't go run and tell April!" she snapped.

Renée's silence suggested that she was thinking of doing just that.

"If you breathe a word of this," Lacey threatened, "I just might let it slip to Doug Mattinsky that you have to go see a shrink in Sacramento every Monday. And I'll tell him why, too."

Renée Henderson was a big, strong, healthy girl, vigorous and tanned. But the blood left her face fast. She turned to Lacey and cried in horror, "You wouldn't!"

Lacey just smiled.

Renée started crying.

"Of course," said Lacey, rubbing it in, "I'll tell Doug you're all fine now. You never even touched your mom with that barbecue fork, and they do wonders at mental hospitals these days, don't they?"

Renée burst into sobs. "You wouldn't tell Doug, would you? Oh, Lacey, don't tell. Please. My life was ruined in Sacramento. Some secrets you just don't tell. Out of decency, if nothing else. Why, even Jess Gardner didn't tell on Michelle Wheeler . . . uh-oh, I shouldn't have said that."

"What about Jess and Michelle?" Lacey demanded.

Renée, who had no tissue, wiped her eyes on the sleeve of her blue polo shirt and said, "Jess broke that date with you because she asked him to drive her to the doctor's office. It was an emergency."

"What doctor? What do you mean?"

"It was an ob-gyn," said Renée, snuffling. "Michelle got pregnant."

"No way! Really? That's why I haven't seen her around. Was it . . . was it Jess?"

"No. He just helped her out by driving her to the clinic. The guy was somebody who graduated a couple of years ago, from what I heard. But don't tell anyone. Please?"

Lacey's heart sank. She'd dumped cute, affectionate, easygoing Jess Gardner purely out of spite. She'd have taken him back in a minute if he'd given her a good reason for breaking their date. He'd had a good reason, too, and a sense of honor.

"I'm sorry, Renée," she said. "Of course I won't tell. Forgive me, okay?"

Saying nothing, Renée got out of the Ferrari and started toward her house, a small white ranch on a small, dusty lot. Renée was still crying. She didn't look back.

"Renée!" Lacey called, to no avail.

Renée went inside her house and closed the door.

Damn!

Tuesday, May 23

CHAPTER 11

Kiki brushed out her thick, shiny hair while she waited for Lacey to pick her up. She hoped that Lacey would approve of her blue chiffon dress, with its puffed sleeves and almost daringly low-cut neckline. When she heard the throaty purr of Lacey's car, she tensed a little.

"Lacey's here, honey!" her mom called from downstairs.

"Tell her to come up." Kiki dashed around, straightening her room. The De Santises didn't have a live-in maid, like the Pinkertons, or even a cleaning woman. It galled Kiki that her dad was so cheap he wouldn't hire in-house help, let alone join the Paradiso-Walnut Hills Country Club. "Why in hell would I want to do that?" the insufferably self-reliant Dom De Santis always asked, when pressed by Kiki on the issue of club membership. "To hang around with a so-called hotshot like Cal Pinkerton? Who buys his ditzy daughter a car she hasn't got the brains to appreciate? Look, sweetheart, those country club types bore me already for free. Why should I pay dues for the same privilege?"

Kiki tossed the pink and white comforter over her pink and white striped sheets, fluffed up her bed pillows, and sat her favorite teddy bear up straight against the pillows. Then she switched on the radio. Buddy Holly was singing.

> *Rave on, it's a crazy feelin',*
> *And I know it's got me reelin'* . . .

Kiki, in a rush, continued getting her room in order. Sometimes she had wondered why Lacey's approval meant so much to her. She had always explained it to herself as just a natural part of friendship. Lacey was her friend, not to mention the most popular girl at Paradiso High. Of course Lacey's opinion mattered.

> *Tell me*
> *You love me only,*
> *Rave onto me!*

concluded Buddy. "That was the man himself," babbled T. J. the D. J., "with one of the goldenest of golden oldies, and speaking of gold, four of the most golden Paradiso girls are vying for the golden crown of Peach Blossom Queen . . ."

Kiki clicked the radio off. She'd heard her name mentioned as a finalist often enough, and she knew Lacey would win for sure. I don't even *want* to win, she told herself. What for? To get a screen test? Yeah, right. She couldn't act her way out of a paper bag. College scholarship? She wasn't sure she even wanted to go to college . . . at least not right away. Kiki De Santis, Peach Blossom Queen, Pretty Peggy Sue? Rave on!

Kiki wondered, as she heard Lacey coming up the stairs to the bedroom, what sort of bit part her friend would get in a movie. Following in her mom's footsteps and everything . . .

"Missed you yesterday, Keek," said Lacey airily, casually, coming into the room as if she were entering her own domain. She wore white pants, a navy blue shirt, and a pair of low-heeled blue pumps. Also a white headband: just the right touch. Lacey flopped stomach-down onto the bed, saying: "Hear you bought a dress. Well, let's see it."

Kiki thought her blue chiffon dress was really pretty. She was *sure* it was really pretty, but still she was a little afraid to show it to Lacey. She went over to her closet, slipped the dress off the clothes bar, and slid off the plastic over. Oh, no! The dress bore a little tag she hadn't seen. REGINA'S ANTIQUES.

111

"Why didn't you tell me you were going to Sacramento?" Lacey was asking. "We could have gone together. I wouldn't have minded skipping a day of school."

Regina's Antiques!

Outside Kiki's room, Dom De Santis was coming upstairs to dress for the day. He always ate his morning bacon and eggs in his bathrobe and pajamas. *So-o* gross. Lacey had told her that the Pinkertons, fully dressed, breakfasted together each morning as formally as if they were dining at a four-fork restaurant.

"We could have gone to Sacramento together," Lacey repeated. It was a mild accusation.

"I just had this impulse," said Kiki. "Mom said okay, so I went."

"So that's the dress," said Lacey, getting off the bed and coming over. "Hmmmm."

Kiki twirled it on the hanger. "What do you think?"

"Put it on."

"There isn't time. We gotta get to school."

"Up school." Lacey reached for the dress and took it from Kiki.

Lacey held the dress in front of herself, modeling for the mirror. "What's this?" she asked, finding the little tag and looking at it. "So," she said, with a smile that was almost a smirk. *"Regina's,* huh?"

"I looked everywhere," explained Kiki, aware that she was babbling defensively. "Nordstrom's. I. Magnin. Letterbee's, even. I wanted just the right Fifties look. . . .

Regina's Antiques was nothing but an old clothes place, maybe half a step up from the Salvation Army. Scratch palace. Cootie coven. Nobody *bought* anything at *Regina's*. That's where you dumped old stuff that wasn't quite bad enough for the Salvation Army.

But Kiki had been so happy to find the blue dress yesterday, and she knew it was not only good but exactly what she wanted. Lacey's reaction—her coolness, her little half smirk—was devastating.

"I'm sure you'll look good in it," Lacey said, shrugging, tossing the dress onto the bed. "Hey! I have to ask you a real big favor."

"Sure," Kiki agreed, eager to get off the subject of the dress, which now seemed a horrible blue rag in her eyes.

"I figured this all out," said Lacey, frowning to show how hard she had thought about it. She sat down on the edge of the bed—somewhat gingerly, Kiki thought—and flashed her warmest, most intimate smile. "Nobody really thinks April can win Pretty Peggy Sue. My only real competition is Raven Cruz. You and I are Pinks. Raven isn't. We can't have someone who isn't a Pink going around with the Peach Blossom crown on her head, can we? Not to mention somebody who does waitress duty at a taco place . . ."

Kiki thought of her mother, who'd been a truck-stop waitress.

". . . and comes to school with chicken *stuff* on her shoes!" Lacey gave Kiki a fetching, pleading look and continued: "So, I was thinking, if you drop out of the competition, I'll win for sure. Nobody should mess with us Pinks, right?"

Kiki didn't know what to say. Certainly, she hadn't expected to win. But she'd never given an instant of thought to withdrawing. Lacey's request came as a complete surprise, but even more aston-ishing was the fact that Lacey appeared to be con-cerned that she might *lose*!

"I don't know," said Kiki, genuinely baffled. "I don't . . ."

Lacey was very reasonable, very understanding. "I know you probably didn't consider withdrawing, Keek," she said. "And I know it's an imposition on you. I'd never even have asked if it wasn't so impor-tant. We don't want somebody who feeds chickens getting a scholarship and a screen test, do we? How will Paradiso look, sending somebody so uncool down to Hollywood? We'd get laughed at. Our Peach Blossom Queens won't be taken seriously anymore."

"Jeez, Lace . . ."

"We're best friends, aren't we? Look, I'd do something for you in return. I have these Madonna tickets for Sunday. You and Bobby could go!"

"You have Madonna tickets?"

"Is it a deal?" Lacey pressed. She stroked the pink ear of Kiki's teddy bear, looking incredibly tense.

Kiki actually felt sorry for Lacey. Lacey was desperate to be Peach Blossom Queen. Kiki hadn't wanted anything that badly in her whole life. Still, Kiki had a nagging feeling that what Lacey was asking her to do was wrong. It was almost like cheating. A lot of kids had nominated her, Kiki De Santis, and she was a legitimate finalist. Even though she wanted to see Lacey happy, it somehow didn't seem right just to withdraw.

"Gee, Lace," said Kiki hesitantly. "I dunno . . ."

Lacey yawned. "I suppose I could ask April to withdraw," she said. "I'm sure she and Spike would love to go see Madonna."

Listening to Lacey, Kiki also heard Bobby Deeter's voice, from the time they'd had a fight about Lacey: *You don't have to follow her around like a puppy dog. . . .*"

"We Pinks have to stay together," Lacey was

saying. "Sticking together has made us what we are, the envy of everybody in school."

"I don't know, Lace," Kiki heard herself repeating. "I'll have to think about it."

Immediately, she felt the piercing power of Lacey's blue-eyed glare. Those eyes could turn to ice in a millisecond. Yet, somewhat to her own surprise, Kiki didn't glance away. Instead, she stared right back. It was Lacey, after a moment, who blinked and looked off to the side.

Kiki glanced at her pretty blue dress, which Lacey had carelessly tossed onto the bed. Suddenly she had an image of herself in that dress. She was standing beside Mayor McNally. He was grinning, beaming, holding the Peach Blossom crown. "This year's winner," he was orating to the vast crowd of people at the festival, "this year's winner, Paradiso's Pretty Peggy Sue, is—"

"Kiki De Santis!" her mom called from down in the kitchen. "You and Lacey are going to be late for school."

"Yeah, Mom," Kiki called back. "Lace, you go ahead. I gotta get my junk together."

Lacey said: "What's it going to be? About the Queen thing?"

Kiki read in Lacey's expression a certainty that the deal was done, but it wasn't. Not yet. She hadn't quit Coach Monfort's field hockey team, even though she hardly ever got to play. Nor had she given up in social studies—her hardest subject —even when it was impossible to figure out how socialism differed from communism.

"I'll think it over," Kiki repeated.

"You do that."

Lacey left the room and went downstairs. Kiki shoved a half-finished book report into her holey old green bookbag, ran a brush through her hair a couple more times, and started toward the door. Then she looked back, saw her pretty, fluffy dress lying on the bed, and returned it to the closet. It *was* pretty. It really was. She'd been so happy, yesterday, to have found it all by herself, so proud to have brought it home.

I don't care what Lacey thinks about it, she thought, heading for the stairs. I look *great* in that dress!

Kiki's father intercepted her, stepping out of the bathroom into her path. His face, half lathered, half shaven, almost made her laugh. But then she saw the "Daddy" look in his eyes: gentle, concerned, and sort of sad. Not *sad* sad, but sad in a way Kiki couldn't describe. His look expressed an emotion that Kiki was vaguely aware she wouldn't understand until she got older.

"Don't do it, Weets," was all he said before

retreating inside the steamy bathroom, with a red towel wrapped around him.

"Weets?" He hadn't called her that for years. When she'd been very little, almost too little to recall, her father had called out, "Where's my sweets?" one day after coming home from work. Scrambling, giggling, absolutely overjoyed, Kiki had run to him, screaming, "Weets! Weets!" as loud as she could. He'd picked her up, tossed her into the air, caught her, and hugged her tight.

The game had gone on for a long time, until one day, very solemnly, Kiki had said: "Daddy, I don't want to be *'Weets'* anymore, okay?"

Come to think of it, the look in his eyes just now, when he'd said *"Don't do it, Weets,"* had been almost exactly like his expression on the day she'd announced her maturity.

And what had he meant today? Kiki knew: He'd overheard the conversation between Lacey and her. He was telling her: Don't withdraw from the competition. Don't give your word against your will. Kiki knew enough about him after almost eighteen years to know how much he respected those who kept their word. He numbered himself among them.

Feeling majorly stressed, Kiki went downstairs.

Lacey, chewing a cinnamon doughnut and holding a tumbler of orange juice, was saying: "Things are a lot different now. When my mother got screen tested, an actress had to work her way up in bit parts. It sometimes took years to get a big role, but Mother married Daddy, so that was the end of it. These days you can shoot right to the top if you get a good role early, and even go on into other fields. Like music."

Kiki felt a rush of resentment. Lacey was so sure she'd convinced Kiki to withdraw. Of course, Kiki thought, she thinks I'm a wimp. Why shouldn't she? I haven't exactly refused to withdraw.

"It's too bad both of you can't win," said Sue De Santis. "It's too bad all four of you can't."

"Right," said Lacey, with a too-bright smile. "Keek, let's go."

Kiki grabbed a bran muffin off the table, and the two girls hurried out to the red Ferrari. "It's too late for Rosa's," Lacey said, gunning down Winding Hill Road. "And I wanted to talk to Raven, too."

"Why?" Lacey and Raven Cruz hardly ever spoke to each other, except to exchange sly barbs.

"She's up to something. Winston Purdy is in on it."

Lacey described what she'd seen Monday morning.

"So what?" Kiki said.

"So Raven's got a trick up her sleeve. I'm sure of it. And believe me, I'll think of a way to find out just what kind of trick it is."

"Well," said Kiki, "I'm sure it doesn't have anything to do with Pretty Peggy Sue."

"Don't bet on it. *Everything* this week has some connection to the festival. Hey! There goes Spike Navarrone. He must be doing over fifty miles an hour."

They had stopped for a yellow light and Spike shot through like a missile, his helmet gleaming in the bright morning sun. Yet another perfect day in Paradiso, with an easy, languid warmth in the perfumed air.

"Spike came on to me yesterday," Lacey said.

"He *what?* He's been dating April for over a year."

"See what you miss when you skip a day of school? He came on to me, though. He's interested. You know how quiet he usually is? How he hardly ever talks to anybody? Well, I got the impression he's not quiet at all if you get to know him. And I wouldn't mind him making some noise with me."

The light turned green. Lacey swung left onto Old Town Road and accelerated up the hill to the high school.

"Oh, Lace!" Kiki exclaimed. "You're not planning to . . . not you and Spike? What would Vaughn say? And April would be so hurt. . . ."

"Maybe I'll just let Spike deal with April. And I can handle Vaughn."

Kiki had to admit that this was probably true. Lacey never had any trouble controlling her boyfriends. If she did something that made a guy angry, she would turn around the next day and be extra nice. She'd buy him a sweater, or maybe a new watch. She'd promise him a couple of hours in the backseat of a car in the scrublands. And for days afterward, he'd follow her around in a worshipful daze.

"There's April right now!" cried Lacey as she shot around Reverend Lovewell's black Chevrolet. "She's a senior, and he still won't let her walk to school. Can you believe it?"

"I wouldn't bother with Spike," said Kiki, as casually as she could. "I'm sure he and April are serious. Besides, he's not your type."

"They're all my type, honey," replied Lacey in her lowest, huskiest voice. She pulled up in front of the school to drop Kiki off. "There's Dwight the Dweeb, out by the flagpole like usual. You can go tell him you're withdrawing from the Queen competition. I'll drive around back and park."

"Ummm," Kiki said. She swung up and out of the low-slung sports car.

"See ya at lunch," said Lacey. "It's the big anti-mall rally. I can't wait to see Raven Cruz fall flat on her face."

CHAPTER 12

Breakfast with the saints, always a horror, was even worse Tuesday morning.

"Why does it take you so long to get yourself ready for school, child?" Sara Lovewell wanted to know. "You're not playing with your freckles again, are you?"

"No, Mother," said April, spooning her oatmeal.

"Getting up so early every day," continued her mother, as if she hadn't even heard. "And this Pretty Peggy Sue business. I just don't know."

April had been surprised, shocked really, when she heard that she was one of the Pretty Peggy Sue finalists. "It makes sense," her cousin, Hope, had said. "You're by far the best artist in school. You even said yourself that Mr. Woolery thinks you'll be a famous painter someday."

Mr. Woolery had told April she could be a

123

commercial illustrator after she went to art school. April thought, however, that it had been Lacey Pinkerton's concern for her, not her artistic ability, that had gotten her nominated.

"But I'm sure it was Lacey and her campaigning for me that made the difference!" April exclaimed to Hope. "It was so sweet of her. I don't understand why some kids put Lacey down for being selfish."

Hope had looked as if she were about to say something, but then she stopped and shook her head.

Lacey was so cool, and she had always been so kind to April—it was an honor even to be in the running with Lacey. April *was* flattered to be a finalist, but she certainly didn't expect to win. If by some unthinkable chance Lacey didn't win, either Raven, who was so smart, or Kiki, who was so nice, would surely be chosen as Pretty Peggy Sue.

"You have just as good a chance as anyone," Hope had said. "Maybe better. You're the only one of the four who has a special talent. That really sets you apart from the others."

I know I have some talent, April thought. But I'm not in the same league as Raven Cruz, Kiki De Santis, and Lacey Pinkerton. Anyway, April had bigger things on her mind, much bigger, than whether or not she'd be elected Peach Blossom Queen.

"I don't know about that Mr. Woolery, either," St. Sara went on. "Your father and I are somewhat concerned about his influence on you."

Mr. Woolery had telephoned the parsonage yesterday evening and asked the Lovewells' permission to take April out to the scrublands on Thursday before school. April had been experimenting with different shades of lighting in her artwork. In her mind, April was already conceiving a series of colored sketches: the scrublands just before dawn, precisely at dawn, and right after dawn. She was planning to do all the sketches in shades of light in which bushes, trees, and wild grass would be suggested but not clearly visible.

Mr. Woolery was excited about her concept. April was too, and she would have been more enthusiastic if she didn't have so much else to think about. The saints, however, were decidedly leery of the whole enterprise.

"Going off alone with a man like that," Reverend Lovewell said, "so early in the morning. I wonder."

Oh, Lord! thought April. If they only knew the truth about me! It occurred to her that somewhere down the road they would have to learn about her secret romance with Spike. She didn't want them to find out. Yet in a way, she really didn't care anymore. They'd made her half crazy with all their worries and puritanical rules and restrictions. Maybe it'd be good for their souls to get shaken up a bit.

"We had hoped you would outgrow this unhealthy infatuation with art," St. Ward continued. "Art is *false worship*," he pronounced in his thundering pulpit voice. April was no longer impressed.

"In yesterday's mail we received," her mother said sweetly, "a whole new batch of brochures from some of the best Bible colleges in the country. I want you to look them over when you get home from school this afternoon. Your father and I are puzzled because you haven't told us the college of your choice for next year."

"Don't you see?" cried April, tears springing to her eyes in spite of her effort to keep them down. "Don't you, at last, *see?* Bible college is *not* my choice!"

St. Ward sighed. "I'll drive you to school. Get your books."

Furious and troubled, desperate to be with Spike, April followed her father outside to the car. The morning was blastingly brilliant. Walking out into all that sunshine was like awakening in the dark and suddenly turning on a light. April winced. All around Paradiso, the peach orchards bloomed fresh

126

and new, row upon row upon row of peach trees, explosions of color stretching into the distance.

On the drive to school, they passed Hope. She walked easily, jauntily this morning. She had, for once, ditched her baggy pants in favor of crisp white shorts and a white University of Nevada–Las Vegas sweatshirt. April gave Hope a tiny wave that St. Ward couldn't see, and Hope nodded in reply.

Reverend Lovewell saw Hope, though, and launched into what April had long ago come to call The Speech. "Stay away from that girl, April," he said.

Too late, Father, April wanted to tell him.

St. Ward drove the Chevrolet up to the school and braked to a stop. April's hand was already on the door handle.

"Can you give me just a few seconds?" her father asked. There was a quiver in his voice, an unfamiliar hint of uncertainty that compelled April to turn quickly and look at him. He'd never been uncertain about anything in his whole life.

"Your mother and I love you, honey," he said, sort of glancing away from her. This was new too. She got called "child" at home, not "honey."

April said nothing, wondering what he'd say now.

But he didn't say anything else, just "Have a nice

day." Anybody could say that. Lacey Pinkerton's mom and dad certainly didn't say such common stuff, like "Love you, honey" and "Have a nice day."

CHAPTER 13

"If it isn't Kiki De Santis," said Principal Appleby, all elbows and knees and scraggly-haired pink dome. "I note that you seem to have recovered from the mysterious malady by which you were assailed yesterday." He laughed—*snort-snort-snort*—and began cracking his knuckles. "Your dear mother sounded most grievously concerned when she telephoned regarding your affliction."

Kiki couldn't decide if Dwight the Dweeb was more ridiculous when he tried to use flowery language, like right now, or when he attempted to sound like a surfer dude. Neither mode of expression fit him, but his plaid sports coat didn't fit him either.

"I feel better today," she said lightly. "Thanks for asking."

The warning bell rang then. Kiki hurried to her

locker to get her chemistry textbook, which she ought to have taken home and read over the weekend. If Mr. Schwob called on her, she'd be a dead duck for sure. "Kiki!" kids hollered, and "Where were you yesterday, Keek?" Usually, she would have shot back tart replies, like "Had something more important to do" or "I totally forgot, do we have school on Monday?" but she was in no mood for screwing around this morning.

"I bet five bucks on Kiki," said Eddie Hagenspitzel. He was standing in front of Hope Hubbard's locker, placing a bet.

"Five bucks on Kiki," Hope said, taking Eddie's wager and writing it down.

What impressed Kiki was that Eddie Hagenspitzel hadn't seen her coming down the hall. He wasn't putting on a show for her approval.

Kiki cut through the student lounge on her way to chemistry. It was a circular, carpeted area between the two wings of the school with soft couches and a conversation "pit," where kids could hang out. Few did, because the weather was always so good outside. So Kiki was surprised this morning to see three of her classmates in the pit, their heads bent over a large, thick book.

"I think that's it," Winston Purdy was saying to Raven Cruz and Denise Guthrie. He was pointing to something in the book.

"But we won't know for sure until tomorrow," said Raven. She sounded excited and exasperated at the same time. "If the film gets back to Carter's on time and the pictures turn out . . ."

They all saw Kiki then. "Hi!" said Raven, as if she'd been startled.

"Hi, Kiki," said Denise Guthrie, in her breathless way.

Winston Purdy merely bobbed his thin head in greeting, but Kiki noticed that he closed the big book he'd been holding and sort of slid it around to the side of his leg. Kiki saw the title anyway, gold letters on red: *Birds of America.* Birds?

Kiki walked on through the student lounge and headed to chemistry class. She wondered what the three of them wouldn't "know for sure until tomorrow," aware that her presence had made them uncomfortable for some unknown reason.

When she saw Bobby Deeter's smile, it made her feel great. She took her usual seat next to him, and he reached over and squeezed her hand. "Missed you yesterday," he said. Just a regular comment, but the thing about Bobby was that he always meant what he said. It was probably why Dom De Santis liked him so much. When Bobby said he'd missed her, Kiki knew he'd really *missed* her. Missed her company, missed having her around.

"Did you get the dress?" he asked.

131

"Uh-huh."

"I can't wait to see it."

"Oh, I think you can," she said, smiling. "Bobby," she said, as big-shouldered, balding Mr. Schwob prepared to begin class, "I've got a little problem. . . ."

"Shoot," said Bobby, looking concerned.

"Okay, troops," commanded Mr. Schwob, "cut the chitchat. It'll keep."

You didn't talk in Mr. Schwob's classroom unless you wanted to spend several hours cleaning test tubes after school.

The subject of this morning's lesson was the behavior of molecules in natural and manufactured compounds, about which Kiki hadn't a clue. Fortunately, Mr. Schwob didn't call on her. So as she pretended great interest, Kiki let her mind wander. Why on earth had Raven, Denise, and Winston Purdy been examining *Birds of America?* And what did it have to do with film at Carter's Drugstore?

CHAPTER 14

Coach Monfort made everybody run two miles on the track during fourth-period gym class, so by the time Kiki got herself showered and dressed, the anti-mall rally was getting started. Skipping the Tuesday menu—Burger/bun w. peas and fruit cup —Kiki walked out onto the great grassy field in front of school. A podium and microphone had been placed next to the flagpole, and several loud-speakers had been positioned on the grass.

The crowd was large and growing larger by the minute. Half the student body milled around, look-ing for sunny spots on the grass. And at least a couple hundred Paradiso citizens were present too. Sheriff Rodriguez, at a discreet distance, leaned against his black and white patrol car, observing everything through his sunglasses. Paradiso was generally a sedate place, but you never knew what to expect when major changes were proposed and big money was involved. As Kiki looked around, she saw several women from town waving a bed-sheet banner on which they had lettered GREENWAY MEANS GREED, with a lot of dollar signs. Kiki recognized April Lovewell's mother, Sara, in the group, and Bertha Carter, wife of the druggist. Huck Spector, the barber, joined them. He wore a sandwich-board sign reading THE BIGGER THEY ARE on the front and THE HARDER THEY FALL on the back.

"They," of course, as anyone in town could tell you, were Huck's longtime enemies, Greenway developers Cal Pinkerton and Lars Cutter. Kiki caught sight of the two men, dressed in business suits, standing near a loudspeaker on the fringes of the crowd. Mr. Pinkerton looked so incredibly distinguished! And Mr. Cutter, Vaughn's dad, had the bod of a teenager even though he was *fifty years old*!

"There you are!" said Lacey, rushing up to Kiki. "Did you talk to the Dweeb?"

Lacey had a whole gang of kids in tow: Penny Bolton, Renée Henderson, Vaughn, Bobby, Eddie Hagenspitzel, and April Lovewell. How would April feel right now, Kiki wondered, if she knew that Lacey was thinking about having a little fun with Spike Navarrone?

And speaking of Spike, Kiki saw him in the distance, racing out of the parking lot on his Harley.

"Ah . . . no, I didn't get the chance to talk to Mr. Appleby," said Kiki in a low voice.

"You didn't?" Lacey's eyes flashed accusation.

"I'll do it later," promised Kiki, vowing to herself that she wouldn't and searching for the guts to tell Lacey right now.

"Yo. Huck! I like your sign! Give 'em hell!" shouted Eddie Hagenspitzel.

"What Huck ought to do," Eddie suggested now, "Is give those Greenway developers a close shave. Get it? A *close* shave?"

"We get it," said Vaughn Cutter, laughing in spite of the fact that his dad was one of the developers.

"Your dad's out there," Kiki told Vaughn. "Yours too," she said to Lacey.

"Daddy's *here?*"

It seemed to Kiki that her friend was surprised. And something else, too, something more. But Kiki couldn't put her finger on it exactly.

"Daddy was in Fresno overnight on business," Lacey said. "I'm glad he got back for the rally."

The word "glad," however, did not match the expression on Lacey's face.

"What was it you wanted to ask me about in chemistry?" Bobby asked Kiki. He spoke softly,

135

almost whispering in her ear. Bobby was always discreet.

"I can't talk here," Kiki told him, with a nod toward Lacey and the others.

"Whenever," he said, putting his arm around her waist.

The noise level on the green increased as still more people arrived for the rally. There were lots more signs too, both pro and con.

Vaughn was talking to Lacey, something about when he'd pick her up for the dance on Saturday. Bobby had turned to listen as Eddie Hagenspitzel regaled Renée Henderson with his misadventures in a Las Vegas casino. "So there I was, with seventy-thousand bucks worth of chips on the table, wondering whether to roll the dice again, when suddenly *right there next to me* was MICHAEL JACKSON, and he said, 'Go for it, dude,' so I . . ."

Kiki laughed. She knew for a fact that Eddie Hagenspitzel had never even been to Las Vegas, let alone played the craps table, but truth somehow never mattered when Eddie was on a roll.

"What's so funny?" demanded Penny Bolton.

Kiki was just a bit afraid of Penny, who was a rumormonger. She knew Penny had spread the rumor about April Lovewell fooling around with Bubba Dole.

"I was laughing at Eddie's Las Vegas bull," Kiki said. "I can see him there at a big hotel someday, doing a comedy act."

"Guess so," said Penny, but without enthusiasm.

An uncomfortable moment of silence passed. Kiki thought she understood. Among all the Pinks, Penny was the most loyal to Lacey. Perhaps she saw Kiki's Peach Blossom Queen candidacy as being unworthy of the Pinks' "All for one and one for all" motto. Maybe Penny knew that Kiki hadn't withdrawn yet from the contest, which Lacey thought was a fait accompli.

Don't do it, Weets.

"So whatcha been up to?" Kiki asked Penny.

"Oh, nothing much. Waiting for school to end. Working at Dad's hardware store. Saturday looks bleak. Hal's got a tournament in Bakersfield. He might not get back in time for the Peach Blossom Ball. But at least we'll be able to go see Madonna on Sunday in Sacramento. Lacey's giving us tickets."

What? wondered Kiki. Oh. Of course. Lacey must have more than two tickets.

Another thought, unbidden, pushed that one aside: It's a *bribe!* Until that moment, Kiki had considered the tickets a sort of friendly gesture, a favor in return for another favor. Suddenly, everything looked different.

"COULD I HAVE YOUR ATTENTION, PLEASE . . ." Principal Appleby stood at the podium, opening the proceedings. The crowd quieted abruptly, and Appleby's surprised honk of snorting laughter burst from the loudspeakers.

"Mating call of the pterodactyl," Eddie Hagenspitzel said. "We'd better hope there's none around out in the scrublands."

Everybody in Eddie's immediately vicinity laughed loudly.

"Pipe down, dudes," warned Dwight the Dweeb, which only led to a new round of laughter.

"This auspicious gathering," orated the principal, "reminds me of the time Winston Churchill . . . no, wait a minute . . . Daniel Webster . . . of the time Daniel Webster, who, you'll recall, was a famous orator . . ."

"Daniel Webster's middle name was Appleby," said Eddie Hagenspitzel. "It's in the blood."

More laughter.

"Pipe down there, dudes!" cried Appleby. "I mean it! Pipe down or I'm taking names!"

"Taking names and chewing butt!" said Eddie.

"As I was saying," the principal continued, "Winston Churchill once observed that in times of trial men are spirits, not animals. . . ."

Appleby rattled on. Kiki looked around. There were easily five hundred people here now. Kiki noticed that Lacey seemed tense. She kept looking in her dad's direction, as if trying to get his attention, but Cal Pinkerton was engaged in earnest conversation with several members of the Chamber of Commerce.

Then Principal Appleby introduced the day's speakers, who were standing behind him at the podium. There was Paradiso's five-term mayor, Artie McNally, a pudgy man with a canny glint in his eye; bony, indomitable Mavis Tuckerman, chairperson of the Conservation League; a man Kiki had never seen before named Edgar L. Standish; and Raven Cruz. Raven looked especially gorgeous, her shining black hair and smooth bronze skin strikingly set off by a simple white dress. Its cadet collar gave Raven a crisp, authoritative look, and the sheath skirt accentuated her trim, lovely figure. She wore white heels, giving her an air of polish and maturity. Three wide bracelets of hammered silver circled her left wrist and forearm, and on her right arm, from wrist to elbow, she wore a startling piece of work that coiled up her arm like a slender serpent. It was, in fact, a miniature cobra made of gold.

Only Raven could get away with something like that without appearing ridiculous.

Kiki was, for a moment, frankly envious. Raven didn't look at all nervous, either. She didn't even

139

have notes for her speech! This amazed Kiki, who couldn't give an oral report in class without a thick handful of index cards.

Mayor McNally spoke first, taking no position but offering a brief history of the historic scrublands and a vision of what would happen if those virgin lands were developed. "Paradiso will not be the same if we build the Greenway Mall," he concluded. "The question is: Will Paradiso be better or worse?"

"Better!" declared Mr. Edgar L. Standish, who turned out to be a Sacramento lawyer and legislative lobbyist representing Cal Pinkerton and Lars Cutter.

"Worse!" maintained Mavis Tuckerman, who sketched a horror story involving thousands of shoppers from all over central California descending on once-quiet Paradiso—"Like locusts!" cried Mavis, shaking her fist.

Then it was Raven's turn. She stepped confidently to the microphone as Principal Appleby said: "Miss Cruz is here to offer the views of some of our students."

"Not *my* view," Lacey hissed. "Who does she think she is, anyway?"

Kiki had the feeling that Lacey had gone a little green-eyed. Already, just standing there and smiling from the podium, Raven was making a stunning impression. The members of the Peggy Sue selection committee, most, if not all, of whom were in the crowd, couldn't help but notice. Kiki felt her own chances of winning diminish, but it didn't trouble her as much as it obviously bothered Lacey.

Raven was speaking now. "I don't believe," she stated, "that the people of Paradiso have been given enough opportunity to voice their opinions on the proposed Greenway Mall. We woke up one morning to learn that our scrublands, which have been untouched for tens of thousands of years, will soon be no more. That's not right. It's not fair. Certainly, it's not democratic. If we don't do something now, we will wake up on another morning to the sounds of bulldozers and cement mixers. So some of us students are going to be circulating a formal petition to halt development in the scrublands. We plan to present copies of this petition to the governor and the state legislature. We will find a way to halt the ruination of a beautiful place everybody loves. . . ."

"Where'll we go to make out if the scrublands get the shaft?" whispered Eddie Hagenspitzel.

". . . and we won't stop working," Raven concluded, "until all the facts come out."

Raven was turning away from the podium, and the crowd was applauding energetically, when Lacey suddenly shot up. She glanced in her dad's direction, then turned on Raven. "You say 'we' an awful lot, Raven!" Lacey shouted, as the applause died abruptly. "Who's this 'we,' anyway? Or is it just *you?*"

Raven spoke calmly into the microphone. "We're Students Concerned About the Mall," she said. "It's open to everybody in school."

"Students Concerned About the Mall!" repeated Lacey contemptuously. "That spells SCAM."

There was some laughter from the crowd.

But Raven, at the podium, was unperturbed. "If you like," she told Lacey sweetly, "you could always organize Students Concerned About Greenway."

Eddie got it before anybody else. "SCAG!" he roared.

Lacey turned scarlet beneath her deep tan. Kiki wondered where all that blood could have come from so quickly.

"You want to know why you're against the mall, Raven?" Lacey shouted. "You want to know? Well, I'll tell you. It's because your dad was once a fruit picker for Pinkerton Canneries. But not a very good one, because my dad had to fire him for incompetence!"

A number of people, upset at the disintegration of the rally, got up and started walking away. Principal Appleby stepped to the microphone, saying: "I'm afraid that's all the time we have, folks."

Kiki caught a look of pure distress on Raven's face. Everything had proceeded so well, but now . . .

"Please sign our petition when we come around," she said, leaning across Dwight the Dweeb to speak into the mike.

The rally broke up then. Some people, of course, were laughing about "SCAG" and about how clever Raven's comeback had been. Others were seriously debating the merits of the mall. They gathered around Raven, ready to sign her petition. Kiki felt that she should stay with Lacey, who was nearly beside herself with humiliation and rage. "That little Mex with her bracelets and everything!" Lacey fumed. "I'm gonna put a bracelet around her neck. Wait and see!"

"It's your own fault," snapped Vaughn, who was usually easygoing.

"What?" demanded Lacey, placing her hands on her hips and glaring at him. "What did you say?"

Everybody—Kiki, Penny, April, Bobby, Eddie—stared. None of Lacey's boyfriends *ever* challenged her. Eddie Hagenspitzel, probably for the first time in his life, was speechless.

"I *said*," continued Vaughn, not backing down a bit, "that you brought this on yourself. *You* picked a fight with Raven. *You* wrecked the rally. And *you* made a total fool of yourself—not Raven!"

Lacey glared at him for another long moment, then said, "Well! If *that's* the way you feel! If *that's* the way you feel, why don't you take Raven Cruz to the Peach Blossom Ball?"

"Maybe I will!" Vaughn shot back.

Lacey stared at Vaughn in disbelief. Kiki saw tears of frustration and rage shining at the corners of Lacey's big blue eyes. Only once had she seen Lacey this angry—the time Emily Gilman had won the talent contest.

And look what happened to poor Emily.

"Okay, Vaughn, honey," said Lacey, in a voice as hard as the nails at Bolton's Hardware. "Hope you have fun with Raven."

With that, Lacey stalked away. Kiki noticed that Cal Pinkerton, alone now, was hurrying away in the direction of his big silver-gray Mercedes. His stride was frenetic, even jerky. He must be angry about the rally, Kiki realized. Then she saw Lacey's shoulders sort of sag for a moment, as if she felt defeated.

But Lacey, as always, rallied. She spun toward the group, pointed, and said: "Penny! Come here!"

Uh-oh, thought Kiki. Rumors comin'.

Penny, her cheerful round behind bouncing beneath her culottes, hurried after Lacey. The two girls headed toward school, their heads bent together, talking.

"Whew!" Eddie Hagenspitzel said. "Better ask Raven to the dance, Vaughn. Or go stag."

"It'll be all right," said Kiki, hoping to soothe things.

"Sometimes Lace just loses it," Renée Henderson said. "It happens to everybody. . . ." She broke off abruptly, oddly.

"Maybe I *will* ask Raven," said Vaughn.

The warning bell rang then. Kiki and Bobby walked hand in hand toward the main entrance. "You mentioned something you wanted to tell me?" Bobby asked.

"Oh. It's nothing."

He stopped walking. So did she. Taking her by the shoulders and looking her in the eyes, he said: "Tell me what it is."

She did.

"I can't believe Lacey had the nerve to even ask you to quit the contest," he said. "You're gonna win!"

CHAPTER 15

When Kiki left school at three-fifteen, Lacey was already waiting in her car, gunning the engine and ready to go. "Let's get out of here," she said, shifting into first and squealing out of the parking lot. "Let's go to your house and make some plans." Apparently, she assumed that Kiki had quit the Queen contest. "I made a big mistake today, but I can turn it around."

"I don't know," said Kiki. "My mom's got company over." This was a total lie.

"Company?" Lacey asked as they shot down the long hill toward town. "What kind of company?"

"Relatives. From the coast."

"The coast?" Lacey was suspicious. "Where on the coast?"

"Carmel." Right.

"Carmel!" Lacey exclaimed. "You know people

there? Why haven't you ever said anything about it? I bet they have a great place. We could go out there and party sometime."

Typical Lacey. Either she spotted an advantage right away, something she might make use of, or she coldly dismissed things and people as unworthy of her time.

"We could go to your house," said Kiki, figuring to stay at Lacey's for a few minutes and then walk home.

"Uh . . . no," Lacey said. "My mom's . . . busy."

Darla Jennings Pinkerton, one-time bit-part actress. Reigning mistress of the Paradiso social scene, such as it was. As if in a vision, Kiki glimpsed an image of Lacey twenty years later, thirty years later, being chauffeured down Winding Hill Road in a big car of some kind. Lacey had become Peach Blossom Queen, been screen-tested, gotten a bit part in a movie, flopped as a singer or never even tried, and . . .

Kiki realized she was thinking of her best friend *as a bit-part actress*! She suddenly knew, in that illogical way you understand a thing you can't possibly explain, that Lacey Pinkerton, in one way or another, was doomed.

And I'm not! Kiki cried inside her mind, like a shipwreck survivor.

"Oh, why don't you just take me home, Lace," she said. "I have to catch up on yesterday's homework, 'cause I skipped."

"Right," said Lacey. "Your blue dress."

The way she said "your blue dress" made it sound as if it were the ugliest, stupidest, *dorkiest* dress in the whole wide world.

Lacey braked for the red light at the intersection of Wing Hill and Old Town. Kiki noted that Huck Spector had hung a big sign outside his shop: SIGN RAVEN'S PETITION: SAVE OUR SCRUBLANDS.

Lacey saw it too. "Let's drive over to Rosa's for a Coke," she suggested.

"No way. I think you'd better stay away from Raven."

"I'll do what I want to!" Lacey snapped. Then, maybe remembering that she needed Kiki's support, she added, "Sorry, Keek, you're right. By the way—"

This is it! Kiki knew. This is where she asks me if I've withdrawn from the competition. "Oh!" Kiki exclaimed, to head Lacey off at the pass, "something interesting happened today. . . ."

Kiki went on to tell about Raven, Denise, Winston Purdy, and *Birds of America*. "I heard Raven say they wouldn't know for sure until tomorrow. Something about film at Carter's."

"I knew they were up to something!" Lacey cried. "And now I'm sure of it."

The light turned green. Lacey let out the clutch. But she didn't turn right onto Winding Hill Road. Instead, she shot forward for half a block and braked to a rough stop in front of Carter's Drugstore.

"What's here?" Kiki asked.

"That's what you're about to find out."

"Me?"

"Right. Whatever Raven's up to has something to do with pictures. I saw nerdy Purdy hand Raven something. It might have been film. And this is the place to find out for sure."

"So?" said Kiki. "What's this got to do with me?"

"I want you to go in the drugstore and ask old man Carter if Raven's film is ready yet."

"How can it be? It's still Tuesday."

"You don't *get* it," said Lacey, sounding as exasperated as a teacher with a pupil who can't add two plus two. "First we see if Raven actually deposited film here. Then we figure out how to get a look at the pictures. I know they're important and that they have something to do with the scrublands. This is not just for *me*," she added, when Kiki showed signs of reluctance, "or even for us Pinks. Daddy will want to know about this. It might have

150

something to do with the mall. I have to do everything I can to help him. You understand," she said sweetly. "You *know* how much he likes you. He'll be *so-o* pleased."

Kiki, who didn't think Mr. Pinkerton cared whether she lived or died, continued to hesitate. "Why don't *you* go in and ask about the film?" she said.

The usual after-school crowd was hanging around in front of the drugstore. Quite a few kids, noticing the lively discussion taking place in Lacey's car, began to look interested. Kiki started to feel like a fish in a bowl.

"*I* can't go in," Lacey was explaining, "because I'm blond. You've got dark hair, not as dark as Raven's, but to an old guy like Jerry Carter you probably look like her. Besides, he can't see so well anymore. I heard my mom say he's got catastrophes."

"Cataracts," corrected Kiki, pleased to know something Lacey didn't.

"Whatever. Come on. Do it, huh?"

Kids were staring. Oh, all right, thought Kiki. She got out of the car. Doing this favor for Lacey might soften the blow of telling her "no dice" on withdrawing as a Queen candidate.

Kiki went into the drugstore, an extremely neat, five-aisled emporium in which you could buy everything from golf-ball-size Jawbreaker candies to sophisticated prosthetics.

Feeling as if she were doing a distasteful, if not dumb, favor for Lacey, Kiki started up aisle two. Shampoos, hair sprays, perfumes, bath powders. There, rounding the corner from aisle three—health aids—was April Lovewell. She seemed nervous.

"April! Hi!"

"Oh . . . hi, Kiki . . ." April scurried on by and left the store as if she couldn't get out fast enough.

"Hi, Mr. Carter," said Kiki, trembling a little at the knees.

The crotchety old druggist, scowling at some doctor's scribbled prescription through thick glasses, looked up. "Yuh?" he grunted.

"Is Raven Cruz's film in yet?" asked Kiki. She was sure he would say, "You don't look like Raven Cruz to me," or something like that. But he just checked a file next to the cash register and said, "Due in tomorrow, girlie. 'Round noon'd be my guess."

"Thank you, thank you," said Kiki, retreating. She was still thanking him out on the sidewalk.

"Well?" demanded Lacey, when Kiki got back into the car. The radio was on KPOP. Elvis Presley was singing "Don't Be Cruel."

"Well, Raven's got some film in there, but it won't be ready until tomorrow."

Lacey shot out from the curbside, made an illegal U-ball on Old Town Road, ran a yellow light at the intersection, and thundered up Winding Hill Road. "Tomorrow you go in and pick up that film," she said. Ordered, really.

"I can't do that. It's not my film."

"Did Carter seem suspicious?"

"No."

"Then I was right. He doesn't know you from Raven. We'll get that film and find out what's going on—"

"No!" Kiki declared.

The Platters were on the airwaves now, singing "Great Pretender."

"What do you mean, 'no'?" Lacey asked. She turned into the De Santises' driveway and stopped by the house.

"I mean *no*. As in, *no*, I'm not going to pose as Raven and swipe her film. And I don't *care* what's on the film! It's her business."

Now I'm in for it! she thought.

But to Kiki's surprise, Lacey stayed calm. She reached under her seat and pulled out a thickly stuffed white envelope. "I never ask a favor without offering something in return," she said sweetly.

Kiki took the envelope from her friend and

looked inside. Another bribe. The gall! She was too angry even to count all those bills. She tossed the envelope onto Lacey's lap.

"No!" she shouted.

Now Lacey looked as if she might explode with anger. "This is all for *us*," she growled, gritting her teeth. "For us Pinks. You're not in the competition anymore, so we've got to beat Raven—"

"I didn't withdraw," said Kiki, meeting Lacey's now-cold blue eyes with effort, "and I'm not going to, either."

Lacey was quiet for a long moment. Kiki could feel her own heart beating fast. The idling Ferrari purred.

"You didn't speak to Principal Appleby?" Lacey asked, in a very, *very* calm voice.

"No, I didn't."

"And you don't intend to?"

"Absolutely not."

"Well," said Lacey airily, "I guess you won't be seeing Madonna then."

"Well, Penny Bolton and Hal Bemis will, won't they? I hear you promised Penny the tickets."

Lacey seemed stung. "I didn't give those tickets to anybody!"

"Yeah, right. But how many people did you promise them to?"

Blood rushed to Lacey's face, glowing darkly beneath her exquisite cheekbones. "Guess you'd better get on into the house and start on that homework, hey?" she said coldly.

Without a word, Kiki got out of the car. Oh, God, I'm in for it now, she worried, wondering what sort of rumor she would hear about herself tomorrow. And all because of some dumb and stupid festival Queen contest.

"Your dress sucks!" hollered Lacey as she revved the Ferrari's big engine.

"Thanks for your opinion, Bigfoot!" Kiki shot back.

Lacey roared away without a backward glance. Buddy Holly was on KPOP again, mourning:

> *If you knew*
> *Peggy Sue,*
> *Then you'd know why I feel blue . . .*

Wednesday, May 24

CHAPTER 16

Paradiso's motto, printed on the masthead of Willa Flicker's weekly newspaper, the *Record*, was "SUNNIEST SPOT IN THE GOLDEN STATE." So when it actually rained, as it was doing when Raven woke up Wednesday morning, the whole town and everybody in it seemed gray and depressed. Also wet. Raincoats were almost unknown to the townspeople. Umbrellas were weird curiosities from an alien world.

Rain, to most Paradisans, was just a downer. But it was disaster to Raven Cruz. Rain to her meant lost time, and time was the one thing she couldn't afford to lose, especially Wednesday morning.

To make matters worse, her mother was sick.

Mornings at Rosa's Café were always hectic: getting the breakfast crowd fed and coffeed-up, the younger kids dressed and off to school, the chickens watered and oyster-shelled. It was a schedule planned down to the second, almost. Papa cooked, Mama waited on tables, Raven dressed the kids and fed the chickens.

This morning the chickens huddled on their roosts, heads buried beneath their wings. Mama was in bed, and the kids were helping one another into their clothes. Carlotta, Raven's fourteen-year-old sister, and Pedro, twelve, were doing the best they could with Rosalita, Manolete, Miguel, and little Orlando.

I hope Mama's only tired, Raven thought as she took breakfast orders from four dripping truckers who had just come in out of the rain. They weren't locals. She didn't know them. Just about the only thing Raven liked about waitressing was the chance to talk to people, especially people from outside Paradiso. *Outside* Paradiso was where she meant to go and live her life.

But these four were too wet or too sleepy or both to say anything but "Gimme scrambled eggs" and *"Huevos rancheros,* lots of hot sauce." Raven didn't blame them, not this morning. She didn't have time to talk.

Rosa's Café was a plain, wooden rectangular building, once a railroad freight car, that Manny Cruz had borrowed money to buy and transport from Springfield Hills to Paradiso. Nobody who didn't know that could ever have guessed, because now the couplings and the steel wheels were long gone, the siding replaced by big windows. Flower boxes with real flowers hung outside the windows. There was a red rose on every table inside.

The roses were made of plastic, but they were colorful and clean.

A long, white Formica-topped counter ran along one side of the café. Along the other side were six tables, each capable of seating four, each covered with a cheery red and white plastic tablecloth.

Raven was mopping a tablecloth when she saw the sleek red sports car pull up in front of the café. Lacey got out. She wasn't with Kiki-the-Clone this morning. Lacey swept regally into the café, removed her beige Burberry coat, and shook a small tide of raindrops onto the floor. Smiling oh-so-sweetly at Raven, she sat down at the counter.

"Iced tea?" said Raven. This would be quick. She'd serve Lacey and get on with her day.

But no. "May I see a menu, please?" Lacey asked. "I feel rather hungry. And you serve such delicious food here."

I'd never know it by the tips you leave, Raven thought. Lacey was notorious not only for her miserly tips but also for her theatrical manner of awarding them. Once she'd given Jess Gardner, whose father owned the town's body shop, a one-

161

dollar tip for doing more than five hundred dollars worth of work on her car. This was after Lacey had dumped him and moved onto Vaughn Cutter. Jess had turned around and bought Lacey a one-dollar get-well card.

Lacey had the menu now, and was studying it with languorous deliberation. *"Eeeuuuw!"* she cried, then, with an oh-so-deadly expression of refined distaste. And with a manicured fingernail, she pried a speck of dried salsa from the plastic-covered menu.

"This must be the appetizer, right?" Lacey said.

Raven wanted to lash right out at her then and there, but the presence of the other customers prevented it. She felt trapped. "Are you ready to order?" she asked, fuming, glancing at the clock.

"Well . . . let me think it over. . . . By the way, I hope you know that you made a complete fool of yourself at that rally yesterday."

Vaughn Cutter didn't seem to think so, was what Raven wanted to say. Denise Guthrie had told her of the spat between Vaughn and Lacey. She didn't think there was much chance of Vaughn's asking her to the dance, but she planned to give him every opportunity.

"I said, you made a fool of yourself," Lacey repeated, deliberately trying to pick a fight.

"Is that so? Are you ready to order?" Again,

Raven felt trapped. She couldn't do anything in response to Lacey's baiting remarks. The other customers weren't paying to see a quarrel.

Lacey seemed well aware of this. "Face it, Raven," she said, "your dad was incompetent and my dad had to fire him."

"I see," was all Raven said.

Disappointed, Lacey finally ordered. "I'll have your wonderful *huevos rancheros,*" she said, "with just a dash of mild sauce. People with your blood can handle hot, but not me."

There was no doubt in her tone of voice that Lacey's opinion of Raven's "blood" was not high.

Raven wrote the order on her pad.

"And also iced tea," said Lacey, "with lemon. You know, I think it's wonderful, all the stuff you do. All those brothers and sisters to take care of. And you must spend oodles of time at the sewing machine, zizzing up those . . . interesting little outfits you wear."

"Thanks," said Raven. She stepped into the kitchen and called out Lacey's order. *"Huevos rancheros,"* she said, "with triple diablo sauce."

Raven busied herself for several minutes, getting the truckers more coffee, filling the sugar bowls on the counter. The kitchen bell dinged. Lacey's order was ready. Raven brought it out of the kitchen

163

ceremoniously and placed it in front of the head Pink. "Enjoy," she said.

"I'm sure I will," said Lacey, reaching for a fork.

Raven watched her take a nice big bite. "It might be just a little bit on the tangy side," she said, waiting.

Lacey suddenly sat bolt upright. "Uh!" she screamed. Her mouth, half open, seemed to quiver. Her eyes poured a flood of tears.

"Something the matter?" asked Raven, managing to look *very* concerned.

"*Whuh!*" yelped Lacey, barely able to see through tears, fumbling around for her glass of iced tea, which Raven hadn't served yet.

"What did you say?" asked Raven. "Can I get you something?"

"Whah . . . whah . . . whaher . . ." *Huevos rancheros* and triple diablo sauce dribbled down Lacey's chin and onto her clean white sweater.

"Oh, *water!*" said Raven. While Lacey gulped and grimaced and drew the head-shaking stares of the other customers, Raven slowly drew a huge mug of water from the counter faucet.

"Here you go," she said, handing Lacey the mug. Lacey flailed at it with both hands, trying to see it from behind the teary film over her eyes.

"Ooooops!" Raven said as Lacey's right hand struck the mug and knocked it onto the counter.

Water spread all over and flowed like a small waterfall into Lacey's lap. "Sorry," Raven said. "I thought you had a grip on it."

Lacey's face was down on the counter. She sucked up the spilled water as best she could. Then, still gasping and sputtering, saying "You! On purpose! Did that on purpose!" Lacey jumped up, grabbed her coat, and fled the café, tears streaming down her face.

"Wait!" Raven called after her. "That was only the appetizer. And your clothes are all messed up. Maybe I can zizz you up something presentable. . . ."

CHAPTER 17

Glancing at the electric clock above the counter, where a half-dozen workers were silently, almost sullenly drinking coffee, Raven saw that it was already seven-thirty-five. *Sacramente!* Time! She'd wanted to get to school early. Yesterday, after the rally, she'd called a preschool meeting in the student lounge for those kids who might be interested in helping get signatures on her anti-mall petition.

It looked as if she was going to be late to the meeting.

If she didn't get the signatures in time, the petition wouldn't be ready for Express Mail in time. The deadline was 5:00 p.m. Thursday afternoon.

And what kid, even the one most eager to save the scrublands, would want to go scrounging around for signatures in the rain?

Also, she had to find time today to pick up the

film at Carter's Drugstore. She hoped that she was right about the film—Winston Purdy had assured her she was—but that too was just another "if."

If the pictures turned out as expected, they had to be included in the Express Mail package to State Senator Miller in Sacramento. Had to be mailed by 5:00 p.m. tomorrow in order to reach Senator Miller . . .

. . . *in time!*

"Papa," said Raven, handing her father order slips from the dripping-wet recent arrivals at table two—three scrambled, one *rancheros*— "I gotta get to school. I don't think anybody else is coming . . ."

The little bell on the café's front door dinged. Somebody *had* come in. *Caramba!*

"Please get just one more, honey," Papa said. "I'll take it from there."

Papa was a short man, powerfully built, with formidable black eyes. His mere presence was intimidating. Calvin Pinkerton, for example, never came near Rosa's Café.

But Raven knew for sure that Papa would never lift a hand—or even raise his voice—against anybody in the family. He was too proud to tell her flat out that there wasn't money for college, but she knew he was praying that she'd win the Peach Blossom Queen contest and the scholarship that went with it.

If Lacey Pinkerton wins and goes around gloating, Raven vowed, it'll be hard for me to keep from strangling her.

Maybe I *will* strangle her, Raven thought, smiling grimly to herself and leaving the kitchen to serve the one last customer who'd just made the door ding.

Raven, for whom self-possession was a source of pride, was surprised to see Kiki De Santis, all alone, standing at the counter by the cash register. Kiki wore an ancient yellow raincoat, buttoned to the neck, and yellow sneakers. *Yellow* sneakers. What color sneakers didn't Kiki have?

But somehow, it didn't look like Kiki. This girl looked different. Sort of worried and determined at the same time. Worry and determination weren't emotions that Raven had ever associated with Kiki De Santis.

"Iced tea?" Raven asked.

"No, thanks," said Kiki nervously. "Can I talk to you a minute?"

Pinks were *never* nervous. It was wildly *un*-Pink to show anything but complete cool. Raven went immediately on guard. This must be some sort of scheme cooked up by Lacey, which Kiki-the-Clone had been ordered to carry out. Raven glanced out

169

the café windows for a sign of Lacey's Ferrari. She saw only the Trooper II that Kiki drove to school sometimes.

"I'm in a rush right now," said Raven. "I've got to get changed"—she indicated her white waitress uniform—"and get up to school."

"Right," said Kiki. "Your petition meeting in the student lounge. I want to sign up. Look, get yourself together and I'll drive you to school, okay?"

Kiki wanted to sign up for the foot-wearying job of door-to-door signature gathering? This *had* to be a Pink trick. Maybe Lacey planned to get her hands on the petitions and burn them or something. I'll play along with this and see what's up, Raven decided.

"Sure," she said, "I'd love a ride. 'Specially with this rain."

She flipped her apron onto a hook in the kitchen, said, "Bye, Papa," and raced across the dusty lot between the café and the family's one-story adobe bungalow. It was sparsely furnished, very clean, but small. Raven shared a tiny bedroom with Carlotta and little Rosalita, who was seven. Carlotta was braiding her sister's hair when Raven rushed in, pulled off her white uniform, and wondered what to wear. Something dark, because of the rain.

"Is Mama very sick?" Carlotta wanted to know.

"Oh, I don't think so," said Raven soothingly,

grabbing a blouse and a pair of pants and hunting up some shoes. "Mama will be fine by this afternoon." She'd done enough mothering in her time to know that the fears of the younger kids could be quieted fairly easily if she herself remained calm and confident. My life is not going to be like this, she promised herself, dressing hurriedly. I'll be Peach Blossom Queen, win a scholarship, go to college, and then law school.

And if I *don't* win Peach Blossom Queen, Raven amended, giving little Rosalita a good-bye off-to-school kiss, I'll find some other way to go to college, become a lawyer, and run for office anyway!

The importance of political office was much on Raven's mind. Taped to the wall beside the mirror at which Raven now brushed her long, straight, shining black hair, was a letter. It was the most important letter Raven had ever received.

Dear Miss Cruz:
Thank you for writing me concerning the scrublands of Paradiso County. As you accurately pointed out in your eloquent letter, environmental issues have been one of my special interests here in the state legislature. Pursuant to your communication, I directed members of my staff to research the Paradiso situation. I am sorry to have to tell you that unless

(1) community opposition to development can be mobilized and (2) negative environmental impact of a significant nature can be proven, the Pinkerton-Cutter plan for a shopping mall could proceed as early as Monday next. If, however, you are able to provide my staff and me with evidence of opposition and the aforementioned negative environmental impact by Friday, May 26, I shall be able to introduce proceedings in the legislature to halt, at least temporarily, any development in the scrublands.

With every best wish for your endeavors, I remain,

Sincerely yours,

Humphrey T. Miller
California State Senate

Raven was very proud of the letter, which made her feel like a responsible adult, even though it meant an awesome amount of rush work. Circulating the anti-mall petition, for all the time it would take, was the lesser of her problems. She had to have proof of "negative environmental impact."

Hoping that Winston Purdy's pictures turned out—and showed up at Carter's Drugstore on time —Raven left the house and trotted in the steady rain toward Kiki's Trooper II. Without half thinking, Raven had chosen to wear a pair of black pants with crisscrossed red stitching up the sides, a red silk blouse Mama had brought from Mexico long ago, and black cowboy boots. As an afterthought, because of the rain, she'd tossed across her shoulders a black cape embroidered around the edges with Aztec symbols. And, of course, bracelets of hammered silver circled her wrists. She considered these old clothes as "rainy day stuff," not entirely conscious of the powerful, even mysterious effect they created. The four truck drivers stared at Raven in admiration as she jumped into Kiki's vehicle.

"Was that the same girl who waited on us?" one of them said. "Naaaah, couldn't be."

Now I'll see what Kiki's up to, thought Raven as the girls set out toward school, driving slowly because of the rain-slippery asphalt.

"You look great," Kiki said. "Everybody admires your clothes so much. *And* your bracelets."

"Thanks," replied Raven. Kiki's compliments had *sounded* sincere, but obviously she hadn't come to Rosa's just to spread flattery around. Kiki still seemed edgy, too, as if trying to nerve herself up for something. I'll wait, Raven decided. "The jewelry I wear is really my great-grandmother's," she said conversationally. "It's been in the family for over a century. Mama says I can wear it until I lose something. So I make sure never to do that."

Kiki laughed. It was a nice, friendly laugh. Raven liked it.

"Want me to turn on KPOP?" Kiki asked.

"If you want to."

"I don't think so," Kiki said. "If I hear T.J. the D.J. tell one more time about Buddy Holly and the Big Bopper and the plane crash in Iowa, I swear I'll barf!"

This time Raven laughed. Maybe Kiki wasn't a phony, super-cool Pink after all. Maybe I've misjudged her, Raven thought. "Well," she said, referring to Kiki's old yellow raincoat, "you're dressed for any emergency."

"This coat?" said Kiki. "It's my mom's. She once worked at a truck stop in Nevada. Sometimes she'd have to help out at the gas pumps."

What? wondered Raven. The mother of a Pink had actually worked? Actual *work* work?

"She was a waitress," Kiki explained. She said it just normally, naturally. She didn't seem to be making a big point of it, like, "My mom was a waitress and you're one too, so we have a lot in common."

The fat tires hissed over the rain-slick roadway. Flat gray clouds hung low over the town, bleak and leaden far off to the horizons. The steeple at Church of Christ, barely visible in low-lying mist, seemed hazy and unreal. Blossoms in the vast peach orchards hung sodden and sad on dripping

174

branches. Paradiso looked strange and different in the rain. Raven wondered, on these gray days, if she really knew her hometown at all. The deceptive thing about Paradiso, she reasoned, seated beside Kiki De Santis on the way to school, is that it's almost always sunny. It takes a rainy day to make you see the other side of it, the dark heart. Bad things can happen here, she realized, just like anyplace else. . . .

VRRRRROOOooooommm!

Spike Navarrone shot past the Isuzu as if it were standing still.

"Oh!" exclaimed Kiki, startled. "I didn't see him coming up behind."

"I think he enjoys doing that to people. I don't know, though. He never says much. I wonder if it's true that still waters run deep. Maybe April Lovewell knows."

"Poor April," Kiki said.

Raven was slightly surprised. Everybody at school was always talking about "poor April" because she dated a boy she obviously liked a lot but had to sneak around with. But Kiki's tone indicated something else, some other reason to describe April as "poor." "Why do you say that?" she asked.

"Oh . . . no reason," said Kiki. Then, as if reconsidering, "Well, I think Lacey's going to make a play for Spike."

"Lacey?" This *was* news! Lacey had never made any secret of her superior feelings toward Hispanics.

"She thinks Spike would be fun to mess around with," Kiki explained, "and now she might need somebody to take her to the dance. After the rally yesterday, she and Vaughn had sort of a fight. . . ."

"I heard about it," said Raven, deciding to make sure she talked to Vaughn today. Raven didn't date much, but she definitely knew that if you wanted to get a guy interested, you had to make yourself available. Guys, it sometimes seemed, couldn't focus their minds on anything not in plain line of sight.

Raven also knew that this time, Lacey might be biting off more than she could chew. "Your friend doesn't really know Spike Navarrone, does she?" Raven asked Kiki. "He won't let himself get used. He pretty much makes his own plans. He's had to, because of all his responsibilities at home."

Raven remembered what had happened between Spike and Michelle Wheeler, the girl who'd gotten pregnant and had been forced to leave school. Michelle had gotten herself in trouble with an older guy. He had showed no interest in marrying her, so Michelle had gone shopping around. Raven, waitressing one night when Spike and Michelle had shared a booth in the back at Rosa's Café, had caught the gist of a long, troubled conversation, which had ended when Spike said: "I've got plans for *my* life. You even *dream* of pinning this on me and wrecking my plans, and you are *history*, babe."

Remembering the way Spike had said *"history"* still gave Raven goose bumps, and not the pleasant kind, either.

Right now, though, she was concerned about how April Lovewell would feel to learn that Lacey was dangling her hook for Spike. "Poor April," she said.

"I know," agreed Kiki. "She really loves Spike, too. And Lacey treats her so coldly. April really admires Lacey. Well, a lot of kids do. Even me. But not anymore. She gets so mean sometimes. Just like that. I wish I knew why. I'd like to help her if I could, but she puts up this wall. . . ."

Raven couldn't muster any particular sympathy for Lacey Pinkerton, so she said nothing.

Passing Ramon's Stop 'n' Shop, they drove by Winston Purdy III. He was on his bike, pedaling furiously and holding a huge black umbrella over his head. Raven expected Kiki to make some sarcastic "Pink" remark about Winston, but she didn't.

Instead, Kiki seemed to tense. She coughed nervously. They were passing Carter's Drugstore now. Raven was thinking about the film, which she hoped to pick up during lunch period today, when

177

Kiki suddenly said: "I . . . I'm not sure how to . . . to tell you this. And I'm not sure if it's important. But Lacey's very interested in some film Winston Purdy took for you—"

"*What?*" said Raven. Actually, she shouted. "How does she—how do you know?"

The film was the key to her whole anti-mall effort! The film was absolutely *crucial*! She realized, instantly, that *this* was what Kiki had wanted to tell her. And she realized simultaneously that Kiki De Santis was a much more substantial person than she'd ever suspected.

Raven listened, flabbergasted, as Kiki spoke about *Birds of America* and what had happened the day before in Carter's Drugstore. "Why are you telling me this?" asked Raven, still a bit suspicious.

"Lacey is Lacey," Kiki said. "She gets away with a lot of stuff just because of who she is and how she acts. And she can be so nice. She really can. But I've never seen her act like this before. And I don't want to see anybody get hurt because of it. Not Vaughn. Not Spike. Not April. And not you."

Raven unaccustomed to trusting Pinks, carefully analyzed Kiki's words. She studied the expression on Kiki's face and considered the tone of her voice. Then Raven decided. Kiki was telling the truth. "Thank you," she said. She would have to keep a very close eye on Lacey Pinkerton today.

What if Lacey went down to Carter's Drugstore during lunch period and made a brazen attempt to get the film?

"Can you give me a ride down to Carter's at lunch?" Raven asked her new friend.

"You got it," Kiki said. "That is, if Lacey doesn't find out and kill me first."

CHAPTER 18

Funny what could happen in just a few morning hours. The day had started great, too. Thirty-seven kids were waiting in the student lounge when Raven arrived, all of them eager to collect signatures for the anti-mall petition. There were only minutes remaining before the warning bell, but Raven was well prepared.

"Paradiso has three thousand, two hundred and seventeen registered voters," she told her volunteers while handing out copies of the voters' list. "We should try to get at least half of them to sign. Senator Miller is already sympathetic to us, and no politician up there in the capital is going to ignore a petition signed by half the voting population."

Bobby Deeter offered to organize kids who wanted to canvass the North Side. Hope Hubbard volunteered to do the same south of Old Town

Road. And Kiki De Santis, somewhat diffident yet determined, said she'd take charge of the neighborhood up on Winding Hill.

"Assign members of your group to areas they know and where they're known," Raven advised, having read—three times—a brochure on door-to-door techniques. "It's harder for a citizen to turn down a request for a signature if he or she knows you or has seen you in the neighborhood. Our goal is at least sixteen hundred signatures. . . ."

"But what if we get waterlogged?" complained Eddie Hagenspitzel, who'd signed on with Bobby Deeter.

Everybody laughed. But Raven had to admit his point. Rain was bad for morale. All day these volunteers would be sitting in boring classes, thinking about walking around later in the rain. She'd be lucky if twenty of her thirty-seven prospective workers actually showed up. The warning bell rang then.

Raven felt pretty good, for about five minutes. She'd just taken her seat in Mr. Raleigh's advanced placement European history class, aware that some of the kids were looking at her in a funny way, when Mr. Raleigh motioned her to come up to his desk. He had an odd look on his face too, sort of puzzled and worried and embarrassed all at once. He handed her a sheet of paper. On it was a long list of vocabulary words and their definitions. It was a list Raven had prepared to bone up for the recent SATs, on which she'd scored 690 verbal and 640 math. She'd tossed the list into her locker after the test and hadn't given it a thought since.

"So?" she asked, figuring some jerk had invaded her locker.

"Perhaps we should step out into the corridor. . . ."

In the hallway, Mr. Raleigh hemmed and hawed. Finally he got it out: "Principal Appleby asked me to speak to you about this."

"Why? It's a vocabulary list. So what?"

His face contorted, as if he'd been struck by an obscure but acute stab of pain. "Dwight the . . . I mean Mr. Appleby . . . found it in his mailbox this morning. There was a note attached. The note said you had the list with you in the examination room on the day of the SATs."

"I did not!" The whole thing seemed crazy to Raven, unbelievable. "Mr. Raleigh, you can't possibly think that?"

He threw up his hands, made a fending-off gesture. "No, no. Good heavens, no. Besides, the note was unsigned. Mr. Appleby just wanted me to warn you that . . ."

Raven understood. All too well. And she understood why some of the kids in class had looked at her strangely. There was a rumor going around. "Raven Cruz cheated on her SATs." But it was more than that. Whoever had started the rumor—and Raven was pretty darn sure who had—was very clever. *She* had wanted to damage Raven's reputation by bringing Principal Appleby into it. Most kids, upon hearing that Raven had cheated, would automatically say, "No way!" or "That's bull." But if the rumor went: "Principal Appleby is looking into some SAT cheating thing about Raven; he got proof in the mail and *everything,*" well, then the old word of mouth would travel at the speed of light. People might mention it over their dinner tables at home. Members of the selection committee would be sure to hear of it. And even if a few believed the rumor—and some will believe *any* wild tale—a kind of vague, unsavory suspicion would surround the name Raven Cruz. "Oh, yes," people would say, "Raven Cruz. Nice girl, very smart. But what about that SAT business? Such a shame. . . ."

Raven barely heard anything Mr. Raleigh said during class. She was both furious and bewildered. Denise was waiting at the classroom door when the period finally ended. Denise, for once, didn't just speak breathlessly. She *was* breathless, mostly with outrage. "I can't *believe* it!" she said. "Can you believe it? Can you *imagine* the nerve?"

"No, I can't. I'm sure she didn't break into my locker all by herself and get—"

"What are you talking about?" asked Denise.

"What are *you* talking about?" Raven wondered.

"The rumor," Denise said.

"Me too. And Dwight the Dweeb got this note—"

"What *are* you talking about?"

"I'm talking about a rumor that I cheated on the SATs," said Raven.

Denise, whose goal was to be a big-city newspaper reporter and who prided herself on knowing "all the facts," was mystified. "That one I haven't heard yet," she said. "I'm talking about Kiki De Santis."

For just a moment, for a shred of a second, Raven thought she'd been had. Kiki had come to the café that morning, acted friendly, driven Raven to school and everything, and then done some horrible Pink thing after all.

"I heard that Kiki De Santis gave Ruth Waverly a green silk blouse," Denise said.

Ruth Waverly, a big-boned, very serious girl, was president of the senior class and a member of the selection committee.

"People are saying it's a bribe," Denise related, "so Ruth will vote for Kiki when the committee meets."

It did sound unusual. Ruth was a much bigger girl than Kiki. There could be no question of Kiki saying, "Here's a blouse of mine, Ruth. I don't need it," or "I don't want it," or "You'd look good in it," or "Wear it on your big date and get it back to me." No, Kiki would have had to go out and buy a blouse in Ruth Waverly's size.

But Raven trusted Kiki now. She was honest. "There must be some explanation," she told Denise. "Kiki De Santis wouldn't bribe anybody."

"We've got to get to the bottom of these rumors fast," said Denise, after listening to Raven's tale of the SAT lie. "The *Grapevine* goes to print tonight. It's all laid out, but I can cut a filler piece on the new boiler and replace it with—"

"Lacey's trying to make me look bad about the SATs. She's using the green blouse on Kiki. I wonder what she'll try on April Lovewell."

"You know," said Denise, "Lacey's far too smart to spread stuff around herself. I wonder who . . . ?"

They looked at each other. "Penny Bolton!" they said in unison.

"She's still doing Lacey's dirty business." Denise shook her head.

They separated for second-period classes, Denise to physics, Raven to study hall. Senior study hall was essentially unsupervised, but second period was

186

too early to screw around and act ridiculous. Most kids slept. Penny Bolton was in study hall, and Raven was looking forward to seeing her. But no Penny. Raven asked Renée Henderson just where the little gossip monger might be.

"I'm sure I have no idea," said Renée, with a sweep of her brilliant hair.

"Well," said Raven, flaring in spite of a personal vow to stay cool, "you tell her she better hope she sees me coming!"

Renée tried not to show it, but she displayed a glimmer of fear.

"Have you seen Lacey?" Raven demanded.

"No," said Renée. "No, I haven't."

Nobody, in fact, had seen Lacey. The reason for her absence dawned on Raven midway through third period, which was anatomy. "I'm so dumb!" Raven murmured to herself. No one had seen Lacey because she was not *in* school this morning. Raven pictured Lacey down at Carter's Drugstore, waiting for the film to come in. If she's not in gym, I'll know for sure, she thought. Lacey had gotten some kind of excuse to sit out gym class all week, but she had to report anyway and loll on the bleachers while everybody else ran around the track.

Raven felt as if she were fighting with one arm tied behind her back.

But then her natural spirit returned, like a shot

187

of adrenaline throughout her body. I'm going to the mat with anybody and everybody who's doing this to me, she promised herself. I'm going to be Pretty Peggy Sue, win the scholarship, and go to college.

Or die trying!

CHAPTER 19

After anatomy, Raven saw Vaughn Cutter in the hallway. He was on his way to fourth period, walking with Hal Bemis and Jess Gardner.

"If anybody's calling anybody," Raven heard Vaughn grouse, "*she's* calling *me.*"

Raven didn't need much of her good mind to calculate that Vaughn and Lacey were still on the outs after yesterday's spat. "Vaughn!" she said brightly, walking up alongside him. "Just the man I wanted to see. Can I talk to you a sec?"

"Ah . . . sure," he said, a little doubtfully. They veered off to the side of the hallway and stopped by a row of lockers. Hal and Jess walked on, although Jess glanced back once, grinned, and winked at Raven.

"I need your help," she said. She was fairly tall, just a shade shy of five foot seven, but she hadn't realized how tall he was until now, standing face to face. His eyes, light blue and crystal clear, were direct. Raven felt her pulse race. For a moment, she forgot what she was going to say.

"What sort of help?" he asked, with a smile that held just a trace of nervousness.

"I need people to help circulate petitions. A lot signed up, but it's raining. Some are sure to fink out."

"I'd like to," he said, "but I have baseball practice."

"You won't if it keeps on raining."

He grinned, as if to say: You got me. "Maybe," he said. "I can't promise."

"Student lounge after school," she said. "See you there?"

He thought it over for a moment, then smiled again, this time without a quaver. "Maybe you will," he said.

Bad weather didn't exist for Coach Monfort. She made the entire fourth-period gym class run around the track in the rain. By the time Raven jumped into Kiki's Trooper II, wet, dripping, and disheveled from the run, she felt like taking on a whole platoon of Lacey Pinkertons in hand-to-hand combat.

"I hope that film is in," she said. "I've got to have it."

Kiki, usually a safe driver, skidded a little as she left the parking lot. "Why's the film so important?"

"I'll explain later."

They got downtown in a couple of rain-spattered minutes. Lacey's Ferrari was parked at the curbside right in front of Carter's Drugstore. So was a white film delivery van.

"Uh-oh," Kiki said. She braked to an abrupt, jerking stop next to the truck.

Raven jumped out of the car and dashed across the sidewalk into Carter's Drugstore. There, in the middle of the Health Aids aisle, were Lacey Pinkerton and April Lovewell. April was holding a plastic Carter's shopping bag.

"Hi, Raven," April said, sort of anxiously.

"Hi, Raven," said Lacey, with a self-satisfied, genteel smirk. She held a crisp, rectangular, white and yellow envelope with SPEEDO PHOTOLABS—SACRAMENTO on the front.

"Why, Raven!" Lacey exclaimed. "You look a wreck! Your cute little gym suit is all soaked and everything."

"I've got to run," April said, looking skittish and embarrassed. "See you guys." She scurried away and out the door.

"You have some pictures there, I see?" said Raven.

"That's right." Lacey made a move toward the

191

door. Raven sidestepped, blocking her path. The two girls glared at each other.

"What's your problem?" demanded Lacey, in her haughty way.

"I have a couple. Does the SAT exam ring a bell?"

"No. Should it? I didn't go to school today. I'm staying home sick."

"You look all right to me. Maybe a nice green silk blouse would make you look even better."

"I don't know *what* you're talking about!" said Lacey, trying to step past Raven again. It didn't work. Raven cut her off next to Bandages and Ointments. In Lacey's eyes now, Raven saw a fleeting hint of panic.

"Had some photos developed, I see?" Raven said.

"That's right. Of me and my dad. The last time we were in Frisco."

"Oh, that's great!" cried Raven, in a deliberately exaggerated tone. "I'd love to see them."

"Some other time," said Lacey. She faked to her right, then slid past Raven in the other direction. "See ya," she called airily.

"Not so fast, sweetie pie," said Raven, grabbing the collar of Lacey's pink windbreaker. Lacey was almost as tall as Raven, but Raven was slender and

strong while Lacey was lush, with that hint of soft-
ness born of self-indulgence.

Raven gave a sharp yank on the windbreaker,
pulling Lacey backward and spinning her around.

"Get your hands off me!" Lacey screamed.

"Huh?" exclaimed Jerry Carter from his perch
behind the counter. "What's going on there?"

Lacey tried to break away from Raven's grip, but
Raven darted forward and grabbed her in a head-
lock. "Mr. Carter," she called, "did the pictures for
Raven Cruz come in yet?"

Lacey was glaring. Her teeth were bared. Raven
could feel her rib cage going in and out, in and out,
like bellows.

"What?" said Carter. "Cruz? What? You got
'em right there. The blond gal got 'em. . . ."

"Give!" said Raven, holding on tightly to Lacey,
who was trying without success to jerk free. "Give,
or I'll crack your neck, so help me God if I don't."

Lacey dropped the envelope on the floor and got
her hands up around Raven's head.

"You even think of pulling my hair," Raven told
her, "and every strand of yours is going to come out
by the roots."

Lacey surrendered then. Raven felt her body go
limp, and released her. Lacey didn't actually cry,
but she looked as if she might.

"What the *hell* is going on there?" yelled Mr.

Carter. "Do I have to call Sheriff Rodriguez, or what?"

"No, Mr. Carter," said Raven, retrieving the envelope from the floor. "No problem. Just a little misunderstanding. It's all over now."

"No, it's not!" Lacey hissed, spinning around and running out the door.

Unable to wait another second, Raven tore open the envelope. Winston Purdy had shot a whole role of film, and every picture was of the same tiny bird. To Raven, it *looked* like the bird in *Birds of America*— red breasted, with patches of gray, white, and red—but she wouldn't be certain until she matched it with the picture in the book.

Moments later, seated beside Kiki in the warm Isuzu, she reexamined the photos.

Kiki glanced over. "Birds?" she asked, puzzled.

"A bird."

"Can you tell me now? Why it's so important?" Kiki asked as she pulled away from the curb.

Raven hesitated. So far, Kiki seemed to be totally honest, seemed *finally* to have seen Lacey Pinkerton's true colors. Raven had learned her lesson in first grade, when Lacey had come up to her on the playground and said, "Get off that swing right now. My father bought it for the school, and I want it."

No, Raven thought, Kiki's definitely not like

that. "If this bird is what I think it is," she said, "we might be able to save the scrublands. We'll know for sure when we match these pictures against the bird in the book, but I think this is the Pacific red warbler. It's on the verge of extinction. If the scrublands are its habitat, Mr. Calvin Pinkerton, for all his money, is going to have a hard time bulldozing even a single bush."

Kiki was quiet for a moment. She seemed startled. "You can do this?" she asked. "Kids can do stuff like this? How did you ever get the idea to stop Greenway Mall?"

"It started when I realized how much I loved the scrublands. They're a lot more valuable than any mall," Raven replied. "I went from there. You can do whatever you want, too. *If* you're willing to work for it."

Again, Kiki was quiet for a time. She drove into the school lot, found a place, and parked. "Wow!" she said then, kind of softly. "Raven, you're right. Why haven't I thought of things that way?"

"I think you've started to," Raven said, leaning over to give Kiki De Santis a big impulsive hug.

CHAPTER 20

It was still raining heavily at three o'clock, and when the final bell rang, Raven found only eighteen volunteer petition circulators in the student lounge. There was no alternative but to proceed, so she gave everybody a pep talk. While speaking, she saw Vaughn Cutter slip into the room, kind of shyly. He stood quietly inside the entry way, his short, blond hair damp from the gym shower, his muscles well defined under a pale green polo shirt. He waited until she'd finished her little exhortation, then came over.

"I want to sign up," he said.

"Great! You live on Winding Hill, right? See Kiki for the voter's list of your neighborhood. She's right over there—"

"Well, I . . . I also sort of wanted to talk to you," he said. "It's about the festival ball."

Quite a few kids were staring, with no doubts at all that Lacey Pinkerton's boyfriend was more than a little interested in Raven Cruz. Raven didn't want to distract them when there was so much work to be done.

"Tell you what," she said to Vaughn, touching his arm, leaving her hand there so he'd know her answer would be yes, "we're all meeting at the café when we're done. Tacos unlimited. Can we talk then?"

Vaughn gave her a slow smile, kind of sweet, even tender. He placed his strong fingers, for a moment, on top of her hand.

"We sure can," he said. "Ah . . . I have to know . . . you dance, right?"

"I dance, all right," Raven said, smiling and looking up into his clear, clear blue eyes.

Vaughn got his voters' list from Kiki and slogged out into the rain.

Winston Purdy had *Birds of America* open to the page where a picture of the Pacific red warbler appeared. Raven took the photos out of their envelope, holding them one after another against the picture in the book. "What do you think?" she asked.

"It's close."

"Close isn't good enough. It has to *be* the Pacific red. What do you think we should do?"

198

Winston shrugged, a gesture that for him was almost a rearrangement of every bone in his body. "I don't know," he said.

Raven decided to gamble and go ahead. "Let's see how many signatures we get," she said. "We might have the right bird here. I think we should mail the petition and the photos to Senator Miller. Remember, we have to get them in the mail by five tomorrow afternoon."

Raven had no way of knowing then that the chances of her dying without ever seeing the results of all her hard work were one in four.

Thursday, May 25

CHAPTER 21

April Lovewell had just arrived home from her trip to the scrublands with Mr. Woolery. Walking among the beautiful plants, April had almost forgotten about all her problems. Mr. Woolery was a good teacher, and with his guidance April saw the light and shadows play in the bushes in an entirely new way. But now she had something important to do—very important.

These are the three most important minutes of my life, she thought, and I'm sitting alone on the edge of a bathtub.

April had read the instructions carefully. About twenty-nine times. The writing on the back of the package said to leave the "Revealer Foil" in the "Symbiotic Solution" for precisely three minutes. April had her bedroom alarm clock, a loudly ticking cream-colored nonelectric job, and she watched with doomed fascination as the ugly black second hand crawled around the dial. The three most important minutes in her life were also the longest. Only two minutes and forty-eight seconds to go . . .

April was in the big old bathroom on the second floor of the big old Church of Christ parsonage.

. . . two forty-four . . .

"April, child!" called St. Sara from the kitchen downstairs. "Hurry along now. Your oatmeal will be ready in a few minutes."

"I'll be down in a minute, Mother," April called through the bathroom door.

. . . two minutes, thirty-three seconds, and counting . . .

"April, child!"

"Yeah, Mom. Hang on a couple of big minutes, for God's sake!" yelled April.

That'd do it for a while. Complete silence from downstairs.

A tear slipped out of April's left eye and ran down her cheek. She brushed it away. The tear came from Real April, who had to be concealed from the rest of the world most of the time. "We want to see a Happy April," St. Ward and St. Sara had been telling her ever since she was old enough to smile. So they—and almost everybody else—got the Happy April they seemed to want so badly.

Happy April was a little goofy, a little ditzy, always worried about her freckles and juvenile stuff like that.

Only three people in the world knew Real April —Hope Hubbard, Mr. Woolery, and Spike Navarrone—but each of them knew a different part of her. They knew that April Lovewell was not the silly girl who'd stripped down to her underwear at Lacey Pinkerton's poker party freshman year and who'd never completely been able to live it down. They knew Real April was not the girl in the white dress in the front pew at church on Sunday, her eyes closed as she fervently sang "Amazing Grace." No, they knew Real April was a real girl with needs and wants, hopes and fears, dreams and ambitions. Like, for example, getting out of this hypocritical, hypercritical town and becoming the artist she wanted to be.

"You can do it," Mr. Woolery was always saying, "because you've got the right stuff."

"You're going to make it big someday," Spike had said, many times. April loved him so much. "But," he added once, "you're never going to get anywhere if you don't stand up to your parents."

Her cousin, Hope, said pretty much the same thing. "What happened between my mom and your parents shouldn't have anything to do with me or you, or what we want our lives to be like. Remember that when you feel down, okay?"

April wished she were more like her cousin, who was really smart without half trying and whom everybody seemed to like. Hope understood Real April and knew that Happy April was a fraud. The only thing that bothered April about her cousin was Hope's opinion of Lacey Pinkerton. April admired Lacey enormously. She was so pretty and cool and confident. Her life was so well ordered and serene. Her parents respected her independence, her right to lead a life of her own. April admired Lacey Pinkerton simply because she had, so obviously, the very things that April would have died to possess.

Hope wasn't so sure about this heroine worship, though. She kept bringing up the strip-poker party, which had *not* been Lacey's fault. Lacey had never done one single bad thing to April Lovewell.

. . . one minute and fifty-two seconds . . .

April had been going into Carter's all week long, waiting for the opportunity to shoplift a kit. No way could she have taken it to the counter and bought it straight out. "I suspected it all along," people would start saying. "She stripped down to the buff at a party freshman year, remember?"

The funny thing was, she'd been more afraid to buy the kit outright than to swipe it. Shoplifting was a *crime*! In order not to be talked about—as if old Jerry Carter cared *what* she bought—April had become a criminal. Moreover, she'd bought a ton of skin cream and freckle remover during the week, waiting for a moment when no one was around to slip the kit into a shopping bag. And after all that planning, all those needless purchases, Lacey had shown up out of nowhere to pick up some pictures, or something. It had been a close call.

The clock's second hand suddenly began to move at an astonishing rate of speed. This must be the relativity that Einstein was talking about, April reflected. How will I ever tell Spike? she thought. He loved her because he thought she had the spark and the drive to get out of Paradiso, develop her talent, and make a life. He had those same dreams for himself, in spite of his desperate responsibilities at home. April remembered vividly—and all too vividly this morning—the night he'd told her about Michelle Wheeler's little ploy. "A girl like that!" he'd said, more bitter and disappointed than angry, but pounding his right fist rhythmically into his left palm. "Can you believe it, April? She gets herself into trouble, which means she's headed down the tubes, and the first thing she thinks of is to try and drag some guy down with her. Let me tell you something: that guy isn't gonna be me. He's *never* gonna be me! I'm getting out of here, just like you. I'm getting out of here *with* you."

April remembered his words very clearly. But even more clearly, she recalled his pounding fist.

April kept her eyes on the clock rather than on the kit.

. . . thirty seconds . . .

St. Sara, from downstairs, called: "Please, child! Your oatmeal!"

"I'm ready to drive you to school!" St. Ward chimed in.

. . . twenty seconds . . .

The Happy Event Home Test Pregnancy Kit, next to St. Sara's iron hair curlers on the bathroom counter, was busy doing its job. It had come in a happy-colored box, which April had torn into tiny pieces and flushed down the john. It was amazing how many brands of at-home pregnancy tests were on the market. Carter's Drugstore stocked them all. And all of them had such optimistic names, like Happy Event. Yeah, right. Early Warning, thought April, would be a lot more accurate. Or Disaster Ahead.

If the Revealer Foil turned pink in the Symbiotic Solution, well, then You're Dead was a pretty appropriate brand name too.

. . . three . . . two . . .

April took a deep breath, held it, and looked.

April Lovewell was truly Pink at last.

CHAPTER 22

April got out of her father's car, walked toward school, and said "Hi!" to Dwight the Dweeb. He was standing beneath the flagpole, next to Winston Purdy's rattletrap bike. Its tires were almost bald, the handlebars wobbly, and the saddle leather shot. Winston had a thin rope coiled around the handlebars, making it seem as if the bike were tied together.

"How ya doon today, April?" inquired Dwight the Dweeb. *Snort-snort-snort.* "How was your peregrination into the scrublands with Mr. Woolery?"

April didn't know what "peregrination" meant, but she got the gist. What surprised her was that Principal Appleby knew. "How——?" she started to ask.

"No problem, no problem," he explained hastily. "I checked with Mark as soon as I heard the rumor."

"Rumor? What rumor?"

"Oh, you know how people are," he said disarmingly. "Somebody saw you and Mark driving out of the Menendez Motor Lodge parking lot down by the scrublands and . . . well, you can guess the rest."

April and Mr. Woolery had parked his car—a distinctive black BMW 318i—at the Menendez Motor Lodge, which was adjacent to the scrublands. They had walked around as dawn came up, studying patterns of light. April had made a few preliminary sketches, and Mr. Woolery had given her some pointers on how to capture what she saw in the shadows and light. That was all. When the sun came up, Mr. Woolery had driven her home to the parsonage.

And at the moment, she had bigger things to worry about than Penny Bolton's latest scandal-mongering scoop, even if she was its victim. April had the real scoop, the kind Penny would kill for.

Feeling vulnerable and blue, and even more alone than she had moments earlier, April went inside the school. Buddy Holly was coming on strong over the P.A., courtesy of "with-it" Appleby:

> *Heartbeat,*
> *Why do you miss*
> *When my baby kisses me?*

A huge stack of just-off-the-presses *Grapevines* rested on a table just inside the door. A gaggle of kids, reading something in it, howled with laughter. April automatically took a copy of the school paper and made her way down into the west wing where the machine shop was. She *had* to talk to Spike. Shop was his first-period class.

On the way to school, as her father droned on about all the usual topics, April's mind had wandered. She imagined herself holding on to Spike, roaring away on his motorcycle to a distant place. Maybe to the orange groves in Southern California. Spike knew orchards. He could get a job. They'd buy a little house—nothing fancy, but very warm and cozy—and April would begin to paint as soon as the baby was born. Spike's hard work would be recognized after not too long a time, and he'd be made foreman. April would offer her paintings for sale at art fairs. People would buy them; demand would grow. Their son—it would be a boy baby, of course—would grow up strong and smart. He'd take over the orchard business that Spike would establish, but . . .

. . . but the problem with the distant future was that it was so . . . far away. Before any of those wonderful dreams could become real, April had to figure out what to do about today.

On her way to the machine shop, April passed

two kids talking in front of their lockers. One was Hal Bemis, and the other, Libby Pitch. Libby was in Mr. Woolery's art class, along with April.

"Well, how's *Marrrk,* huh, April?" asked Libby.

"You two play a little poker out there at the Menendez?" asked Hal Bemis, with a wicked snicker.

Running away with Spike to a comfy cottage in the orange groves seemed very, *very* far away.

In the corridor just around the corner from the machine shop, three girls April didn't know were jabbering excitedly. She thought at first that they were talking about her and Mr. Woolery also. But no. "Didja hear? Didja?" one squealed. "Vaughn Cutter asked Raven Cruz to the festival ball!"

"No! No way! What'd Raven say?"

"She said yes. Isn't it awesome? Lacey Pinkerton's nose is gonna be so far out of joint she'll need a crowbar! God, I *hate* her!"

April walked past them without seeming to pay any attention. Some kids *hated* Lacey?

"Raven Cruz collected over twenty-six-hundred signatures on her petition," one of the girls was saying. "She's *so-o* excited. She has to send the junk up to Sacramento or someplace by five o'clock today. . . ."

April felt happy for Raven, whom she didn't know very well, but who was always friendly. Having seen again the beauty of the scrublands just this morning, April didn't want to see them paved over. One of the few points of agreement between April and her mother was their opposition to the proposed Greenway Mall.

"See Spike?" April asked Marlin Connery, a huge, heavily muscled farm boy. Marlin was in shop with Spike. Marlin flipped the matchstick he had between his teeth from incisors to canines and told April, "Spike's gonna be a little late this morning. Had to get his ma to the doc."

Another late night at the Blue Hawaii. "Thanks, Marlin," April said. Nothing to do now but go to first-period bio and wait. She *had* to see Spike.

April got to the classroom well before the bell rang. Sitting there alone—and feeling *really* alone —she opened Denise Guthrie's *Grapevine*. She'd heard yesterday's rumors about the green silk blouse and the SAT, and now she saw what the kids at the school entrance had been laughing about. Ruth Waverly, senior class president and a member of the selection committee, who'd supposedly been bribed by Kiki De Santis, had published what she titled *A Small Fable*:

Once upon a time on the highest hill in Flowerland there lived a Pink Witch. She was very beautiful and she had everything she wanted in the world. Then one fine day the Rulers of

Flowerland offered a golden crown to whoever should be judged the most worthy lady in the kingdom. "It is I," said the Pink Witch. But to her great horror, two others came forward to claim the golden crown: the Dark Princess and the Lady of White Shoes.

The Pink Witch was furious. "How dare they?" she shrieked, throwing such a terrible tantrum that the earth moved.

Now, the Pink Witch had in her court a loyal jester named Copper. "Copper, my fine fool," said the witch, "We must find a way to make the Dark Princess and the Lady of White Shoes appear unworthy to wear the golden crown of Flowerland. I believe I have found such a way. Some time ago, the Lady of White Shoes had a green silk gown that was far too large for her to wear. She gave it to one of Flowerland's rulers. Very recently, the Dark Princess was able to answer a great number of riddles put to her by famous scholars in a far-off land called Princeton. Copper, my fool, do you see what we must do?"

"Yo, witch," replied Copper enthusiastically, "even Stevie Wonder can see that."

And so it came to pass that the Pink Witch sent Copper into the kingdom, where rumors were spread about the motives of the Lady of White Shoes and the Dark Princess. But the people of Flowerland were judicious and wise. They did not believe false rumors. The Pink Witch did not receive the golden crown.

She threw such a terrible tantrum that her father, to appease her wrath, had to take her to the land of Frisco on a silver bird, where, fer shure, dudes, she spent a fortune.

April was shocked. She really was. Ruth Waverly was suggesting—no, she was coming right out and saying—that Lacey had put Penny Bolton up to spreading rumors about Kiki and Raven! Penny, everybody knew, was so loyal to Lacey that she might have spread a few stories on her own, but Lacey would never have been behind it.

This was *mean*!

April also noticed that the fable did not include, as a contender for the golden crown, a "Lady of Red Hair" or "the Speckled Princess." Well, there'd been no rumors about her . . . except for the one about Mark Woolery and the Menendez Motor Lodge!

It hardly matters much right now, thought April, dismissing the whole business from her mind. *I gotta see Spike!*

CHAPTER 23

She didn't see him until lunch—Thursday menu: Franks 'n' beans w. fruit cup. Even then, he didn't show up right away. April got in line, saving Spike a place, and shuffled forward with the rest of the kids. It was a strange feeling. There she was, with a baby growing inside her, with her whole life in turmoil, *and none of them knew!* The other kids chattered away about the Peach Blossom Festival, upcoming exams, who'd just had a fight with whom, and what they were going to do during summer vacation. All of those things seemed so alien to April right now.

April's mind drifted back to that spot beneath the Ponderosa trees on the hills above Old Smuggler's Road. That was the "special place" she and Spike went to. That's where "it" had happened on a balmy night—she'd calculated—twenty-three days earlier. Spike had been so sweet that night, even sweeter than usual, and it had seemed the most natural thing in the world to do.

Even now, in spite of everything that had happened and all the unknown things that had yet to be faced, April would never forget the kiss that had started everything, a long, slow, dreamy journey down a blossom-scented tunnel, which suddenly turned upward. Wrapped in Spike's arms, April found herself traveling skyward at incredible speed, and then she was soaring, soaring in absolute stillness and splendor. Somewhere, far away, Spike was asking, "You okay? Baby, you okay?"

She hadn't possessed the breath to answer, so she'd just nodded.

"Don't worry about anything, baby," Spike had said, still holding her tight. "We'll always be together. That's the only thing that matters. You're the best thing that's ever happened in my life."

April had felt like a true queen that night. Peach Blossom Queen wasn't even a close runner-up.

Now, standing in the cafeteria line she wasn't sure *what* she felt like. She felt as if she were shooting upward again, but this time in some immense rocket over which she had no control. It seemed to her as if Spike were the captain, the master of her fate and soul.

She was standing there, peering about for a sign of Spike, when Lacey swept toward the cafeteria.

Janice Campbell was with La[...]
derson, and Penny Bolton, o[...]
seen and read the *Grapevine* [...]
gave no sign that it had both[...]
through the halls of Paradi[...]
trailed by ladies-in-waiting.

"April!" she cried exubera[...]
been looking for!

"Here!" she continued, thrus[...]
lope at April. "I just won't be able [...]
spent half the night awake, trying to th[...]
appreciate them most."

April took the envelope and flipped it ope[...]
third-row tickets to the Madonna concert on [...]
day in Sacramento!

"I really can't . . ." she started to say, thinking
that there was no way her parents would let her go.

"Now," said Lacey, with a smile so big and
bright and warm it could have melted half a glacier,
"now not a word. You just take them, okay? Have
fun."

Lacey moved on to the head of the line—somebody *always* let her cut—and April just stood there,
looking at the tickets. The whole scene had been
very public. Lots of kids had seen. April hoped that,
finally, they understood. Lacey Pinkerton was not
the "pink witch" depicted in the *Grapevine* fable.

219

nice person, and a good friend. Kids
     ⸺tand that.

     of them didn't. "Didja see that?" April
     ⸺ say. "Lacey's trying hard to make her-
⸺ood."

     right," another girl replied. "After that
     the paper. She's got her nerve. The whole
     knows what a pretentious phony she is. If
     ⸺ur dads didn't work for Pinkerton Canneries,
     ⸺y Pinkerton wouldn't rate for a dime."
"Every dog has its day."
"Time's a'comin'."

They were just jealous. Every girl in school
wanted to be like Lacey Pinkerton. April certainly
did. Or had, anyway. Her life, very suddenly, had
veered off onto a completely different track. High
school, and the things of high school, seemed very
far away now.

Then Spike was there beside her. "Hi," he said
as she let him slip into line. His presence, as ever,
made April feel warm and safe and confident. She
knew, when she told him the news, that he
wouldn't ask the questions guys ask in the romance
magazines and on the bad TV movies, questions
like, "How did it happen?" and "Are you sure I'm
the one?" He knew how it had happened, all right,
and he knew he was the one.

He talked about his mom while they went

220

through the line, got their trays, took the franks 'n' beans. She'd been "out"—he never mentioned the Blue Hawaii Bar—and she'd had a "little spell." Dr. Bates, from Linden Hills, was at the farm right now. Spike had an excuse to leave school for the afternoon. He'd only come in at all because there'd been a paper due in social studies. He had a $B+$ now, and was trying to whack it up to an $A-$ at least before final exams.

"You're not saying much," he observed as he followed her to an empty table way in the back of the caf'. Half the school was eating lunch outside. But April always ate in the caf' with Spike, because he was on the state's lunch program for kids from poor families. He didn't like to be on the program. He hated it, even. Still, he had to eat. His mom wasn't bringing in any dough, and his dad certainly wasn't mailing cash home from Folsom Prison.

April, still saying nothing, placed her tray on the table and sat down. Her stomach was in knots; she couldn't have eaten a single baked bean.

"I've got something very important to tell you," she said, her voice cracking as she struggled to find the right words.

"Yeah?" he asked, looking up. "What?"

"Please don't be upset."

"I'm not upset. Upset about what? *What?*"

"I think I'm pregnant," she said. She hadn't

221

intended to say it that way. She'd planned to say, "I'm pregnant." Flat out and honest. *She* was talking like a girl in the romance magazines.

He just stared at her for a second, his brooding, dark eyes turning darker as she watched. Her heart dropped like a rock, slipped out of her body, rolled across the floor, and curled up into a dry little ball in a cafeteria corner.

April wanted to say "I'm sorry," or *something,* but she'd used up all available words just then.

"I'll handle it," he said. "I'll think of something."

At first, April was slightly cheered. He would stick by her at this time of crisis. He *would* think of something.

Yet almost immediately, she began to wonder. *What* would he think of to "handle it"? Neither of them had dreamed of—much less planned for—this mess. Spike's future was as much on the line as her own, and she knew how desperately he was counting on the future.

"It'll work out," he said, his eyes dark and unreadable. "It'll work out one way or another."

What did that mean? Again, April felt her hopes dwindling.

"Let me do some thinking on it, and we'll talk later. Damn! If I didn't have to get back to the farm and see about Mom. Look, I'll leave a note in your locker, okay? Where we can meet?"

April nodded. Spike often left notes in her locker. The combination was 32-18-7. His birthday (March 2), his age, and a lucky number. "Or maybe something else," they'd often joked.

"I hate to have to leave you," he said, looking worried. "You gonna be all right?"

She tried to speak, choked, nodded, and then got out a "Yes." It didn't sound like much, but it was "yes." He kissed her on the forehead and, leaving half his lunch uneaten, hurried toward the cafeteria exit. Lacey Pinkerton stopped him as he went past her table. She smiled and said something. Spike smiled and said something back. Then, with a final little wave in April's direction, he was gone.

He was gone before April could lift her hand to wave back.

CHAPTER 24

No one who saw April Lovewell that afternoon, neither teachers nor students, noticed anything unusual. If you said, "Howzit goin'?" she'd say fine. She'd say, "Watch out for Mrs. Ferris in the library. Must've had a fight with her husband or something." April answered right away when Mr. Blaisdell, the psychology teacher, asked her to distinguish the ego from the superego, and laughed as much as anyone else when Eddie Hagenspitzel did a deadly accurate imitation of Dwight the Dweeb doing an imitation of Don Knotts.

Inside herself, though, April was on a crazy, wild roller-coaster ride to hell and heaven and back. One moment, she knew everything would work out fine. The next moment, she saw herself in the country poorhouse, or on the street corner, begging money to buy her baby food. St. Ward and St. Sara would drive by in their black Chevy, saying, "Turn thy eyes away from her, for she has sinneth beyond redemption." In psychology class last quarter, April remembered Mr. Blaisdell saying that sometimes people who got themselves in some sort of bind—got fired, lost a spouse, became real sick—turned suddenly to religion. Not me, April thought. I've been there. Spike and I will make it through this by ourselves.

Hope sat across the aisle from April in Mrs. Tugwell's English class. Several times, April almost worked up the courage to tell Hope about her problem. Hope would certainly listen sympathetically. She might even have some ideas about how to handle this mess. And Hope was obviously in a very good mood. While Mrs. Tugwell rattled on about Ophelia's suicide, Hope slipped a note over.

I heard Jess Gardner still doesn't have a date for the ball. Is that right?

April scribbled a "Right" and passed the note back. It was a simple, normal, everyday little note, but it seemed to April like a message from another world. Dates for Peach Blossom Balls no longer counted in the land where she now lived.

Do you think he'd take me? Hope inquired. *Why not?*

226

Think I should ask him?
What have you got to lose?
MY NERVE!

They both giggled, enough to make Mrs. Tugwell turn around and glare. Then April leaned across the aisle and whispered: "Can I see you after school? There's something important I have to tell you about."

"Sure," Hope replied.

After school, though, April couldn't find Hope. She was feeling a little better by then anyway, her emotional roller coaster on an upswing. Of course things would work out. Of course Spike would think of something.

But Spike hadn't returned to school. There was no note in her locker. She hoped something serious hadn't happened to his mom. Phoning him was impossible. The Navarrones couldn't afford a telephone, not to mention a lot of other things. And *I haven't got a cent to my name either,* she realized. *We're really in great shape to start a family.*

"What's wrong?" asked cheerful Penny Bolton, walking down the hall and past April's locker. "You look like you could use an upper."

Does it show that much? April worried. "Oh, just tired," she lied.

Penny stopped to chat. Like Lacey, she seemed

227

not at all bothered by the *Grapevine* article. It was astounding how blithely some people handled all sorts of pressures and travail. If anything truly bothered Penny Bolton, she kept it to herself, even her sister's death.

"Have you heard?" asked Penny.

"Heard what?"

"Uh-oh," said Penny, looking uncomfortable. "I thought you'd heard. I thought that's maybe why you looked so down."

April's heart dropped into her stomach, maybe even lower. Something had happened to Spike! He'd wiped out on his Harley! He'd rammed into a Mack truck while speeding home to his mother!

But no.

"Lacey asked Spike to the festival ball," said Penny, looking sadder than St. Ward at his basset hound best. "I thought you knew."

April almost lost it then. She knew Spike had gotten sick of sneaking around to see her, even when they went to their "special place" in the hills. He wanted to be a normal guy doing normal things with a normal girl, like hanging out at Rosa's Café. Like taking a girl home and kissing her good night outside her door. What was so wrong with wanting that?

April saw, with shattering clarity, that the sneaking around, the always being alone together, had

228

created a kind of hothouse atmosphere. In that fiery little environment, she and Spike had gone further than they might have otherwise.

How could she blame him if he wanted to go out with Lacey Pinkerton? Who didn't?

Lacey must have asked him to the dance when he'd stopped at her table in the cafeteria, just after April had told him that . . .

"No, Penny," April said, "I hadn't heard that."

"Oh!" exclaimed Penny Bolton. "I'm so-o sorry . . ."

"Sure, Penny. Of course. I know you are."

I have been such an idiot! April accused herself as Penny Bolton twitched her little butt down the hall and out the east wing exit. *Did I listen when Hope tried to warn me? No!*

But there is one thing I am gonna do . . .

You can't. You don't have the nerve.

I do have the nerve. I've got nothing left to lose. I'm gonna go right on up there to that big house on Winding Hill Road and I'm gonna tell Lacey Pinkerton off! I don't care who's there to hear me when I do it, and I don't care if Lacey and all her toadies laugh about me for years to come. For years to come, my life'll be a wreck anyway. So I'm gonna do it, come hell or high water. Hell, St. Ward would say. St. Ward, you don't know anything. If

229

Aunt Leanne made it on her own and raised a kid as nice as Hope, I'll do that too if I have to.

April realized she was thinking in a way that, for her, was out of the ordinary. She'd never in her life been strong willed or aggressive. She realized that she hadn't discussed this with Spike yet, either. Hadn't heard his side of the story. Well, his side of the story could come when it came. She recalled, behind the bleary eyes of memory, how Lacey had said, "Have another glass of punch, April. Just another teeny-weeny little glass." She remembered Lacey grinning and laughing, dealing the cards. "April, you lose again. You'll be down to your panties pretty soon."

Now too, after four years of pushing it into the back of her mind, April remembered a moment in the locker room. It was the Monday after the already infamous strip-poker party. And she'd asked Lacey Pinkerton, "Did you say anything? Did you? Everybody's talking about me. They all know. Somebody must've told. It wasn't you, was it?"

She ought to have asked, "It was you, wasn't it?"

She ought to have said, "It *was* you, you pink witch!"

I'm going up that hill! April vowed.

As April walked down Old Town Road, a car pulled up alongside. She recognized the old maroon Jaguar that Vaughn Cutter drove around in.

"April, want a ride?"

Raven Cruz sat in the front seat next to Vaughn. She was holding a large manila envelope. In the backseat were Kiki De Santis and, of all people, Winston Purdy III.

"No, thanks. I'll walk."

"C'mon. Hop in. We just have to stop at the post office, then we'll take you anywhere you want to go."

For an instant, April thought of asking them to take her out of town to the Navarrone farm, so she could talk to Spike. Too many complications. She dismissed the idea. "Thanks anyway. I can use the walk."

"Okay. See ya."

The Jaguar pulled away. None of the kids in it had said anything about Lacey and Spike and the festival ball. Maybe they didn't know yet. Or maybe they were just not saying anything, being polite.

April reached the intersection and started up Winding Hill Road. It occurred to her that she hadn't been all the way up the hill since freshman year, the night of Lacey's notorious birthday party. With hanging around at school, looking for Hope, and the walk itself, April didn't come in sight of the Pinkertons' huge Victorian until around five o'clock. When she started up the long lilac-lined drive, she had an impulse to turn around and go back.

Just then, a gleaming sedan backed out of the garage and started down the drive toward April. She ducked back into the lilac bushes, which, like everything else in Paradiso, were wild with blossoms.

The sedan passed within a half-foot of April's hiding place. It was the big Town Car Lacey's mom got driven around in. April saw her own reflection in the glistening paint on the car. She caught a glimpse of the chauffeur, wearing a little billed cap, and got a look at Darla Pinkerton in the backseat. She wore dark glasses and sat up straight. That was class for you, real elegance, April mused ruefully, thinking of the Pinkertons' fine, well-ordered lives. Nobody in their family told somebody else to go to hell, or sat on the edge of a bathtub waiting for a Happy Event.

Knowing that Mrs. Pinkerton wasn't home emboldened April for her confrontation with Lacey. The red Ferrari was out front. It was probably too early for Mr. Pinkerton to have come home from work yet. April didn't see his Mercedes, but the garage doors were closed.

She was just about to ring the doorbell, having readied herself for whatever would come, when she heard a kind of strangled scream or something from around the side of the house. Then there was an awful crash, followed by another cry.

Acting instinctively, April ran around the side of the huge white rearing house, past banks of manicured rose bushes. She recalled, from the night of the party, a big glassed-in sun room on this side of the house.

"Daddy! Plleeease!"

April heard Lacey. Screaming. And Mr. Pinkerton's voice: *"Embarrash me in fron' of the whole damn town, will you! I swear I almosh died . . . !"*

April, throat dry and heart thundering, heedless of thorns, wriggled in beneath roses and pressed her face to the sun-room window. Just in time to hear the wicked hiss of Mr. Pinkerton's belt, which he whipped through the air, striking Lacey. She was backing away from him. The end of the belt lashed around her hips. She cried out.

"Daddy!!!"

April's senses were operating on maximum. In an instant, she saw everything: Mr. Pinkerton's rage, Lacey's pain and fear, and the two whiskey bottles on a coffee table near the TV. One of the bottles was empty, the other nearly empty. Mr. Pinkerton's face was scarlet. He moved awkwardly, stumblingly, as he pursued Lacey across the room.

". . . give you ever-thin', every-thin'!" he was

raving. *"An' look what I get in return. 'Barrass me in fron' th' whole town. . . ."*

Lacey turned away from him, attempting to flee. He swung the belt again, catching her viciously on the backs of her thighs. She screamed, stumbled, and sprawled forward, coming to rest at the window outside of which April cowered beneath the roses.

Mr. Pinkerton threw his belt across the room and sagged down into a chair.

April held her breath. Inches away, on the other side of the glass, Lacey lay sobbing, her hands over her face.

Then she removed her hands and opened her eyes.

She saw April.

Never in all of her life had April seen the hate she saw then. Lacey's blue eyes widened first in startled surprise, then narrowed with fiery hostility. April had *seen* Lacey humiliated. She'd been a witness. So now April knew that all of Lacey's life was a fraud, a pretty, painstakingly maintained facade behind which were savageries and deceptions.

She'll never forgive me for what I saw, April understood as she backed out from under the rosebushes and started down the long driveway. April knew for sure that she could drop off the ends of the earth now, just like that, and Lacey Pinkerton would only stand there and wave goodbye.

April also knew that she'd better take a fresh look at her own situation. Her own parents at their carping, fretful worst, were not one-tenth of one percent as bad as Calvin Pinkerton. They weren't perfect, but at least they didn't live a lie.

What I'll do, thought April as she walked back down Winding Hill Road, is go over to school and see if Spike left a note in my locker, and maybe I'll run into Hope along the way. Then I'll go home and try to work up the courage to talk to Mom and Dad.

It was funny. As far as April knew, this was the first time she'd ever thought of Ward and Sara as "Mom" and "Dad."

She also wished that, when her father had said, "Your mother and I love you, honey," at school Tuesday morning, she had told him that she loved them too.

Friday, May 26

CHAPTER 25

Hope heard the *slap* of Jess Gardner's sneakers as he raced toward her and the lumbering *thud* of Eddie Hagenspitzel. She felt her mouth open in a silent scream—her voice frozen in terror. Hope heard a high-pitched ringing as her vision faded to darkness. She fell weightlessly down a long tunnel. . . .

When she came to, moments later, Jess Gardner was on the floor beside her, cradling her in his arms. "It's okay, Hope," he kept saying, "it'll be all right. It'll be all right. It's okay. I'm here for you. . . ." But his face was numb with horror and disbelief.

No. It wasn't true. It couldn't be. God, please, this was just some gruesome nightmare. Hope's breath came short and shallow and fast. She couldn't get enough air. She shivered uncontrollably, her body trembling with cold in the warm morning.

Hope didn't want to look, but she couldn't help it. There on the polished corridor floor lay the cold, motionless body of April Lovewell. Around her neck was the cord that had choked the last breath out of her.

"April!" Hope screamed.

"It's okay, I'm here for you. . . ." Jess whispered.

"April! No! No!" Hope's cries echoed off the walls in a heartbroken wail.

April was dead—murdered. Stinging tears streamed down Hope's cheeks as she clung to Jess, sobbing helplessly for her dead cousin.

Saturday, May 27

CHAPTER 26

Willa Flicker, editor of the Paradiso *Record*, was beside herself with excitement. She was in the *Record*'s tiny editorial office in the Pinkerton Building, which didn't provide much room for a big woman like Willa to be beside herself. She was trying to decide which of two major stories ought to be on the front page of her next issue. April Lovewell's murder, to which neither Sheriff Rodriguez nor anyone else had a clue? Or the Greenway Mall?

Willa had on her desk a clipping from the Sacramento *Bee*.

State Senator Humphrey T. Miller failed today in his attempt to block development of Greenway Mall in Paradiso. Miller, a longtime opponent of what he calls "environmental rapacity," told the *Bee*: "I thought we had a good shot. Local reports indicated that the Pacific red warbler, a bird on the verge of extinction, inhabited the native scrublands on which the proposed mall is to be built. Unfortunately, photographic evidence of the bird's presence in the scrublands is inconclusive. We will continue our efforts."

Reached at his home, Greenway developer Calvin Pinkerton stated: "This bird business is ridiculous. The Greenway Mall offers a boom era for our whole valley. I know a lot of people around here signed petitions. But that doesn't mean anything. People don't know what they want until they get it. Everybody is going to love Greenway once it's built."

Raven Cruz, student head of the anti-mall campaign, disagreed. Miss Cruz said: "We're not stopping for a minute. We're going to save our native lands. And the red warbler is out there, singing to us every day."

Willa read the clipping a second time, and then a third. She'd always dreamed of landing a job on a big paper, maybe the *Los Angeles Times*, when a major story hit. She knew a big story when she saw one. And now she had two of them staring her right in the face.

Raven Cruz was just a kid, yet she'd been able to obtain the attention and aid of a state senator.

But after consideration, because it was so shocking, so mysterious, Willa chose the murder as her front-page story. She sat down at her worktable and blocked out the headline. It was an easy job.

WHO KILLED PEGGY SUE?

S0-CFN-037

World Without End

World Without End

"A lush and sinewy tale of three friends-lovers whose
lives are traced over a 30-year period. One of the most
notable novels of 1981."

THE NEW YORK TIMES BOOK REVIEW

"For the reader, Francine Gray's WORLD WITHOUT
END is a voyage of rediscovery. It is the rediscovery that
the deepest experiences of life are to be found in friendships....It is surprising perhaps that her theme should
seem so fresh and nourishing, considering that friendship
is the oldest and most precious of the arts."

Norman Cousins,
THE HOLLYWOOD REPORTER

"Clearly the work of a richly talented writer."

NEW YORK DAILY NEWS
review by D.M. Thomas, author of The White Hotel

"Francine du Plessix Gray should win a large following
with this novel. Her sturdy theme is examined with care.
She writes with an almost old-world elegance without
being precious, richly evoking place and character."

NEWSDAY

"Gray likes character and does it ravishing justice....
She cuts to the core of the familiar and unfamiliar
circumstance. As ideas and insight pour out of her,
Gray's breathless tone is held in check by her vivid
images."

CHICAGO SUN-TIMES BOOK WEEK

"It is almost old-fashioned in its romantic vision."

ST. LOUIS POST DISPATCH

SELECTED BY BOOK-OF-THE-MONTH CLUB

Also by
FRANCINE du PLESSIX GRAY

Lovers and Tyrants

World Without End

FRANCINE du PLESSIX GRAY

PLAYBOY
PAPERBACKS

WORLD WITHOUT END

Copyright © 1981 by Francine du Plessix Gray

Cover illustration copyright © 1982 by PEI Books, Inc.

Published simultaneously in the United States and Canada by Playboy Paperbacks,
New York, New York. Printed in the United States of America. Library of Congress
Catalog Card Number: 81-85255. Reprinted by arrangement with Simon & Schuster.

Books are available at quantity discounts for promotional and industrial use. For
further information, write to Premium Sales, Playboy Paperbacks, 1633 Broadway,
New York, New York 10019.

ISBN: 0-867-21079-6

First Playboy Paperbacks printing August 1982.

To Ethel, Joanna, Rose

My deep gratitude to the American Academy in Rome, whose generous support and great kindness enabled me to finish this work in peace.

The author gratefully acknowledges permission from the following to quote:

Random House for Yevgeny Yevtushenko's poem *Babi Yar* from Olga Carlisle's book *Poets at Street Corners*.

Penguin Books Ltd. for the use of lines by Vladimir Mayakovsky from *The Penguin Book of Russian Verse*, introduced and edited by Dmitri Obolensky, copyright © 1962 by Dmitri Obolensky: from "Conversations with an Inspector of Taxes about Poetry," and "Unfinished."

Horace Gregory for *The Poems of Catullus*, translated and with an introduction by Horace Gregory, copyright © 1956 by Horace Gregory.

Famous Music Publishing Companies for the lyrics to the copyrighted song "That's Amore." Copyright 1953 by Paramount Music Corporation.

Miller Music Corporation for the lyric from "Down Argentine Way" by Mack Gordon and Harry Warren, copyright © 1940, renewed 1968 Twentieth Century Music Corporation. All rights administered and controlled by Miller Music Corporation. Used by permission.

Ecco Press for Robert Haas's poem "Against Botticelli" from his book *Praise*, copyrights © 1974–79.

Part One

Friendship is here, my heart
Richer than love or passion.

CATULLUS

i

The Russian walked with his arm linked through Sophie's, a man with soft brown eyes and a scar on his left cheek. She had been in love with him for three hours. Since childhood she'd often fallen in love with visions, strangers, ballet stars, on the occasion of a fleeting glance. She had known very great loves that lasted a day and a night. The park lay before them luminous with fog. A large romantic park, empty benches, beds of tulips scintillating with recent rain, lamplight shimmering on an immensity of moisture. The path stretched ahead of them to what seemed infinity, all end obscured, terminated only by a distant bank of vapor or low clouds. "I'd like to walk to the end," she said, "which may not exist." His glance was sentimental, swift. "We shall order it to cease existing." They had met that afternoon in Leningrad at a recital of folk dancing which Sophie attended alone. From the very beginning of this trip she'd decided to be alone some part of each day. "Where have you been you nomad," Edmund and Claire scolded her the next morning, "why do you leave us like that?" They seemed peeved, as if she were turning on some pledge. During the folk dancing Sophie had wept. Girls in early puberty veiled in white gauze had glided across the stage with steps floating and minute, their hands twining and twisting like snakes turned into flowers, like aquatic

9

plants waving in an ocean storm. And children in black Cossack costumes on the tremulous edge of manhood had shot across the stage like glints of coal, dancing their nascent ritual of seduction with fiery sabers, with proud and furious glances, with postures of fighters. Sophie had wept over her lost childhood, her solitude, the pain of growing up in America, the beauty of these dancing children entering like fierce swans into the storms of life. But then the next part of the spectacle upset her even more, oh the second part of it was awful. The curtain had reopened on a stage bathed in the fruited glow of Western nightclubs and an all-girl rock band singing Elvis Presley. They ranged in age between ten and fifteen, they played on synthesizers, trombones, trumpets, electric guitars, they made a din which Sophie found atrocious. They were dressed in the navy-and-white costumes of Young Pioneers, with bright red cravats about their necks; they still wore high white knee socks and flat little-girl shoes with buckles. Boom pah-de dada they sang, thrusting towards the audience their bodies made lithe by Soviet calisthenics, muscular pelvises, budding breasts. Boom dada they shook their shoulders, lasciviously trembling, winking. So perhaps Sophie wept again thinking their youth is being ruined, their civilization is just as corrupt as ours. That's when the Russian came to sit next to her asking was she alone in the city, could he help. Sophie didn't know what to say. "Stalin would die," she whispered, nodding towards the stage, "Lenin would die." He frequently smiled. He had gentle, ironic eyes. "Khrushchev mightn't have liked it either." He wore a brown shirt open at the collar, he lived in Moscow, he'd come to Leningrad to attend a congress of cardiologists. They walked together down Nevsky Prospect. When the rain started pouring they went to dinner in a large café where another band of adult men played acid rock and Sophie put her hands over her ears, saying over the platters of cold fish, "Look here this is crazy you're importing the worst poisons of our culture without taking . . ." There was a great burst of thunder, the dining room was plunged in darkness, the band stopped playing, waiters hurried about with many candles, shouting. "You have made the poisons stop," he said. For the rest of their dinner the lights wavered softly on and off as if powered by the energy of a small erratic wind. All in his face was soft and faunlike, tendrils of thick hair curling over wide temples, brown eyes that taunted hers with the flirtatious glances of bygone movie stars. "Indeed the rock music does not become you, you are more like a tango, I shall ask you many questions about your life."

"In New York I rise at four A.M.," Sophie said. "I have a two-hour television program every morning five days a week, I get to the studio at six, read the wire reports, finish the morning's script, talk to the producer . . ." "You are very famous and you earn as much as some football players and soon you will have your portrait on the cover of *Newsweek*." "I've already had that," she said. He looked amused and very tender. "Is it great freedom?" "Perhaps it is solitude," she said; "isn't great freedom also great solitude?" He shook his head at a slant, not clearly yes or no. "And what do you do in the afternoon?" "In the afternoon I go home and nap and read more newspapers still. . . ." What papers? Ah if I tell you you'll get a lesson in American geography, the *Boston Globe*, the *St. Louis Post-Dispatch*, the *Philadelphia Inquirer*, the *Chicago Tribune*, the *San Francisco Examiner*; why so many? We Americans are drunk on information, I'm beginning to think it's one of our national diseases. . . . Why have I come to Russia? Oh you ask so many questions Vladimir Ivanovich! . . . We've come to Russia together Edmund and Claire and I, best friends since adolescence, we've come here to recapture . . . we've come here to figure out how to live the last third of our lives; after forty-five there isn't much left but friendship is there, only friends will tell you the truths you need to hear to make the last part of your existence bearable. . . . Have I been in love? Oh that's been the disaster of my life. It should never be a disaster? What a flirt you are Vladimir Ivanovich! I could give you an excellent Marxist reading on romantic passion; those who still look on romance as the main ingredient of the good life are brainwashed by the bourgeois propaganda machine, victimized by a defunct capitalistic ethic that gluts on the permissive excesses of our decadent literature. . . . How's that, passing grades? . . . Do I dream at night? Yes I have primitive, simple dreams, they're often nightmares, I dream of being precisely the opposite of what I am, there are many children about and I must cook for fourteen and I'm constantly out of food and everyone shouts at me, but we must stop this immediately, in my métier I'm the one who asks the questions. . . .

He said: "I shall take you to see old friends who will make you happy." And so they had walked down the banks of the Neva to visit a small traveling circus that had just arrived to town. A thin scar ran from Vladimir's temple to his ear; in his youth he had published several volumes of verse. Sophie put more perfume on her wrists, wishing for everything with this man. The circus troupe lived near the river in a one-room trailer cabin at the center of which there was a table laden with champagne, wines, sweets. Two thin blond girls in trapezists' costumes were arranging cakes into neat little rows. The manager of the troupe kissed the doctor on the cheek and said, "I want you to meet my new juggler and hypnotist; he can put people under a spell for five days, he's cured insomnia, stopped them from smoking for the rest of their lives." "Let me also show you some tricks," the hypnotist called out, "let me show you." He disappeared into a closet and came out again in a white brocade jacket, carrying his kit. He made six orange

Ping-Pong balls disappear and took them out of his mouth two at a time, he made them disappear and found them in Sophie's pockets, he made them disappear and pulled them out of the doctor's ears. The blond trapezists wore tight lavender T-shirts which matched the great arcs of violet paint on their upper eyelids; they sat on the same chair with their arms entwined about each other's waist. The juggler put his Ping-Pong balls under some dishes, lifted the dishes and said see there's nothing there anymore. The thinner girl snuggled her chin into her friend's shoulder, their faces melded together like a single head distorted in the vision of fever, their dark red mouths loomed immense in their wasted faces. "Like a Picasso," Sophie whispered. The doctor agreed. "Nineteen three, blue period." Later the Russians recited poetry, Blok, Mayakovski, the doctor's own verses. When Vladimir Ivanovich recited poetry, standing up, eyes closed, his chest rolled outwards like an opera singer's, his voice took on a different order of nature —the rolling of streams over pebbles or the mysterious language of macaws at night; he spoke his song an octave higher than his other voice and for that time the circus actors stood captive in their poses, frozen as in death, the trapezists' pale long hair lay entwined like one mass of wheat above their violet bodies . . . and then after a long while the doctor-poet's eyes opened, he smiled at Sophie and talked to her in human voice again. "Oh, oh," Sophie retorted when he said Americans knew no poetry by heart, "I'll prove you wrong, I'll start with Yeats! 'That is no country for old men. The young in one another's arms, birds in the trees—those dying generations . . .'" But then she felt her tears storm up again, couldn't finish. Vladimir stroked her arm. "I have translated Yeats for our literary gazettes; for a while it was forbidden here but slowly things are changing. . . ." He was bidding his friends good night. And she went out with him again into the park.

The evening was luminous with fog, still luxuriant with her hopes for his touch. You're the victim of romantic fiction Claire and Edmund had told her for thirty years, you're like Madame Bovary; lately at every new quickening of her body she'd thought no more, I never shall again . . . "I believe in staying in my country and fighting for change," the doctor was saying; "there are little advances and freedoms which would have been silenced in the fifties; we must work step by step, like good liberals; I have a column in one of our literary gazettes every month, I plan very carefully, I try to test every limit. . . ." Scintillations of moisture still garlanded the linden trees, the empty benches seemed to fade into the gravel on which they stood. "Several times a year when I'm depressed I go to the country in the south with the Gypsies," the doctor said; "everything is let loose, it's like the Ivan chapter in *The Brothers Karamazov*, we sing and drink all night, sometimes so much that I remember nothing, but in the morning I am quite like new, reborn. . . ."

"I used to be able to do that too," Sophie said, "but no more, no more. . . ." And then she startled at the sound of footsteps in the gravel a few alleys behind her. She imagined the guide of the tourist group she and Claire and Edmund were traveling with, turned back expecting to see his stocky frame, the boreal eyes blazing behind thick spectacles; it was only an aging dog shuffling across the park. "You are so naive, so sheltered," the doctor laughed; "if you want to avoid them you must never look back! When you go out of the Union as I sometimes do you're followed by two men, one from your own country and one from the country you're visiting, you call them . . . goons, right? I have two goons when I travel, two *doppelgängers*; it is amusing to have them meet, to set them off against each other and then reconcile them; actually they're very lonely people, they know how hated they are by everyone, sometimes I feel sorry for them. . . . Perhaps we should liberate the goons; you would say goon lib, right? But perhaps you've already had too much liberation in your country; I think everything is so permitted there that nothing is erotic anymore, isn't that true? Here we're so puritanical that men and women are forbidden to be in a hotel room together after eleven at night unless they're married, so we take many trains, much is forbidden so all is very passionate. . . ."

"We are very puritanical," he repeated flirtatiously as they continued to walk. "We have many boundaries, limitations. Trains . . . When we're very serious we take the Trans-Siberian. When all is permitted nothing is desirable; it must be very sad in your country. . . ." The fog lifted, the Neva River glimmered from under the tall oaks bordering Decembrists' Square. He went on for many hours talking about himself, like most men she'd ever desired. His therapies, his translations, his periods of censorship, his survival. Whether or not they became lovers for one night is irrelevant. "I had an extraordinary evening," Sophie reported to Claire and Edmund at breakfast. "I had a long talk with a Soviet man who goes to the Baltic States when he's in a really acute depression, Latvia, Estonia, can you imagine, those are their sanatoriums, their paradises!" "Fancy going to Riga for a breakdown!" Claire exclaimed. "I'd rather be in Moscow for mine," Sophie said. "Come my loves it's time for our morning swim."

June 1975, brilliant dawn sunlight, primeval mud of the river. Against the flank of the Fortress of Peter and Paul, once a prison for dissenters against the Russian czars, there stretches an expanse of sand which now serves as bathing beach for the population of Leningrad. The three tourists comment on the irony of the site, on the beauty of the view it offers. Above the flat indigo mirror of the Neva, Peter's city oscillates in a phantasm of marble and of malachite, a prodigality of spires, turrets, coronets and eagles, of golden and enameled roofs shimmering like the variegated scales of a giant lizard. " 'It has been noted,' " Edmund reads from his guidebook as they sit beneath the fortress walls, " 'that no site in the world is less favorable to the founding of a metropolis than these 101 islands set into an impetuous river and constantly threatened with destruction by a glacial sea.' " "A despot's fantasy!" Sophie exclaims. She slips off her shoes, walks to the shallow water at the riverbank, slides her blouse over her head. Claire still lies in the shade of a tree, reading her guidebook. Edmund has thrown his clothes to the ground and stands in his bathing trunks by the riverbank, staring at the water. They are all three forty-five years old. Sophie's frame small and powerful, waist finely modeled, breasts with the ripe fullness of Titian's nudes. Claire's limbs spindly as those of a young deer's. Edmund's lithe tight body is that of a man who has a fastidious concern for aging.

Claire has turned around and stares upwards towards the fortress wall.

"Hurry up Clairsie you're the last one in as usual!"

"Thirty years of waiting for you, we're fed up!"

Edmund plunges into the river. Sophie wades in after him. Claire puts down her book and starts undressing after having picked up the contents of their satchels, which fell to the ground in a gust of wind. (In hers there is a small Victorian tortoiseshell comb mounted in silver, a biography of Mahatma Gandhi, a photograph of a long-haired teenager in a Radcliffe T-shirt; in Sophie's, a peperback entitled *Women and Sexism*, a variety of leaking ball-point pens which have colored a composition notebook various shades of mottled blue; Edmund's briefcase contains a 1915 edition of Baedeker's *Guide to Russia*, a Russian edition of the works of Pushkin.) Claire slowly slips off her jeans and wades into the river. "It's colder than the island in April!" she calls out.

"Freezing," Sophie shouts, "strictly for polar bears!" She swims a vigorous backstroke, arms flailing, chanting, "I love summer, I love summer!" Claire (who has also been known from earliest childhood by the name of Pebble) keeps her arms folded over her breasts until she starts to swim. There is a rich smell of dead leaves underfoot, across the river the Winter Palace gleams with its pale green hue of ice and verdure, death, rebirth. All is still gaiety this morning and reclaiming of childhood, all is still bathed in great playfulness. "Where is Edmund?" Sophie calls out when he has been out of sight for half a minute. "Where are you my pet?" An anguished cry here, a burst of laughter as he grabs her legs from under the water and emerges beside her to clutch her waist.

"Ah there he goes Hermes the teaser, always trying to catch us underfoot!"

"Welcome to St. Petersburg my loves!"

Sophie kisses Edmund's forehead and swims a languorous sidestroke towards Claire, her curls glinting copper in the sun.

"Best come out soon or you'll get chilled the way you used to Peb . . ."

"Like that time we first went swimming together off the sailboat . . ."

Claire: "Were we fourteen?"

Edmund: "No, no, fifteen, it was 1945!"

Sophie: "Eddem's right, forty-five."

"We used to talk a lot about reincarnation."

"Peb wished to be Saint Francis."

"Soph wanted to be Rosa Luxemburg."

"And Edmund wanted to be reborn as a work of art."

" 'Once out of nature I can never take . . .' "

" '*Shall* never take,' Sophie darling, you've gotten that line wrong since we were fifteen."

ii

Nantucket, 1945

Cribs, collies, playpens, golf bags, campers' tents, riding gear and even ponies, clamming equipment, picnic hampers, movie screens, radios, sand pails, bags of diapers, barbecue grills—the Nantucket ferry came in twice a day from the Massachusetts mainland redolent with tribal plenitude; its sleek-limbed families tended to be large, the one-child family was rare, the childless and the single seemed almost barred from the vessel. And at least once a day Edmund persuaded his mother to walk to the ferry to watch it disgorge its exotic cargo of American summer. Edmund and Mara were already at the landing when the ship's last horn shouted out towards the island, sounding as if the whole world had put its mouth to a whistle, staring at the vessel as if it were a foreign nation unto itself. They played a game, the kind of game often invented by two persons who share a solitude: Arguing in three languages as they observed the emerging crowds, they chose *la famille la plus magnifique* to emerge from the ferry, the one with the most children, the longest blond hair, the handsomest dogs, the tallest father, the most gleaming braces on its young ones' teeth, the largest barbecue equipment, the fullest station wagon.

They walk towards the ferry every day down holly-hocked lanes, down lustrous streets whose cobblestones impose upon traffic the stately gait of an early age, past flower vendors displaying in horsedrawn carts the splendor of red zinnias and purple gladioli.

The mother is tiny, birdlike in figure, the top of her head barely reaching her son's ears. Melancholy eyes of a Byzantine icon looming over chiseled cheekbones, black hair severely parted in the middle and carefully braided, tresses winding like a small jet crown about her exquisite pale face; and always an ornament in that hair, a feather, a tortoiseshell.

He has just turned fifteen; has cornflower blue eyes framed by very long dark lashes; wears a gray flannel vest under his blue blazer, a silk ascot about his throat; is fond of his first pair of sunglasses, which he practices putting on and off with a debonair gesture. His thick dark blond hair is worn quite long for that decade, resembling photographs of certain nineteenth-century Romantic poets.

He reads to her from a guidebook as they walk:

"*Ecoute*, listen! 'In the early nineteenth century the men of Nantucket stayed away for years on their whaling ships, hardship came frequently to these heroes of the high seas who often had to resort to cannibalism when their stores of food ran out . . . "Thar she blows, thar she blows," this was the eagerly awaited cry of the lookout, the harpooner threw his instrument with all his strength deep into the back of the huge beast . . .' "

He's stopped walking and tilts back, lifting his arm like a harpooner.

" '. . . the boat drawn by the whale bounced about in a shower of spray, the treacherous journey often lasted for many hours as the gigantic mammal swam miles across the sea, sometimes the whale attacked the boat instead of diving, it could smash the vessel with one blow of its tail or try to grab it in its enormous mouth. . . .' "

Edmund closes the book, breathes deeply, runs for a hundred yards down the street and rushes back towards his mother, waving his arms with well-being. "Freedom!" he shouts in all his languages. *"Liberté! Svoboda!"*

". . . so here we were, Claire, two penniless European refugees whose only previous respite from August heat had been to spend a week in a modest inland boarding-house run by childless Russian immigrants. Nothing much in store there for me. My mother enjoyed the proximity of an Orthodox church, and of some damp woods in which we held interminable discussions about which mushrooms were safe, how much roulette to play with this delectably free food. I can't say I wasn't surrounded by affection; the spectacle of a woman who's struggled alone to bring up a child is touching to anyone but a monster . . . a former colonel of the czar's artillery gave me tennis lessons, Moscow gentry eking out their living catering piroshki tutored me in Russian poetry in return for my painting their portraits. And the rest of the time I drew everything in sight while they gambled at their perennial game of gin rummy, which began at nine in the morning and often went to midnight. . . . Great bursts of extravagance of course, as soon as anyone sold a memoir about his days in the Cadet Corps or pawned off a family diamond there was a big party for the entire Russian community of Bridgeport, impecunious balalaika singers doubling in as waiters shuffled about very drunk, flies unzipped, as they passed the vodka. I used to think that Providence drove me towards you due to my severe case of asthma. But the fits of coughing and sneezing which seized me when I was fourteen were probably a rebellion against the fact that my only summer companions had been these dotty experts on Pushkin and Glazunov—off to the ocean the doctor told Mara unless you want your son to end up like Marcel Proust—so money was somehow found to get us a vacation on the island, ah yes she'd won hundreds of dollars at gin that spring, that was it. . . . Here it is 1975 and I can remember it as if it were yesterday, walking down Nantucket's streets towards your house in a trance, staring at all that tribal gaiety, the long-haired children swinging from oak trees, the beautiful children chasing each other down the rose-filled lanes, the shouting tribes of young running out of tennis clubs flailing their rackets, their puppy-warm shoving, whispering, sharing of edibles—childhood is a prerogative of the rich my dear; there was something both exciting and forbidden about entering your life, some kind of treason to the frugality of immigrant life. . . .

"No no Peb it wasn't guilt, it was . . . the sheer excitement of the previously denied. The few friends I'd made in school were freaks such as myself, little middle European émigrés gifted at the harp or the cello, and here we were, my God, going to lunch for the first time with what Mara had described as '*une des familles les plus magnifiques en Amerique*.' I guess you and Soph had just enrolled the previous winter at her ballet school and that's how our mothers met; why didn't you phone them even earlier, I asked, we've already been on the island for a week—one must be proud in this world, she answered, one must never let the rich think one needs them; I pondered that one a long time, it may have led to many an ornery mask I chose for myself—I'll never forget the quick sly smile she gave me as she said that, and then her query as to whether I'd remembered my watercolors, a miniature set she'd given me for Christmas which could fit in my pocket, oh she'd rather starve on black bread than buy me anything but New York's most elegant watercolor set. . . ."

"That's the way I remember my first glimpse of you, brush in hand . . ."

"And I remember that just before we reached your house the ferry's horn rent the air and we ran towards it to engage in the most central ritual of our week-old island life; we ran to stare at the ship unloading its riches as if they were nourishment for our starved eyes. . . . I guess what struck us as most exotic on that ship was an entity so foreign to our own lives, the father, the American dad expostulating and supervising and explaining seabirds to his sons and reprimanding the little ones about toilet performance and overlooking the safety of every item in his bursting-with-goodness station wagon—here was Mara, orphaned when she was still young and widowed before I was ever born, and here I was the precocious monster who'd immunized himself against the possibility that there might be any better life on earth than the seclusion he'd shared with his mother since birth . . . so when I met you that first day I was totally awed by the mysteries of family life, like an explorer coming to some new continent whose rites of bonding are radically different from those of his own. . . ."

"I remember how beautiful you were, and how terrified."

The ferry has spewed out its humanity, the families are driving their hoards towards the island's heart. With a sigh Mara glances at a piece of paper in her purse. Edmund puts on his dark glasses. And they walk towards a seaside street a few blocks west of the ferry landing.

"Attention at lunch today," Mara says, "you must admire this island with passion; in this country you must always admire and they have curious polite way of thanking you for admiring."

"What splendid cobblestones, what a chic horse, what a heavenly church."

"Not so sardonic please."

"What a chic church, what a heavenly horse."

"*Tishe*, quiet," she snaps in Russian. "You have great trend to irony. . . . I repeat, don't forget that proper Americans have exquisite manners. . . . I admired Fifth Avenue bus once near ballet school and Mrs. Sanford said thank you, thank you."

The Sanford house comes into sight a few hundred yards later, as hulking as the ferry that loaded nearby, equally celebrant of a confidence in childhood and in summer. Edmund stares with grave curiosity at heaps of croquet mallets lying on the lawn, bicycles of many sizes lined up against the garage wall, swings and hammocks strung from several trees, the two-foot-high cast-iron blackamoor holding out its hand for an imaginary horse.

"I protested that I have another lunch appointment," Mara says as they approach the door, "so you can meet this wonderful family alone."

"But . . ."

She blows him a kiss and disappears as swiftly as a swallow.

He stands at the front door taken aback, feigning to inspect an enormous sign in the shape of a ship's prow that wears the residence's name: SEALARK. A smiling black woman in white uniform opens the door and invites him in, church service has gone late, the Sanfords have phoned from the Yacht Club to say that they'll be a little delayed. Nantucket's bells are tolling twelve, the sunny living room declares its owners' great enthusiasm for the animal world. Many beasts prance across its chintz curtains and slipcovers, its ashtrays and china cups strive to imitate the shapes of frogs and various forms of birdlife, a wooden merry-go-round horse serves as portmanteau for dozens of Windbreakers. Edmund walks out onto the terrace, admiring its vast view of Nantucket Sound, sinks into a chaise longue at the water's edge.

Island's church spires melting and shimmering in the

noon haze like palm trees in a desert mirage, boats of all sizes and shapes proliferating like fireflies on the sunny water, rataplan of tennis balls, shouting of children, flap of furling sails from neighboring houses. Two retrievers run onto the terrace and start licking the span of skin between Edmund's socks and the bottom of his flannel trousers. He might have dressed too formally; he hurriedly unfastens the buttons of his vest; if he ever becomes rich he can wear tennis shorts to Sunday lunch. Smaller vessels bobbing like petals on the glass of the harbor, grandiose black schooner sweeping into view labeled in gold letters, *The Churchill*. Taking out his drawing pad, water from the sound, delectable sweeping of colors on thick grainy paper, melon hue over the space intended for the harbor, think of Turner's landscapes, of their melding earth sky water into one aqueous reality, a passage of brackish green and then of blue and brown for the shallow dun-hued water suckling at the Sanfords' landing. A sharp arch of black for the curve of the schooner gliding towards the lighthouse, struggle to suggest the harbor's activity without lapsing into literalness, each boat must fuse into the sea the way a rock melts into its forest quarry. . . . Leaning down to the terrace's edge to clean his brushes Edmund hears a rustling sound at his side. Two young girls of his age stand by the side of his chaise longue, each extremely beautiful in her own way.

From the perfect oval face, over the aquiline nose and the finely modeled, arrogant mouth, very pale eyes stare at him with a grave inscrutable gaze. Claire Sanford has already been described to him by his mother—without Edmund knowing precisely what Mara meant—as "a great Puritan beauty." Her long brown hair is hugged to her head as tightly as a seal's from the perspiration of running. Her breasts barely bud under a tight little white sports shirt. And she clutches to her chest a terrified young white rabbit, with eyes the hue of crushed raspberries, whose paw is bandaged onto a wooden splint.

The other girl, full-breasted, luminous gold-speckled eyes, a curly mop of tawny hair, a powerful nose, stares with great curiosity at Edmund's drawing.

"I'm Claire Sanford," the thinner one says. "I'm Sophie Ross," says the other.

Both have extended their hands. And Edmund, startled, throws his watercolor into his lap and reaches out a hand to each of them.

"You're painting our view!" Claire exclaims.

"Do you feel any affinity to Manet?" the full-breasted one asks.

"No, more to Monet actually."

"Oh but you don't have an accent," Claire says with a pout, as if deprived of a promise. "Meet Mr. McKenzie," she says as she thrusts the rabbit's good paw towards Edmund. "He broke his leg and I put it into a splint." A curiously breathless way of speaking, fast clarion spurts.

"He's so beautiful!" Edmund cannot get his voice above a whisper as he caresses the animal.

"Thank you! You can stroke his head, too."

When shall we lose our nervousness, our habits of solitude? Edmund remains lounging in his chair, rhythmically stroking the trembling animal whose ears are glued to its head in terror at the sound of the crowd that's begun to stream into the house; oh I'm as terrified as you are Mr. McKenzie. The tribe running in from the outdoors seems to range from adolescence to late middle age, they doff their Windbreakers onto the rocking horse, help themselves to cooling drinks, swarm about with the ease of persons who have known a house since early childhood. Repeated voicings of the words "Plinker and Babsie, Plinker and Babsie"; these must be the familiar names reserved for his older hosts, Claire's parents.

Manners returned by the familiar sight of elders, Edmund finally springs to his feet to greet them.

"Welcome aboard!" Paul Sanford exclaims. He is a tall tanned man with burgundy pants and heavy spectacles.

"So nice so nice to have you with us!" The slight blond woman holds out both hands to Edmund. "How heavenly to have you with us!"

Even on that seaside day she stands on very high-heeled shoes which give her a frail, tottering walk. A large sun hat shelters her pale hair, her kind, drawn face. And then behind her that chattering bevy of cousins, nephews, uncles, nieces whom Edmund studies with the same curiosity he bestows upon the magnificent families who emerge from the ferry's innards. Phrases of American politeness still foreign to his ears, warm compliments on his English, his blazer and his watercolor of the harbor, what does he think of Renoir, of this first trip to Nantucket? The elders' curiously swift intimacy.

"When I was ten my father took a splendid house near your birthplace, overlooking the Rhine," he hears Mr. Sanford say. "We were four boys in the family, we had more fun that summer than any other summer I can remember."

"Do please tell your dear mother how thrilled we are with Mr. Fokine's Ballet School, and how beautifully she plays the piano there."

"My oldest brother was six foot five," Mr. Sanford adds as he hands Edmund a glass of lemonade, "he was captain of the St. Paul's hockey team, he went on to Yale and made Skull and Bones. . . ."

"Claire's older brother," Mrs. Sanford interjects, "who died three years ago, was also a promising athlete at St. Paul's . . ."

"This island is a knockout remedy for the glums," Paul Sanford cuts in, changing his spectacles; "happiness can become a way of life, young man, it must if we're to survive!" "How is your dear mother, how sad that she had another luncheon appointment." "She's frightfully busy, as always." "How attractive! What a great beauty she is!" "Thank you!" The martini in her thin-stemmed glass, the trembling of her frail hand, the ringing of a lunch gong.

"Bless us O Lord in Thy ever increasing Mercy," Plinker's voice booms over the bowed heads. "Make us plentiful in grace and strength bless those of our leaders who've helped to spread justice and peace unto the world General Eisenhower General MacArthur our great allies Winston Churchill Field Marshal Montgomery increase our fruitfulness and bring our enemies to the side of justice in order that they may enjoy the fruits of Thy bounty . . ."

Everyone: "Amen."

"How many languages do you speak?" Sophie ventures in the flurry of after grace. "Four." "Let me guess, French, German, English *et quoi d'autre*?" "Russian." "Oh my you could have interpreted at the League of Nations!" Sophie, Claire, Edmund and Cousin Jeff have a bridge table by the bay window to themselves. This fourth young person seated with them raises his head from a studious dissection of his chicken and stares at Edmund with particular amiability. Jeff Howell is many inches taller than the other three occupants of the table and Edmund surmises he might be seventeen years old. Crew-cut light brown hair, affable chestnut eyes, coach's whistle hanging from a string about his neck, T-shirt announcing that he attends Mr. Sanford's old school, St. Paul's. Edmund is particularly fascinated by the solidity of his neighbor's feet; as he tries to bring forth his best conversation and confines his considerable nervousness to the restless twitching of his own legs under the table he's aware of the unchanging angle of Jeff's large impeccable white sneakers, as triumphantly still as the

Chippendale breakfront covering half of the dining-room wall. The revelation that Jeff is in some way related to Claire—he was orphaned at fourteen, Plinker is one of his two legal guardians—affects Edmund deeply. How privileged to be an intimate of this quicksilver creature who emanates such mystery and distance, who seems to draw a circle about herself to break the spell of her own remarkable beauty!

"So, how was church?" Sophie is the one who always seems the first to speak. "Impeccable I hope?" "Quite lovely really," Jeff says. "And you don't go?" Edmund asks Sophie. "I'm not Christian," she says with ease. "It's a terribly pretty building," Edmund offers. "I belong there," Claire says, eyes still cast down on the rabbit hovering on her lap. Jeff throws a wary smile at Edmund. "I saw your eyes, Jeffrey Howell," Claire cries out angrily. "When did you leave Germany?" Sophie asks Edmund in the suave adult tone of one who knows when to change the subject. "Oh the Nazis cleared us out in 1937, then we went to Paris and they chased us out of there in 1940 towards Portugal . . ."

For a time all three give their attention quite single-heartedly to Edmund. Had he been in the Blitz? No Pebble, Jeff corrects, that was Great Britain, he came from Germany and France. What town did Edmund live in in Germany before he went to Paris? Munich? Ah, the Munich Pinakothek! Sophie exclaims. Sophie's hair is like that of a marvelous feline, a lioness or tigress, its curls winding in soft tendrils about her neck. "What did your father do?" she asks Edmund. "I'm not quite sure, perhaps I didn't have one." "How exotic!" Sophie says in a throaty whisper. The other two stop eating, stare hard while he quickly asks Sophie, "What does *your* father do?" "He works with talent, he's an agent for all kinds of artists. . . ." Edmund is attacking his chicken, not visibly impressed, so she shakes her curls and adds, "I mean he's an agent for singers, dancers, playwrights, violinists, all kinds of fascinating people, oh he so loves art! . . ." Sophie speaks in a hushed, modulated, almost conspiratorial voice, she eats avidly, pausing every few minutes to scrutinize the room, whispering precious shreds of information into Edmund's ear when Claire and Jeffrey engage in one of their frequent disputes. Claire's a fabulous pianist and she's never lost a tennis match . . . Claire's refused to eat meat since the age of eight . . . Claire's her best friend in the world and she, Sophie, is not only Claire's best but her *only* friend, Claire's funny that way, very solitary. . . .

Claire wears a pale blue satin ribbon in her hair. She stopped eating early in the meal, having picked at a few mouthfuls of vegetables. Is Edmund more fascinated by her beauty or by the plenitude of her world? "At Christmas I shall visit *cousins*," she spouts upon a discussion of the school holidays, "I have cousins in Detroit, Milwaukee, San Francisco, Dallas, Philadelphia, Wilmington, Baltimore . . ." "*Ma fleur*," Sophie interjects, "you may even have cousins in Peru!" "Why, dear heart," Claire whispers, mimicking Sophie's throaty voice, "I bet I even have some in Madagascar!" She turns to Edmund and he will always recall this as the moment he first fell in love with her: the way she said "Madagascar," the little teeth as white as the first crocus and as delicate as a rodent's flashing under the glory of the beribboned chestnut hair. "Have you, Edmund, ever been to Madagascar?" she asks, staring at him with those glacial periwinkle eyes many hues paler than his. "I keep meticulously away," he answers, "from all islands which begin with the letter *M*."

The girls' laughter resounding in the room, Jeff smiling widely too. Sophie: "You speak English so beautifully, Edmund, you have only the very lightest of European intonations." Claire: "I take advanced French at Spence, and Sophie's in intermediate." Sophie: "And when we go away to Ethel Walker's next year I'll *join* you in advanced. Claire's Mademoiselle only left her last year, Edmund." Jeff: "Pebble, I remember you also had a German nurse when you were a little kid, she made the niftiest Christmas cookies." Edmund: "So you've known each other all that long!" Pebble: "Since we were born, literally." Jeff: "Not precisely that long, silly, I'm three years older than you are. . . ."

Clamor of ice in fine-stemmed glasses, a dream of crystal, whispering aprons of maids offering lemon sherbet, many voices clang over the fragile china, Babsie and Plinker, Babsie and Plinker. In the dining room's sea-struck light the adults' sunned faces are as florid as bloodstains in the snow, there are bright little yachting flags in the lapels of their jackets and shirtwaists. "Uncle Plinker are you thinking of coming to join us in Hobe Sound next Christmas with Uncle Charlie? . . ." "No sweets, actually we're thinking of going to the Bahamas now that the war is over and we can travel more freely. . . ." All this Edmund hears, observes, particularly Paul Sanford's voice booming over their heads as he organizes the pleasures of the summer's last weeks, American dad supervising reprimanding counseling, is April's morning sickness better today, a little brandy after lunch could do the trick. . . . Masticate, chump, swallow he urges a four-year-old nephew seated on his lap, eat your vegerino, duck. . . . And that gastric upset of Douglas's, bicarbonate of soda, sporto, the old remedies are the only humdingers, always a stubborn streak in you Doug just like Pebble; it's been some years since Pebble has listened to advice about *anything* in life. . . .

"I guess the next thing that amazed me that day is the sight of your bedroom, Peb, that stark little bedroom devoid of the frills and flounces of girlhood, denuded of any traditional belongings save for your Books of Common Prayer, your crucifix and that hospice for stray animals you'd built up there . . . every week you managed to imprison a sea gull, some field mice or chipmunk, pleading broken wings or ulcered tails; the room was filled with the sad pink eyes of rabbits gazing out from behind cages, the voices of possibly healthy sea gulls screaming for their liberty. . . . 'You're much better now my sweet' you said to one of your birds and then you screamed back at it in such perfect mimicry of its voice and were so pleased with the fits of laughter that besieged us that you went on to imitate the mouse's, the chipmunk's squeal with equal virtuosity. . . . Olaf your retriever was there, panting excitedly on his mattress, and I asked you whether you were going to be a veterinary and you said oh mercy no a pianist or perhaps a missionary, and Sophie raised her eyes to the sky with an exasperated air and Jeff blew his whistle and said let's get some exercise, Soph be a peach get the basketball give it your . . ."

"Your one oh oh."

"Yes, and Plinker was standing on the lawn among all the cousins, April and Doug and Katrinka, April with her glossy pageboy and mean little overbite and her Long Island way of saying 'That would be so nifty, dearie . . . .' Plinker organizing a clambake for the following day and a picnic sail to Siasconset for the day after, I'll get the big boat ready early in the morning so we can catch the breezerino at low tide; and before I knew it I was on a sailboat for the first time in my life, both Sophie and I, city folk not made for all this smart WASP stuff getting wretchedly seasick in the rising wind. . . ."

In the next weeks, the next years, Edmund would witness the lengthy preparations of Babsie Sanford's empty busy days, the strained, tinkling sound of her laughter as she passed coffee at Sunday lunch, bracing herself for her solitary weekly visit to the Nantucket cemetery. Not allowed to mourn in her own house, forbidden to mention the name of that child who had drowned before the family's eyes in a sailing accident, she would spend many hours of the week preparing a bouquet for her son's grave and spend the afternoon there quite alone, unseen, unheard. The rest of the week Edmund observed her tottering about the business of Sealark in those high-heeled shoes which shackled her movements like little chains, protecting herself from the sun with a multitude of veilings and wide-brimmed hats. Edmund often accompanied her to the Main Street Market early in the morning, when the flower vendors' stalls opened, to find just the proper hue of amethyst and violet gladioli to mix for her Sunday bouquet. Then she returned to the beloved vegetable garden which Plinker seeded every spring to pick herbs and greens before the sun could reach them and wandered sweetly through the house, singing the Anglican hymns she'd learned from her father, a bishop of Boston, making still more flower arrangements for every one of the child-filled, guest-filled rooms, myosotis plumaria delphinium columbine. She was frail and protected like an idol, she painted her sadly smiling mouth a deep shade of ruby red, occasionally she sat on the beach in a large straw hat watching her adopted flock gambol, her hand resting on her husband's shoulder as he accompanied her to the ocean's edge, and that was the way she spent her summers save for those days when she fell into the cyclic depressions she had suffered since the death of her older child.

Babsie Sanford, in the early moments of her seizures, sits on the floor of the sunny living room trying on a variety of hats and costumes, becoming a heroine of one of the many novels she and Plinker had read aloud to each other when they were first married, when Plinker was a junior partner in his Wall Street firm and their children were small and perfect; she becomes Catherine mourning Heathcliff, Dorothea chiding the chilling Casaubon. Then she would rise to dance alone in the center of the room, singing her hymns in a high childlike drone, stockings torn, hats askew, her seizures came suddenly. "Would you just go away if you were I, dear Edmund?" she had said one morning as he helped her to carry an armful of vegetables and flowers from her garden. "Would you be able to just trust yourself to the Holy Spirit and *leave* all this happiness?" Within the next half hour Edmund found her seated on the floor of the living room in an ancient ball gown, took her to her room before phoning the Yacht Club to get Plinker home immediately. She was not violent. One called a doctor and kept her under sedation for three days. Everyone in that house was gentle, Edmund soon realized, save possibly Pebble.

Claire at the piano practicing a difficult Mozart sonata as Sophie and Edmund turn the pages. Upon faulting on two successive chords she slams her elbows and fore-arms violently upon the surface of the keyboard, shouting imprecations, creating cacophonies that make all her animals startle in fright. Many months occur between such outbursts, when her glacially exquisite composure dissolves to reveal a shouting demon whom no parent and few friends can calm. It's as if the Mademoiselles and Fräuleins who'd educated Claire Sanford, striving to fashion the most perfect lady of their careers, had left untouched some unruly darkness that was beyond any-one's control. After an initial temper, or sensing the first symptoms of one, she'd often run into the dunes, the beaches of the island and stay there alone for many hours. Edmund once found her on such an occasion, seated cross-legged like a Buddha on a distant beach, nose to the wind, eyes opening once an hour or so as in a trance. He'd sat in the grass and stared at her, wondering what it would be like to suddenly purge oneself of all anger and rage as she seemed to do in such moments. He asked her later whether she'd been praying; she'd answered it was "more than that," she loved church but the old Anglican prayers didn't satisfy her, after each fit of anger she wished for "a complete and total purgation of myself," she could not further define the nature of what she sought—that particular evening she'd come home with effusive apologies to her father, as she always did after a disappearance, throwing her arms about Plinker and offering a large basket of wild berries she'd picked for him on the moors of Siasconset.

Edmund, Sophie and Claire race up a long dune at sunset. On the beach below Plinker has built a bonfire for his Sunday picnic. At the age of seventeen Edmund will be five foot ten or so, with a nascence of ruddy hair on his slender muscled chest. He strives to win the race after giving his two friends a handicap and struggles mightily up the slope, feet slowed by the deep sand. His hair is the hue of a young lion's mane, there's determination on his face and an ironic smile. Sophie trails Edmund and Claire, laughing and lagging considerably behind. She is sturdy and sleek-limbed, all in her is opulence and delectation of ripeness, her ringlets of hair are hardened by sun and salt to a metallic glint. "You stinkers you're cheating Edmund don't let me down!" Claire is almost up to Edmund, her long chestnut hair waving about like a curtain of silk, as he arrives at the crest of the dune Edmund gives his hand to Sophie while stretching out his left foot to trip Claire; all three fall into the thick dune sand, laughing and pummeling each other's bodies, feasting on the remains of each other's childhood. This could have occurred in the summers of 1946, '47, '48. The island of their happiness stretches at their feet, wealthy and gorse-covered, splayed with the spikes of many churches and hot stretches of wild roses in full bloom. At six o'clock on Sunday evenings Nantucket's oldest church bells play church hymns. " 'Amazing Grace, how sweet thy sound,' " Claire sings in a high clear tone over the shouting of Sophie's and Edmund's voices. And Jeff's, Plinker's voices answer her from the group gathered on the beach below: " 'I once was lost but now am found . . .' "

Edmund becomes good enough to play tennis in club doubles but can never quite manage to beat Pebble. Whenever he leads her three-two in singles her stubborn little chin protrudes in even more determined manner, she returns his strongest serves with a top-spin backhand that sends him flying to the corner of the court, managing a weak dribble which she smashes with such force that the ball bounces three feet over his head, irretrievable. "You never double-fault, do you Pebble?" he mutters as they pass each other at the net. "You never double *falt*," she mimics his trace of foreignness as she runs past him; "why rabbit love I haven't double-faulted since I was six years old." And the phrase charms him as much as her way of saying Madagascar. The few times he's led her four-two she's become all the more tough and ethereal, all the more imbued with those qualities that addict him to her. She goes on to lob to Edmund's backhand, she covers the whole court with a few paces of her coltish legs, she recoups to four-up. She aces him three serves and leads him five-four and breaks his service handily in the last game of the match. . . . But no victory is essential, for Plinker and Babsie waft Edmund in their kindness, Plinker and Babsie have made a vocation of this spot of earth and seem to rule over the very island air which has returned to Edmund the art of breathing.

"I always wondered why they adopted me with such fervor, Peb . . ."

"We were traditionalists, E.R., you were our perfume of Europe, our scent of a still more ancient order. . . ."

"Oh I must have been like one of those exotic animals fed dainties by a monarch, a court jester of sorts with my watercolors and my Voltaire quotes. . . . After all seriousness was suspect at Sealark wasn't it, happiness wasn't a choice but a civility, a distillation of good manners. . . ."

"They force-fed it to me until I almost died of it, Eddem; it was the principal excellence of character they sought."

Throughout his wretched winters Edmund looks forward to the voice of Paul Lincoln Sanford III (vice-president, Clark Dodge and Co., member of the Stock Exchange, chairman of the board of trustees of St. Paul's School, vice-chairman, National Multiple Sclerosis Society, member Knickerbocker Club, Dartmouth Club, Metropolitan Club) booming out grace over the beginning of Sunday lunch.

Almighty Father grace our house as we've honored Thee in Thy tabernacle bless our land with honorable industry sound learning and pure manners save us from violence discord and every other evil way . . .

Bless our summer's work most Merciful Lord and grant us seasonable weather that we may gather in the leisure of our land we humbly beseech Thee to behold visit and relieve Thy sick servant Elizabeth Sanford for whom Thy prayers are desired . . .

Heavenly Father preserve the integrity of Thy chosen land stretch forth Thy almighty arm we pray Thee to strengthen and protect the servants of our government particularly Thy servant Thomas Dewey give him courage and strength in the toil ahead . . .

(At times Plinker asks Jeff to say grace; Jeff is awfully good at grace because as the family says he's "a born educator.")

Almighty and most Merciful God we pray that Thou govern and guide the minds of Thy servants the teachers of this nation bless all those who teach and those who learn and grant that in humility of heart . . .

iii

Aged twelve and fairly short of stature for his age, Edmund decided to play an active role in improving his mother's disastrous finances. He placed the following notice on the parents' bulletin board of the Horace Mann School, where he'd earned a scholarship upon his arrival to the United States:

> Young émigré from war-torn Europe will give private lessons in French, Russian, German at modest charge of one dollar an hour. Phone on weekend nights—555–5942

Still barely five foot two, he dressed in as mature a way as possible and deepened his voice to conceal his youth, not minding if he was thought to be a trifle dwarfed. He prepared his sternest expression as he stood briefcase in hand at his client's door, and would be most severe about students mastering rules of grammar before approaching the art of conversation. ("Being a traditionalist I believe in structure before emotion Mrs. deKay. Say after me, please, *le* bras, *la* tête . . .") He departed after assigning a formidable load of homework and was extremely stern with students towering a head above him who did not finish their assignments. In Edmund's last three years of high school Sophie Ross's mother, an aggressively warm, bountifully painted woman who proved to be one of his most industrious pupils, decided to take German lessons to aid the Richters' calamitous finances. ("But next Sunday Mrs. Ross I want you to memorize the past, present and future tenses of the verb *töten*, to kill.") Babsie Sanford engaged in Russian lessons for the same philanthropic reasons, a project rendered difficult by her incapacity to follow any consecutive stream of thought. "I forget my name in Russian, dear?" "Elizabeta Ivanovna." "How attractive!" "I've stressed that we mustn't speak any English at these sessions; I've taught you that 'how attractive' in Russian is 'kak ha-ra-scho'; repeat after me, please. . . ." "Cake horror-show." "No, no, Elizabeta Ivanovna, repeat again, please. . . ."

"My childhood? Oh I survived as best I could," Edmund would say in his early twenties, "seeing I was the only son of a possessive, single, extravagant woman. . . ."

"The only son of a Slav of exuberant emotions . . ."

"Oh don't tell me about the Russians," he'd shout out years later when he could bear to remember, "their primal fecklessness, their hunger for extremes; I know more about Russians than anyone else west of the Dnieper, that omnivorous spirituality that's like a case of constant drunkenness . . . their extravagance . . . their extravagance! Let me tell you a story.

"It's one of my earliest memories of the United States. Good Friday of Holy Week. Easter sweets are brought us by two impoverished White Russian princes, friends of Mara's from Munich days, who attempt to support themselves in New York by catering Russian delicacies. Rain pouring. The princes are of indolent disposition and detest all modes of public transport. They've taken a cab from their flat in the East Twenties to ours in the West Nineties, and keep it waiting at the door while they chat with us over tea. Tea in our frugal household remains an elaborate Russian ritual, served in tall glasses, accompanied by blackberry jam and nostalgic talk of how much more flavorful it was brewed in samovars abandoned three decades ago in St. Petersburg. . . . The raisin-studded dome of the golden koulitch and the pearly pyramid of pascha are duly admired, memories are recalled of Chaliapin's last performance of *Boris*; after an hour or so Mara delicately hands our friends a sum of eight dollars. I go out to accompany them to their cab and observe that its meter registers the sum of thirteen fifty; the princes are many dollars poorer than they'd been before they started making the cakes and yet they appear delighted—deeply moved, in fact—by the afternoon's transaction and the visit that attends it . . . this event was repeated every Good Friday in equally whimsical fiduciary style. A parable, perhaps, for the mayhem of penury which my mother also imposed upon our own lives. . . ."

"I love that story Eddem, I don't think I've ever heard it before."

"There are things it helps to only remember later. . . . I'll tell you another one Sofinka. Well you know what a modest living Mara eked out pounding out Ponchielli for you and Peb to do your arabesques to, a pittance really . . . nevertheless our average nightly schedule went something like this: the Shakespeare Repertory Company on Tuesday, the Philadelphia Orchestra's all-Handel program Thursday, Gieseking at Carnegie Hall on Friday, an obligatory opera on Saturday . . . to hell with such fleshly amenities as nourishment, dental checkups, warm clothing, all of that recedes before the meticulous nurturing of aesthetic sensibility; let's limit ourselves to meat on Saturdays and fast on buttermilk all other nights, let creditors keep knocking at the door, *les gens bien* must be capable of humming most major symphonic tunes, spouting poetry in at least three languages, discussing all aspects of theatrical repertory . . ."

"Poor angel, now I understand why you've had such problems with your teeth; you should still watch them, you know."

"Listen here it is 1975 Sofka and I remember as if it were yesterday that musical voice of hers pleading with our landlord, 's'il vous plaît Mr. O'Malley a single woman with a child one more week until check comes in . . .' but even at the age of eleven I was a more effective cajoler than she was, having been steeled since early childhood to protect my frail little mother from prehensile hostelers in Munich, Paris, Lisbon . . . 'For shame for shame Mr. O'Malley,' I'd shout, 'expel two orphans and you call yourself a Christian? . . .' yet even such an ultimatum wouldn't deter us from continuing our feast of spectacles, standing in the middle of our filthy little rooms hastily nibbling on a piece of black bread to make the eight-thirty curtain at Carnegie Hall, Town Hall, the Philharmonic . . . you know, Soph, long before I even met the Sanfords there was one ritual I missed in my life more than any other, the sight of a family seated in a proper dining room. How I gloated over the most conventional images of American family life—Thanksgiving covers of *The Saturday Evening Post*, Christmas spreads in *Woman's Home Companion*, ads for silver in *Life* mag . . . Ah for the gleam of a decently roasted chicken, for two forks laid at the ends of a table, for any ritual of stability in the New World . . . Instead of which constant threats of eviction or all heat turned off when the rent went unpaid and we'd resort to the princes' living room, 'Ai ai Alexander Maximovich can you put us up for just a few nights until I receive check from Monsieur Fokine may God ever bless your kindness Alyosha . . .' no penury could deter her from continuing her Sunday-afternoon gambling parties, to which she invited every seedy émigré she knew who could be in some way useful in perfecting my education . . . you saw them there yourself during your occasional visits to our blini parlor, the creeps who'd hovered over Mara ever since we got off the cattle boat, offering their devotion, their dandruff, their decorations from the Crimean War . . . and what did they get along with their flapjacks and their lecherous glances at my mother's beauty, caviar by the tubfuls, do you hear, Soph, the only protein I saw all week . . . let's not even speak of Easter and Christmas Eve, which brought a mayhem of increased rabble off the streets, for each one of whom Mara had bought a tiny present and wrapped it as intricately as a Fabergé egg; since they all brought friends and relatives I was constantly sent into the bathroom to relabel gifts received from guests a minute ago and redistribute them to unannounced visitors; all this made an impression, you see they must always impress, impress . . ."

"Unfair Eddem. Generosity reigns alongside excessiveness in the Slavic soul."

"Don't talk to *me* about Slavs, they've always a need for barbaric display to show off their status, their style . . . actually we might have survived frugally enough without those gambling parties, as if she had anything to gamble with!—on those days I'd escape to the Frick or the Met with my books and watercolors and gloat over the Vermeers and dream of that brilliant artist's career she'd designed for me; I'd stay there till closing time and even then when I came home there they still were screaming, 'Geen, geen,' gambling at preposterous sums like a dollar a point . . . there were those three nights we spent on a park bench to avoid our landlord because the few friends who could have put us up were off catering Stroganoff for some wedding in Bridgeport or playing the yearly chess match up the Hudson at the Tolstoi Foundation; after each of those nights we spent in the park I fainted punctually as I got to school, just before my nine o'clock Latin class, whether out of undernourishment or out of sheer protest I don't know

. . . on those Central Park days I'd go to Fokine's from school and watch Mara play Mozart after her work hours, tears streaming down her face, whether out of rage for what was happening to us that week or nostalgia for the brilliant musical career she'd given up for me I'll never know either . . . then we'd spend our evenings at the Automat until the place closed down, oh how she reversed the habitual pattern of parents torturing their children! . . . 'This lack of anything I have to give you will kill me,' that was her tune, 'Ai ai *dousia* when will you ever forgive me for the little I've had to give you? . . .' Every half hour I'd go to the Automat machines and steal us more cups of tea to calm her; I'd found some metal plugs which handily substituted for nickels; God Soph don't talk to me about the Russians' primal attraction to suffering, their love for the fainting sensation of approaching the abyss, now do you understand my adulation for that Sealark tribe? One eternal picnic, childhood returned to me as a gift, the bliss of their repose!"

"Look at the color of the Neva, E.R. . . ."

"Yes, superb, pure indigo with a trace of zinc white . . . anyhow something usually happened to rescue us just before a final disaster. Mr. Fokine advanced a month's salary or Mara's luck turned and she'd clean up a few hundred dollars at her Sunday gin game, or else we'd meet a protector at a social gathering held by some White Russian group we used to cultivate to get a free bowl of borscht—the Association of the Knights of Saint George, the Association of Russian Cadets Graduated Out of Russia, the Association of Russian Imperial Naval Officers in America, oh how she loved to see me shine at those affairs, you should have heard me! 'I agree with you Countess Schouvalov Tolstoi's treatment of your great-grandfather was not as favorable as some other historians'—'I do think Countess Potemkin that Rimski-Korsakov's importance has been overstressed at the expense of Borodin's. . . .' 'How enchanting your son is Maria Petrovna, what a success he'll be in life. . . .' Here I was, gorgeous little monster humming obscure Monteverdi airs, bowing to women's wrists, impeccably attired in flannel hand-me-downs from some recently deceased White Russian colonel, a perfectly normal quadrilingual child who'd acquired his own peculiar tactics of survival. . . ."

"Yes, all those lessons you had to go through dear heart, even when you were fifteen, we were so awed."

"The lessons! I suppose that's in part what she planned her Sunday largesse for, apart from her own passion for gambling. Barely a guest escaped from her tiny salon who couldn't offer me free lessons in some form of self-perfection . . . the voluminous graduate of the Moscow Conservatory who rapped me on the knuckles for my awkward phrasing of Haydn and threw her arms around me ten seconds later weeping for forgiveness. . . . As for drawing, painting! When I was thirteen she judged the training at Horace Mann insufficient and some Ukrainian card shark who made his living designing de Pinna's windows came to teach me still life, exposing me to a Middle-European style in which threatening bananas and melancholy eggplants were given every possible tragic modulation. . . ."

"What I remember best about Mara are her extraordinary hats."

"Yes her hats, straight out of the St. Petersburg Emily Post, another way of retaining style and caste . . . a lady can't be seen in the street without a hat and every kind of place requires a special texture, color . . . beige felt for weekend errands, velvet for Saturday-morning museum outings, tulle and feathers for the evening and a new assemblage of hats every season so that no one could think we weren't well off, big joke . . . well here she showed an extraordinary sense of economy—have you ever known them to be consistent? We'd spend our

Saturdays riding the city's subways to get the cheapest possible fine materials for *les chapeaux*; until I was fourteen or so I was particularly delighted with our search for feathers because their colors were so beautiful; I still have this dream that Mara and I are in this huge warehouse in Queens totally walled and ceilinged with feathers, plumage of hundreds of varieties of wild birds, russet pearl shimmer of turtledove, emerald brilliance of pheasants' neck, a glorious dream . . . and then those egrets and wisps of tulle brushing by my nose each time she turned her head when she sat by me at the ballet or theater in her only black dress, sat there with that haughty bearing of a beautiful woman who knows she's being admired and has no intention of acknowledging it . . . aspiring suitors were always visible, in and out of the theater; how I shook with rage when they grazed their mustaches to her wrists . . . I wheezed and sneezed terribly in any public place and she found this most disturbing to the performance; meanwhile the nose-blowing kid at her side was wondering whether his crazy life was dictated by his mother's aesthetic appetites or by her need to escape the bleakness of her tiny rooms or by her dedication to honing that chef d'oeuvre she wished me to become. . . ."

He'd never forget those nights spent on the park bench, the bowel-deep hysterical yelp of ambulances and fire trucks piercing the darkness as he lay head to head with his mother on a bench they'd found near the West Nineties, the alternating whir of her sleeping breath and of her low quiet sighing and occasional sobbing—he'd pretend to sleep soundly through the night so as not to hear her mutters of remorse, what have I ever given you *dousia* but ruins, dreams—across the fragile forest of the park gleamed the apartments of the very rich, Fifth Avenue, Central Park South, lamplight played on the sooty leaves of the budding trees—while behind him stretched streets strung with the shops where he'd been castigated for his mother's mounting debts, series of shops he'd sworn to never enter again, walking fifteen, twenty blocks to find a new grocery to buy their buttermilk and black bread in—South of him at Columbus Circle the electric ribbon of news blazed out the world's events around the clock, JOHN L. LEWIS ORDERS END OF COAL STRIKE, CONGRESS VOTES TWO BILLION TO UNRRA, BORIS KARLOFF MARRIED IN NEVADA, JOAN CRAWFORD DIVORCES THIRD HUSBAND, HAPPY EASTER, Happy Easter ha-ha—he'd lain there aged sixteen and muttered never never again this is not going to be my destiny and had dreamt of his sporadic life with the Sanford clan—Claire's glacial concentrated gaze as she played Mozart with Jeff hovering over her to turn the pages—Sophie's sturdy legs dangling over the edge of the pool golden eyes twinkling saying guess what's new and exciting Eddam, Barrault's coming to New York next fall and next spring Dad's bringing over John Gielgud—Sophie whom everyone teased about being secretly in love with Edmund performing one of her fabulous swan dives into the pool after saying with her mischievous smile someday I'm going to marry you Edmund someday—Jeff's booming protective voice as he treated them to the horse show every Christmas careful crossing the streets kids careful crossing the street —Plinker's tall heavy body hovering over the vegetable garden as he mulched his beets and lettuces—Sitting at movie houses during Claire's and Sophie's vacations to see *Mayerling* for the fourth time, each of them pretending they'd cried less than the other two—going to church with the Sanfords on summer Sundays watching them share the thin fragile wafer of the Anglican Communion —during those nights on the park bench he'd even missed the uppity athletic little cousins, April, Katrinka, that fringe of the tribe whom he'd never bothered to charm and who still saw him as a dangerous foreign

substance saying in their Locust Valley lockjaw you
should improve your backhand dearie if you want to play
club tennis—he heard the ecstatic graciousness of Babsie's voice as he unveiled some new portrait he'd done of
Claire, Claire at the piano, Claire holding an animal
under her arm—lying on that park bench all he could
think of was oh God let me return to the haven of their
order, the repose, their crystal, their rectitude, the neatly
aligned knives and forks of their Sunday dinners.

In less critical times Edmund and his mother slept in two
small adjoining rooms—Mara's convertible couch in
what she insisted on calling *le salon* was surrounded by
the armful of curios she'd brought from Europe, a few
icons and family photographs, her aquatints of St.
Petersburg, Edmund's silver christening cups—she'd
never deprived him of her presence for a single night,
had never gone anywhere without him except to earn her
daily bread, he'd known no separation and no rivals
—aged ten as he drifted into sleep he'd considered the
possibility of being an immaculate conception as readily
as other children fantasize about being adopted, the
phrase *causa sui generis* had entranced him in his first
year of Latin, Godlike child his own First Cause who
might have willed himself—aged thirteen and suddenly
grown an inch taller than Mara, his arm gallantly linked
through hers as they walked through the Metropolitan
commenting on Giotto and Botticelli, he was still not
aware that their frugal, precious solitude could ever
cease—fathers, who were they, obsolete entities who
would have taught him to admire statues and aquariums
—a father might have been one of the indolent laggard
Russian gamblers of his mother's salon or an American
fanatic who would have taught him to sit up straight,
throw a ball, be bored—I am the son of no man he
occasionally thought with satisfaction.
    Every Sunday, in the opaque, incensed darkness of the

Russian Orthodox cathedral at Ninety-seventh Street, Edmund knelt before the icons whose large, melancholy eyes resembled his mother's—he stared at the crowd of immigrants who bowed and sank to the floor and constantly moved across the church to cross themselves before another image of the virgin, at the bearded bejeweled priests in pink taffeta robes swinging their censers before the mass of muttering, chanting, seething flesh—he stared at Mara's frail body prostrated on the cold stone floor, in remembrance for beloved dead whom Edmund didn't recall and whom she refused to discuss she lay prone on the floor arms extended to the altar —later they shared the thick fragrant bread of the Orthodox Communion, a basso profundo intoned the dark chant of forgiveness, Edmund docilely knelt by his mother's side, his hand touching the worn cloth of her coat, and wondered about the dead ones for whom she so beautifully wept.

Bare facts: The kind faces that stared at him from the silver-framed pictures interspersed among her icons were those of his grandparents. Flight from St. Petersburg, 1922. His grandfather, a musicologist of some repute, had been able to teach part time in a Munich lyceum. His grandmother had tutored young ladies at the harp and they had both died of typhoid when Edmund was three. Little else: "It's all too old, too sad." Yet also this: Mara had conceived Edmund at the age of nineteen with the aid of a German poet of Jewish origin whose photograph she kept alongside those of her parents and who had died before Edmund was born, aborting her promising career as a pianist; and leaving his son little else but his baptismal name. Or so Mara said. When he passed the photograph of the writer to whom she'd assigned that role (in adolescence he'd compare the mournful, fine-boned face to Kafka's) he'd often salute it with a gesture of defiance, as if to say damn it why didn't you live on at a distance to at least write me the truth?

He only knew that the first Edmund Richter lay shrouded with some curse of art which Mara preferred not to discuss.

Mara had even chosen to derive her son's patronymic from her own father's name, so his full Russian name was Gedmund Petrovich; I am Gedmund Petrovich he'd struggled with since the age of four.

But none of this reticence for what she called life's important issues! Constant discussions over tea and jam with the destitute teachers of piano, violin, painting, Russian history: Mightn't the pain of exile be redeeming to our spirit, we struggle so hard that our soul might become fuller than those of the privileged who've never known any suffering. . . . Nonsense Margarita Petrovna forget such priestly teachings, suffering can only debase us . . . ah no Alexander Maximovich I don't agree, suffering can purify us and refine our vision of the world. . . .

When did it go wrong with poor Mother Russia was it really 1904 and 1917? Or should we trace the roots of the tragedy to the Decembrist disaster of the 1820s? Did the catastrophe begin even earlier, was Peter the villain of the piece when he raped pure integral Russia and gave birth to that Westernized hybrid that made revolution inevitable and landed us on West Ninety-second Street?

Mara would kiss Edmund's paint-stained fingers when he came home from art class, saying you will save me yet, you will save us all.

That garland of distinguished noble Russian names often held to his ear in childhood Vorontsov Yusupov Dolgoruki Kutuzov Scheremeteff we are distantly related to a distant branch of the Kutuzovs (oh don't tell me about their very special brand of snobbism, their need to hold on to ancient caste systems long ago put in the grave). Years afterwards when he'd have to trace the migration of paintings across Europe to the halls of the Hermitage the garland of names would return to his ear

like a childhood refrain, Kutuzov Scheremeteff Dolgoruki Vorontsov.

I had no father to kill no family to hate no milieu to
reject he'd joke with friends much later, what an Oedipal
void!

Gedmund Petrovich Richter was reared by and for a
woman; he'll become one of those interesting late
twentieth-century persons who detests the segregation of
the sexes, who feels deep loss without the company of
women, who'll never find joy or interest in barrooms,
poolrooms, men's saunas, team sports or the late-night
elation of whiskey poker chips cigars, he's the kind of
man who'll spend much time holding a woman's hand
saying for heaven's sake let me help you with this
problem Claire darling, you've got the blues Sophie
sweetheart and I'm going to pull you out of them,
Francesca Dorothea Tracy Arabella, you're in trouble
trust me I'm your friend.

There comes an age when the son's clinging embrace
becomes a light brush of the cheek, when he must start
abstaining from the magic of his mother's touch. As
single women we are particularly shaken by this sever-
ance, we rebecome barren, singularly fragile. A year or
two after Mara had introduced Edmund to the Sanfords
she began to show interest, for the first time since her
son's birth, in the attention of other men.

New York City
April 29th, 1948

Delightful Margarita Petrovna!

I'm filled with happiness at the news of your
fiançailles! I hope you'll be eternally happy with
Mr. Exter and that you'll invite me soon to meet
him at one of your Lucullan Sunday-night feasts!
Congratulations also for Eddem's fabulous college
acceptance and thank you so much for your note

about Smith, I'm going to major in French so as to catch up to you know who! Mama and Papa send their warmest wishes and hope to salute you soon.

> In a bourrée of kisses,
> Sophie Ross

> New York City
> May 5th, 1948

Dearest Aunt Babsie,

It is with sorrow that I put this pen to paper, for it is with the principal purpose of announcing the news of my mother's impending marriage. I apologize that I cannot assume anything but a funerary tone for this somber epistle. Voltaire referred to the first honeymoon as La Lune de Miel and the second one as La Lune d'Absinthe. I hope they start with the latter.

Elizabeta Ivanovna, I look on you as one who's been a second mother to me in the past three years. How clearly I remember that first time I walked to lunch at Sealark, how indelibly inscribed in my memory is every gesture of your great thoughtfulness! Gratitude for your note about my scholarship to Columbia; I'm sure the letters which Plinker wrote to recommend me were of immeasurable influence and I hope to grow increasingly worthy of your esteem as the years go by. I'm thrilled about Pebble's own good news about Bryn Mawr (your daughter stinks as a correspondent by the way, owes me a good half-dozen letters in this last term alone). I think she should study a lot of philosophy along with her music, her contemplative side is most curious. . . . As for my curriculum, I plan to major in art history and paint on the side, waiting for the day when I can find an equitable balance between being an artist with a capital "A" and supporting myself without the threats of imminent disaster for which my mother has such talent. . . .

Grisha Exter was actually a tall, dapper, prosperous art dealer of half-Russian, half-Bulgarian origins who had frequented Mara's salon for some years, and for whom she'd broken all precedents by allowing him to escort her, the year before, to the Annual Benefit Ball for the Orphans of White Russian Cavalry Officers. A shock of graying hair hulked over his owlish, handsome face, at which he stared fastidiously in a mirror before entering any room. He claimed to have a doctorate in art history from Heidelberg and carried a residue of calling cards in his wallet, brought from an earlier exile in Italy, engraved with the words Dottore Gregorio Exter. ("The veracity of this distinction, Aunt Babsie, cannot be checked with any more certainty than some historians' claim that Galileo had a mole on his left forearm.") He was widowed, bowed deeply to women with a trace of clicking heels and sold voluptuous eighteenth- and nineteenth-century nudes to New York's growing postwar art market. His favorite expression was "order, discipline above all" and he had an annoying habit of instantly disposing into precise parallel alignment any objects that lay before him—pencils, spoons, toothpicks, pieces of bread. By 1948 Mr. Exter had traded enough Lancrets and Greuzes to own a small brownstone on the East Side on whose ground floor he had an office and a showroom. Fluent in four languages, knowing enough art-buying New Yorkers to have been invited out to dinner many nights of the week as a bachelor, he had chosen so exquisite a wife that he was asked out even more often as a married man. No more of Mara's spectacles! Dinners are where Grisha meets his clientele. Edmund finally had most of those amenities he'd missed during his years with Mara—worn clothes inherited from many a generous Obolenski replaced at Brooks Brothers, teeth decayed through Mara's spendthriftiness recapped by the Park Avenue dentist of a man he hated, punctual meals served by a Filipino houseboy at a candlelit, silver-burdened table—and claimed to despise it all.

Aged eighteen we're still plagued by those adolescent questions about parents, do they make love, how often, how? Sometimes Edmund heard a shuffle of whispers as he came up the stairs at night, a muffled, plaintive conversation. Pausing in the stairway when he returned from a late class a year or so after Mara's marriage he'd heard a long low moan emitted by a voice that resembled his mother's. He shifted his weight, his satchel of books came crashing onto the floor, a door opened and his mother stood above him at the head of the stairs in a luxurious white satin nightgown, braids undone, mass of dark hair falling to below her waist. She'd coarsened considerably since her marriage, that skin once as delicately pale as a magnolia petal had taken on an unhealthily florid hue. She smiled at him with all her old tenderness and a new shyness; I was worried about you *dousia*, did you fall? Her voice was blurred, her body exuded a newly sweet smell, that of a browning flower, an overripe fruit . . . "It's nothing, only my briefcase, the books toppled out. . . ."

Edmund helps Babsie Sanford thread her tapestry needle. The Sealark living room is filled with bouquets of roses and carnations, with paintings of sailboats, retrievers, prizewinning horses. Plinker and Jeff sit by the fire, Plinker gently strokes Claire's head as she lies at his feet with an arm about Sophie's shoulder, looking at an album of last summer's photographs. "Are you happier than you were last summer, Edmund dear?" Babsie asks. "Insanely happy, Babsie dear, how couldn't I be, I've been listening to April yipe out her toilet training theories, satisfying Sophie's insatiable need to swim while Pebble plays her eternal sets of doubles with

Jeff . . ." "So you aren't happier? . . ." "And my mother is safely tucked into her new little palazzo with her bordello Louis XV and a man who would surely bore for Bulgaria if the Bulgarians ever had a Varsity Boring Team. . . ." Babsie puts her needlework away. To the end of his life Edmund would remember her eyes the color of dried grass, the tears that threatened to gather in them when she sensed her goal of family bliss thwarted. She smiles, claps her hands. "The Game, the Game," she calls out, "let's play the Game!" "The Game's a super idea!" April cries.

Everyone at Sealark has always agreed that their Game is the world's most amusing one because it brings such fresh and novel insight into people's character. All you need is pencil and paper and six or more to play; Jeff is always assigned to explain the rules to newcomers, for he is "a born educator." Everyone helps to choose a list of questions, like for instance: What would you order as a last meal before your execution? How would you start a conversation if you found yourself stranded in an elevator with Albert Einstein and Shirley Temple? Scribble each answer on a little piece of paper, your niftiest printing, please, then fold the paper and pass it to your neighbor, everyone's on their *honor* system not to peek. When everyone's filled in all the questions Babsie and Plinker will collect all the papers and take turns reading them aloud . . . then everyone tries to guess which player wrote each entry . . . the winner is the one who recognizes the most authors, an extra snifter of brandy for the winner . . . what would you say if you were seated at the Debutante Cotillion between Louis XIV and Toots Shor, between George Washington and Gloria Vanderbilt?

Staring out of the window at the moonlit sound, Edmund nurses his fourth brandy and watches the Nantucket ferry emerge from darkness, white and gigantic, the bride of night, moving with a swiftness amazing for her bulk. All shines so vividly tonight, white steeple of the church the tribe attended that morning, white vessel lumbering towards the Sanford clan so united, so meticulously studious of each other. . . . Edmund takes the first slip passed to him by Katrinka ("Print neatly dearie you tend to be so sloppy"). Query: "Who would you rather have been more than anyone else in the world?" "Machiavelli," Edmund writes. April hands him a slip several questions later. ("You haven't *won* yet this summer dearie.") "What do you hate the most in the world?" the question reads. "God," Edmund writes in large, clear print. Then he sits back staring at the ferry through the spiraling vapors of his English Ovals while Babsie and Plinker start reading the answers.

"Question: 'Who would you choose as your traveling companion if you were to spend six months in the mountains of Ceylon?' Answer: 'Katharine Hepburn.' "

That must be Jeff! How many hands for Jeff? Sophie, Edmund and Pebble for Jeff. Katrinka and Babsie say it's Douglas. Plinker says it's Edmund. Plinker tabulates.

"Capital fun!" Plinker reads the next query. " 'What's your favorite pastime on a rainy night?' Answer: 'Sitting up with Tom Dewey at the Plaza Oak Room.' "

That must be Plinker! No silly that's only Jeff or April pretending to be Plinker! Who's for Plinker . . . for Jeff? . . .

"Let's go on, it's all such heaven!" Babsie picks up the next slip. "Question: 'What do you hate the most in the world?' The answer is . . . oh no!" She drops the paper on her lap.

"What is it, dear?" Plinker demands.

"No!" Babsie repeats.

"Are you quite sure you feel all right, my angel?"

"I just don't know what to say."

"What's the *question*, dearie?" April asks.

"What do you hate the most in the world?" Babsie whispers.

"And what's the answer?"

"God."

A hush on Sealark. "Pass me a cigabooo," April whispers to Katrinka. Jeff twirls his coach's whistle, Claire nervously presses her retriever to her chest.

"God!" Babsie repeats. "I mean, who . . ."

"What in heavens are you saying?" (Plinker)

"Someone in the family says they hate *God* more than anything else in the world," Babsie whispers.

"They're just kidding, dearie." (April)

"They're just joking, Auntie." (Katrinka)

"I think it would be a lovely idea" (Sophie) "to separate into backgammon schuettes."

"Or go for a celestial swim." (Claire)

"Don't protect me, Santa Clara," Edmund calls out as the eyes of the tribe rest upon him. "Who in hell but I would say that?"

"Perhaps you're only an agnostic, sporto," Jeff suggests.

"Not at all, dear Jeffrey. I wish my disbelief to have the violence and passion of faith."

"Are you saying you're an atheist?" Sophie asks in an excited whisper.

"And what's an atheist? An atheist is a God-obsessed maniac who witnesses God's absence everywhere, a man with deep religious convictions who truly *believes* in the nonexistence of God."

Deep silence.

"A religion which doesn't call upon you to get out of the armchair or the church pew, why that's the ideal of everyone in this room . . . the usefulness of religion is that it allows you to believe in God without ever *thinking* about Him. . . ."

"I don't mind thinking about Him," Jeff offers. "By all means let's discuss God, fellow. . . ."

But Edmund prefers to hold forth alone. He stands up

now, his voice performs exaltedly beside him as if it were stalking the stage like a great bear.

"Your contentment with well-being, to use William James's astute insight, protects you like a carapace from any thirst for transcendence. . . . You're so sure to find him at the hour of your death that you keep him rigorously away from your lives. . . . Only the deepest skepticism can save us from being atheists, and I utterly refuse to be a skeptic."

"What about . . . what about saints?" Claire ventures.

"Saints, dear Disappearance Act, are created by people in *spite* of the Church, and they're made to be devoured by crowds, like angel food cake. But let me finish . . . what is purer than belief in the Void? To be certain that there's nothing is the most pristine faith of all!"

"It's quite clear that the fellow has had too much sun . . ."

"Alas no, Plinker! If I were mad I'd be the genius my mother wishes me to be and genius isn't easily arrived at, one must merit it by serious suffering, by trials firmly traversed . . . genius listens to Orphic voices and writes under their dictation . . . let's put an end to the exalted imbecility of these proceedings. . . ."

He stumbled over his chair and fell, and by the next morning when he woke up with a severe headache he'd quite forgotten the rest of his peroration.

Claire was practicing her piano when Edmund came into the library the next day. She was playing Mozart. He couldn't focus well that morning. His last memory of the previous evening was of being tucked into his bed by the two girls. Her playing was particularly tempestuous; she stopped in the middle of a phrase and stared at Edmund, clamped her arms down on the piano keys with a crash of chords. "You're desperate this year!" she shouted. "Why in heck are you so impossible this summer, can't you be *sane* like us, conform to certain *basic* rules of behavior?" "Oh look who's talking, Mademoiselle Blithe Spirit who feels free to roam the moors for hours at a time while the family turns the island inside out looking for her. . . ."

Without losing her grace of gesture—amazing!—she started flinging books at him across the room. "You and your goddamn artistic uniqueness," she shouted, "you and your damn European individualism!" Bam! he thought, there it goes, our first tantrum alone. "Stop that Pebble will you stop that immediately, you're not used to being talked to are you, they've always thought you were too special, too frail to curb, but I'm not going to stand any shrews around me!" She continued to throw, tears welling in her crimson face. He searched for ways to control her. She turned towards the wall to reach for more books to hurl at him, he ran across the room and grasped her by the shoulders. He shook her very hard, pressed her trembling body against him, felt the arousal which tortured him many times a summer when he touched her. "Why do you attack me like this, Peb, why?" She fell onto a sofa, her hair spread out like a length of brown silk. "Because I love you," she sobbed, "because you're my brother, my best friend, and I want you to be perfect!" She trembled with a soft undulating motion, he sat down by her, put his arms around her, kept his body pressed against hers.

Sounds of Sealark mornings flowing into the room from the summer outside, Babsie humming a hymn as she snipped flowers in her garden, Plinker giving April's daughter a lesson in seashells, here's a limnet sweetheart . . . Edmund cupped Claire's face in his hands, put his mouth to hers for the first time. She responded warmly at first, clutching him to her. "Someday you're going to marry me, Pebble," he whispered, "someday you'll marry me and you'll never have tempers again." She drew away from him brusquely. "I'll *never* marry!"

she whispered fiercely. "What if I don't ever want to marry anyone?" "Oh you'll marry Jeff or someone like that all right, that's what they all want. . . ." "Never, never anyone!" "All right then, promise, you keep that promise Peb!" "I swear!" Her swift alternations of mood always alarmed him, he held her shoulder as lightly as he could. "If you promise not to get married then I never will either, ever. . . ." Surrounded with that tribal love he'd so envied she was much more solitary than he. It was the first time he'd come to that knowledge.

Claire is lying on the dunes posing for Edmund. She wears tennis shorts and a brief white halter. She's bent one leg at the knee, as Edmund has asked her to, folded her left arm under her head. It is a year later, they are both twenty years old. They have built a bonfire in the pit of the dune on a windy, cool afternoon in late August. The flames flicker on her bare flesh when the sun goes in behind a cloud. Edmund squats a few yards from her at the grassy knoll of the dune, his sketching pad leaned against a piece of driftwood. She has sat for him like this since the age of fifteen, reading, holding her animals; and the passivity of the act seems to suit her calmer moods. What strikes Edmund most about her body in this spring of her flesh is its continuing childlike delicacy. The legs are long and thin as a filly's, the waist hung extravagantly high. The most singular feature of her face are the enormous eyelids which arch over her pale eyes and give her face part of its haughtiness; he tries to draw those lids, is unnerved by the difficulty of rendering their fragile curve.

"Peb, don't fidget so!"

She stills her head. Her eyes are cast down as if she were absorbed in studying a grain of sand.

He whistles a Mozart aria, struggles to render the delicate slope of her neck. "At times when I draw you I need to destroy you in order to recreate you . . . there's this new idea that realistic art is bourgeois because it's an imitation of reality but when it's good it's anything but that, it's a total recreation. . . . I'm mentally killing you right now Pebble, I'm annihilating you in order to make my image even more perfect than you are. . . ."

She gives a startled, excited little laugh, stares at him with curiosity as she sifts sand through her fingers. He studies the curve of her delicate, arrogant mouth. The underlip is thin and severe; the fully modeled upper lip curves faintly upwards, as if readied for a mimicry, an ironic smile.

"I'm going to need that hand in a second, Pebble."

She puts her hand back on her leg and continues staring at him for a few minutes with her huge crystal eyes. When she begins to speak again he knows that she's about to offer one of her rare moments of unleashed candor, one of those monologues she sometimes indulges in with little need for attention or exchange.

"I'm going to *need* that hand, you absolutely must lord it over all those around you, mustn't you, Edmund, you do love to tyrannize. That's one of the things you relish about my having to sit for you, it's the only time you have me quite in your power, you try to dominate all women around you because . . ."

"Trying to be analytic? So damn unWASP of you."

"Don't interrupt me like that. I think it can be dangerous, such a desperate need for power as you have. Look at the storm you raised when you lost your totally exclusive place in Mara's heart, scenes out of *Othello*, or the way you tease Soph; she's so insanely in love with you she'd go live in Madagascar at the flick of a lid from you and how you adore that, it's the aspect of your character I distrust the most, your need for total control over others . . ."

"A few more hors d'oeuvres for the oral stage."

"Don't always tease me, E.R. . . . You see as a

pacifist I have to constantly reexamine all forms of power . . ."

"Power! Dear Clair de Lune, do you realize how much need for power there is in your kind of pacifism? . . . Your need to lord it over the animal kingdom, your utter inability to accept a defeat in tennis . . . that's all the likes of you and Jeff and April can think of anyway, compete compete, you and your cute WASP violence. . . ."

She stares at him, squinting, as if he's drawn a difficult problem on the blackboard.

He whistles again. "Speaking of violence, I saw such a strange show the other day by one of these new abstract artists, a guy called Pollack, Pollock? Nothing but webs of black and white dribbled about bare canvas; if that's the direction painting's going I may have no place in it. Sorry, get that leg up again, Santa Clara."

Only in certain Tanagra statuettes glimpsed in museums has Edmund seen the same frailty of proportion, in those little clay figures with breasts like small hard apples that hold a ritual animal under their arm. Strange creature! Swept by waves of rebellion against the family he craved to belong to, feeling the transience of a tourist in the world which had rescued his childhood . . . Claire the glacial center of his adopted tribe enmeshed in her growing network of world causes; Edmund don't get mad but I flunked bio this term by trying to stop all dissection at college, Eddem please come to a Ban the Bomb demonstration in Philadelphia next Sunday. . . . Her massive urge towards the oppressed, her disdain for the strong, the privileged, her own class. . . . This is what had made her friendship such a privilege, a gift, her aloofness from all she'd been born to, her disdain for most of the alliances of a normal adolescence. . . . Save for her adulation of her father she was rejecting it all as rigorously as she had denuded her childhood room; you never knew how the rich would work out their guilt. . . . He'd recently referred to her revolutionary impulses for justice and compassion as "unique to the conscience-stricken, repentant aristocracy"; she'd given him the same perplexed intense stare she was giving him today, fastidious student deciphering a classroom problem, but now her huge eyelids lowered again, the sideway arch of her neck signaled that she was resuming her blast of candor. "As if it had all been a bed of roses for Mara! You're unfair to her, Edmund, you only started your bouts of erratic behavior when you stopped being the absolute and only center of her life!"

A bored, jaded tone: "I still am, you know."

" 'Still am, you know. . . .' Look at how sensitive you are about it. . . ." She raises her head, shakes her curtain of hair. "I want you to know something . . ."

"And I want you to know that it hurts to have a best friend withdraw the way you do, Claire; you can create hell around you, you and your goddamn notions of world love and peace."

"I've hurt you?"

"Oh Pebble, you know perfectly well you've hurt all those who love you by your withdrawals, your aloofness!"

She lowers her eyes and retreats again, her chin shaking a little. She remains still for many minutes now, posing superbly, unbudging, head held farther down than before, heavy eyelids almost closed; the tension in her limbs makes the intersection of her neck and shoulder more difficult than ever to draw. The ligaments of her neck flow smoothly towards the beginning of the frail collarbone, where they're interrupted by the trite ribbon of her halter top. Edmund draws that transition of neck to shoulder over and over again, erasing after each attempt, never reaching the fluidity he strives for. He curses, takes out his penknife and whittles his pencil, stares at her again; the pose has become strained and wooden.

"Damn anatomical problem that neck-to-shoulder passage. Take off that silly top you're wearing Peb, I want to see your breasts." She makes no motion, does not raise her glance.

"If you move your arms you'll disturb the pose; I'll do it for you." He walks to her and slides his arms under her torso, unfastening her halter. "Listen, I've been doing this at the Art Students League since I was fourteen."

"Doing? Doing what?"

"Drawing from the nude female model. That's considerably better, without those damn straps getting in the way."

Without saying a word she put her arms to her waist, unfastened her shorts and pulled them off. In a few seconds she had lain down again, one arm cradling her head. He continued to draw, stunned by the frail tautness of her body. She had resumed the pose with total obedience, one leg stretched out on the sand and the other leg bent, fully exposing herself. Her pelvis, as flat as a dish of milk, stretched down to a triangle of pale auburn hair. Above her high, tiny waist her curiously large nipples were the nacreous rose hue found deep inside a whorled shell. Her eyes now lay fully upon his with a blank, heavy-lidded, questioning stare that seemed almost drugged. And for a while the artist's eyes she stared at continued to confront her with an intense, disinterested gaze.

He had straddled her and pinned both her arms behind her. The extremely brief resistance she had offered left her hair covering her face. He gently put her wrists together above her head, brushed her hair back and put his mouth to hers. He slid his hand over her pubic hair, gently rubbing the lonely ridge of flesh with his thumb and forefinger. The sun disappeared behind clouds, the light of the bonfire swept over her face. It had the same expression of dispassionate interest with which he had stared at her for the previous hour. Edmund stripped and forced himself against the smooth wall of her orifice, pressing repeatedly against her while she bit her lip in pain. "It's all rather difficult," she said with an ironic smile. He stopped thrusting to put his mouth to her nipples, he continued to rub the ridge that lay like a tiny boat in its sea of fur. He watched her eyes close, her breathing quicken, he put his hands under her buttocks and forced himself against her again a few times with all the strength he could muster. She cried out, her eyes opened, her face tightened and reddened as it did when she was about to have a fit of temper. He continued to thrust, amazed by the exquisite tightness of her orifice, so different still from the ease of the whores he had gone to a few times since beginning college. Her breathing quickened again and she began to share in his movement, thrusting towards him. But her initial pain had softened and disabled him. They lay still in each other's arms. "I'm sorry," she whispered, "perhaps it wasn't precisely the way it should have been." "It was perfect," he lied. He tenderly kissed her eyelids many times, her cheeks, her mouth. And then in a gesture that did not seem to particularly startle her he bent down to kiss her, sweeping his mouth over her bitter little blood.

They searched for Claire Sanford that night as they had searched a few times during her childhood. Riding on top of the fire department truck, Plinker screamed her name throughout the island until the far end of Great Point while Edmund ran through bogs and fens on his own search with her name on his lips; the wind breathed like a lion in the pastures of Cotuit, in the red clay of Sankaty bluffs the wind moaned that she had drowned in the surf. In the middle of the night Edmund slept for twenty minutes in the pit of a dune and then hitched a ride on a truck and continued to shout her name through the stubby moors of Siasconset. He ran down the beach where

Plinker and Jeff had once taught him to catch the surf, where summer after summer he had lain on his raft like a stalking panther waiting for the whitecaps that would carry him most violently to shore. But she was neither there nor in the forest of pitch pines in the middle of Quidnet where he continued to shout all the names he had given her for five summers; My Botticelli, Santa Clara, Miss Elusivity, Clair de Lune, Disappearance Act he called out, clouds of gulls scattering at each outpour of his voice. His breath came short, an alarming wheeze returned to his lungs. He returned to the dune where they had lain the previous afternoon, searched for the indentation in the sand which marked the precise spot where her body had lain and fell into it, sobbing. The morning sun was high and for an hour he lay face to it, eyes stinging from wind and sand. The toll of her innocence, of her crazed search for purity. His guilt. His force. Her submission. Such a simple thing. Thrusting into the virgin rock, sword in a scabbard. Yet she was the one who had made it possible. He was older by three months, he must protect her forever . . . these concerns later lost their gravity when he lay stunned by sun in the lion-colored dunes where they had long held their picnics and their races. Lying in stupor in the sand, staring at the island of his only childhood happiness in the silvery light of the Nantucket noon, no disasters, no serious sins seemed possible. The church bells tolled "Amazing Grace," the horn of the afternoon ferry shouted towards Nantucket, announcing its beautiful vacationers, its plenitude of sand pails and summer furniture, its adulation of childhood. . . . Claire Sanford's disappearance did not last particularly longer than those of her earlier youth. She returned the day after she'd run away from Edmund on the beach, in time for tea, bearing armfuls of plums she'd picked for the family by Hummock Pond. She had just *felt* like spending the night alone in some secret dunes of hers which she'd loved for years. . . . Tears

welled in her eyes when she heard that her vanishing had
caused Babsie to be put under sedation; she ran upstairs
to her parents to offer her effusive apologies, one of her
rare bouts of solicitude.

iv

One travels to the Soviet Union in 1975 with young marrieds deeply in love, California orchid-growers recovering from painful divorces, aspiring photographers eager to document every Art Nouveau building in Moscow. Some Americans travel there to buy cheaper vodka or lacquered boxes ornamented with leaping Cossacks and melancholy maidens. Others simply come to Leningrad to say they've been somewhere new and sit in dusty blue buses chewing on toothpicks while the rest of their guided tour leaps out to inspect the battleship from which the Revolution's first shot was fired. It is amply explained to travelers in the literature that accompanies their visa applications that they are forbidden to bring marijuana to Russia, change American money at unauthorized sources, photograph airports, bridges, tunnels, power stations or railroad stations under penalty of imprisonment; that it is wise to bring flat rubber sink stoppers for Soviet bathtubs, disposable lighters, ballpoint pens and panty hose as tips for hotel employees; that they can under no circumstance travel in the Soviet Union without the company of one of the crisp, efficient government guides who process foreigners through the demanding Intourist schedule. In the twenty-four hours since they've been in Leningrad, Claire, Edmund and Sophie have already visited the modest three-room log

67

cabin where Peter lived while supervising the building of his city, a museum that houses ten centuries of Russian icons, the site of Alexander II's assassination, the innards of the battleship *Aurora*. Sophie, the most restless member of the triad, also wishes to take a taxi on her own to visit the arcade where Gogol's protagonist is said to have ordered his greatcoat, the train carriage now encased in glass at Finland Station which brought Lenin back from exile. "Stop it, Soph, you're going to bring us out of this country on stretchers!" But she shakes her copper curls, laughing and threatening to go off on her own, talks them into choosing one more place to visit; they've loved each other long and are inured to her amazing energy. Edmund and his women take a cab to the pond of Tsarskoye Selo, where Sophie suggests a swim as it's been her habit to suggest everywhere since she was fifteen; but upon the tourists taking off their shoes some guards run up to announce that bathing here is *zaprishchino*, forbidden, what do the Americans think they're doing? It takes Edmund's carefully remembered Russian to assuage the enforcers of the law. So while the rest of their Intourist group visit the Annual Exhibition of Soviet Farm Technology the three friends simply lie in the grass talking about their long adolescence together, and stare at the lake which shimmers at their feet in a phantasm of swans, oak trees, minareted follies as in the effluence of a giant's tranquil breath.

Later that morning they climb into the Intourist bus a few minutes after the rest of its passengers, as they had the previous day. "Late again," one of the guides calls out, "Dr. Richter's party is very often late!" That guide's name is Irina. She has a splendid head of long dark curls and a languid air, is wafer-thin for a Soviet woman, smiles sweetly in between her bouts of reprimanding. Whereas the other guide of Intourist Tour No. 137 Destination Tbilisi-Kiev-Leningrad-Moscow is a squat and handsome man with large imperturbable eyes and a copy of *Pravda* perpetually folded under his arm. Edmund, Claire and Sophie wave greetings to the acquaintances they've made in the past five days and sit down together in the rear of the bus. Ahead of them are the plump, loquacious Zabars, who work on Seventh Avenue and whose favorite vacations seem to be spent in countries whose regimes they can relentlessly criticize —Romania, Bulgaria, Albania, Hungary. To the left is Mr. Jones's group, an eight-citizen-strong delegation of Rolls-Royce dealers from Florida who wear shiny little tags on their lapels saying Silver Shadow, rush onto the bus before anyone else to sit in front for the best view and shop relentlessly, being already burdened that noon with flowered shawls and crates of fragile tea sets. As for Ted Weicker, he teaches political science at a very liberal prep school in the Northeast. He discusses Soviet politics elaborately with his wife and often points out aspects of the Soviet system he finds superior to our own; you've got to hand it to the welfare state not an elderly citizen unemployed look at those fine old ladies sweeping the streets clean as a whistle.

"Professor Richter," Irina says before switching on the microphone for her morning talk, "you will agree that your 1915 Baedeker takes decadent attitudes towards central facts of our history?"

"Allow me the indulgence of my profoundly bourgeois nature, Irina Grigorievna; I promise to be less guilty of deviations after you take me to the Hermitage."

"On Monday when repair is over, Dr. Richter, have more disciplined patience. . . ."

Irina smiles, proudly pats her American jeans, switches on her microphone. "Upon arriving yesterday, gentlemen and ladies, we learn that Leningrad, formerly called St. Petersburg, was founded by Peter the Great in 1703 to open windows towards Europe . . ."

"Venice of the north," Mr. and Mrs. Weicker whisper in unison.

". . . regime of Czar Peter built St. Petersburg at greater human sacrifice than any other city since barbaric times, a hundred thousand men lost in the task . . ."

"It's like the Sleeping Beauty," Mr. Zabar says.

"Like flowers encased in a glass paperweight," Mrs. Zabar agrees.

"And now this morning we are on way to visit Petrodvorets or Peterhof, impressive palace designed to be a country home of Russian rulers, built from plans of French architects, correct, Dr. Richter, enlarged and finished by Italian Rastrelli in 1746. Always take attention gentlemen and ladies as you descend from steps of bus. . . ."

Tourists are recommended to photograph the famous cascades of water which rush down over six steps of colored marble to a majestic central basin. At the basin's center they much admire a gilt bronze statue of Samson tearing open the jaws of a lion, symbol of Peter's victory over invading Swedish troops. We will now visit Peter's little villa Monplaisir, which stands a few hundred yards from the main palace. It was in the emperor's nature to frequently seek escape from the splendor that surrounded him . . . Peter was six feet ten inches tall and suffered from grave spastic fits, possibly epileptic . . . the czar was a big joker and punished any guests who arrived late to dinner by forcing them to drink a liter of vodka in a single gulp, in one gulp! And here is the tankard from which guests sometimes drank themselves to death in this little cottage Peter built to escape the luxury of his great palace . . .

". . . as we depart, gentlemen and ladies, please note again extreme beauty of forty-five gilded statues and of cascade in front of palace. . . ."

Photographs: Claire Sanford in blue jeans next to a gesticulating statue, immense pale eyes cast towards the

Gulf of Finland, straight brown hair flying in the wind —Sophie Ross squatting on a park bench holding an ice-cream cone, speckled gold-green eyes squinting in laughter, teeth very white in the strong squarish face —Edmund Richter in faded denims, extremely handsome man of forty-five with longish, slightly graying dark blond hair, points his arm magisterially at the wrestling Samson.

That second afternoon in Leningrad the members of the Richter party plead headaches and excuse themselves from a visit to the Museum of the History of Religion and Atheism to walk arm in arm through the city's streets. Claire and Sophie photograph lime-hued, pale blue palaces, poets remembered in stone or marble at the edge of verdant parks, citizens in worn uncouth clothing standing in lines on Nevsky Prospect to buy a piece of fresh fruit, portraits of Central Committee members strung on banners across the avenue. Sophie still wears her babushka and dark glasses so as not to be recognized too soon by other American tourists as Sophie Ross of the *Good Day America* show. She notes that Soviet teenagers are wearing their hair long, American style, that the overwhelming majority of bus and trolley drivers are women. "Macho attitudes are something else here, Peb," she waves her notebook; "women make up eighty percent of the factory workers and of the medical profession but they're still coopted into a full load of housework and guess what's the only available birth control device, a diaphragm that only comes in one size . . ." Claire keeps straightening Sophie's babushka, which tilts askew when she gets excited by her research.

Edmund walks a trifle behind the women and often hums Russian words under his breath; his first language swells towards him from the lilt of surrounding voices, bittersweet with memories of childhood smells and tastes, of his mother's gardenia scent and steaming kasha. He murmurs returning words like a child caressing a bedtime fetish, words of tenderness, titles of novels. *Dousia*, little soul; *Voina i Mir*, *War and Peace*. Towards the end of the avenue they see their guide, Evgeny, staring at a slender display of Western literature in the windows of a bookstore. He holds a little red umbrella on his arm as he walks towards them, gestures almost forthcoming. "Can I help you, is there anything I can do for you?" "We're looking for a lovely park bench to sit on," Sophie says with her radiant smile. "Preferably with lilacs," Claire adds; "we've been friends for thirty years and we've come to your country . . ." "I would suggest Decembrists' Square." The Russian points towards the Neva with a friendly wave of his umbrella unaccompanied by any change in his hooded gaze.

They choose a park bench near the river. Primness, grandeur, melancholia, solitude of Peter's city, fragility of artifice, beauty frozen and embalmed. Buildings shimmering in the palest light, in the albinic heat of early summer. A pitiless sun hovers perpetually over Leningrad throughout its white nights, its skies remain frozen in the color of tea roses, towards evening the river turns to hues of geranium and crushed mother-of-pearl.

" 'For six months of the year all the Neva's water freezes into a bitter layer of ice,' " Claire reads from Edmund's Baedeker, " 'and the wet hostility of certain winter days induces into Petersburg a mood of Dostoevskian despair.' "

A young man and woman court each other with shy, brief kisses on a nearby bench, four young gymnasts in yellow tights practice their somersaults on the lawn, a child skips rope down the park's graveled alley.

Edmund talks about the gesticulating statues surmounting the roof of the Winter Palace to the right of the square. "They're so measured, Grecian, don't you think, so foreign to this Nordic light, like hostages exiled from some Mediterranean mountains . . . and the austere lines of the long buildings almost glacial, right, so at odds with the sweet tint of their hues, primrose yellow of the Admiralty, pale sky-blue of the Smolny Cathedral . . ."

They've reached that bend of early middle age in which the tyrannic, longed-for past is the immediate seducer and the future looms as fearsome.

Sophie is always the first to face it.

"I've got to break out of the hell of the past ten years, it's been one long backpacking trip for me, a nomad's existence, a succession of hotel rooms decorated in group-sex modern . . ."

"Even after the bezzazz of success?"

"As I was trying to tell you yesterday before you enthralled us with your rap on Pushkin, it's been lonelier than ever."

"It's been a rotten time for me too," Edmund says. "I had very mixed emotions of longing and terror about coming here, certain memories remain painful even after all these years . . . but I've spent the past year living on some kind of a brink, I don't think I can go on with what . . ."

"Edmund, don't fuck up again, don't leave behind the glorious career you've spent twenty years building up!"

"Soph sweetheart let's leave the confrontations till a bit later in the trip, okay?" Claire says softly. "Let's keep away from all unnecessary violence. . . . I think I'm just beginning to pull things together but I came here to be sure I'm going to do it right; I've too often felt on the edge of an abyss, like . . . Eddem, do you remember that day you almost drowned in 1950?"

"How could I forget, wading into the ocean that August evening after one of your disappearance acts, the surf was heavy, I was dazed, brutish, as I swam out each wave rose towards me like a great dark cavern framed by glints of foam . . . I'd no idea how far out I'd gone, I'll never forget those murderous tender arms that braced my shoulders and steered me back to shore while the two of you stood at the water's edge, shouting save him, save him Jeff . . ."

"Oh shit," Sophie says, "just when we were getting up the nerve to talk about the future."

They walk back arm in arm towards their hotel.

v

Postcards:

Florence, Italy
June 27th, 1951

Dearest Sofinka—I've seen few things on this trip I more crave to share with you than the Convent of San Marco, all those cells with Angelico frescoes on their walls, one more glorious than the other, paradisial voices mingling in unison over the city. . . . How's our own island paradise this year? I was torn, torn about the decision to go abroad this summer, but my mother's gracious offer of a trip to Italy is essential to my work and you must all be more relaxed without my twice-an-August acts of desperation . . . write soon my sweet and let's have a family reunion the moment I step off the boat. . . .

Florence
July 2nd, 1951

Clair de Lune—I don't gave a damn for the salvation of your soul but if I could capture in one moment of my work the luminosity of the violet-robed angel in the Fra Angelico I stared at yesterday just after reading your quest-for-purity missive I'd be a happy man. It's the one in which the angel bends towards the virgin with a gesture of warning, hand sed in alarm as if to say it ain't all good news kiddo, there's a rough road ahead . . . which brings me back to the theme of your blasted little purity: Until you can name the furies which lurk behind your passion for abolishing all weapons and your didactic avoidance of even Campbell's beef consommé (not to speak of your impatience with most of your fellow humans and your extremely complicated views on keeping your life untainted by sexuality) you'll still have a tough uphill climb to whatever anyone could call salvation. . . .

> Rome
> July 15th, 1951

Sofinka darling—Must share one of my life's great windfalls with you, I'm faced with the exciting and terrifying prospect of making my debut in the New York art world this fall . . . a chap who runs one of the better little New York galleries came to see my studio class last spring and just wrote a letter offering me a show in November. I hope you all turn out en masse!

> Venice
> August 15th, 1951

Pebble of the Running Brook—Deep gratitude for the superb Swiss hunting knife you sent me for my birthday; I might just carve up my steppie and serve him for dinner to Maman at Russian Christmas; don't you think that would be one-upping the Greeks? The honeymoon couple whizzed by here last week on their way to Baden-Baden to take the waters, which Mara badly needs, for I must share the painful astonishing news that she's taken to dreadful bouts of drinking since her marriage; can you imagine that beautiful angel taking to booze though she's secure for the first time in her life, she who never touched so much as a drop of sherry until she started her life of idle luxury, it's as if we've had no peace since we ceased to starve. . . .

Lovers, children, heroes, none of them do we fantasize as extravagantly as we fantasize our parents. It may have to do with our need for their immortality. The souls of offspring know what they want, have their own perverse knowledge, nest in layers of deceits, seldom daring to fly out until it is too late. Later, later next year I'll figure her out again Edmund would say, later later there's plenty of time. After his migration to the Sanford clan Edmund would have wished Mara to have a windfall from some White Russian foundation and otherwise retain her life unchanged, pouring tea more frequently than ever for the cake-making princes, intensifying (platonically) her friendships with his teachers of piano and Russian poetry, continuing to stand in line for tickets to her spectacles, continuing to pound out the "Dance of the Hours" for the pliés of wealthy young American beauties. Instead there was the giddy new Mara wandering through the house in florid housecoats, pretending to water her plants, praising her Grisha's fields of expertise (the technique of nineteenth-century aquatints, the iconography of French landscapes), occasionally packing thirteen pieces of luggage labeled G.E. to travel to Baden-Baden, Saint-Tropez, the Paris Ritz. Edmund had moved out of Grisha's brownstone to live in the Columbia dorms the fall Claire and Sophie left for their junior year abroad, pleading easier access to classes and studios. It was not until the day he came in for a morning visit and saw Mara tippling vodka at 11:00 A.M. that he realized he'd avoided being alone with her for more than half an hour in the past year. He began to notice many mannerisms of the novice drunk, repeated pleadings of migraines as an excuse for one more, proclivity for those silver cups of Grisha's which she could pretend at a distance were filled with consommé or juice. It dawned on him that he'd never even bothered to find out how Mara spent her days. She'd severed all ties with previous émigré friends to frequent Grisha's prospective buyers, stopped participating in any charitable Russian causes, read increasingly less. She indulged in numerous new whims—Paris clothes, illustrious resorts, luxurious restaurants (oh don't talk to me about their sudden shifts of temperament, their excessive capriciousness!). "Of course my angel, absolutely everything you want my angel," Grisha exclaimed as he entered her room with his crisp cavalry step after the houseboy had brought her her breakfast tray, acceding gallantly to forty-case lots of vintage champagne, frequent reupholstery of their entire house.

Some months after he'd caught her with her morning vodka Edmund accepted Mara's invitation to lunch on the occasion of her birthday. They meet at "21," where she seems to lunch almost every day with wives of Grisha's clients. ("So *nouveau riche mon chou*" she'd said about that establishment during their years of penury, "not for proper people like us or the Sanfords.") Mara in a Maggy Rouf dress which Grisha had bought her in Paris the previous summer. The aigrettes of her velvet hat brush Edmund's face with bittersweet recall of their Saturday search for feathers. Waiters bowing deeply as she heads for her accustomed banquette, the faint leaflike rancor already on her breath. Mara reveling in the same glossy Brittanic splendor Edmund enjoyed at the Sanfords, oak paneling and gleam of sumptuously aligned silver, splendor of crystal, files of uniformed, cast-iron blackamoors. Mara immediately runs down the restaurant crowd for Edmund; of late her conversation has been restricted to extraordinarily trivial international gossip, who frequents which ski slopes and which Zurich gallery, who's acquired the most amusing butler, lover, chef, plastic surgeon. She starts being very loquacious on her second glass of Pouilly-Fuissé; *à droite*, she exclaims with a sweep of her hand, is a man who owns most of the tin mines in Bolivia, *à gauche* is an English duchess who's about to play the Beast in Cocteau's next film; she'd visited Grisha's gallery the week before last and was most serious about purchasing a Segonzac . . . and at the back of the room, her voice rises in excitement, is a famous beauty married to a Venezuelan oil magnate—the husband is a handsome extremely sad man who only speaks to his cat; a few weeks ago the cat died after the magnate discovered his largest oil deposit to date and he's now the world's most silent billionaire . . . their Paris house is said to have a library with a fireplace of sterling silver, floors of stainless steel and genuine tortoiseshell bookcases . . . that's where this great beauty takes her men now, two or three times a day, on a library couch upholstered in genuine black mink; she'd come into Grisha's gallery recently looking for Degas pastels and had found them overpriced, a stingy bargainer, but he was hoping to soon sell her a little Derain . . . Mara is summing up the room on her second bottle of wine now, "No more Degas," she giggles, "all the oil in Venezuela, *La Belle et La Bête* . . ." She stops laughing and stares tenderly at Edmund, not quite focusing, as if his eyes were twin cribs. He stares back priggishly. Reversal of classical tensions, this happens to us increasingly, puritanical children scolding giddy, hedonistic parents . . . she gives an exasperated sigh, pleads with her son to have a zuppa inglese, orders a triple espresso. Is she ecstatically happy in her new orgy of idleness, utterly miserable, shall we ever know?

The tactics of the rival can be cunning. Grisha tries to capture his stepson's goodwill by vociferously approving every opinion or watercolor he brings home ("*Ton fils est un Chardin*, what order and discipline, *du pur Chardin!*") "*Cher ami,* who do you think is the greatest painter who ever lived?" he asks upon snaring Edmund out to lunch at the Plaza Men's Grill. What an idiotic question Edmund thinks. "Well, perhaps Titian," he blurts out. "*D'accordo, d'accordo,*" Grisha exults, "your answers always brilliant but I've always wanted to know *why* he's the greatest." "Look at those loose, revolutionary brushstrokes, he was the first to liberate painting from the tyranny of line. . . ." "Remarkable, brilliant, thank you!"

"Actually Titian's late period was totally misunderstood for centuries," Edmund expounds at the Plaza another time over a third sherry. "Except perhaps by Rembrandt?" "Precisely," Edmund says to the beaming stranger across from him. "No one understood late Titian until Rembrandt . . . you're spoiling my mother to death," he adds. The pale cavalry eyes stare back, eyes he's never bothered to plumb, has simply overlooked, disdained. "You're indulging her every caprice, encouraging the full extravagance of that anarchic Slavic spirit, that's been your way to keep her totally in your power . . . ." The man's eyes suddenly severe, cynical. "It wasn't an easy life she led alone with you, was it? Can't we have a little charity, *cher ami*?" "You and your talk of order and discipline," Edmund says, downing his sherry. "Discipline for youth like you; as for Mara, let her be, she's finally resting, *elle s'amuse!*"

Sitting on a bus riding uptown to play a tennis match at Columbia Edmund dozes and dreams briefly about Mara's afternoons. She flies over the city like an enormous zeppelin, her newly majestic body painted like that of some tribal statue; she points with her old sweet laugh to all those places in the city where he'd like to find her between the hours of two and six: sympathizing with fellow émigrés at the Tolstoi Foundation, addressing envelopes at the Foundling Home for the Orphans of Exiled White Russians . . . the bus jolts to a stop, he wakes and realizes that she's in none of those places, that she's finally indulging fully in that ancient passion for gambling which she chooses to keep hidden from him, that Grisha will retain his power by letting her continue the vodka, the cards, the desperate boredom that's gnawed at her since she ceased a life of hardship, as if such obsessive temperaments fall to pieces when released from the discipline of survival, can only feed nefariously upon themselves . . . oh Mama you're so good, so educated, can't you get interested in cancer or in the Alliance Française, the extinction of rare animal species, can't you give lectures at the Cosmopolitan Club, there's only one thing left that can draw us back together. . . .

New York World-Telegram, November 22, 1951

The work of Edmund Richter, a precociously gifted painter who is still an undergraduate at Columbia University, reassures us that the realist tradition is thriving notwithstanding the fashionable new smears beginning to spot 57th Street like an epidemic of measles. Richter's remarkable land-scapes—informed by considerable technical skill and lyric precision—are bound to make an important contribution to contemporary art. His oils of Italy and Nantucket are particularly striking, and present the sensuous surface and the attention to detail of a young Corot.

Everyone gave parties. The show sold out. There were fetes for Edmund at the Exters, the Sanfords, the Rosses. At his mother's house, over a lavish buffet of cutlets

Pojarsky and chicken Kiev, Edmund asked to renew acquaintance with the genteel companions of his adolescence. His teachers of Pushkin, Mozart, tennis, still life, the cake-making princes and the graduates of the Moscow Conservatory mingled with the cosmetic manufacturers and Seventh Avenue designers described by Edmund as Mara's new milieu. In the Rosses' lush interior of mahogany and polished brass ("*nouveau riche* but so warm," Mara always judged them) operatic divas and stars of the Broadway stage raised their champagne glasses to the young painter. And at the Sanfords' apartment at River House, a small black-tie dinner was attended by whatever cousins lived within traveling distance of New York and were not fighting for freedom in Korea.

"Having always been passionately fond of Europeans, I have grown to be particularly fond of this young man who has graced our seaborne domain as a friend—nay, almost as a son—since his fifteenth year, and who like so many Continentals is destined to make a noble contribution to the culture of our blessed country. May we drink to your success, to your wealth and fame, young fellow; I raise my glass to one who may become—nay, I insist, *will* become—the American Gainsborough. . . ."

Plinker has twinkled his glass over the cherries jubilee, tuxedo looming majestically over the candlelit Meissen. At the toast's end Edmund catches a glimpse of Claire hanging lovingly upon her father's words, standing to applaud the toast, clapping. And the arched curve of her back, the rigid regal thrust of her head reminds him of some tiny German figurine that twirls under a glass dome upon the turn of a key. There's something about her adulation of her father, something of the obedient Teutonic princess about her that moment which frightens him.

But ah what triumph Mara has upon reading Edmund's reviews, upon witnessing the sales of his paintings! Mara enjoys a great, brief happiness that winter, for the central goal of her former life (the cultivation of genius) is being fulfilled. "*Il sera* Delacroix, *er wird* Brueghel, he'll be Tintoretto."

Five weeks later, at the end of Christmas week, Mara was struck by a cab as she swayed down the street from one of her mysterious afternoons in town, and died three days later of internal hemorrhages, with a minimum of pain.

Edmund stayed with her at St. Luke's Hospital until the end, clutching her hand, refusing to look at the face of the man who thought he had loved Mara. She had been struck in the abdomen and remained in a coma for much of the remaining time.

In a moment of consciousness the day before she died she whispered to Edmund that she wanted him to fix her hair. "Braid it," she said with great difficulty, "the way you did when you were little."

Edmund carefully brushed the burnished mass of sweat-matted hair onto one side of the bed. Working deftly at the first braid, he recalled those Saturday mornings when they had settled in their first American rooms and Mara had let him tie her hair with a bright red satin ribbon which gave her the air of a schoolgirl at a Russian Christmas party. "You're just like my sister this way," he'd said when he was eleven as he'd added a sprig of holly to the ribbon . . . this time he had asked the nurse for some strips of white cotton with which to tie the ends of her hair. And then he had turned her face gently towards the ceiling again, laying each dark braid decorously on the pillowcase. She gave the beginning of a smile. "Thank you, *dousia*," she whispered. Grisha was gazing out of the window, a pearl of tear trembling at the end of his peaked nose. "It was so beautiful, so short," Mara managed to say again to Edmund, speaking very slowly in Russian, her lips straining painfully towards his ear. Precisely *what* had been so short, Edmund urgently wanted to know, what did she consider so beautiful? Life in general? Their love together? Her love with the other one? Had he been too harsh towards her in the past years? Shouldn't he have allowed her the luxury of idleness after those frantic years of scrubbing and scrimping, of plotting his scholarships and his lessons? Couldn't he keep his damn little diligence to himself, continue lavishing affection on this extravagant generous creature whose surface alone had been altered? He started speaking to her but her eyes had closed again. There would be no more words from her; and a few hours later Edmund knew that he must call a priest. Sunday service, to which he'd refused to accompany her since the age of fifteen, about which he'd driven her to tears by deriding it as the opiate of the masses, had been the only unchanged ritual of her new life with Grisha. So a bearded deacon in black cassock and tall square hat came from Ninety-seventh Street and held the crucifix close to her face, chanting for a few minutes about life eternal, anointing her forehead with an umbrous ointment redolent with incense.

Kneeling by Mara's bed, becoming oblivious to his surroundings, as if he were trying to go into coma with her. Conscious only of the lingering warmth of her hand as he keeps it clasped to his cheek, of the occasional pleading of nurses who beg him to eat, take air. Shaking his head angrily at the touch of any hand, refusing to open his eyes or lift his head, remaining on his knees notwithstanding the doctors' urging that he lie down on the cot set up for him in Mara's room. They're gentle with him, do not force. Her husband seems to come and go, sobbing elegantly into a handkerchief, muttering about having to call friends, pressing soup and coffee upon him. No sense of how long the man remains in Mara's room during that last day. A nurse was shuffling sheets, another bustling about the room. It's all over, a doctor's voice spoke softly into his ear. He lifted his head and realized that they had just finished closing Mara's eyes. This was his last vision of her: Mara's brow was deeply furrowed, as if she'd just squinted intently into the sun. The vigorous chin jutted forward more stubbornly than ever, reminding him of those childhood photographs taken of Mara with her mother by some embankment of the frozen Neva, wrapped in muff and furs, already confronting the camera with haughty irateness. Edmund stared hard at the willful features. In an atavistic impulsive gesture he moved his hand slowly over her face in the sign of the cross, three times, in the manner of the Orthodox Church. *"Cher ami, cher ami,"* Grisha was sobbing towards him. But Edmund was already running out into the winter night, not looking at Grisha or even bothering to take his coat, thinking of nothing but his need to retain his numbness as long as possible.

It was a Sunday, shortly before midnight. He ran. He ran shouting down 114 Street, controlled enough to know that he was running on an empty side street rather than on a well-policed avenue and that he had only a few moments in which to give free rein to his voice. "Peb, Sophie," he cried out repeatedly, "Sophie, Peb, where are you?" He turned the corner into Broadway and stopped shouting, ran south and tried to schedule his next several hours. Sophie was abroad with her parents, dining with Dame Edith Evans, John Gielgud. He knew where Pebble could be found every Monday morning at 9:00 A.M. during vacations; his only problem was what to do with himself before he reached her. He rushed down Broadway, aware that he was running at even pace, elbows at his side, left arm raised in symmetrical rhythm with right knee, like a trained runner. Young orphaned desperado immigrant with over-long dark blond hair rushes down Broadway in the middle of a warm winter night past the bookstores where Claire and I searched for rare editions of Emerson in our high-school days, past the New Yorker movie house where a few spring vacations ago I took Sophie to see the *Children of Paradise* three times in one week; every ten minutes or so when his breathing became labored he paused to lean against a wall, staring at the streets of his childhood, let's salute the pharmacies in which druggists refused to sell us cough medications because of nonexistent payments, pay tribute to the Café des Artistes where the Rosses take us to brunch with shimmering coloraturas. At Fifty-seventh Street he turned left and east and ran through the familiar block of the Art Students League. Stopping for a second in front of the school, where he stared numbly at one of his watercolors exhibited in the window, he realized that he had run with only two or three interruptions for some fifty blocks. He continued sprinting east on Fifty-seventh Street, passing the painfully familiar stoops of Carnegie Hall, the Russian Tea Room, Mara's former ballet school. He ran past the expensive Fifth Avenue stores at whose windows Mara had stared with her curious gaze of envy and disdain during their childhood walks. He swerved south on Lexington Avenue, east again on Fifty-fourth Street, and started looking for a bar. After passing a half-dozen possibilities he stopped at one on First Avenue filled with men and ordered a double Jack Daniel's, straight up. He drank it slowly, not feeling the fire. It would be weeks before he could face Grisha or the solitude of his student room, the only gesture to live for, the only bridge that could span the abyss, was to fall into Pebble's arms and then, only then, allow himself to go. Until we find her we must suspend all thought and continue to run or else fall into a deep short sleep. He paced the bar as he downed his bourbons, disdaining the men's whistling and appraising, their softly mouthed hoots and whispers. He needed a bed for a few hours of the night and wished to remain precisely in that part of town, near the building where Pebble played tennis every Monday morning of her vacations. After a half hour of refusing propositions he started a conversation with a pale hairdresser who'd accosted him by asking him what sign of the zodiac he'd been born under. "Taurus, like Michelangelo." His companion had spent four years in a Catholic seminary and was presently obsessed with problems of astrology and transmigration of souls. He took Edmund to a comfortable third-floor walk-up furnished with numerous photographs of Greta Garbo. A few hours later Edmund woke before the stranger, dressed quickly, ran out. It was one of those warm January days of springlike haze that precipitate the thawing of December snows. Edmund took up his sprinting pace again and ran to the familiar building by the river.

As Edmund came towards Pebble in the River House Tennis Club she stood alone at the base line of a court, practicing her serves, a basket of balls by her side. He stared at her, wishing for the first time in days that he had some pen and ink. There was a superb curve to her spine as she leaned deeply back on each serve to throw the ball into the air, her torso then swooping downwards with violent acceleration as she brought her racket smashing onto the ball. She was absorbed in the gesture, rehearsing it very rhythmically, pawing the ground with her sneakered foot for a few seconds before engaging in the dual motion of languid leaning back and furious downwards thrust. He watched her through some thirty serves before calling out to her, aware that in her straining for perfection she was capable of repeating the same gesture 80, 120 times in one practice session. And then he cupped his hands and yelled, "Pebble, Pebble." The voice returned to him across the courts, faint and piping, not quite his. And he realized that he could not tell her yet, that he had to remain in motion for a few more hours, even with her.

"Edmund, where have you been, rabbit?" She had turned around, dropped her racket, opened her thin arms towards him.

"I've come to play tennis with you," he yelled. She ran towards him and put an arm on his shoulder, stroking his hair. "That's super, why didn't you call me ahead of time? Do you want me to cancel my opponent, she's not due for half an hour, shall I call?" "Yes, yes, please, Pebble." His arms trembled. "Please call, and find me a racket and a pair of sneakers, will you?"

She ran to the dressing room with a skip and a hop, saying, "You look like something the cat brought in. . . . I haven't told you I'm playing some Stravinsky for the first time. . . ." He continued to stare at her body as she ran; she wore the same little white shorts in which she'd posed for him a year and a half before, she'd grown thinner since adolescence, looked more ephemeral than ever. Edmund grabbed Claire's racket from the floor, played the ball fiercely against the backboard . . . "Take that, you bastard," he muttered, talking to death. "And that and that and that." It was the first time he beat her at tennis. He was driven by some force of rage more demonic than any in his memory; the ball is his enemy, the ball is Grisha who had snatched his mother from him and spoiled her to death, the ball is Edmund himself who'd failed to understand Mara and cure her, it's that own grief of his which he must remold into some anger with which he can at least survive. There's no possibility that day of missing the ball. His rage fills him with as much agility as strength; even when Pebble is at net smashing it deep into his backhand corner he manages to return with a deep unretrievable lob, scooping up the ball and keeping it in patient enough contact with his racket to send it flying in a high curve that swiftly dies behind her at base line. His agility causes her considerable amusement, she laughs after many of her netted returns. "E.R., where did you learn that brilliant lob? Who in heavens have you been training with?" He leads her four-three. She rallies, her chin angrily thrust forward, and breaks his serve on a double fault. But in the following game he breaks her serve and the score stands at five-four. "Historic moment my dear," he says at the net as they change sides, beginning to feel a terrible lightness, "I'm going to beat you, Santa Clara." She sticks her tongue out at him mockingly. "Oh no you're not. But I don't know what's gotten *into* you." Changing her tactics, she returns his serves with short, choppy strokes that force him up to net and tries to pass him wide, with deep drives down the line. But he reaches every one of them as if his arms were an extension of his rage. And she can only return two of his serves anyhow. The other three are aces, and he's won the set. "What *has* gotten into you, Eddem?" she cries with eminent sportsmanship. And she leaps over the net to hug him. But he's run to the back wall and knelt against it, sobbing.

"My angel, what's wrong," she cried, kneeling beside him. He told her. For ten minutes or so he let her hold him against her, his head cradled against her fragile shoulder. As he sobbed and shouted his imprecations he realized that it was one of the few times he'd cried since he'd stubbed his toe at the age of seven, that Mara had protected him from many of childhood's griefs while denying him much of its pleasures. His sorrow expanded, he broke away from Claire and rocked uncontrollably on the floor, his body coiled. When she attempted to raise him off the floor he retreated from her, rocking even more uncontrollably in a corner of the room, attempting to knock his head against the wall. After having shouted for help she offered her self as a buffer zone between him and any surface he was trying to attack, letting him knock his head violently against her body as he attempted to destroy himself.

* * *

New York City
March 2nd, 1952

Beloved Sofia Larionovna,

What an unthinkable trip, of course you could never have come all the way from England for Mara's funeral (it's about the first time I allow myself to pronounce or write those words). Thank you for all your notes, and for worrying about me the way you have. Sorry I haven't written yet. This is just about the first time I'm even allowed to write. I've very little memory of the first weeks, to tell you the truth I don't even remember the funeral. I'm told that on top of the incredible asthmatic attacks I was under immense doses of sedation. As you know Pebble took several weeks off from college to take care of me, and between her and Babsie . . . I barely pulled through without needing a psychiatric ward. I myself had to skip more than two months of school, shall perhaps be allowed to resume in a fortnight. But thank God my thesis was already almost finished and that was the brunt of this term's work. Pebble is talking about going to England again after graduation, which worries me. Will you tell me whether she's apprised you of such a plan? Her reasons: the old stuff, "finding herself" away from her formidable conformist clan, et cetera. Well, thanks for writing so often. Sorry I sound so limp, etc. *"La chair est triste, hélas, et j'ai lu tous les livres."*

Yr. Edmund

New York City
June 15th, 1952

Sofka,

Congratulations on being in love again! Next

time I hope you choose a man with a name more interesting than John Dillon, something truly beautiful like Hyman Levine Farina. That way if your endless appetite for broadening your identity involves a rediscovery of your Jewish roots you could change your name back to Mrs. Hyman Farina Levine. Yes, Pebble is going abroad, God damnit. On July 1st. For the whole year. With the craziest plan you can imagine: working as a secretary to be independent from her family while she continues her piano training! So I'm right now a little desperate. As for Babsie and Plinker it's their retirement year, they're going to live in Arizona because the medics say it'll be better for Babsie's nerves. What a good idea for you to work for the Democratic party in California!

Yr. Friend always   Edm.

New York City
June 22nd, 1952

Mon Clair de Lune,

I am drunk, dead drunk, I became willfully drunk so that I would have the guts to write you what I haven't had the guts to write or say *à pleine voix* for some years; I promise to go to bed and sober up and reread this letter before sending it, but it's the only way I can get up the courage to say that I love you madly, I will never be able to love anyone again, I offer myself to you here and now, do with me what you will, immolate me, marry me, torture me, but the one thing you cannot do is to deprive me of your continuous presence by my side and your continuous power over me. . . . I am at your feet as below an altar, the altar of my expectations, my desires, my ambitions. . . . I hurl my body towards you as a man who throws himself from a burning building,

I beg for you the way you beg your Lord for daily bread, all this I could not say when I took you to the ship yesterday. . . .

Next morning: Whew! What a headache! But I'm glad I got it out. What I'm really doing is asking for your hand in marriage, in an outrageously serious way. I don't need to elaborate on bourgeois reassurances such as: The penury I suffered as a child makes me all the more determined to support myself in a consistent manner; what with my assistant teaching at Columbia and the support of a good art gallery I'm as ready as anyone is to offer you a hearty independence from your family, one which would be immensely more helpful to your musical career than the insane course you're presently launched on . . . forgive the inane digression. Let's say that I give you a few months to think about all this, even in the glaring light of dawn I can soberly repeat that you are my life, my blood, my only hope, etc.

New York City
July 17th, 1952

Dearest Pebble,

No need to say how miserable I am at this moment without so much as a postcard. I realize that you're as wretched a correspondent as can be found on this planet, that you're a solitary explorer by nature, that this European venture is one more step in your chimerical search to break with all that's closest to you. I also realize that I may have done something foolish in my letter of some weeks ago. I confronted you with the vehemence of my passion, which is the human ingredient you probably fear the most. I wish to stress that I could remain as chaste in a marriage, if you should so wish it, as

Abélard would have remained if he'd been shipped back to Héloïse after his disastrous deprivation. So I'm proposing something quite innovative: a radical extension of friendship into a *vie à deux* which would enable me to be constantly in the presence of a being as necessary to me as food. . . .

New York City
August 16th, 1952

Sof dear,

So Mr. Farina wasn't up to porridge? How sorry I feel for him! Miss Elusivity has been gone for over eight weeks now and hasn't written a word to *anyone*, not even to her parents. A good lunch with Jeff the other day, all aglow after his heroic Korea bit, Purple Heart ribbon blooming on his chest like violets in springtime, rather at loose ends for the time being and thinking of going to Oxford for grad work in history. Write soon, dear heart. . . .

New York City
August 22nd, 1952

Dear Claire,

In light of the letter which I posted to you fully two months ago, and of the rather important decisions I brought up in it concerning our mutual destinies, I really find it extraordinary that you have not had the charity or manners to pen a reply. I acknowledge that I'm deeply in your debt, that you saved my life last winter (but then your entire family probably saved my sanity over the course of the past many years). Yet I do not see that a sense of satisfaction about having been admirable towards someone should release you from all continuing decency. I feel right now as if you had pulled me out of the icy ocean only to deposit me on a small parched island with a tree bearing one tiny palm for sustenance . . . that palm being the distant hope that sometime in the next month you might grace me with the nourishment of your words. . . .

New York City
September 8th, 1952

Hey, Frozenpuss,

"Some people fancy they're being natural," La Rochefoucauld once wrote, "when they're merely being boorish and rude."

Yours,   E.

New York City
September 25th, 1952

Dearest Soph,

I really miss you too, very very much. Gratitude for your many heartening letters. What are your plans for autumn and winter? (To answer your query: I'm staying put, of course, to begin my master's thesis and to earn my daily bread, which I do by teaching many charming morons, truly visual spastics, to draw apples.) And so I thrill at the very thought of being reunited with you in the city sometime soon. I'm so eager to see you that if you can't make it farther than Chicago I'm ready to hitchhike out there to meet you halfway! Let me know!

New York City
October 19th, 1952

There's really more craziness in you than I'd expected, Peb, and more meanness, and more smallness. If I don't hear from you in the next two weeks what can I do but capitulate? . . .

October 23rd, 1952

Sofinka

Can't tell you how thrilling it is to know you're soon coming East! Have you made up your mind yet about the exact date of your arrival? If you haven't I *command* you to. . . .

New York City
November 7th, 1952

Beloved Sofinka. It really is ghastly about Adlai but . . . Ecstasy! You're arriving! I've got to run off to class, just want to acknowledge the receipt of your beloved last letter and say that I'll be meeting the Chattanooga on November 22nd at Penn Station, and I can hardly wait until you rush into my waiting arms. . . .

They began living together the following month.

vi

Through the open window of the Intourist bus Claire smells wafts of lavender and thyme, she opens her eyes and sees the calm, massive landscape of Soviet Georgia hulking before her like a temple, blazing in the still heat of noon, a fragment abandoned on the altar of light —they're driving through tall stands of birches that alternate with vast fields of red poppies and white nicotiana, the bus halts before a drawbridge, a cloud of insects emits a long, shrill droning that sweeps the ground like a wind—then there's a stand of pine trees and tall ferns as dark and silent as the ocean floor; look at that forest so pristine and still Sophie whispers by her side, it has the isolation I'd like to find someday in Nepal, Tibet—What a novelty Claire says, that's how I wanted to live for decades and now you're the one looking for solitude—Sophie is tired this morning and claims not to have slept a second of the night, keeps her head on Claire's shoulder; well at least I wouldn't be giving anyone grief by splitting would I Peb?—That's your first dig of the week Claire says I haven't given people much of a break is that what you're saying?—Bet your sweet ass you haven't Peb you haven't—Explain me to myself Sophie I want you to explain, it began when I was very little sitting in churches, there were too many moments when I wanted to leave behind all I knew for a new life in which I'd feel more worthy—I often think back to a time I was walking on a beach with my father, I was eighteen, he sat down on a rock and said you're all I've got in the world Peb and you'll be the end of me yet, all I ever wanted for you was to be happy, the tears came down on that large kind face and it was as if a rock were melting before me, the memory's so painful that I didn't recall it until we were all in our middle thirties and I was completing the destruction of that safe world he'd wanted for me—You've always struggled for a total liberation from the world you were born into Claire darling—A search that was Utopian, perhaps harmful to others, right Soph? I spent a couple of decades working on a totally wrong model of perfection, nutty, totally misled!

Georgia is the first leg of their Soviet journey, the bus rambles through a pale golden fire of noon light, the day so brilliant that they seem to be moving across the bottom of a huge crystal bowl and the world's light refracts with myriad force in a great circle about their heads—Sophie has closed her eyes and Claire wraps her sweater around Sophie's shoulders—the Rolls-Royce dealers are asking Irina whether there are bank accounts, zoos, fire trucks in the Soviet Union; "The Soviets are still Asiatics," Mr. Zabar says to his wife, "impossible to understand them in our Western terms," and Edmund is reading to Mr. Weicker out of his 1915 Baedeker—their guide Evgeny sits across from them on the bus dressed in a frayed suit of pale grayed blue, his hair bluntly cut as a sheaf of wheat—if one looks straight into his spectacled eyes they don't so much return a gaze as a fleeting reflection of a grain of world, a passerby; throughout this country Claire has seen many men with his terrified untrusting eyes, with that stare which seldom fastens on the eyes of another human but seems to hover fearfully at some point in midair—Do you remember that first Ban the Bomb demonstration we all went to together in

Philadelphia? she says to Sophie, the pickets waving, you and I were cheering the speakers while Edmund was sketching faces of people in the crowd and we kept saying this is serious Eddem please be more serious —Sophie stretches, yawns, you're a walking contradiction Peb aren't you, you attack the idea of power yet you've fucked up our lives by having exceptional power over us—Well nothing's tormented me as much as my relations with others Claire says; for a few decades I didn't think I even needed any others—You preach nonresistance Peb and you're a fighter by temperament, your abhorrence of force is coupled to an extraordinarily aggressive attitude towards life!—Yes yes very complex that all came as a great surprise Soph; pacifists are filled with a lot of inner violence, yet beyond the force of my love for my daughter, for you, for Edmund, I've little to trust in except my nonviolent means; we've always got to see the enemy as capable of conversion, awaken and startle him into openness—look at Evgeny, I know he's been programmed to fear and hate us as the enemy but I'm determined to discover a chink in his armor so I sit here doing a kind of psychic auscultation of him, trying to figure out where the chinks might be—

From the beginning of their trip Sophie and Edmund have noted that Claire has retained her old manner of engaging in long sentences with little need for attention or exchange; she speaks her thoughts out loud, pale eyes staring straight ahead of her, sometimes continuing to talk while her companions have wandered off to study a building, photograph a view. In this she has changed less than any other member of the triad, in this they might be disappointed. This is their third day together and they still delight in discovering the new gestures and phrases of each other's middle age ("that constant clearing of your throat hem hem has little to do with childhood asthma Eddem it's just another dreary academic tic"); they are like vacationing siblings who dramatize the most

minute changes in family behavior. Claire's perorations
are as interchangeable as ever with her internal musings;
if interrupted she will simply lean back against the back
of a chair or bus seat and withdraw again . . . for
instance, that day in Georgia:

". . . the only thing pacifists have to work with is
their tactic of moral jujitsu, Sophie; once we've palpated
the opponent's armor, so to speak, discovered its chinks,
we've got to throw him off balance by some act of
humility or trust . . . we smile as we pass the machine
guns and we carry no armor, we're steeled with a totally
different kind of inner guile . . . you know what A. J.
Muste said on the eve of World War Two, he got up
in Quaker meeting and said if you can't love Hitler
you can't love any man, just think how difficult that
is. . . ."

"You're making the mistake of considering love as an
emotion," Edmund remarks as he comes to sit beside
her. "It is, in fact, an attitude."

An attitude! Edmund has always had a way of turning
things around on their head, practicing his own brand of
moral jujitsu, Claire's holy zeal for humanity in the
abstract! The pious luxury of loving enemies! She won't
answer him, she leans her head against the back of the
bus seat and shuts her eyes; there she goes Sophie says,
bye-bye for a while.

". . . Ladies and gentlemen, we are approaching our
destination, village of Mtskheta, earliest mythological
home of the Georgian people. . . ."

Irina, the tour guide, has switched on her microphone
for her little midday lecture, she's wearing her best
American T-shirt and the word Levi's is prominent on
her tiny left buttock—The Rolls-Royce dealers lean out
of the bus snapping pictures of horses; Irina dislikes
ancient history and she sniffs into her tissue as if the
mountain air were poisoning her—"This is said to have

been first Christian outpost in pagan times until fifth
century . . . ai, what else, proud mountain people had
military and commerce connections with Greece, Rome,
Persia . . . and now gentlemen and ladies before continuing our sight-seeing we're going to take refreshment
in typical old-fashioned little Georgian garden. Evgeny
Sergeievich, do see that everyone gets off properly.
. . ." The group descends into a luxuriant garden filled
with roses, dahlias, foxgloves, mallows, every seasonal
flower of a tumultuous European garden—they're beck-
oned to enter the little house that attends it; the owner sits
in its dark cool interior, a smiling, aged Georgian with a
black cap on his head who offers his guests fruit juices in
delicate crystal glasses—Claire sits on a rock outside of
the old man's door, needing the air, the mountain view,
observing her companions inside—Edmund puts his
arms around Sophie in one of those asides he offers when
she's depressed, "Oh Sofka this is what Voltaire was
talking about, cultivate our eccentricities, our most
repressed desires! This is the way I'd like to end my life,
painting landscapes and tending a garden as beautiful and
useless as this man's"—but Sophie stands still in one of
those new moods of gloom and withdrawal Claire can't
decipher; in the past day she'd mostly talked about where
she'd travel at the end of their Russian trip, which route
to take home, "Why don't I fly back via Copenhagen?
I've always wanted to see that part of the north, or
maybe I'll fly to Italy, drop in on the Rome office and
catch the end of the film festival in Cannes; come along
and we can rent a boat to Sicily"—then moments of
depression they can't decode, her long solitary evening
walks; her moments of delight seem disciplined, en-
forced, like that brittle cheerfulness of her TV appear-
ances which has cloaked her numerous crises, Sophie at
7:00 A.M. the month after her last husband died, flashing
to Claire and ten million Americans her extraordinary
smile, every curl of her head perfectly sculpted, saying,

"Good Day America, more violence last night in strike-ridden Uganda, the Panama crisis is growing to a head" —this creature of total freedom and great solitude who strides through American cities in a turban and dark glasses to avoid autograph hunters; for years Claire had marveled at the tenacity of her affection—Sophie had always been there with her insistent voice, her huge tenderness, her monumental appetites, ah if anyone had the tenacity to get through to the dead Sophie could; in their twenties they used to imagine Sophie broadcasting séances, "Guess who I contacted last night, George Bernard Shaw, John Stuart Mill"—the invasion of Normandy Edmund used to call Sophie's tumultuous entrances, accompanied as they were by a stream of questions and announcements, "Peb how are we going to help the Hollywood Ten, Eddem please explain to me the *ultimate* meaning of Eliot's *Quartets*"—"After the age of forty there isn't much to live for except friendship," Sophie'd announced yesterday and they'd all agreed. "It took me some traumatic years to learn that," Claire said; "you were way ahead of me Soph; for my first twenty-five years I hadn't learned friendship the way other people haven't learned to swim or ride a bicycle; in those years you and Edmund were the only ones whose stubbornness was great enough to claim me, whose voices were tenacious enough to break through my solitude; in the long run Sofka you may have been my humanity"—They were in the sleeping car of a train bound for Tbilisi, 1:00 A.M., Sophie her head in Claire's lap, Edmund lying on the opposite bunk—"Look at it this way," Edmund said, "friendship is freer of deceit than any other bond because there's little power, profit, material pleasure in it"—"What about the free consent," Sophie exclaimed, "no oath or duty, total self-determination!"—"It's perhaps the most pacifist emotion we can have," Claire noted; "look at the Quakers, a Society of Friends"—and then Edmund had come up with something very beautiful, friendship is that state in which we most resemble the society of angels promised us in catechism, in which we can share the truth of our inner thoughts in total freedom and abundance . . . that's just what I came here for Sophie said I sure hope we can start soon and then they'd all fallen asleep.

Vineyards stretch ahead for miles towards a violet mountain—Evgeny sits on a bench a few yards away from Claire, bent forward, self-absorbed, rapping his knee with a copy of *Pravda* which he holds furled into a narrow roll—his approaches to the Americans are meted out in some meticulously detailed program of behavior —"Can I help you?" he asks each time he sees one of his group walking unaccompanied through a Soviet town, "Is there anything I can do for you?" The Zabars assure their fellow tourists that Evgeny spends his nights writing up reports on the Americans but the image ignites no anger in Claire, she sees a creature haunted, hunted by the fears and temptations of survival—the mission lying ahead of her in Moscow might help to save the life of a man who was once as docile as Evgeny; whatever attempts her companions make to keep her from it she's determined not to avoid its complications—one of hundreds of thousands of men incarcerated in this country, Edmund's already warned her, a symbolic gesture, risky, futile—

"Oh I wish I could take home one of those lovely brooms that old woman is sweeping the street with," Mrs. Weicker says. "Ted look what a gorgeous broom!"

"You could eat off the sidewalks in this country they're so clean."

"Soph where on earth did you pick up that odious habit of constantly drinking from water fountains abroad, you're going to get hepatitis!" "Stop always using that word odious Peb, it's so Cambridge, Mass."

". . . Intourist never tells you what hotel they're ever taking you to on your next stop," Mr. Zabar explains to

Edmund; "that's so no one can ever look you up in case you've got friends or relatives in this country; it's the same in Hungary Czechoslovakia East Germany Poland."

That evening on the way back to Tbilisi, Irina and Evgeny have arranged a typical Georgian banquet for the American tourists. It is held at a cooperative farm nestled at the bottom of a pleasant valley. There are vineyards nearby and groves of olive trees shimmering silver in the early evening light. Evgeny takes over from Irina at dinnertime. "Georgian hospitality is renowned throughout our Union for its warmth and old-fashioned charm . . . throughout the nineteenth century our Russian poets came to Georgia to receive inspiration for their verses and restore their health . . . Georgia was our muse as Italy was for poets of the British Isles. . . ." A long narrow table is set in a woodland pasture and laden with many flowers, with heaps of tomatoes, onions and cucumbers, with dishes of Oriental eggplant and cheese pies, with little glasses for vodka and larger ones for white and red wine, with bowls of garlic cloves cooked to such subtle lengths that they attain the crisp blandness of water chestnuts, with abundances of fresh figs, pears, peaches, pomegranates and slender crescent-shaped loaves of fragrant bread. Sophie wades knee-deep in a nearby stream, picking more wild flowers for the table. "These people might be poor," Mr. Weicker comments, "but what a sense of community!" The Rolls-Royce dealers delight in learning to drink their vodka in one gulp and shout many *Na Zdarovies* to their Georgian hosts. The hosts praise their local wine as the best cure for arteriosclerosis, schizophrenia, impotence . . . the chief source of their astronauts' courage . . . the principal source of the Georgian people's longevity . . . many toasts are exchanged.

"To the health and happiness of our American guests!"

"To Georgia!" (Edmund) "To this remarkable handiwork of nature!"

"To the noble ideals of Western democracy!" (Arthur Zabar)

"To the shared concerns of our two great traditions!" (Ted Weicker)

"To the increase of our mutual trust!" (Claire)

"To your eyes, Clara Pavlovna! To her beautiful eyes!"

"To détente," Sophie drinks, "to world peace!"

"To your beauty, Sofia Larionovna! To her beauty!"

"To our Georgian women! To their tenderness . . . their suffering . . . their patience . . . their fortitude . . ."

("Does he want the shishkebab in his face?")

("Hush, Soph, hush.")

"To the children of Georgia!"

"To the children of America!"

(". . . the little beasts . . .")

("Shut up, Eddem.")

"To the future!"

As they walk back towards the bus after dinner Evgeny stops before an enclosure in which there stands a young buck deer. The animal thrusts its lustrous black muzzle through an interstice of the gate and the young Russian kneels down to caress it. "*Dousia*," he whispers, "*lapachka* . . ." He walks about the pasture stuffing chestnuts in his pockets, feeds them to the deer. Claire stands at his side. "Oh how lovely Evgeny Sergeievich, how lovely!" The animal picks the chestnuts delicately out of the man's hand, rubbing his muzzle against his wrist. "Isn't he beautiful?" the young Russian whispers. "How could one ever kill such a creature? Ah I've never understood hunters, Clara Pavlovna."

Irina claps her hands, calling them to board the bus.

Evgeny takes off his glasses, blows on them gently as he continues to whisper to the animal. Claire turns around to look directly into the Russian's unshielded eyes, which still remain boreal and abstract.

vii

On weekends in their New York studio apartment Edmund constantly drew and painted Sophie in the nude. She would remember those years as her life's most perfect moment. He would remember them as his period of odalisques. He painted Sophie in bed in the poses of Renoir's late canvases, a vase of roses by the night table; of Goya's *Maja Desnuda*, arms behind head, breasts trembling warmly in the air. Dictatorial, he did not let her talk, often made her read during the pose so that she would not continually confront him with her questioning gold eyes. She posed with magnanimity, with genius, with a sybaritic abandon. Even when engaged in the most menial tasks there was a tension between the languor of her gestures and the piercing attentiveness of her gaze which made every attitude she struck a painter's dream. Later she would give her poses a self-conscious skill ("Do you want me this way? My arm lower down?") which lost some of their original power. But he would never forget the amplitude and instinctual grace of her movements that first year, Sophie seating herself at a table by the window in just the right Vermeerian light, Sophie reclining on pillows in billowing pants and turbaned head, legs crossed like Delacroix's harem women. The feature of her face which fascinated him the most was the large, fine Roman nose that dominated her softly modeled oval face. It made an abrupt little departure from its bridge, jutted forwards briefly like Giuliano de' Medici's in the Botticelli portrait. It intimated a force, a streak of masculine independence, which had not yet manifested itself in her life. After many odalisques, Edmund concentrated on Sophie's face and painted numerous heads of her, struggling to capture that peculiar still-hidden force of her character: Sophie in a velvet cap, like Raphael's brooding young man; Sophie's copper curls cascading to her shoulders and adorned with a circlet of flowers like Rembrandt's Saskia.

She loved the intensity with which he stared at her when she posed, the crouched taut intensity of a hunter stalking prey from a thicket. She would have wished for that same intensity of gaze in every one of their moments together, for she was one of those women who'd entered life believing in fierce elemental passions, lived through a few brief ones already, sensed that her central tragedy might be to never live such an idyll with an artist called Edmund Richter. She'd waited for him quietly and long —she'd waited for him, to be precise, since the age of fifteen when they'd first met on the terrace of the Sanfords' house, since that moment when she'd come upon him in his outlandishly formal poor boy's blazer, water-color brush in hand, lifting towards her his defiant and awed immigrant's gaze. She'd accepted the evident centrality of his love for Claire with a cool, complicated patience which had to do with her own adoration of Pebble; she had not so much resented Claire as she had lived in a fatalistic hope that one day the cycle of their infatuations would somehow be broken, shaped anew. Like most women who are capable of long and deep-seated passions she had a genius for secrecy, self-control. Edmund only came to understand her constancy when they started sharing a bed and looked upon it as admirable but awesome in its perseverance. So it was that Sophie could finally be a Muse to her long-awaited artist, breathing as quietly as possible under his heavy intent gaze as she posed, staring with pretended detachment at his chiseled face under its mane of wavy dark blond hair, the high cheekbones which he enjoyed ascribing to Tatar blood, the thick dark lashes which made his very dark blue eyes all the more inscrutable.

If Sophie sometimes fell asleep during an afternoon pose it was because she'd had frequent bouts of insomnia since childhood, a recurring, needling sleeplessness impervious to any medical diagnosis, in which she even had a kind of pride, attributing to it her omnivorous reading of most nineteenth-century novels ever published. When Edmund woke in the morning she'd already be watching for him, mass of copper curls richly tangled on the pillow next to the koala bear that was still her bedtime fetish, exuding towards his awakening senses her faint scent of musk and essence of roses and her radiant smile, springing up swiftly to make his breakfast, clean his studio, perform the menial tasks any of us would perform if we'd been educated to believe that our highest destiny is to bask in the closely reflected glory of a genius.

Glory! He'd never known anything like that adulation for artistic success, performance, fame, which she'd inherited from her family. He often joked that this had been the cause of her insomnia, that since childhood she'd been kept from sleep by fantasies of the great men who lay in store for her. Like her parents she wept whenever she heard applause; he'd never seen anything in his life like the Rosses' reaction to applause; it could be Lukas Foss's Bach Partitas heard on the portable radio they carried to the beach, E. E. Cummings reciting his poetry at the 92nd Street Y, rave reviews of some art show on Fifty-seventh Street, a crowd clapping for Eglevsky's window leap in *Le Spectre de La Rose*; at any of these occasions tears would rise to the Rosses' eyes at the sheer sound or symbol of applause, applause. Edmund compared their adulation of artistic success to servants' infatuation with the alcove secrets of royalty, deplored its effect on the woman whom he now thought of as his most admirable friend. Yet he remained awed by the intensity of Sophie's interest in all that he cared for, the spiritual attunement of a lover whose body foresaw his every need . . . Jewish women, soft-thighed, seldom athletic, dutiful daughters . . . their nutritional reverence for the man of culture . . . Waiting for their artist (dead or alive) with monumental solicitude . . . Muse with legs constantly opened for his enjoyment, breasts trembling over him like bread loaves warm from the oven.

At night he often dreamt of Claire's stingy, Anglican little athlete's body.

Earliest recollections of Sophie's family, 1946: Edmund and Mara, Claire and Babsie visit together for the first time at the Rosses' apartment on Central Park West. The two girls huddling to each other shoulder to shoulder. Babsie: "What a heavenly home you have Mrs. Ross!" "Thank you Mrs. Sanford." Mara: "Ees divine house" (and in an aside to Edmund, "Parvenu, but so sweet"). Camilla Ross: "I hear your husband does a gorgeous business downtown Mrs. Sanford!" Babsie: "Oh thank you Mrs. Ross!" Throughout this ill-matched gathering Edmund stares at Camilla and reflects that he's never seen anyone so extravagantly adorned outside the operatic stage. Her kind, shrewd face is surmounted by an Athena's helmet of brilliantly lacquered hair, bangles clang on her limbs like many cymbals, she reminds him of the finale from *Salome*.

Larry Ross is short, sleek, mustached, plump and lustrous as a bullet. One finger of his left hand is missing, the result of a scuffle with police in the 1920s, when he worked as a union organizer to support his

parents while occasionally attending City College. He
became an unsuccessful actor, left the stage to work as
press agent for a few Broadway and film stars. By the
time Edmund has come into Larry's life he's added
numerous musicians and playwrights to his clientele and
even some novelists who hire Larry to ensure handsomer
reception of their work. "Self-made man, former leather-
tanner, child of the New York ghetto," the *New York
Post* describes him; "Larry Ross has become one of the
country's busiest impresarios." His mustache and thinning hair are now groomed twice a week at home while
he roars out orders by phone to some minion agent in
Pasadena or purrs to directors of the Comédie-Française,
his library is upholstered floor to ceiling in the tartan of
the McPherson clan, there are signed photographs of
John Gielgud, Sir John Barbirolli, Ralph Richardson,
Leslie Howard, Sir Laurence Olivier on the Rosses'
piano, their immense collection of polished brass—
doorknobs, decanters, candlesticks, lamps, mortars and
pestles, wall sconces, beakers and salvers—demands an
auxiliary force of five domestics before every one of
their lavish parties to acquire its proper polish. Resting in
the Rosses' library or guest room during the frequent
bouts of migraine that follow his mother's death Edmund
has ample opportunity to observe the mogul's schedule.
At seven every morning Larry reaches for the telephone
from his bed, grizzled and swollen-eyed, not from
alcohol of which he never touches a drop but from that
sheer mania for fame which began to torture his face in
early middle age. He first calls London, Paris, Berlin, to
be sure he catches clients before their lunch hours and by
nine thirty works his way to New York trade, impatient
for that exquisitely harassing noontime when he can
track down artists in Europe, New York and California in
the span of a single hour.

During Larry's hunt in prelunch Europe, Camilla
brings him his velvet dressing gown, his *Variety*, his

breakfast tray; and several hours later, when he has moved to the other two phones set on the desk overlooking Central Park, she brings him his lunch. From twelve to two Larry is at the summit of predatory joy, interspersing Paris, New York and Los Angeles talents during his manicure, searching through Europe for elusive actors whom he wants on Broadway the next season ("Where is Barrault? What do you mean you can't find him, hunt him down, track him, catch him before the day's over!"). He persuades Paramount to buy the film script of a new novel for which Bette Davis would be perfect; he reassures nervous conductors: "Wait till you preem at the Met, Maestro; you've already got a double page all set to go in *Newsweek*!" In late afternoon, European trade asleep, New York about to fold, Larry Ross is left to savor California until 8:00 P.M., when he emerges from his bedroom triumphant from his day's work and nostalgic for still more. "Oh Camilla *Liebchen*, if we could only crack Japan I could be working until midnight! What do you think about going to the Orient to hook up to the Kabuki?" If they are not entertaining or scouting for talent at a new show that night they dine quietly in front of the television, discussing the day's successes; or they talk about Sophie, apple of their eye, that beloved child of their middle years upon whom they lavished the finest education for art and womanhood available in the United States.

"I'll give you a big party for your next exhibition, Edmund Richter; whom would you rather have at this party, twenty young actors, twenty young sculptors, twenty playwrights?"

"How's our wunderkind?" Larry Ross bellows when Edmund walks into his flat. "How's my Botticelli, how's my Holbein?"

"Monsieur Renoir, I've bought you a warm coat on sale at Russeks, we women know! A wonderful buy, my

pleasure! Your poor mother would have fainted if she'd
seen you in that thin jacket in midwinter!"

"Sophie, you don't realize what a phenomenon your
father was in his time; it's rare we understand parents
while they're still alive, that's the tragedy of it, they fall
together like pieces of a puzzle only when it's too late.
. . . Larry was a prodigy peculiar to our 1950s, one of
the first guys who wanted to create a cult of artists in a
country which had disdained most artists with Puritan
brutality . . . what was his favorite word Soph?"

"Magic, remember Eddem?"

"Exactly. He collected artists' personalities the way
other moguls used to collect horses, racing cars, Queen
Anne highboys, but for more sacramental reasons, the
artist's presence was his talisman, his ride on the silver
horse, his only infection of immortality. . . ."

From some celebrities—mayors of growing cities
searching for an orchestra—Larry Ross made money.
From others—painters, writers, musicians—he was
happy to only make transcendence. Even light at the
Rosses' lavish parties, provided exclusively by the glow
of some sixty candles, has the aura fitting to an atmosphere of worship. Candlelight, much muted candlelight, and the throaty, secretive whispers Larry has
coached his wife and daughter to assume in the presence
of genius. One cannot stress enough the gracious pious
hush, the liturgical reverence, of Camilla's and Sophie's
voices when they introduce guests to Larry's collected
talent: "Leonid Berman, over there by the piano, is the
most exciting person to come to ballet design since Bakst
. . . Irwin Shaw, by the window talking to Gertie
Lawrence, may be the closest thing to Hemingway in our
decade. . . ." Groomed in Larry's art of creative intro-
ductions, how adroitly the hostesses pilot conductors
towards up-and-coming baritones, William Faulkner towards movie tycoons looking for a Great Writer's script!

In these rooms resplendent with bordello textures and churchly lights, the fifteen-year-old Sophie had learned to pass canapés with such poise that the director of the St. Louis Symphony might readily return another time to stare at her plunging young breasts and be snared into a contract with the Detroit Symphony. Sophie, aged sixteen, maneuvering the caviar about the room: "Mr. Williams, *The Glass Menagerie* is the most transcendent *pièce de théâtre* I've ever seen!" "Mr. Bernstein, I do think the largo movement of Mahler's Seventh gains unequaled beauty in your hands!" Sophie of the early breasts and golden eyes, how skillfully she'd been trained at the novel glory of seducing artists! And all around her Moët et Chandon pouring, salmon gleaming in their platters of polished brass, Lauritz Melchior and Ava Gardner singing a duet beside a piano strummed by Gian Carlo Menotti, Shirley Booth and Salvador Dali hovering over the caviar, Lucrezia Bori and Truman Capote playing backgammon at a neighboring table, a clipping from last week's *Daily News* prominently displayed next to a brass tankard saying Talent Magnates Larry and Camilla Ross Entertain Lawrence Tibbett and Irwin Shaw in Their Plush CPW Home, Larry bellowing "I'll get you from the Jay Thorpe level of the stage to Bergdorf's!" Camilla Ross emerald-lidded graciously smiling in a mountainous gown of purple brocade whispering "You must return next Thursday, we're having Sir Wildestein, one of England's most gorgeous patrons of theater, and the German ambassador . . ." (a knowing pause) ". . . to the UN."

Editors of *Life* magazine seduced into writing a feature story on the new conductor of the Chicago Symphony, authors achieving a desired transition from Harper's to Random House at the flick of a Larry Ross introduction.

"Head of Philip Morris Corporation, meet the dancing wonder of the City Center Ballet and wait till this little genius hits Kentucky to preem in your auditorium!"

"Publisher of the *Los Angeles Times*, meet the most magic tenor of the San Francisco Opera!"

"Director of the St. Louis Museum, I want you to meet the most promising young painter in America! Just look at that masterpiece by the window, Maestro; couldn't you just reach out and eat that fruit it's so real? . . ."

The artist Edmund's work was most often compared to was Chardin. Pellucid tonalities, lyrically precise rendering, tight lustrous textures. Edmund enjoyed a mastery of the most ancient archaic recipes of the painter's trade; he found the modern world odious for its capitulation to immediacy, facility. He painted on wooden panels of five plies of maple to retain the full luminosity of old masters' gesso techniques. He mixed his own grounds. He began by steeping two and three-quarters ounces of rabbit or hare's skin glue in a quart of cold water; the glue was soaked overnight and turned an opaque greenish-gray as it swelled to three times its volume. It had to be slowly heated in a double boiler; he cooked his potions in the morning when Sophie went to work to spare her the acrid smell, though she claimed it was pleasant; he was ever amused and touched by her accommodations. The glue was poured into a pot containing the chalk or whiting, stirred continually for an hour, strained through several layers of cheesecloth. After brushing the mixture onto his panels Edmund completed the smooth ivory perfection of his painting ground by rubbing it down with several different grades of sandpaper. He used imprimaturas of pale Venetian red mixed with egg yolk, rendered his values in umber and white before applying any further color. His portraits of the ebullient Sophie were brooding, imposing, reflective. "Richter's paintings achieve their classic character by their virtuosity of execution and an emotional detachment remarkable in an artist of so young an age. . . ."

* * *

Sophie could not run their ménage without bringing home six bottles of wine at a time, five pounds of peaches, three armfuls of flowers. ("Oh those zinnias against your purple cape, just sit the way you are Soph, don't move, don't move. . . .")

Her college teachers had claimed that she was destined for one of the most brilliant careers of her generation of women "if she could only focus at considerably greater length on any one of her extraordinarily varied fields of interest."

She swooped with equal appetite upon the latest tidbits of quantum physics, jazz history, Marxist analysis, social biology; her weight had as much variety as her information, her mercurial body waned by scores of pounds as she dove into another week-long fast of grapefruit or papaya. On other days when she sat cross-legged on the floor gorging on her favorite crème brûlée, Edmund saw in her the lustful conniving impulsive child he cherished more than any of her personae, the fat greedy kid who needed to savor down to the last lick every delectable tidbit of opera, friendship, literature, ballet, anthropology, swimming fests, haute cuisine. She was phenomenally industrious; Edmund insisted they share their rent and refuse Larry's magnanimous offers of support; though none of her jobs lasted for more than a few months she'd accepted Edmund's decision that she must "emancipate" herself from her parents. She taught modern dance at a trade school in the Bronx. She previewed shows for a TV magazine. She volunteered at the Upper West Side Democratic Club. She decided she might have a flair for fashion and became a lingerie buyer at Bonwit's. She rebelled against the decadence of that and worked at a welfare center in Harlem. She'd been the star of Ethel Walker's swimming team, she swam fifty laps of an Olympic-sized indoor pool daily to stay in shape. When she'd saved enough of her earnings to stop working for a few months she studied African dancing with Katherine Dunham. "Oh God, Soph, what next," Edmund moaned as she returned from each novel foray with a torrent of praise about its possibilities. "But E.R. you've known since the age of five you wanted to be an artist, the rest of us have to find ourselves. . . ." She took recorder lessons for some weeks and their tiny rooms whined with the flattened notes of "Greensleeves." She took acting lessons and their rooms stirred with the muffled, groping sounds of Method exercises. ("You are a blind girl. Palpate the face of a Greek youth . . . of Cyrano de Bergerac . . . of a baby . . . of a sleeping stranger . . . of your father . . .") One day she rode uptown on the subway and got a job as a reporter with the *Amsterdam News*.

"Now that finally is a *great* idea; you're a born journalist, Soph, you've got a mind for news like no one else."

She had the obsession of all modern youth, she wanted him to remember her as his life's greatest lover. Candlelight, fresh flowers, Coquilles St. Jacques, Pouilly-Fuissé, the art books she collected for him on the coffee table, the wide deep bed, her Tiffany glass shimmering like harem silks, Brahms playing softly in the background, the rituals of undressing, shall I dim the lamp sweetheart, would you rather in the dark . . . She was puzzled by the total readiness of his sexuality and of his simultaneous independence from it; her touch stirred him with ravishing instantaneity, he pounced upon her with such tenderness that she often thought she'd achieved the heat and beauty of ideal passion. But over the months she realized that the impulse had to come from her and her alone, otherwise he'd go to sleep, his eyes staring at the ceiling until they closed. She continued her tactics of discretion, diplomacy: he could have been trying to allay his recent sorrow, dreaming of his own future glory, thinking of the canvas he wished to prepare for the next day, having an occasional thought about Claire, she never asked. Her sexuality was industrious, intense, she studied the newest manuals meticulously to memorize directives for novel positions and sensations, she rehearsed her sensuality like a summa-cum student cramming for exams, she turned and twisted on her artist, alternating largo with moderato vivace as she thrust down upon him at a fabulous variety of angles, riding astride his pensive body like a jockey trying to whip up a steed. She purchased books on erotic Indian temple sculpture, mounted Edmund upon a corner of the bed and moved her haunches fervently upon his as she made him sit up with her legs locked about his waist. She put her mouth to him and circled her tongue languidly about the tip of his sex, one of her most perfect moments was to hear him comment on her artistry, yet one morning she woke up crying. "You never grab me in the middle of the night," she wept, "how can you love me if you don't *wake* me sometimes?"

In the winter of 1953 Edmund finished his master's thesis, "The Concept of Artistic Genius from the Renaissance to Our Time."

The artist is the man viewed as most dangerous to Plato's Republic precisely because he partakes of so much Godliness, because his poetic gifts are the result of divine possession and the making of his painted forms so arrogantly imitative of the Creator's own work. . . .

World's most cursed and most blessed, hospital case and prophet, tippler of absinthe and victim of nineteenth-century alienation, he will finally be banished, via the route of Romanticism, to the exile of Bohemia, Tahiti or hashish. Hooligan and seer, heretic inebriate and scapegoat for our sins, he will

continue to be held as the complex object of our
derision, envy, love. . . .

Most reviews of Edmund Richter's exhibition of November 1954 praised his "masterful control of naturalistic drawing," his "formidable skill for working with veiled transparencies of color." "In an age when the slapdash sham of nonobjectivism seems to be swamping the New York art world, Richter offers a breathtaking reaffirmation of the realistic tradition. . . ." A few periodicals were less favorable. In an issue that featured a monumental Franz Kline abstraction on its cover *ARTnews* admitted to Richter's virtuosity but dismissed his work as "complaisant oils depicting strong and pretty women in a nostalgically realistic style that could have been achieved anytime in the past one hundred years."

Edmund reacted very poorly to all criticism. Sophie referred to this as his tragic flaw. "They're beginning to want scandal and aimless ferocity, precipitate violence instead of the freedom of discipline! If that's the direction it's all taking I'm pulling out!"

There were always those parties for him at the Rosses. Sophie still cringed whenever he criticized her family. "Wasn't that the niftiest do last night, don't you think Larry Tibbett is sure to buy that big still life of yours?"

"Listen, Soph, one more mention of those artist-gobbling talent mongers I meet at your family's and I'll puke. If I have to sit through one more of those evenings I'm going to pull my pants down in the middle of the evening and play 'Jingle Bells' on your piano with my . . ."

She was an obedient dutiful daughter; he'd singled that out as *her* tragic flaw; she'd avoid his eyes for hours.

"You're the most magnificent model any artist's ever had," he'd say to console her. To placate her he drew her climbing out of a bath and draping herself in towels, as in Degas's great pastels. He often muttered as he drew, it was a habit of his, he sometimes murmured French cynicisms which confounded her. "Damn this business of art, Soph; in all that's useless one must be divine or cease altogether. . . ." When she didn't understand his meaning she gave him one of those smiles that made all other women's smiles pale in comparison; she had spectacular teeth, a little prominent but small and finely modeled, with a cleavage between the two front ones which she adored to hear him say was a traditional mark of great sensuality. He admired the firm ampleness of her flesh, its Rubenesque paleness, her patience. Patience! How often he'd felt her eyes upon his throughout the night (pale, the color of lightning) like the eyes of small hungry animals piercing the darkness one sees in drought-stricken country.

"How's my Botticelli and my daughter his magic model? Have I gotten you tickets to the swellest shows this week!"

Edmund ruefully mused that a season with Sophie was not unlike a season with Mara, minus the penury: Cossack choruses one night, Habima Players from Tel Aviv the next, Gieseking at Carnegie Hall, Japanese puppets, the Vienna Boys' Choir, she cried at them all when she heard the applause.

Once in a while after a cultural sortie Sophie liked to go to Larue's, to the Stork, "Just to see who's new and exciting there."

> *Sambas, rumbas:*
> *If you're romantic senor*
> *then you will surely adore*
> *Argentiiiiiiina (tsk tsk tsk tsk tsk tsk tsk)*
> *I'll bet an old castanet*
> *that you'll never forget*
> *Argentiii-iiina*

* * *

> *When the moon hits your eye*
> *   like a big pizza pie*
> *That's amooo-oooooooré*
> *When the stars make you drool*   .
> *   just like pasta fazool*
> *That's amoooooooooooré*

Journal American, January 2, 1955—Sophie Ross, beauteous strawberry-blond daughter of talent magnate Larry Ross, was sighted at the Maisonnette the other night with art-world wiz-kid Ed Richter, and rumors that they'll soon say their I do's are burning the grapevine to a crisp. . . . Sophie's celeb-hunter dad played a role in podium-bender Leonard Bernstein's decision to sign up for another season at the Phil. . . .

Camilla Ross loved to take "the children" with her on her brief vacations in the sun.

Haiti in 1955 . . . Patou's Joy ("The Costliest Perfume in the World") emanating from the women's pink tweeds as Edmund followed them out of the plane towards Oloffson's limousine . . . Sophie reclining by the pool, ogled by all men in sight, displaying her majestic milky flesh, the luxuriance of her underarms . . . Edmund sunning himself between the two women, wondering what he would do with himself the following year.

Lying beside Sophie at nights Edmund often tried to recall those black days after his mother's death when he couldn't even remember the pet name of that other beloved young woman who'd never left his side. What are those inanimate objects after which wealthy Gentiles call their daughters, he'd kept muttering during his illness, Muffin, Fiddle . . . Fern . . . Brook . . . what's the name of those objects one finds in a brook?

A curious thing had happened in the months of 1954. Edmund began to draw and paint multiples of Sophie. He could not invent any more poses for her. He sensed he had explored and exhausted the total entity of that patient malleable body. He was now painting her repeatedly in the same identical pose, arm under head, knees chastely drawn up, eyes not cast down on a book anymore but staring out of the canvas with a haunted, intelligent gaze. He simply did the same painting over and over and over again, varying only the tonality of the undercoat—raw umber, terre verte, sienna, red ocher, grisaille. During the week, when she was out working, he used the same principle of repetition in his still lifes. He painted precisely similar arrangements of vase, fruit, tablecloth in multiples of four, eight, sixteen, thirty-two canvases.

February 1st, 1955

Jeff old boy,

Happy New Year and how are you? I hope your Oxonian studies are all you'd expected them to be; the first thing I'll do when I have the courage to travel alone again is to visit the Ashmolean down the street from you, three Brueghels of unsurpassed beauty right there. . . . I've had a super year selling out two shows and indulging in the prehensile hospitality of the Ross clan. Listen, that talent-gobbling world of the Big Apple is getting to be more exhausting than ever. Consumption of artists a sacrament of success, like fatness for tribal chieftains. Will you eat your artist now or shall I wrap him for you? I've been consumed as artist à la Crème, sautéed with walnuts, boiled and fried (a recipe I frequently have to impose on myself in order to survive). Sophie's sweet as hell and very sexy, whatever that means. I feel like a bejeweled stud, like one of those bulls the Egyptians deified and embalmed near the pyramids of Gîza. . . .

So that's how *I* am. It's seldom that I write you, of course, without inquiring about Miss Elusivity. I received no more than one brief card last year. It's so hard to know how she is, with Babsie and Plinker in Arizona. I hear that Sealark is rented for a three-year term what with Babsie so ill and that she's feebler than usual. *News* please! Shall we ever see our Paradiso again? Listen lifesaver, stay well and do know that there's always a daybed in our living room for you; we've moved three blocks east to Charles Street, with a large studio skylight this time, quite out of Puccini. . . .

Best always, etc.   Edm.

At times Edmund and Sophie looked at slides of Nantucket together: Jeff in his Harvard-crew shirt, coach's whistle about his neck, masterminding a volleyball game at Sealark. Babsie with a spray of rosemary and zinnias in hand, looking surprised. Eighteen-year-old Pebble embracing her father as he hovers over his vegetable garden, her face nestled in his shoulder. Once Edmund caught Sophie staring at the picture of Claire with an expression of fascination, passion, anger, things so complex he felt too weary to decipher them.

Sixth Avenue and Tenth Street in the late evening when Edmund increasingly walked out for a few hours to be alone: whistling of cabs, garrulous voices from the Cedar Bar, brushes and canvases stacked up in the window of an artist supplies' store as in an ossuary. One night he started his first postcard to Claire in almost three years while leaning against a streetlamp. He addressed it Angelface, tore it up, threw it into the trash basket in front of the Women's House of Detention.

He often feared that he forced Sophie to pose as much as he did to allay her devouring solicitude, to halt her invasion of him. So he started their weekend poses early in the morning, made her sit until the moment they had to get dressed for the opera or the Habima Players. When would this beauty exchange the happiness she knew with him for some prolific maternity? He would go to visit her, a decade hence, in some vintage New England mansion. There'd be a plethora of concerts, lectures, aproned maids, savvy young Finnish nannies for her children, first editions, poets in residence, pedigreed Weimaraners, a kind and philanthropic Wall Street husband hovering admiringly in the background. Increasingly voluptuous of body, she would stand over Edmund at the poolside, calling out the year's purchases and accomplishments, her chairmanship of the Connecticut Democratic Party Committee, her rescue of three community theaters. He would lie in the sun and softly whisper, "You plague me with your abundance, you plague me with . . ."

Her smell of rose water and moist animal fur. Her nimble loving hands repairing his shirts, massaging his neck, whipping up delicate mousses in their little kitchen.

At times he adored her.

The threat of her flesh and of his growing anguish on winter weekend afternoons, when the waning light of early dusk forced him to stop painting at four o'clock . . . listening then to Mozart or just talking, his head on her lap, pleading that his eyes were too strained to do anything else . . . he'd seldom known anything as remarkable as her genius for listening; like many men's sisters she was the central anchor of his life and its most perfect constancy; how often he wished that she could have been his sister . . . but such a fantasy would have been offensive to her, totally beyond her understanding . . . so he talked about his fears of being an artist behind his time, perhaps he was a born teacher like they said Jeff was. . . . "No, never, never!" she cried at such prospects and he realized he was threatening something as sacred to her as her faith in great passions. . . .

Early in the spring of 1955 he purchased a Siamese cat. He called it Vico.

"If only I could start everything all over again," Edmund said to himself, aged twenty-four.

During that last year with Sophie, Edmund developed a habit of sleeping away his moments of acute distress. Sleep was his refuge, his haven, his exile from all decisions. Living with this admirable woman plagued with insomnia he could go to bed at midnight and sleep until two o'clock of the following afternoon, paint for a few hours, go to bed and sleep again until ten o'clock the next morning.

Upon his last show he was interviewed by *Newsweek* and several other periodicals. He enjoyed saying things like "Great painting nourishes *the soul*." Others of his answers were cryptic, ornery, tended to amuse reporters. "You're presently the boy wonder of the New York art world, but don't you fear you might be painting against the tide of fashion?" "The artist's business is with eternity, not costume."

London
Ash Wednesday, 1955

Sophie darling . . . how joyful to put your dear name down on paper again. . . . I just finished writing Plinker and Babsie and telling them how profoundly I'm beginning to miss the States after this almost three years' absence. . . . It's been very very hard as you and Eddem predicted studying full time while working, and there have been all kinds of essential political activities taking up my time. . . . Last December for instance I went on a 200-mile Ban the Bomb march from London to Nottingham, the spirit of the crowds was so beautiful, imagine one thousand persons determined to march together that distance, and Sir Bertrand came to address us as we started from the London Mall. . . . However I caught a frightful pneumonia and was laid up for almost three months with it, which is why I failed to send you proper season's greetings.

. . . I might have been in very bad shape if Jeff hadn't come to the rescue with a decent doctor, I was so far gone that they kept me in hospital for weeks where I got all kinds of lectures about the dangers of vegetarianism etc. . . . There was that first week when Jeff said it was really hit or miss. . . . Well anyhow don't worry it's all over, it sounds as if you and Eddem are having a celestial time together, I'm presently practicing Schumann but each time I hear Myra Hess play I realize it's utterly hopeless for me to aspire to the art! A big hug to you and our rabbit love and tell him I'll write him myself very soon. . . .

The quality of Sophie's flesh: on the best days Rubenesque in its sumptuous whiteness, like milk or whey, utterly luminous . . . on other days her flesh seemed to take on the hues of fruit gone too ripe, like Renoir's late nudes, which he had come to detest.

Suddenly at 5:00 A.M. on a spring morning in 1955, it was a Saturday, he ran out of their flat and ran all the way to Fourteenth Street and then up to Pennsylvania Station; he sat down in the first train he saw without having the slightest notion of where it was going, it took him all the way to Harrisburg, Pennsylvania, where there was nothing to do but take a guided tour of the Hershey chocolate factory, he was the only adult not accompanied by a child, it was just a week before Easter and acres of liquid chocolate were being poured into molds of rabbit and egg shapes, he stood over the ocean of brown ooze and wept because he was reminded of Mara's extravagant Easter feasts. ("Every man is born," she used to say, "but outside of Him who else had the imagination to rise again?") He wept thinking of the eggs she'd painted in such delicate silken hues, of the Russian princes sitting over their pascha and koulitch and swallowing small teaspoons of raspberry jam while sipping tea from tall glasses . . .

When he returned the next day Sophie was in bed reading, smiling, bravely pretending she hadn't cried, cheek resting against her childhood fetish.

The following morning he was finally able to write a postcard:

> New York City
> April 4th, 1955

Sweetest Claire!

Do you realize what a horror show it would be if you didn't take care of yourself and got to the Harp Farm ahead of schedule, can't you just see the hundreds of jerks who would come to your funeral, your great-uncles from Detroit and all your lousy reactionary Republican relatives converging on Sealark, the whole goddamn moronic mob of them Cousin April with her Locust Valley lockjaw saying "yes dearie, it's so nice to see you dearie," and don't tell me that scene would be nifty, kind of neat, delish, swell, keen or crackerjack, it would be strictly lousy, nothing but a floppola. . . . Oh Angelface write me which boat or plane you're taking. . . . .

viii

Sealark's summer tenants obligingly vacated the house a week early for Claire's late summer wedding, which remained a very small and private affair because of her mother's death that spring.

Standing at the front door upon arriving, Edmund watches Plinker hovering at the gate of the abandoned garden. He has not seen him in over three years, since the weeks after Mara's funeral. Plinker wears heavy spectacles. He has just turned sixty-five. His eyesight is said to have been failing. His face has turned an unhealthily yellow hue that could be the combined legacy of age and strong sun. He stares at the abandoned, weed-filled patch where he used to instruct young ones in the profitable growing of lettuces and zinnias, he looms tall and scowling at the garden gate, cane in hand, as if planning the reconquest of his domain. Edmund starts to walk toward his friend. It takes Plinker a while to recognize him. He puts on another pair of spectacles as Edmund approaches him and the gesture is as grand and lonely as that of a sea captain raising his binoculars to identify a distant vessel. He's recognized Edmund, he hobbles majestically towards him, arms outstretched, half yelling, half growling his ancient jibes and greet-ings. Passionately fond of young Europeans! Does Ed-dem remember all the times he'd been sick on his sailboats? Remember that time when he got poor Babsie so upset during the Game? Remember that afternoon Peb disappeared in the dunes and they ended up searching for Eddem too in the fire truck?

Oh does Edmund ever remember.

Well, what else could you have done but let that garden go to weed? What would have been the use of keeping Sealark open with poor Babsie so ill and all the lovely young people grown, and Claire away on one of her crazy searches in England? Thank God, at least that was over, Jeff had brought her safely out of it, that's one consolation Plinker has had since Babsie's death; now Plinker could finally plan his next few years of retirement; they'd rent Sealark for another few summers and he'd go back to Arizona—splendid golf club out there, a lot of fellows of his own kind, knockout place for the glums. And in a few years when the Howells returned from England he could move back to New York, live at the Harvard Club in winter and help reopen Sealark in summer; by that time there might be one or two little Howells to help out with, right? There'd be a new generation to enjoy good summer fun, a lot more beach picnics and clambakes . . .

In his excitement Paul Sanford switches two pairs of spectacles on and off his nose with great speed.

. . . but he mustn't go on about himself like that, how is dear Edmo, is he happy, we've all got to live somewhere, there's breakfast and dinner and so on, is he taking proper care of his digestion now that he's in some ghastly artist's flat? Is he making friends in his new life, always very important to pick the proper friends at his age. . . .

"I wish you were my father," Edmund says.

Paul Sanford takes his long-distance spectacles off slowly and puts on the other pair, staring at Edmund with curiosity. Edmund turns around abruptly and walks back to the house.

Plinker looming at the altar, crying as he gives his daughter away.

Edmund has not seen Claire either since he accompanied her to the *Queen Elizabeth* three years ago. She has not grown any thinner, thank God, and her body is hued that pale tint of honey from her few days' stay at Sealark. Her hair is longer and very lank, surprisingly unkempt for this occasion. Her superb face is as untainted by makeup as when she was fifteen. Even on this day she seems to have given no thought to her appearance.

"Oh rabbit love I've been happy enough in London but do I really have enough talent for the piano to make a career of it? . . . And besides with the world the way it is there are so many other things to be done. . . ."

"Jeff has a small comfortable post teaching at a boys' school in Wiltshire, two hours from London; he's always loved the country life. . . ."

Jeff has tenacity, oh boy does he. Like Sophie.

They stand at the reception line.

Claire wears her grandmother's wedding dress. Sophie, maid of honor, wears a gossamer number shot through with blue-and-green iridescence, like a pheasant's plumage. She lifts her arm to adjust Claire's wedding veil, the two women clutching at each other in a long embrace, the flesh of Sophie's underarms pale as alabaster.

Claire's breath on his cheek as he kisses her: like that of a child being put to bed. "Good luck, cookie," Edmund says. She smiles.

Cincinnati, Atlanta, Boston, Philadelphia, Baltimore, each wedding gift shines roundly on a long table, objects she'd rebelled against since childhood, Spode, lace tablecloths, Tiffany silver.

Edmund, champagne in hand, looking at Nantucket Sound: Would they procreate, could she ever grow large with Jeff's child?

April to Edmund, wry little smile: "What a dull

wedding, dearie, this place is dismal with poor Babsie gone."

Sophie: "She's done the only thing Plinker wanted her to do, marrying Jeff."

Someone tinkled at the piano, Plinker perhaps, a bit of Cole Porter. As the piece ended, Edmund saw Claire rise and clap, smiling adoringly at her father, and again there was something rigid, Teutonically obedient about her frail little torso, like that of a toy doll spinning under a little glass dome. She scared him anew then, with her dual quality of obedience and rebellion.

How splendid Jeff looked as they cut the cake! His head had an air of elevation which fairly added to his stature. Shimmering with blue and whiteness, he looked like those perfect young American fathers at the head of the Thanksgiving table whom Edmund used to admire on *Saturday Evening Post* covers in his childhood. Perennial coach, eternal husband, docile consumer of all that's sold to us as happiness. . . . Claire, on the other hand, did not fit in. She was dreaming, staring out to sea as she had when Edmund found her hiding in the dunes of their adolescence, steeped in some communion with God knew what. "We're cutting the cake, Claire," Jeff said. And took her wrist and made her grasp the knife and strike it into the heart of the pearly white mound. He smiled and put his mouth to Claire's cheek. She waved her hand at the camera. There was a look of triumph on Jeff's face which Edmund decided had something brutal about it. He hated him. He admired him. He wanted to kill him.

Edmund took another drink and walked alone to the terrace. Gossamer boats speeding in the harbor like insects skimming a pond, thudding of tennis rackets on the court next door; he hadn't played tennis since that Monday morning when he'd beaten Claire three years ago, he might never play again, he might get successful and play constantly, he might explore the North Pole,

learn Sanskrit and Hebrew, it was time to change a life.
. . . He stripped off his clothes and dove into the bay.
He swam furiously towards the gold-and-black hull of a
yacht still called *The Churchill* moored several hundred
yards out at sea. That Muse with whom he'd hoped since
childhood to share the struggles of an artist's life . . .
He was terrified by the helplessness of his desire and of
his rage, by the threat of capitulations still to come. I am
now obliged to deal with certain unsufferable certainties.
Under my masks there's little guile, every betrayal is a
little death, I fall upon the thorns of life I bleed, I take a
short vacation from pain and have two years of perfect
orgasms and fall again on the same thorns, will there be
nothing between birth and darkness but a mire of
imperfections?

"Goddamn tribe!" he yelled as he swam out into the
harbor. "The fucking goddamn tribe has her by the
throat!" But this time the water was as flat and calm as
that of a child's tub and no one needed to swim out after
him. They just went about the business of finishing that
rather dull wedding.

Buffalo, New York
September 17th, 1955

My darling Sophie,
    You've been my beacon, my life, my survival.
You've been my manna and my daily bread, the
miraculous substance that saved me in my time of
starvation. And if I left during your sleep it's
because I'm too much of a coward to do it any other
way, because I was in a stage of despair and need
which transcends any rhetoric of love. I slipped out
of our haven somewhat the way I left last spring,
went to Penn Station and took the first train I saw
without even knowing where it went. Roulette, my
little dove, roulette, there's much of the Russian
gambler left in me . . . this time I took a few

belongings, college papers and dear Vico, and we ended up in this town which I've always associated with the vulgarity of honeymoons in general and of Niagara Falls in particular. Tomorrow I take another train to San Francisco and Berkeley, where I'll start a doctorate in art history as soon as they'll let me. I'm sorry if I haven't prepared you better for this, but you might have guessed by now that I was being tortured by needs vastly at odds with the domestic bliss you so artfully brought me. . . . I may be rationalizing my brusque departure by thinking it was as essential to you as it was to me. . . . There's much growth to come to you and I was always stifling it beyond forbearance, only talking about my own goddamn needs and my uniqueness; you've got to concentrate mightily on yourself after three years spent with a virtuoso of narcissism . . . I'll write soon, I'll write often, oh I know I have a lifetime of explaining to do. . . .

Ever your own   Ed.

Berkeley, California
October 1st

Sweet Sofka,

Here I am holed up in a bleak student room after a long day of washing dishes at the local Howard Johnson's, still on pins and needles waiting to hear about the doctoral program and desperately needing to talk to you . . . having explained why I left the sweetest refuge ever offered me I must tell you why I also had to leave the vocation I cherish as much as life—i.e., why I decided to cease painting.

I'm enough of a traditionalist to believe that the function of religion and of art is to help transcend the pains of life and make bearable the cruelty and senselessness of nature, that the task of the artist is to infect others with his emotions towards reality. And that this function can only be fulfilled by noble, finished, serene works rather than by the increasingly tortured fragments presently dragging the viewer into the maelstrom of our suffering.

But these may be outdated reactionary ideals, Sofka, it's possible that the creation of beauty has become obsolete, that the harmonically complete masterpiece is irrelevant to the fluid mayhem of the contemporary world. . . . Certain things are no longer possible as the devil said to Dr. Faustus. And when I look at the oeuvres of Messrs. de Kooning, Pollock, Kline now thriving on 57th Street I predict that their raw primal violence and celebration of the void will prevail, we're domesticating the outrageous, we've reentered one of those periodic cycles of rebarbarization that recur through history and America's giving the world a dose of barbarism socko this time. . . . I forecast about twenty years of its reign.

Yet you see Soph I hope that my kind of painting may resurface in a few decades, I refuse to indulge in the luxury of alienation, I believe that an art of equilibrium and celebration will recur and I'll wait my turn . . . meanwhile I prefer to make a masterpiece out of my own life, dedicate it to teaching the kind of art I'd have created in a saner time.

This is the only way I can think of surviving in this marvelous country which leaves the artist utterly free to influence absolutely no one.

A creature more superb than you will never again come into my ken Sofka; you've been the most constant, steadfast component my quarter of a century of life. . . .

Berkeley
November 15th

Sofka: I got into the doctoral program that begins
next February! And they'll even give me a teaching
assistantship which can keep some cash flowing in.
. . . I forgot to tell you that in order to get a totally
fresh start I gave away most of the lucre I'd earned
from those shows to worthy causes favored by two
of my disappeared Muses—the War Resisters
League and the Tolstoi Foundation. . . .

Berkeley
December 19th

Merry Xmas, my sweet love, I think of you every
day. No, I don't expect any news of you yet, I know
I've been a shit; I also know that time will heal all
present pain. I keep thinking of the plenitude I
abandoned when I left you; I also think of how
things would have developed if we'd followed the
luxuriant course of the past years. I remain content
with my decision because of the glum predictability
such a life would bring: I would have ridden the surf
for a few years in that talent-devouring cafeteria of
your father's which contaminates rather than alle-
viates the artist's solitude . . . we would have led
an "interesting life," which is the ideal of many
idiots. . . . Irwin Shaw, Ray Bolger, Oscar Ham-
merstein and whatever brilliant professors you pick
up in your varied courses of study would have
turned up at our first child's baptism . . . within a
few years I'd be filled with the jaded singsong of an
artist radically out of step with his time. . . . I see
myself tragically consuming yogurt to keep ulcers

at bay after six hours of teaching basic drawing in some dreary Middle Western college. . . .

Now for a few questions I must ask about *you*, whose destiny is as precious to me as mine. Have you ceased dedicating your life to a member of the male sex? Are you being less generous, more self-centered with your admirable energies? Have you quit thinking that fucking artists is going to lead you to a higher state of reincarnation? All these conditions must be met my darling if you're going to find the happiness you deserve. There are too many rich little Jewish girls around whose greatest dream is to marry an artist when they grow up and when they're twenty-one their daddy buys them the largest toy artist at F.A.O. Schwartz, a six-foot-two artist with real vinyl teeth, real plastic hair and a genuine corduroy suit; every morning the little heiress winds up her toy with a big key that fits to the small of his back and says have a good day dear, off to your studio now . . . unfortunately I've felt just like such a toy in the past year; I'll find you easier to live with when you start fulfilling some of your own considerable talents sweetheart; you happed on a half-Jewish nomad who's got too much rage in his heart to afford being a retail item in your dad's booming celeb factory.

Leaving you I feel like an adolescent who suddenly, painfully must abstain from the magic of his mother's touch, must sever himself from this source of nurturing to achieve his true strength and avoid the scarring of dependence. . . .

More very soon my darling, I'll be watching for your syndicated by-line in the *Daily News*!

Moderato, with sincerity
Edm.

Berkeley
January 4th, 1956

Beloved Sofia Larionovna,

I miss you as desperately as ever; I feel I owe you a still clearer reading of why I had to flee the dreadful power of your family's protection.

I'll start with the following incident: It was the fourth anniversary of Mara's death last week, and suffering a deeper solitude than I've ever known, determined to suffer through it stoically, I went to Mass for the first time in many years and watched people indulging in the most archaic, ancient desire of mankind, which is to eat the God.

I suddenly grasped, with unprecedented clarity, the power of our unending desire to devour the Godhead and its symbols. How did tragedy and all other art arise? Out of religious sacrifice, out of the universal need to both placate and consume that which is most sacred and to appropriate part of its power. And I understood that it is the artist's risk, precisely because he has a trace of the divine in him, to be in some way destroyed by society.

Take it from there; what happens in a society as profoundly desacralized as ours! It has nothing godly to consume anymore *except* the artist! Oh Sofka will the world ever resolve its curious ambivalence of love, envy, appetite, hatred for us! What duplicitous ways you've found to destroy us, either by letting us starve (as we did in our noble nineteenth-century garrets) or else by devouring us (as you presently threaten to do).

Well I'll tell you kiddo, I'd rather starve than be eaten, anytime!

What's most terrifying of all is our willingness to sacrifice ourselves for you to resolve your ambivalence, to purge you of your hatred and earn your exclusive affection and esteem. Oh, we'll do anything to forge your love, in life and in death, we'll destroy ourselves in drugs like Verlaine, we'll drown ourselves in booze like Scott Fitzgerald and Dylan Thomas, we'll do anything to satisfy the myths you create for us. . . .

And you wait and see sweetheart it's going to get worse and worse with your dad's spectaculars glamorizing our destruction, we'll alternate being buffoons and media martyrs, Truman Capote will pull his pants down and piss right on television, Irwin Shaw will buy a fistfight with Larry Rivers on the Jack Paar show; by the 1980s the expiatory devouring act will be brought directly into your living room, ladies and gentlemen; artists will commit suicide right on the idiot box to keep your love.

Hoc est enim Corpus meum right on the telly kiddo.

Oh Soph dear Soph I left this racket just in time!

To return to what I wrote you a few months ago:

I hope that my turn will come again; that we shall once more be capable of celebrating the beauty of the created world; and also of preserving our sanity by holding society at bay as a worthy adversary instead of capitulating to its greed.

Until that day I'm using the most expedient recipe yet found for the artist in our times: "Exile. Silence. Cunning."

Part Two

The theme was richness over time.
It is a difficult story and the wise never
choose it . . .

ROBERT HAAS,
AGAINST BOTTICELLI

ix

Upon arriving at Kiev from Georgia, Edmund, Sophie and Claire are taken to see the statue of Prince Vladimir, founder of Russia's oldest city. His statue stands among tall beeches at the site where he once offered Slavs the choice between Christian baptism and death by drowning. At least that is the way Evgeny tells it. Below Saint Vladimir, the Dnieper flows the color of flawed amber, russet beeches lean towards it like penitents from shoals of dirty sand; nothing special here in the way of bathing, Sophie comments, let's not even try it in this city. As they ride to the center of town Irina points to an eighty-nine-room palace built in three days to comply with the whims of the second-to-last czarina, who never set foot in it, after all. Eighty-nine rooms never used, all that money, labor at the expense of the Russian people! A few members of the Intourist group ask if they can visit Babi Yar, burial place of over a hundred thousand persons killed by German occupation forces. Evgeny stands mute at the request, swatting flies with his copy of a folded *Pravda*. Don't even think of it, Irina says, that's over an hour from Kiev, farther than any cab accepts to go, so . . . visit impossible. But Edmund gets a few taxis on his own. And the Americans get to Babi Yar with no problem, seeing it is in the center of the town, ten minutes from the hotel.

At Babi Yar a bronze monument now dominates a majestic ravine in which the victims lie buried. Arthur Zabar takes over as guide: During their occupation of Kiev, Nazis massacred some eighty thousand Jews here and went on to exterminate Ukrainian and Russian resisters. But the site was ignored until the early 1960s when Yevtushenko made it famous in a poem: "There are no monuments on Babi Yar, A steep ravine is all, a rough memorial."

Soviet authorities have tried to suppress the fact that Jews were the first victims to be singled out at Babi Yar. Arthur Zabar thereupon puts on his yarmulke and reads a prayer in Hebrew from a little book covered in white vinyl which he keeps in his shopping bag. The Americans stand heads bowed for a few minutes, staring at the cenotaph. The sight is awesome. The tortuous summit of the bronze monument depicts a prisoner trying to burst from his chains. Even after thirty years the ground at Babi Yar remains brown and barren because of the massive chemical effect of quick-lime poured upon decomposing bodies. There are only a few shreds of dried flowers at the monument, Sophie notes; visits must still be very rare, little will ever grow in this terrain. Claire and Sophie pluck blades of grass thrusting through the cement of the walkway and place them at the statue's feet. "Ten minutes from the hotel door to door and they tell you it's impossible," Ethel Zabar says as she replaces her husband's yarmulke in her shopping bag. "According to that party slave who's herding us around it was two hours out of town!" Arthur Zabar exclaims. "What kind of human rights can you expect," Claire asks, "in a country where lovely girls like that are forced to lie for a decent living?"

The next morning they take a plane to Leningrad. As they drive towards their hotel from the airport Edmund recognizes from his mother's aquatints the yellow walls of the Smolny Institute which served as Bolshevik headquarters in 1917. He has a recurring dream of Mara in which they walk down Leningrad's streets looking for her childhood home near the Smolny; they never succeed in finding it; in successive dreams it's been destroyed by Red troops, German artillery, has been superseded by a hospital, an exhibition hall of Soviet farm machinery . . . Edmund wishes to grab Sophie's arm and tell her that Mara's childhood home must be right near here, near the Smolny, but Sophie and Claire are arguing again with Evgeny about religion. A narcotic vagary doomed to disappear, Evgeny says, just as Karl Marx put it! How can you say it's disappearing, Claire protests, look at the babies being christened in your country, the churches often filled! You take the Marx quote out of context, Sophie adds, he called religion "the heart of a heartless world," and only then does he call it "the opium of the people. . . ." Evgeny smiles and compliments Sophie on her interest in Marx. At the back of the bus the Rolls-Royce dealers talk about their newly purchased balalaikas and the pleasures of the trip; isn't it gorgeous traveling through a country where there's no graffiti, no pornography on any walls? Sophie has slept well and is in cheerful mood, banters with the Weickers, who're great fans of her morning show, about détente and the average income of the Soviet factory worker. Edmund stares at the nursery-blue hues of St. Nicholas Cathedral, at the sumptuous lilac tints of the sky surrounding its gilt domes. These days he cannot be exceptionally moved by a landscape or the hue of a wall without wondering what pigments he'd have mixed to render it. "I do not know which to prefer," he recently wrote Claire in a letter which he considered profoundly Slavic, "my suffering before or after the cessation of my art. It is not so much joy which leads us to paint or write but terror of our death, fear of not leaving enough claw prints on the dunes of time; sorrow lies on either side, the act of art is strung between two poles of pain. . . ." The tenderness of St. Nicholas' walls could be rendered in cobalt blue mixed with a very small dose of white, sky would need a trace of cobalt violet, church's marble pilasters have a rose tint prone to alizarin or madder. Dulcet sweetness of Leningrad's hues the most striking first impression; what brutal history is cloaked with a more ambrosial palette, siege of the early 1940s, men boiling leather briefcases into a sticky mass for their dinner, stripping off wallpaper paste to get at its traces of potato flour, more dead of hunger than in any other city in history after Stalin's purges had already carried off millions. Azure palaces, mourning mothers, icy foreheads of starving children, Shostakovich conducting to packed houses, musicians' breaths exhaling clouds of white fog in the freezing concert hall. . . . As the bus rumbles alongside the Neva, Edmund watches the first sun worshipers leaning against the cement of the river's embankment; in this most heroic of cities hundreds of survivors have stripped their bodies and lean against stone walls, eyes closed, lard-hued flesh begging for June's first warming rays; how many summers do they have left, how many do any of us have before it will be decidedly too late to find grace or rebecome what we could wish to be?

"Your mother was from this city, Dr. Richter?" Evgeny's spectacles still shield the curiosity he evidences towards Edmund's party.

"Ah yes Evgeny, my esteemed foremothers were suffering women who taught the harp to your grand duchesses. . . ."

"My parents are dead also," Sophie tells Evgeny, "they ruined my life and I loved them greatly; don't you think most parents have a way of destroying us in some symbolic way . . . oh I suppose you don't subscribe to such Freudian ideas Evgeny Sergeievich?"

"Today gentlemen and ladies we are going to visit Fortress of Peter and Paul. . . ."

The bus is loaded, ice-blue, packed with memories.

Irina smiles at her flock, smooths her American jeans, switches on her little microphone. "On way to fortress I urge you please to notice famous Winter Palace Square, largest public space in world after People's Square in Peking. . . ."

Professor Richter is again assured that the group is scheduled to visit the Hermitage Museum on Monday of next week. He is urged to take note of the interior of Peter and Paul prison, forbidden to visit of public until the Revolution and surely not included in his 1915 Baedeker. "One of the first prisoners to be executed there was the only son of Peter the Great, who had rebelled against the czar's reforms and was put to death by his father's own hand. We shall also see the cells once inhabited by Dostoevski, Gorki, Kropotkin, Lenin's brother, Alexsandr Ulyanov . . ."

"What do you propose to do about that dissident, Peb?"

"Everything I can obviously; he's on a hunger strike in one of the worst jails in Russia and I'm trying to reach his friends ahead of time so I can arrange to meet them but I can't even get a phone connection to Moscow. . . ."

"And what precisely can they do?"

"Give me a report on the exact state of his health so we can start putting pressure on to get him out of jail. . . ."

In the heat of the late afternoon Edmund had paused in Decembrists' Square to admire the statue of Peter perpetually defying the pale sky, stopped at a flower vendor's stall to buy fresh tulips for his women. He'd walked into Sophie's room after a brief knock; they were lying in a large double bed, Claire reading, half reclining on a pillow, Sophie bared to the waist, her head on Claire's lap, trying to have a brief afternoon sleep, splendor of two women's flesh joined in ancient affection, sensuality of sheets rumpled in great heat. "What's new and exciting, Professor, what beautiful flowers you've brought us!" And then Claire had started discussing her mission again.

"Since this damn tour only gives us four days in Moscow, I've got to make some contacts ahead of time. . . . The tenacity of this Baklanov, thirty-five years old and he's only been at liberty for fourteen months of his adult life . . . systematic hunger strikes to protest ill treatment of his fellow prisoners, confined to solitary in the freezing winter . . ."

Edmund stares at the Neva flowing beneath their room, darkening violet in the early-evening light. To recreate the curious dark sweetness of that sky, like lilac blossoms about to unfurl! A deep cerulean at this hour. The water a Prussian blue. Two women in black babushkas in an ocher yellow boat in the middle of the water. He toys with the pistil of a white tulip. "Peb take a rest for a change why don't you? Why can't you forget a bit about your missions on this trip?"

"Forget about my missions!" Claire leaps up, paces the room. "When will you ever leave your alabaster tower, Edmund!"

"Now listen you're not going to drop out of our tour and start getting followed by the KGB; this isn't a country in which to exhibit your virtuosity at guilt Pebble; you only have to be here for two days to realize that oppression is as great as it ever was under Peter the Great, who often decapitated two hundred dissidents in one afternoon with his own hands. . . ."

"What cynicism, Edmund, what does that have to do with my conscience, not a tinker's dam!"

Her pale face made more inscrutable by its walls of straight brown hair, for years he'd compared her to a medieval city-state, self-sufficient, impregnable.

"It has to do with the fact that you're a tourist of suffering, my dear, the way I've become a tourist of art, the way our Rolls-Roycers are tourists of Russia, the way Sophie is a tourist of everything. You've been saving asthmatic sea gulls since you were a child just to ease your damn little conscience. . . ."

"Apologies for your own passivity!"

"If I wish to bury myself in the difficult task of reclaiming our friendship on this trip it's my privilege to do so, so don't try to make me feel guilty about being an inactivist who prefers to remain where it *was* at. . . ."

"Please E.R., please Pebble, let's stop this!"

Sophie languorously brushing her mass of copper hair, pacifying them with weary dutifulness.

"You're both behaving as if we were still at Sealark; I didn't come on this trip to serve as some sort of Security Council . . . let's not be late for dinner again and bring a sweater, Peb. . . ."

Edmund said other things as they walked to dinner through hallways walled in scarlet damask, hung with bright fairy tales and scenes of the Neva at every time of year. You pimp with your purity don't you Peb, you know your problem sweetheart you've been trying to be a saint much of your life but you won't make it because you only love that part of us that can be saved . . . saints are one of my favorite subjects, you can't help but be a specialist in saints when you're an art historian, I collect them, I'm an aficionado. . . . They're tumblers of sorts, people who know how to turn one hell of a spiritual somersault . . . but your somersaults have been abortive Peb, as if you'd lost your balance in midair and landed aslant on the wrong foot. . . . She'd walked ahead of him with her air of being unaccompanied and having no one to listen to; he'd reflected on the dilemmas facing three persons in middle age who've had a lifelong obsession for each other; Sophie had followed close behind them, pretending to be buried in a Russian grammar.

That evening the tourists are taken to see Leningrad's circus on ice. Edmund, Claire and Sophie sit with the

clapping Zabars, the delighted Weickers, the gilded
Rolls-Roycers among bands of round-cheeked Russian
children. They watch seals dueling, clowns and poodles
pushing baby carriages, trained bears in sky-blue skates
playing hockey games. The youngest bear acts as goalie;
he swings smartly at the puck with his little stick when it
comes near his cage; when his wobbling ankles fail him
the crowd cheers, the circus trainer rewards him with
handfuls of fresh fish. There is much clapping and
shouting among members of Intourist Tour No. 137
Destination Tbilisi-Kiev-Leningrad-Moscow. "Now you
will see romantic ending," Irina promises. In the evening's last act a ballerina in glistening white tutu whirls
about the skating rink surrounded by a flock of trained
white pigeons. She holds a large hoop through which the
birds fly in and out, in and out, like planets gone berserk
about the gravitation of a star, briefly settling on her hair,
her wrists, her breasts. An acrobat in white satin pants
glides into the arena, seizes the ballerina onto his
shoulders. He holds the hoop while she makes her
exquisite movements through it; the ballerina now circles
about her partner like a luminous satellite, hair flying,
stretching her limbs into great écartés and arabesques.
She stands on tiptoe on the hoop he holds, defying
gravity, performing amazing gyrations in the air, and the
pigeons become a third planetary circle, still gliding
about her body to settle briefly on her breasts, her wrists,
her hair. "Three rings of light," Edmund whispers to
himself. Which may be nothing but a reflection on the
harmony he'd like to achieve on this trip with his life's
two loves.

Their favorite time of day in Russia is after 10:00 P.M.
For after emerging from the ballet, the opera or whatever
other spectacle they have been taken to they receive the
guides' permission to walk back to the hotel alone
instead of returning by bus with the rest of the group.
Dawn through the night, dawn until dawn, in Lenin-

grad's white nights the sun follows them like the KGB; when they exit from the theater that night the buildings have sunk into a torpid haze of dark fruit hues, the sun still throws a slice of pale gold across the rooftops of the bloodred Mariynsky, the lime-green Stroganoff palaces. Still silent and trailing behind her friends Claire stops walking and sits alone by the edge of a canal. They are by the church built on the site of Alexander II's assassination, its dark-lozenged brilliance glints like coal in the light of night. "As the czar stepped out of his carriage a second bomb was thrown, the czar collapsed, face splattered with blood, once again as so often in St. Petersburg the snow was red with blood." Edmund stands by the embankment, wondering how long to let Claire brood alone. He walks to her and sits down by her side, his hand on her arm. And she buries her face in his shoulder for a minute. Edmund, Sophie and Claire walk through the city hand in hand again, talking about the islands, the games, the pains of their long adolescence. One detects no other serious tensions between them yet, not too many complications. They have loved each other long, their happiness in being together is as luminous as the white pageant they have just observed. It is the beginning of another beautiful Russian night.

x

On a July afternoon in 1959 Edmund stands in Rome's Villa Borghese Museum with a sheaf of notes scribbling some last thoughts on his doctoral thesis. He has chosen as his theme Titian's painting *Sacred and Profane Love*, which depicts two beautiful young women who resemble each other like twins but differ vastly in costume. The figure at the right of the vast canvas is nude save for a white loincloth, the other protagonist is sumptuous in a gown of white-and-crimson satin; they sit on the rim of a sculptured marble basin towards which a Cupid leans to stir the basin's limpid water. Many precursors of Edmund's labor had spent years of their lives debating the ironic symbolism of the women's vestments—was it the nude figure which Titian meant to embody Sacred Love, the vested one who personified profane and transient lust? (R. von Marle, *Iconographie de l'Art Profane au Moyen Age et La Renaissance*, The Hague, 1931.) Numerous scholars domiciled in Leipzig or Stanford had dedicated themselves to the single issue of dating the canvas (1514? 1515? Right before or after Titian left the workshop of his teacher Giorgione?) And a few doctoral candidates of Edmund's unbridled ambition had elaborated on the *paysages moralisés* depicted behind the two beauties—dark wooded hill dominated by forbidding fortress brooding behind the figure of Profane Love,

serene verdant pasture surmounted by church steeple
stretching behind Sacred. (S. Schramm, *Die Früe Bilder
von Tizian drucke*, Leipzig, 1920.)

Let's not fuck up with our usual love of confrontation,
E.R., don't strive for any revolutionary new views,
always a risk as an opening aria . . . also avoid
possibility of jealous positivists yiping against subjec-
tively self-indulgent speculations . . . stay quiet, formal, earn the comments "impeccable, irrefutable" . . .
just sum up most honorable findings to date and add
some stirring insights of your own into Neoplatonism of
Titian's vision—

—T's central theme is the tension between two
kinds of Venuses, two kinds of love: (1) Chaste
Sacred Love, *Amicitia, Caritas*, that higher form of
bonding only reached in deep but nonphysical
relationships versus 2) Sensual Profane Love,
which Romantic agonists later upheld as the central
ingredient of happiness——Brief elaboration
needed on Renaissance's revolutionary attitudes
towards nudity, its rejection of all medieval preju-
dices against the naked form—by 1515 the nude in
art personifies the most exalted and *spiritual* attributes, Friendship, Genius, Soul, Clarity, Eternal
Bliss——Include crucial historical background
overlooked in earlier studies of *Sacred and Profane*
—greatly stress general distrust of romantic passion
throughout mainstream of Western philosophical
tradition, right until nineteenth century's disastrous
glorification of it—up to then friendship rather than
love was seen as cornerstone of human happiness
—Aristotle: Transience and destructiveness of venereal appetites, capacity for friendship is only measure of human virtue/Cicero: *Amicitia* more valued
than either power, honor, wealth/Montaigne sums it
up for the Renaissance a few decades after Titian

paints *Sacred and Profane:* Love is "an impetuous and fickle flame," whereas the fires of friendship produce "a gentle and universal warmth, moderate and even"—

While traveling through Italy in the summer of 1959 Edmund enjoys staying in those modest *pensiones* in which aging couples, week after week, keep bottles of mineral waters and amber medicines on their tables. There is an orderliness, a delectable monotony about such establishments which reflect the pace of his own recent life. An order from Napoleon Bonaparte issued on the occasion of a soldier committing suicide for love has hung over Edmund's desk in Berkeley for the past few years: "The First Consul notifies his Grenadiers that a soldier must conquer the pain and vulnerability of his passion." Like many of us who've known the ending of an ardent dream he's come to think of himself as steeled and stoic, able to control all future lust. In such moments we may extend our disaffection to the entire race, conceive for the future of our species a Utopian breed that will live in perfect control of all fleshy desires while tranquilly performing increasingly noble mental work. . . . During his years at Berkeley little emotion has stirred Edmund, save the bittersweet memory of three childhood friends he's not yet dared to revisit and the blissful prospect of academic glory. He's already spent much labor on, drawn much applause for, meticulously documented papers on the iconography of medieval ivories, on the disputed meaning of clocks (reminders of life's brevity or symbols of a rising middle class?) in seventeenth-century still lifes. "Recipe for academic success?" he wrote Claire and Jeff shortly before leaving for his summer in Italy. "Charm the wives of those professors instrumental in voting you tenure. Head directly for the silvery-haired, old-school gentleman scholars whose pianos are littered with photographs of

themselves with dear B.B. at I Tatti; they still hold the
fort, thank God, at most departments from Berkeley to
Cornell. . . . Don't omit enrapturing some of the useful
faculty wives you might find most dreary, medievalists'
spouses bovine with domesticity, blue-jeaned *guerillères*
beginning to agitate for civil rights. Achieve repute for a
good table, be noted for amusing little sauces, heed
Oscar Wilde's dictum that a gentleman is one who is
never unintentionally rude.' . . ."

When staying in his Italian *pensiones* Edmund eats his
dinner alone, a book at his elbow; and then walks out
slowly into the streets of Rome or Padua, stopping at a
café to study closely some architectural landmark and
savor the prospect of the assistant professorship which
will be his the following fall when he hands in his
dissertation.

Upon arriving in Florence he'd checked into his *pensione*
and walked to the Convent of San Marco to revisit its Fra
Angelicos. He arrived at half past twelve, the convent's
doors were closed, he remembered that some museums
in Italy close at noon on Saturdays. He sat down on a
park bench adjoining the convent, unaccustomed to
suffering a flaw in his rigidly structured schedules, and
tried to decide where to go next. In the Badia Church
some blocks away Dante used to see Beatrice at Mass, in
the Strozzi Palace nearby the medical student Savonarola
had been brought to God after a severe disappointment in
love. Church bells clanged, pigeons gathered in droves
upon the statue of a nineteenth-century cardinal that
faced Edmund's bench. He observed the preening of
males before indifferent, scurrying females, their irides-
cent green chests and bright rose beaks, the luminous
pink eyes that blinked like signal lights in a laboratory. A
few young men in blue jeans sat at the feet of two
silver-haired duennas, chatting. Italians, their respect for
the dignity of elders . . . he and Sophie and Claire

would turn thirty the following year, terror of reencountering a past; Sophie might be in Florence this very minute; in a day or two he'd try the *pensiones* she'd be likely to have checked into. . . .

Wisps of cirrus clouds hovered over the city like angel's lungs. An orange bus stopped and discharged a child in green licking on an ice-cream cone, two embracing tourists studying a guidebook. The pigeons flared upwards in a fusillade of feathers. Edmund rose and walked slowly towards the Bargello to revisit Donatello's *David*, feeling sudden loneliness. Shopkeepers drawing down their blinds for the weekend, bare-legged Swedish tourists clanging with metal canteens and cameras, autumnal palette of ocher and mustard palaces simmering in a great August heat. He reached the Bargello through narrow side streets, avoiding the crowds on the main squares. An adoration of the early Sienese school hung in the main waiting room, angels' faces modeled in apple green under the spread of rainbowed wings, mouths open in song or wonder. He climbed the staircase slowly, hoping for the same burst of emotion he'd received from the *David* eight years before.

He walked to the main room and stopped at its open doorway, startled and joyful. In front of the Donatello, a few yards away from him, a young woman leaned against a pillar in a pose of some exhaustion, kerchiefed head held down. Her brooding air made it clear that she didn't see the streaks of sunlight on the gallery's floor any more than she noticed its statuary, that she was engrossed in urgent deliberations of her own. She lowered her satchel to the floor, whipped off her kerchief with an exasperated gesture. Her cascade of copper curls confirmed Edmund's suspicion and he walked swiftly towards her, stood behind Sophie and put his hands over her eyes. She spun around and fell into his arms, her body much frailer than he remembered.

"Angel I just got the letter about your being in Italy, I was about to go to your *pensione!* I've looked for you everywhere, in Modena, Parma, Vicenza!"

"But those aren't the places with important Titians," he whispered, kissing her many times, holding her shoulders at arm's length to better study her face.

"Four years!"

"Why didn't you also write me where I could find you, funny one?"

"I wanted to leave it to Providence."

A few new freckles speckled her marvelous nose.

"Providence has been kind, let's travel together a lot. . . ."

They slept again in the same room for the following three weeks. Edmund renewed acquaintance with the arsenal of objects Sophie carried with her on all trips, he remembered them from their earliest adolescence. Postcards of Chartres, Spanish shawls, harlequin masks, she'd always pack a few of these curios even for a weekend, as if she needed them to anchor her nomadic nature; barely had she walked into a hotel or guest room —Nantucket, Haiti, Florence—she unpacked her magic identity kit, draped a mantilla over a lamp, rearranged furniture, cloaking the most banal room with her intense, domestic sensuality. On this particular journey her first gesture was to shift furniture about again, bring two single beds together, yet how careful she was to remain passive, serene! Edmund would usually kiss her good night with great tenderness after they'd read in bed for an hour.

She fastidiously studied every subtle change in his body, his face. His cheeks were ruddier, his mane of hair made more golden by four years of California sun. He'd grown even leaner and more muscled, tempered his body more fastidiously than ever, his moodiness had neither increased or decreased. Sitting in squares in front of their favorite churches—Santa Felicità, Ognissanti—they talked effusively about their current problems, mostly his. Ah what a life Titian had, it was paradise on earth! Such an artist didn't lick boots in the salon of some whimsical patron, he was often a grand seigneur himself; Charles V made Titian a Count of the Lateran Palace, gave him a knighthood, what have you, rulers from all over Europe paying visits to his studio . . . he wasn't yet quite sure how much biography to put into his thesis, there's that legend about the emperor himself leaning down to pick up one of the master's paintbrushes. . . . The motto on T's coat of arms bore the words "Art is more powerful than nature," the Romantic nonsense about artists' suffering was still a long way off, such an artist dealt in lumber and grain, invested in real estate, gold, jewelry. . . . There's a marvelous description of the freedom with which he worked when he reached his seventies, he used brushes as big as broomsticks and his fingers, even the palms of his hands; Vasari observed that he painted "like God when he created man." . . . He could do whatever he wanted, Soph, they left him alone, they let him work into the fervor and loneliness of great age. . . . She smoothed her hand over Edmund's forehead, reconnoitering the familiar grain of his forehead under her palm, the two small chicken pox scars on his left temple, he often kissed her hand and talked about the course in Renaissance he was about to teach that fall; by the time he was thirty-three or so he might well get tenure, he'd set himself the goal of thirty-eight years of age to be chairman of his department. . . .

They made love a few times in the three weeks they were together. Twice they went to Arezzo. Edmund couldn't remember the location of the church where Piero had painted his frescoes on the Miracle of the Cross; it was one of his more petulant days; Sophie kept pointing in the direction of the main square but he complained that she could not read maps, refused to ask directions. They arrived ten minutes before the sacristan was scheduled to close the doors; once in the church he refused to answer Sophie's questions about the iconography of Saint Constantine's dream. "Just look and enjoy them, don't try to explain everything out of existence." He complained that he'd remembered the frescoes better lighted, more grandiose, she understood how intensely he cultivated his moments of high emotion for art, that these were the only passions left to him. Later he stroked Sophie's hair and apologized, gave her the little lecture she'd craved. "That dream of Constantine you were asking about . . . the Tuscans excelled at depicting hallucinations, phantasms, dreams from the beyond . . . the Franciscan Revival, its gospel of unearthly joy was their chief source of inspiration. . . ."

That afternoon they sat in a café while Edmund sketched the fronton of the cathedral. He'd planned to do nothing but finish his thesis during this trip; he'd only started drawing as a way of protecting himself from Sophie's solicitude, aware of that nutritional respect she had towards the act of art. He drew no persons, no landscapes, only architectural details from facades of buildings, friezes and roundels, fluted pilasters and stone rosettes. She checked on his materials, pacing and talking to him while he worked, observing that he drew as meticulously as ever, with the same number three pencil on Arches paper.

"Have I ever learned self-reliance in my past few years as a journalist, Eddem; I love to work the overnight shift while the rest of the city sleeps, live in counterpoint with everyone else, share eight A.M. cocktails with the guys from my news desk under the Third Avenue El. . . . Yes, you're right, it finally keeps me safe from my family's invasions, one more Wagnerian diva and I'd have gone into my own *Liebestod*. . . . Eddem, I'd like to become the first woman bureau chief of a European capital or the first anchorwoman to direct the coverage of

a presidential election. . . . I don't care what Kierkegaard says about journalists, you overeducated boob; I
don't give a damn whether we'll turn the late twentieth
century into one immense voyeurist experience, you're
so perverse, you really are, you're the one who inspired
me to be a reporter. . . ."

Another day while Edmund drew, Sophie read him a
note that she'd just received from Jeff:

"I'm writing to announce glad tidings of great joy. Peb
and I are knitting tiny garments! We did want you and
Plinker and Eddem to know as soon as all was totally
safe. I've got her under wraps, she's seven months along
and feeling nifty. The schoolwork here continues to be
very satisfactory and we're carding splendid blankets
from our own sheep. . . ."

He was squinting at the thick, bristling stones of the
Strozzi Palace. She scrutinized his face, terrified at the
prospect that it would show pain, equally perplexed to
find it impassive, inscrutable.

"Anglican romanticization of nature as vulgar as it's
misguided," he muttered, "stinking with baa-baa sheep
and bunny rabbits playing croquet on the lawn."

Lying awake in the dark one night during their stay in
Florence she compared herself to a hunter waiting before
dawn for the most desired brilliant mallard to rise out of
the darkling water, then rebelled at the image's violence
and the metaphor was wrong anyhow; she had long
auscultated her patience, was ready to wait for him for
many more years—she often thought she'd absorbed
some of Claire's pacifism in her search for great love; her
motto was watch everything, mend when you can, lie
still when you're helpless—during that stay in Florence
she'd pretended to be utterly content with her present lot,
her rising career, her new self-reliance—she lavishly
praised Edmund for all this; only he could have emanci-
pated her from dutiful filial acceptance of her parents'

fame-starved lives—she never shared with Edmund the agonizing weeks she'd spent after his departure to California, her decision to only work night shifts for a few years to make a radical break with all that was most familiar and dearest to her in the city—neither did she share the letters she'd received from Claire a few weeks previously; throughout her pregnancy Claire had had great depressions, seemed unable to leave her house, had barely opened the door to go outside. . . . "I feel more starved and solitary than ever, Soph, stranded in flesh as in quicksand . . . will this be my only future, more cradles, more of my poor mother's carefully nurtured acres of lettuce and potatoes? . . . Soph dearest, do write me often and I'll write back faithfully; I who've always been so aloof and self-sufficient, I need you more than ever and probably more fiercely than you've ever needed me. . . ."

As Edmund fell into his deep easy sleeps he was aware that Sophie might lie awake in one of her frequent bouts of insomnia, humid and superb, still waiting for her once-and-only artist. He kept remembering those last nights in New York a few weeks after the Nantucket wedding during which he'd meticulously prepared suicide at the side of this woman for whom he had immeasurable love and esteem. In between his extravagant orgies of sleep he had outlined diverse plans for self-destruction in order to escape his growing anguish, replace the death by smothering which her solicitude threatened him with. Pills are too messy he'd mutter, drowning takes too much courage, pistols are better, ah, that neat tiny bullet hole in the last minutes of *Mayerling* which symbolizes the impossibility of any lasting happy love. . . . What will become of her? he often wondered in the summer of 1959 as he watched Sophie pacing up and down a piazza while he drew; what would be the fate of this best friend for whom he had such an ambivalence of love and terror? She'd redirected her indefatigable tenderness, thank God, towards the problems of the world. She paced about the streets while he worked, conversing with passersby or reading newspapers with the aid of an Italian dictionary, returning with disparate shreds of information: Italians feared a vacuum in Lebanon, ten thousand Algerian refugees migrated to Tuscany in the past two years, largest atomic plant in Europe about to uproot the sheep-farming economy of the Modena region. You've improved Sofka he muttered to himself as he drew, you're on the right road all right, you're more terrific than ever, but he never told her in so many words. He often castigated himself for his lack of heart.

On their second to last night together he lay on his back, kept from sleep by the knowledge that she was staring at him across space as she had so often in New York, with the piercing eyes of an animal making its way through the darkness. He tightened the sheet around his shoulders and told her he couldn't marry her yet. Oh I know, I know, she whispered, almost laughingly. And how does my Sofia Larionovna always know, what makes my girl so smart? I've learned that's the way much human desire works Eddem, people are always pursuing some great white whale, that which they can never have, the way you're still wanting Claire, the way I've wanted you . . . oh don't pretend that's all passé Edmund, I know just what Peb means to both of us, she's what Captain Ahab was hunting for, solitude, self-containment, perfection . . . that's why I've chased her too, we all want the unreachable; Claire's my closest friend but I doubt if she can ever belong to anyone or anything except those dunes and moors, those causes . . . oh don't worry about me in the least Eddem and don't be disillusioned, you haven't hurt me a bit during this particular segment of our life together . . . I know just what I'm saying Eddem you'll probably continue hurting women left and right as a revenge against being abandoned by Mara and Claire . . . yes I know all about the new Edmund, he's tough, brittle, knows precisely the kind of success he wants and is wearing some kind of mask that he's not quite comfortable with yet . . . oh stop that phony baloney about we Jews being so psychoanalytic, who else knows you as well as I do, how much do women mean to you Edmund, I mean, are you homosexual . . . no of course you wouldn't be lying here beside me if you were totally that; I suppose you consider yourself bisexual. . . .

The musical voice, the lilting diplomatic tone in which she discussed French novels. Dawn had washed the hills beyond the cathedral with a tinge of melon hue. Edmund was dressing, pulling on his shirt.

"I think most artists are narcissists, sweetheart, and even though I may never paint again I'll always remain an artist, I'll nurture my narcissism with utmost solicitude, water it, prune it, give it exotic plant care. It's enabled me to survive through thick and thin. As a narcissist I might prefer to wake up next to someone in whom I see a pond-clear reflection of myself, man or woman. And as an artist I'm rather fond . . ."

He drew the curtains open.

"I'm awfully fond of the sheer aesthetic symmetry bisexuality presents, though I much prefer women."

"I'm flying back to New York tomorrow, Eddem, and leaving New York next month."

He spun around. "When did you decide that?"

"About a minute ago."

"Well I'll be damned. What a monkey you are."

"I want to move around for a number of years, be a nomad again."

He stood over her bed, took her hand.

"Oh, Soph, don't lose what you've gained in the past two or three years, you've become so centered, so strong, you're on the way to becoming everything I'd ever hoped you'd become."

"Thanks for the last minute handout."

"Can't you trust me a little more, Soph? I have so little of your goodness, your greatness of heart, when will you realize how stingy I am about showing my love? . . ."

He pulled at a forelock of her hair, as he'd done to tease her since they were fifteen.

"Cross your heart and hope to die . . . I'm going to sit there in Berkeley hoping that you won't become a Rockette next, or the first woman astronaut."

"That might be cosmic."

"Sweetheart, I'm going to sit in Berkeley waiting for you to become another Marguerite Higgins, promise that you'll continue being even more of what you are now. . . . Soph, you're my best friend, my most trusted love, you're much of the little I have in the world, however rough a time I give you. . . ."

He sat down on the edge of her bed, ruffling her hair. She still smelled of musk, of essence of roses. She brushed her hand over his chest, unbuttoning the shirt he had just put on. He leaned down to kiss her, thinking this is a mystery I'll never understand. He knew again the ecstasy of her mouth enfolding his sex, of her tongue lapping at him like a suckling at the breast. She knew he had loved her absolutely, if only for an hour, which may be the longest it ever matters.

The next day, having several hours to spare between planes on his way back to Great Britain and the United States, Edmund stopped in Rome's Villa Borghese to take a few last notes on Titian's *Sacred and Profane Love*. One beauty shimmering in white-and-crimson satin, the other sumptuously naked to the waist, holding in hand a flaming torch that points to heaven.

— Careful to refute any earlier theses which posit antagonism between personifications of Sacred and Profane Love—It can't be overemphasized that Sacred looks at Profane with unbounded depths of affection—one could even suggest that the Cupid stirring the water at the picture's center could be homogenizing the principles represented by the two women—support Panofsky throughout, stress admirably sane Renaissance view of human emotions embodied in this canvas—relate briefly to disastrous contemporary ethos, we aren't yet prey here to the odious modern dichotomy between deviant and "normal" sexuality, between genital love and "platonic" friendship—Renaissance ideals embodied in Titian's vision present a vastly different view of human bonding—Human affections seen here as a vast rich spectrum in which *Amicitia*, *Caritas*, *Eros*, *Philia* can freely flow into each other, can take on many modulations within the life-spans of persons bonded by great and lasting friendships (see Marsilio Ficino, *Opera, et quae hactenus extetêre*, Basel, 1576).

xi

Idyllic exile, Edmund's Tahiti! In Berkeley in the spring of 1963 Nobel laureates design new bombs on a hill fabulous with jasmine while whistling melodies from Beethoven's string quartets. Fraternity men still lurch about the campus at 2:00 A.M. singing "Violate Me in the Violet Time in the Vilest Way You Can." Professors with doctoral theses on "The Crystallography of Radium" or "The Phenomenology of Hegel" are giving Mario Savio straight A's on his semester before leaving for their beach cottages in Sausalito. Edmund's seminars are held in rooms redolent with the smell of eucalyptus or (according to his whim) upon lawns aflare with the blossoms of hibiscus and frangipani. Scores of acolytes line up at the door of his office at dawn of registration day to be ensured enrollment in his classes. They delight in his mellifluous delivery and his meticulous concern for each student's progress. They enjoy that mastery of the ironic jibe (inevitably conservative in tone) which enlivens Dr. Richter's lectures and his annotations. Most contemporary art? "Apocalyptic wallpaper." Andy Warhol? "The Leonardo of Boredom." "Syntax is a faculty of the soul," he scribbles in the margin of a paper. "Only the most naive of humans," he comments to another victim of progressive education, "believes that there is something under heaven more important than convention." In this dusk of American innocence Edmund sees only hills dense with vegetal splendor hovering over San Francisco Bay, lemon trees bulging with gold in his backyard and the growing possibility of becoming another Kenneth Clark.

There lives in Berkeley in the early 1960s a tall, blond, suntanned professor who fascinates Edmund because of the sheer abundance of his happiness. Luke Edwards earned tenure at the age of thirty-three, has won every sailing regatta or tennis tournament in sight, is considered to be the West Coast's most eloquent lecturer on William James, has earned literary success by publishing delicately autobiographical short stories which center upon the unexpected felicities of his domestic bliss. As if this copiousness wasn't sufficient! Luke Edwards also claims to have found God. An ordained minister of the Methodist Church, he obligingly holds chapel services one Sunday out of two to enable the university chaplain to engage in his own regatta races. Edmund's friendship with the Reverend Luke Edwards enables him to draw the following conclusion: His own happiness in California is not one whit smaller than that of this creature graced with every attribute of human bliss.

"I've bought a modest little cottage overlooking the water," Edmund tells his colleagues, "with dreadfully mixed feelings about becoming a bourgeois landowner. . . ." The phrase charms persons of all persuasions, but at heart he feels no ambivalence whatsoever. His dinner parties (seductive candlelight, Russian delicacies remembered from Mara's days) are esteemed as the most delectable in town. He forces tulip bulbs, studies antique catalogs, has become a promising collector: Etruscan vase and XVIIIth Dynasty Egyptian bronze bought for a song from an unseasoned West Coast dealer, Tarascan statuettes bartered for a few dollars in Mérida. "I advise charming young San Francisco art lovers on the availability of Seurat drawings," Edmund writes to Jeff's country retreat in Great Britain. "I adore being seen with famous beauties, I've become skilled at many new levels of survival . . ." (it's with Jeff that he fully shares the delights of a worldly success which his other two friends might dismiss with Puritan disregard, involved as they are with their own searches, causes . . .) ". . . my occasional bouts of romantic interest are pragmatic and comfortably brief; last term a sophomore with the breasts of an Ingres sewed marvelously, a graduate student with a Botticelli profile helped me cook masterpieces. . . ." When Edmund returns to his sunny cottage the cat Vico pounces softly onto his master's shoulder, rubbing his stubbly whiskers against his neck in way of greeting. He climbs upon Edmund's lap as he sits at his desk correcting papers and gently digs his claws into his master's lap to reassert his presence. Edmund often stares at the animal as it lies coiled in satisfaction on his windowsill, roaring its pleasure at the sun, and compares its furled contentment to his own. Shall we ever know passion again, Pussums? How should we look upon the disappearance of our elemental urges? Shall we say relief, ambivalence, a faint regret?

There also lives in Berkeley in the 1960s a large, garrulous professor of Russian literature who rubs himself against all things Slavic like a chilled animal seeking the fire's heat, and has no other passion in life save for women. John Mirsky is immense and bearded, lives in a state of constant crisis, prefers to engage in all activities in the supine position, and like the characters of the novels he lectures about seems to be forever suffering from some final agony of belligerence and passion. Visiting him one steers between mounds of Lermontov, Pushkin, Tyutchev volumes that threaten to avalanche the visitor like the crumbling walls of a ravine; one finds John lying on his dusty couch moaning his adulation for a newfound love or a newly discovered poem. He lavishes his most passionate monographs on the critical moments of the briefest and most disastrous destinies —the last poem written before Lermóntov's fatal duel, the last letters written by Esenin before his suicide. John's been to Russia a dozen times, agonizes each time over the betrayal of his revolutionary forefathers' dreams, swears never to return but reapplies for a visa eighteen months later, revisits Moscow to wallow in the agony of still another disillusionment. His women can be frail, pimply freshmen or voluptuous divorcée flutists, he seduces them into his book-crammed lair for a few months, lets himself be battered by the pains of their infidelities or by the nascent bliss of one of his. And after a tempestuous dissolution reburies himself in his dusty rooms to write a new monograph on Gogol, Gorki, Gumilev. Upon peaks of emotion his large saturnine face erupts in patches of violet like the mauled cheeks of a boxer; turbulent passions or demanding translations manifest themselves like stigmata on his body, making him look as if he'd spent the night street-fighting in the streets of Yerevan. His immense, bearded form looms over all as he walks through campus, and by the triumphant or dejected cast of his head Edmund can always tell whether Professor Mirsky is living the end of another splenetic union, the bliss of a new one or the dejection of a womanless week. This is the way Edmund had met him: standing alone in a narrow abandoned stack of the Berkeley library bellowing out for his own solitary delectation some lines of Mayakovski's: " 'The sea is ebbing . . . The incident is closed . . . Love's boat has been shattered against the life of everyday.' "

In his lonely womanless moments John lavishes on Edmund his intense affection, bringing him rare Georgian vodka, exotic brands of tea he'd bought a decade ago in Kiev. After recounting the denouement of his last passion he lies supine on Edmund's couch, continuing to roar out more beloved lines: " 'Ah for that woman who brings us delectation/After having fully tortured us for decades . . .' " There are many discussions of love, death, the redemptive power of suffering and passion.

"The older I get, dear John, the more adamantly I support the view that mankind is distinguished from other varieties of fauna and flora by its capacity for total sublimation. . . ."

"*Niet, niet!*" his friend shouts.

"Ninety percent of the power attributed to sexuality is not so much an instinct as the work of man's imagination, his ability to fantasize . . ." "*Irunda*, nonsense!" "But look at animals! Their lack of imagination is the major trait that distinguishes them from humans, and many species only copulate once or twice a year. . . ." "*Oujas*, horrible thought!" "When will you wean yourself from the tyranny of romantic love that's strangled us for two hundred years, all a lot of Wertherian nonsense, dear boy!" "But there it is, big as the Winter Palace twice a day," John bellows.

The cat jumps off the windowsill, rubs against Edmund's ankle, walks towards the kitchen to signify his sense of approaching dinnertime.

"Most lust is a creation of our imagination, a form of literature!" Edmund shouts from the kitchen, stirring his borscht.

"And what else is there to live for save literature?" John yells back.

"I've said *niet* to the tyranny of the imagination, Ivan Maximovich, I believe we may soon see a mutation, a new race of postsexual men . . ."

"Utopia, monstrous reverse Utopia!"

"Will you not agree that the excitement, the anxieties, brought you by the erotic are more important than sex itself?"

Moans, unintelligible splutters of rebuttal in several languages.

Late at night they exacerbate each other's Slavic temperaments, stand on tables to drink toasts.

"Ah if you could only meet that exquisite creature whose betrayal cured me of all lust, Ivan Maximovich . . . I drink to her who has purged me of all future passion!"

"And I drink to the resurrection of every venereal drive in your body, Gedmund Petrovich!"

"To the defeat of the demon of desire!"

"No no, you desiccated monk, to the eternal Venus!" John drinks.

"Ah yes, to the embrace of chaste celestial sacred Venus!"

"You will see, Abélard, you will see!" John shouts back.

It happened this way: On the first day of semester a tall, frail creature with an abundant mass of golden hair made a tempestuous and belated entrance into Edmund's class in nineteenth-century French painting. Standing close to her a few weeks later in her apartment, where she'd asked him for a drink to advise her on Impressionists inherited from her husband's family, he saw her eyes as an unnaturally pale green, the hue of new moss at spring thaw. Within their first hour together Simona made it clear that her husband was in California much less than half the year, and was insatiably engaged in developing new terrain—carving up the Sardinian coast with descendants of the Aga Khan, buying hunting lodges in Kenya, Ceylon. She spilled her life to Edmund with much tossing of her splendid hair, seeming to have already documented herself thoroughly on his, often drawing similarities between their two fates. Ah she had been plagued by much misfortune! Her mother (Hungarian, an angel) died when she was eight, at the war's beginning. Her depraved Italian father left her in the care of erratic aunts, who in turn had her brought up in a series of provincial convents. *Dio* the horror of it, the beatings, the near-starvation diet of sweet potatoes and sour grass tea! Her first lover—the wretch—at least served the purpose of financing her acting lessons, which she was sure would have been her true, brilliant vocation if destiny had been less atrocious. But at Papa's command she was married for mercenary reasons at age eighteen to a little count who measured his descent from the ninth century. She had left him the following year—he was the greatest bore in Europe—and spent two years in Paris writing poetry at the keep of an art historian who was finishing a book on Byzantine mosaics. She adored art historians, she could never stress enough how she believes in Edmund's genius. . . . Later there had been a specialist in eighteenth-century tomb sculpture . . . anyhow, last year she married the half-Italian scion to a San Francisco fortune, this man called Craven who leaves her comfortably to herself with a few servants when he goes parachuting in the Himalayas or dives for coral in the most barracuda-infested reefs of the Caribbean and has already discarded two earlier wives who desired bourgeois marriages. . . .

At least that is the way she tells it. Weeks and months later, as Edmund cups in his hands the frail face dominated by shrewd jade-hued eyes he thinks he knows what binds him to her. I am finally staring at a face which holds some shreds of my own childhood: in this sun-drenched haven which only glimpses the century's pain through some crazy course in the history of film she offers me some continuity with my own past, some shared pool of history and suffering . . . but the green eyes do not stare back with the same recognition. Simona is seared, unaffectable, living solely for a tenuous survival which she's decided to ornate with as much novelty as possible, white Jaguars, numerous travels, rare drugs and wines. In between her trips to shoot rapids in Peru or hunt leopard in Nepal she prefers to make love to

Edmund on a fur rug in front of her fireplace. Pale long-limbed body, flesh boyish or prepubescent in its frailty, mane of flaming hair spread on a velvet pillow in the light of the dying embers—new items in Edmund's collection of the exquisite. Their meetings are neutral and torrid, unswept by any emotions except her whims for new sensations and his desire to break her will. . . .

"*Nou*?" John asks.

"Orgasm is another business of the brain, dear one, a way of gaining more information about ourselves. . . . But, oh, how she exploits the frailty of my ego. . . ."

"I know, I know! This creature as obdurate as granite is begging you to sculpt her destiny, correct?"

Will Edmund please help Simona to find her true essence? she begs him; she's always had to live in a loathsome state of dependence on men, it will never cease until she finds that precious vocation she's been struggling to find all her life. . . . Is she an actress, an artist, an art historian? This Sophie he often talks to her about, who helps support her old sick parents so nobly and has just won a big prize for her writing, how did she go about finding herself as a *paparazza*? Perhaps that could be a career for Simona, should she try that next? Only Edmund can help her look for the real Simona Danielli, a daughter of the depraved Roman aristocracy who might only have a few more years to live . . . she expresses these quests in a mongrel mix of languages through the persistent haze of Turkish cigarettes, her eyes glowing with intensity, in whatever moments she is not attempting to enlarge her still fitful grasp of the nineteenth century. As Edmund satisfies himself on Simona's insatiable body he only begins to feel her in his power when the balance of pain and pleasure she demands verges on danger, when he takes her with as much brutality as his body can muster after inhaling rarities that make his heart beat at double its normal rate.

In between Simona's frequent trips he sleeps ten hours a night, meticulously supervises dissertations on "Cycles of Martyrdom of Saint Agatha in Italian Painting," "The Iconography of the Railroad in Nineteenth-Century French Art." At the art historian's conventions that annually fill the halls of Hiltons in Chicago or New Orleans, Professor Richter, index fingers delicately joined towards his new blond beard, participates in panels on Caravaggio or presents papers resurrecting the reputation of Guido Reni. ("Richter's trimmed his hair!" young women professors in the audience whisper adoringly. "I liked it better when it was more Byronic. . . .")

Some months after they had started torturing each other Edmund and Simona went to spend a weekend at a seaside hotel in Big Sur which Simona wished to visit because she might eventually interview Henry Miller there; she could begin her career as a *paparazza* that way. . . . Edmund had looked on this stay as an occasion to dissuade her from flying to Katmandu where she planned to join her husband on a two-month hunting trip. With a force of desire which he'd seldom before experienced he seized her many times a day, upon waking, in a quiet sea-lapped cove, before their dinner outings, testing his power over her by trying to make her promise that she would spend the summer in Berkeley rather than accompany Craven to still another nature-depleting trip to an underdeveloped country. But Simona insisted on everything, Machu Picchu and frequent stays at the Gritti and the Plaza-Athénée, she desired her master's degree and her Edmund and her tenuous ability to talk volubly about Courbet; why should she relinquish any of these freedoms for the sake of one brilliant member of a sex she detests, *Sono tutti stronzi!* She seemed to skirt the edge of emotion on the last day of their stay at Big Sur, her limbs twined about him like tendrils of fire about a log, she swore her eternal dedication to his body . . . but the next morning she insisted on returning to San Francisco, where she must pack for that trip to Katmandu.

They returned to Berkeley the day before Sophie was scheduled to arrive for a brief visit on her way back East from Hawaii, where she'd spent the past year writing a series of articles on the fiftieth state. "Statehood is outrageous!" (her last letter). "Do you realize that these blessed islands are blossoming into one of the most powerful outposts of the military-industrial complex . . . American imperialism cloaked by a seductive veil of sunshine and flowers . . . creating one of the most monstrous racist pentagons on earth? . . ."

"How nice to be able to catch a glimpse of you," Edmund had answered the previous week as he despaired over Simona's threatened departure. "It's far from the ideal time for me but I'll meet that 10:50 Pan Am flight from Hawaii on May 12th. . . ."

There are few moments more brutal than those in which a fantasy we have evolved over months, in moments of great solitude, dissolves upon the instant of encounter. Sophie had envisioned Edmund standing alone at the gate of her flight, guarded but smiling, embracing her with that heat of gesture always more ardent than any words he could ever offer.

The tall lanky woman at Edmund's side had a mane of gold hair that recalled the abandoned creatures of Pre-Raphaelite paintings, was dressed in thin floating vestments that gave her a surface of glimmering plumage. Her long pale hands shook slightly, she smiled perpetually, seemed determined to immediately charm the visitor. Edmund chain-smoked and never took off his dark glasses, reminding Sophie of those times in their adolescence when he wished to seem most inscrutable and mature. Sophie decided to remain equally inscrutable.

Simona's interest in her seemed to make Edmund uncomfortable. He soon became garrulous.

"The ocean is quite beautiful," Sophie said as they sat down to lunch in Sausalito.

"The sight of unenclosed water is barely tolerable."

"Ah *ottimo, ottimo!*" Simona exclaimed. "I adore the Edmund who hates nature, it is divinely comic!"

"What do you do for a living, Simona?" Sophie asked.

"You never, never ask that in Europe," Edmund snapped.

"What do you do in America, then?"

"Let her be, let her be! She's a little sincere but sweet, so sweet!"

"I'll tell you what she does for a living, Soph, she collects art historians' cocks, the way Catherine the Great used to collect very tall generals. Jewish art historians documenting early Christian amulets, Harvard WASPS writing monographs on Ravenna mosaics, she's had them all . . ."

"Have you been to Caracas, Sofia, or to Bucharest? There's no reason not to go to Bucharest, the Brancusis are magnificent. . . ."

As they gave her a brief tour of Berkeley, Sophie kept asking questions which seemed to bore Edmund and Simona extremely, how many Chicanos had entered California since 1960 she wanted to know, what was the average yearly income of the Chinese working in San Francisco, weren't students at Berkeley beginning to activate for students' rights?

". . . and you have so many independent beliefs; it is wretched to depend on some dreadful male as we are forced to do in Europe, particularly if you hate men as much as I do; presently I am nothing but another bibelot in the life of a man who goes about ruining nature in as many parts of the world as possible; he insists I accompany him on his shooting trips and it is amusing and helps me get rid of my anger. . . . You're beautifully self-composed, Sofia, and you esteem yourself to be very strong, yes?"

"I'm getting there," Sophie said.

Simona flew early that evening to Katmandu. Edmund was co-hosting a party at the Faculty Club that night for a colleague who was leaving for Harvard. When he came to pick up Sophie at her hotel at 9:00 P.M. he seemed to be still another person from the guarded fragile Edmund she'd lived with in Florence, the moody irate one she'd shared earlier that day with the Italian. There was a forced radiance about him.

"We'll be an hour or so late to the party," he said as they got into his car. "That's approximately when I like to arrive to these academic dos. . . . You seem to be in absolutely terrific shape, Sophie darling!"

"And except for the terrific new beard you're a perfect mess, I think."

"What are you talking about? I'm in stupendous form!"

"What are those ghastly things you're chain-smoking? I've never seen you smoke that way before."

"You're mad, honeybun, I've always smoked, I started chain-smoking at Sealark when we were sixteen."

"Cut out the macho. What are those smelly black things you and that Italian poison your lungs with?"

"Black Sobranie, the world's most expensive cigarette . . . so listen, out with it, what do you think of her?"

"She's very beautiful, and perhaps not as perverse as you romanticize her to be. A beautiful lost child."

"She's actually *quite* corrupt, and filled with utterly demonic complications."

"She's your great red whale, and I hope she gives you hepatitis. It's slower and safer than a suicide attempt."

By this time she was steeled to her life's search, as he smiled and tugged at a forelock of her hair she knew that he was hiding his surprise at her new measure of impudence.

As she walked into the crowded room with Edmund he immediately became its center of attention, his head stood magisterially above the level of the crowd. He stood radiant and seemingly immense at the door, lingering there as if he wanted to prolong the impact of his entrance; the crowd seemed to turn towards him like many delicate metal filings realigning themselves around a magnet, the sweet domestic classicists' wives with braided hair coiled chastely about their heads, the tall tanned archaeologists with yachting pins in their lapels, the tall sunned English professors who'd forgotten to take elasticized tennis bands off their wrists, they all turned towards Edmund. Sophie suddenly understood that need for instant and forever-assured approval which had led him to early success and early exile; that evening she thought she understood almost everything. He was making the rounds of the room, introducing her as his oldest childhood friend, "the closest thing I have to a sister," "the apple of my eye," "star reporter for the *New York Post*," "my very own house radical," he said another time. He hugged colleagues, kissed their women on both cheeks European fashion, made appointments for the forthcoming week, tennis matches, boating excursions. Time came to make a toast for the departing colleague, it was Edmund, always Edmund, who was asked to make the first toast. "This is not to say that it is impossible for Jonathan to simultaneously retain the deep affection of the Berkeley and Harvard community . . . it is rather to say that Jonathan has a greater capacity to preserve the affection of those two great institutions than any other Rembrandt scholar I can think of . . . I drink to those disciplined savants, to those noble alcoholics of the single object of Jonathan's incomparable dedication who will save our great academies from the growing

barbarism of our times. . . ." Edmund does everything
with such style, no one can afford to give a birthday party
without him in Berkeley because his toasts are so unique,
has Sophie seen his little collection of pre-Columbian?
Each piece acquired for a song, what an eye! Sophie had
to talk for a while to a voluminous hirsute Slavic scholar
introduced as John Mirsky. "Grandiose man this Richter," he roared out to her, "the mainstay of my existence,
can't you resurrect him, resurrect? . . ." At one point
Sophie saw Edmund hovering alone at the bar, hands
clutching the rail as if suddenly seized with some great
anxiety he couldn't share; he was bent over the bar going
"aah, aah," a strange sibilant drawing of his breath; this
lasted for a few seconds and then he went to the mirror,
ran his fingers quickly through his hair before returning
to the crowd his brilliant smile.

As they came into his flat at 1:00 A.M. the cat's soft
pounce upon Sophie's shoulder, its intense and immediate recognition of her ("eight years, Vico," she whispered, "eight years!"), gave her a moment of pain.
Edmund opened a split of champagne. She lay on a
corner of his bed, staring at the exquisite little clay
statues on his mantelpiece, blank lunar faces, archetypal
arms folded over pure narrow chests. He sat at her feet
with his head in her lap, saying the Tarascan one at the
right is probably a votive figure, some deity invoked at
the time of human sacrifice . . . and then he turned up
towards her and before either of them had undressed
pulled up her skirt and buried his head in the thick hair of
her sex, spread its lips apart with his subtle tongue, a
tongue like a muscular flower petal that had a power, a
languorous rhythm she had never known about; you are
my Orient, this he often said, you're my favorite of all
human substances, we'll meet like this as long as we
live. Later his tongue and his sex explored every orifice
of her body, the night seemed dissected by their flailing
limbs, she had the image of insects gone crazed on some

drug, mandibles whirling in all directions, mouths screaming for new angles, new chasms, we drone in ecstasy as we straddle the same road or lie furled, receiving bliss from distant hands, the other watches, columnar and vigilant, enjoying the joy he's offering, lying still in the expectation of his own pleasure, our limbs rotate like the arms of a compass, any dawn becomes awesome with the monotony of more desire. There was a new skill and delectation in his lovemaking which saddened her profoundly.

The next morning as he drove her to the airport they were affectionate, matter-of-fact with each other; this also was their manner, to act like two siblings who must discuss some family affairs before leaving each other for a stretch of time.

"Any recent news from Great Britain?"

"Jeff carding his wool and curdling his whey while Peb goes on her sit-ins and ride-outs for disarmament, gets dragged from Trafalgar Square every few months in the company of Sir Bertrand . . ."

"And they're due back this summer, do you know when exactly?"

"Early September. Going straight to New Hampshire, Jeff will be teaching near Concord. . . ."

"Oh God, at that ghastly stuffed-shirt St. Paul's of his."

"Don't knock it, Soph, few such islands of civility left! I've been writing our lifesaver a lot, heartily sharing men's problems. We made a pledge to get very drunk together every seven years; I'll have to look in on them next summer."

"I hope you look in on me too, you may be in for a few surprises. . . . You know, Edmund, I have no idea of who you are anymore and I'm not sure you know either; I've barely known who you are since you stopped painting."

He kept his eyes on the highway, gave an annoyed shrug.

"Art, art . . . in all that's useless one must be divine, darling, and I didn't have that much faith in myself, or in the future. Do you miss posing for me, Sofinka, you were the most stupendous model. . . ."

"Yes, for some reason I adore to pose . . . how do you conceive of your future these days, Eddem?"

"I'd like to write a lasting work, quote unquote, on some grand theme like the nude in history . . . in twenty-five years Harvard can give me a splendid Italian villa to curate, like B.B.'s . . ."

"*Perfetto*. Your career as a dandy is already off to a smashing start."

"I'll have a *dueña* to take care of me, a mother figure in mended cashmeres who paints on velvet. You'll come to stay and I'll pour tea on a terrace amid rows of cypresses, surrounded by the most beautiful men and women in Europe."

"You're certainly enjoying your motherfucking power trips over the local rabble."

He gave her that glance of guarded surprise, threw his cigarette out of the window. "Yes, three or four years of teaching can give you the Pygmalion complex if you're any good at it. How about you, sweetheart? How do you foresee the next years?"

She reached into his pocket and lit a cigarette; she hadn't smoked one for years.

"I wish to be superbly taken care of. If you knew how depressing it's been to spend three years as a roving reporter living in sleazy motel rooms, trying to fall asleep to the screech of Greyhound buses and the whining of icemaking machines . . . and then the loneliness of the evenings, solitary meals month after month in motel restaurants watching teenage organists with foot-high mops of bleached hair play the 'Dance of the Hours' on electric organs, feeling too bushed after a

twelve-hour day to walk more than twenty yards from
my bedroom at night. . . ."

"You're so admirable. Why didn't you tell me more in
your letters?"

"You're not the easiest person to communicate with
anymore, dreamboat. . . . Larry lost every penny he
had and went deeply into debt besides, some dreadful
movie deal he got swindled into, and Mama had a cancer
operation . . ."

They'd sat down at the airport's coffee shop.

"You're even braver than I thought, Soph, tell me
more."

"I've often worked until dawn taking on extra free-
lance assignments to support them through all this." She
became silent, head bent down.

"Why don't you stay over an extra few days and talk it
out with me, Soph? Let's go back to town this instant."

"Your kindness smacks of duty. I do think you've got
enough to deal with as it is."

"Please, Soph, please stay."

"We've got to do some of these figurings out alone.
. . . It's just that it's not a life for a woman, Edmund."

"Well, perhaps it is, for an extraordinary woman."

She started to laugh, knowing it would forestall tears.

"I don't want to be extraordinary yet. . . . All I want
is . . . what's that word the Italian uses so well?
Repose! I want repose, I want to lie back like an Oriental
courtesan and be fed champagne and pomegranates
around the clock, servants bringing me fine shawls in the
evening, I want to shut my eyes and just live, just
live . . .

". . . live a life with *style*!" she shouted, banging her
fist on the table.

"Oh, God," he said, "you're going to do something
totally idiotic again if I don't do something about it."

Her flight was being called. "Let me go," she said.

And then, as she kissed him good-bye:

"I saw the most marvelous graffiti on a wall in Berkeley yesterday. One of them said The Future Isn't What It Used to Be."

xii

Please note the central floor plan of all Russian churches, Edmund says, always in the form of a Greek cross, four arms of equal length—unlike the space of your Roman rite, which draws the eye in a long directional impulse towards the altar, the Orthodox liturgy focuses on the area right beneath the central dome—and this dome under which the community worships, moving about with uniquely anarchic Slavic fervor, is the symbol of the Dome of Heaven, the dwelling place of God—this central design might be said to express the Orthodox's immense stress on community. . . .

The pathways of the silent muddy town are sodden with recent rain, the church bells of delicately gilded Novgorod seem to have stopped in midcadence; Claire says it's as if some carefully timed poison had steeped into the veins of an entire population and just this morning put it to sleep. Do not even try to go into any church, Irina says, it is all under *remont*, repair, ah, don't ask me why so much is always in a state of *remont* in our country, Sofia Larionovna, you always ask such difficult questions!

The four of them had left Leningrad at dawn that morning. Above the worn brown seats of their train compartment hung photographs of a fiercely bearded Lenin, a statue of Pushkin surrounded by beds of tulips.

"Today I am in my playful mood," Irina announced as she distributed a breakfast. "I've spent two nights in my home in beautiful large city and I'm in my most gracious mood . . . I shall give you little quiz. What is the name of the river we're passing on which Leningrad is built?" "Volga!" the three tease her. "Naughty, no breakfast. On what boat was the shot that was heard around the world?" "*Aurora!*" "Good children, chocolate for all. . . ."

The train rumbles towards Novgorod through the flat solitude of the northern plain. Vast fields lined with curtains of birch trees as fragile as the limbs of insects, immense lakes swathed in mauve mist of dawn, their boundaries invisible; I can't tell whether this landscape is dull, Claire says, or whether it has a melancholic beauty I can't grasp. . . . "I'll cheer you with recent Soviet statistics," Irina says. "Every minute in the Soviet Union nine babies are born; women still outnumber men by some twelve percent because of the Great War; our women hold seventy-three percent of positions in education . . ." ". . . and eighty-seven percent in public health," Sophie adds.

"How well informed you always are, Sofia Larionovna!" Irina wears a T-shirt with the words Disco Beat on her left breast, shiny high-heeled black shoes which she keeps wiping with her tissue, a long hunter green skirt with matching jockey cap set on her carefully crimped hair. Claire has said she can't detect a single chink in her armor. Edmund has talked about the narcissism of the new Soviet women. Irina twists and turns her head seductively at her Americans, pouting and smiling, fingering her curls. "Another point! Our per capita income has increased by twenty percent since 1974, our gross industrial production has risen by twenty percent . . ." ". . . and only ten percent of Soviet women report ever having had an orgasm," Sophie says languidly. There's no telling what Irina ever chooses to hear. She continues handing out cucumbers, buttering

slices of black bread. In the past year alone fifty-four
million people improved their lives by moving to better
apartments. The favorite visiting places of foreign tourists are one, Moscow and Leningrad, two, Kiev, three,
Tbilisi, ai ai why you wish to go to sleepy Novgorod is
beyond me but it is my duty to make you happy, yes?

Ai ai I met the most wonderful Soviet man two nights
ago in Leningrad, Sophie says, he was handsome and so
much wiser than I. Are you married, Irina Grigorievna,
and do you still live with your parents? I live alone with
my mother and my *babushka*, we are what do you call, a
matriarchy. . . . Are you looking at beauty of landscape, Clara Pavlovna? When you look at fields of
Muscovy do you feel Russian, Professor Richter?

Oh yes, yes!

Edmund: Novgorod means "new town" but it's actually
one of the nation's oldest cities; in the twelfth century
Novgorod claimed some thirteen hundred churches and
is said to have been saved by a miracle . . . when the
Prince of Suzdal besieged Novgorod the citizens hung an
icon of the Virgin Mary on the gates, arrows flew upon it
thick as rain but it remained unharmed, and real tears ran
down the face of Our Lady . . . so upsetting the
attacking army that it fled . . . four centuries later,
however, the prosperous town went into decline when
Ivan the Terrible butchered half its citizenry to suppress
an uprising, choking the river with dead corpses . . . by
modern times a population which once totaled 400,000
had fallen to some 850 souls. . . .

Bulbous church domes of celestial turquoise or blazing
deep blue like firmament of clearest night, conical domes
in the shape of Oriental warriors' helmets, oval domes
the flat dark green of forests just before sunrise, freshly
gilt domes surmounted by great gold crosses strung to
each other by ropes of golden chains, monasteries the

hue of tea roses imprisoned in crenellated battlements of bloodred brick, above the locked doors faint frescoes of resurrection, threatening prophet, frail Saint George, Virgin staring with terror at the announcing angel. The gilt is freshly blazing, the paint as lustrous as that of a new toy, but all doors are shut, no one in the streets, one single child fishes in the river by a dormant monastery, all dressed up and nowhere to go, Irina says, that's nice American expression I just learn, and rain, rain, go away . . . Irina steps slowly, delicately on the cobblestones of Novgorod, often bending down to wipe her shoes. She moves in the frail sepulchral rain as on a field of broken glass, walking with delicate crablike motions to avoid the troughs of mud. She's proud of the new skirt and cap she inherited the day before from the Zabars after she'd roundly scolded them for dropping out of the tour to visit synagogues. And when she finds a stretch of dry pavement she moves like a mannequin on a fashion runway, with rhythmic swaying of her slender hips, pointing disdainfully to different churches: Monastery of St. Anthony, Church of the Purification, Church of the Assumption, Church of St. John the Compassionate . . . as her Americans photograph domes and towers she paces slowly at Sophie's side, takes a large mirror out of her bag, licks her lips, adjusts her jockey cap. "*Sa démarche langoureuse m'ennerve*," Edmund says; they sometimes speak French to each other, like characters in nineteenth-century Russian novels. Church of St. Perpetua, Irina waves with her long manicured hand, Monastery of the Holy Spirit, Church of the Transfiguration. We should soon move on Gedmund Petrovich I'm frozen to the bone, I think it's time for a cup of tea, there at left is the nunnery where the czars sent their wives when they were too tired with them, ai ai, what terrible times these were. . . .

                              *   *   *

You can't go in, you can't go in, the old woman says as
she slowly brushes her broom across the steps of the
cathedral. The caretaker is dressed in black from high
felt boots to wool headkerchief, a bunch of keys clangs
at her waist, she sweeps banks of dust and dried grass off
the steps of the church. You'll never go in, you'll never
go in . . . Why can't we go in little mother Edmund
pleads, we'll be very quiet, we'll stay two minutes but
the interdiction becomes a chant, a litany, it is forbidden,
forbidden . . . she keeps her head down, sweeping at
the dust and shreds of dried flowers. Her legs are
swaddled in high bands of felt, her kerchiefed head nods
in rhythm to the chant, the only sound in the utterly still
town, closed, closed, there'll be no going in, there'll
never be any going in. He's a professor Claire says, he
teaches the history of icons at a great American university, this is our favorite country after America. There'll
be no going in, no going in at all the old woman sings
joyously; she stands squarely in front of the cathedral
door, squinting fiercely at the visitors, all locked up, all
locked up forever. Phenomenon of refracted power,
Sophie whispers, is she ever proud that she can keep us
out. We've made her year Claire says, we've given her a
happy year.

   Edmund: Well if we can't go in we can at least talk
about it. . . . Claire, Sofka, come stand in front with me
here—even more than in the West the Slavic Church
serves as an icon, an image which shares in the divinity
of the archetype it represents—and in this country the
Church has always been seen as a redeeming community
of love in which the individual is relatively unimportant
and helpless—Irina Grigorievna don't fret dear, we'll get
our tea, we'll get it in a minute (Ai you're freezing me
Gedmund Petrovich, though all you say is remarkable)
—The Russian nation has always seen itself as a mystical
organism outside of which there is no salvation, Edmund

continues; its ancient communitarian roots give us many clues to what's happening here today—the Slavs never recognized Greco-Roman concepts of private property, the generosity, the hospitality you still shower us with today, dear Irina, manifests that unique sense of brotherhood—there was never any room in Russian society for our Western notions of individualism and individual salvation—

All utterly brilliant Gedmund Petrovich but let's . . .

All utterly brilliant but abstract, so abstract Sophie cries out, what in heaven's sake does it have to do with your own life Edmund Richter? When have you ever lived for anyone but yourself, when have you been capable of love for community?

She stands in front of the cathedral, notebook and pencil in hand, suddenly shouting, a gilt dome framing her Titian hair, her angry golden eyes.

All you've been for years is a graduate student of yourself, the rooms of your life upholstered with theses on the iconography of dead game in Early Dutch still life. . . .

Soph . . .

You and your goddamn Tarascan statuettes and your delectable *millefleurs* pattern Meissen.

Look who's talking Soph! As if you hadn't had your share of ultrabourgeois hedonistic splendor!

You and your drugged contessinas, you're as splendid an example of late twentieth-century narcissism as anyone I can think of!

You wear you candor like a campaign button don't you Sofia, have you only come on this trip to lacerate us with your outdated insights?

Don't talk to her like that, Claire shouts at him, leave her alone!

Ever since childhood Sophie and he had criticized each other with brutal clarity but Claire had abstained from any criticism of Sophie, as if she were a sacred precinct of her life which must remain untouched, and now they were both shouting together at him.

Leave Soph alone!

You and your gigs on Chinese bird deities, when have you lifted a finger for anyone since we were in our twenties?

What banal clarity Sofka, why are you throwing me back to what I may have been fifteen years ago? I've come to think that art historians are nothing but glorified undertakers tiptoeing about searching for more corpses to embalm, I've come here to try and transform my life when there's still time and when I turn to you for help you're usually off on one of your solitary night prowls. . . .

I don't believe in the kind of transformation you talk about Edmund, all we can do at this late stage is apply a little aspirin and Band-Aids to our various cancers. . . .

Soph you're the one who seems to have no more need of others whatsoever, which I find morally and metaphysically abhorrent!

Children, children, stop! Claire shouts.

You can't go in, you can't go in the old woman sings, sweeping banks of dust back towards the steps of the church, you see no one will ever go in.

They walked back to the station a half hour before train time and went to the buffet for tea. Its door was ajar and a sign said Open from 11:00 A.M. on. A Verdi aria played on the radio, floating from the little room like a summer breeze. A large blond waitress stood behind the counter, her hair teased and lacquered like an operatic diva's, her lips painted a dark shade of ruby red. She leaned against a vitrine which displayed arrays of radishes and beets, coarse red caviar and smoked fish. The music blared, photographs of Soviet ski teams hung on the walls, the little room was bathed in a seductive roseate light. We'd like some tea, Irina said. We're closed! the waitress

called out. Then why are you here? Irina asked. I'm
telling you there's nothing! the waitress shouted, nothing
to eat, nothing to drink! Then why do you stand there all
dolled up with all the lights and music on and that fake
food on your counter? None of your business, there's
nothing left, nothing whatsoever! The Verdi blared, the
caviar gleamed under the rosy lights. Why is there
nothing? Irina exclaimed, I want to know precisely why
there's nothing! *Remont*, the woman shouted back,
remont, we're in repair! And why are you forever
repairing? Irina cried out, since my childhood I've never
heard about anything but *remont*, the Hermitage is in
remont! My grandmother's heating system has been
three months in *remont!* The waitress seized one of her
plates with a threatening gesture. Irina swiftly ushered
her Americans out of the door and led them towards the
train, her needled heels clicking angrily on the stone
embankment.

Ai what a situation, what a state we're in Gedmund
Petrovich . . . when we can know when our buffets are
open then we'll have true Communism.

Once settled on the train she was quiet, and after
straightening her hair in the mirror she bit her lip and
looked contritely at the landscape.

It's so wonderful to travel in a country that's even
more fucked up than ours Sophie said.

Within a few minutes of the train's departure they
were all falling asleep.

As he dozed off Edmund thought of all the violent
women he'd seen in the Soviet Union, shouting, forbidding, force-feeding propaganda, instilling the little order
there was in this most anarchic of nations or perhaps
making the disorder even more intense, women beating
up their men when they led them out of bars by the scruff
of their necks; a few days ago he'd seen a salesgirl
bludgeoning a man until blood spouted from his head for
stealing a bottle of vodka from her counter, last night in

Leningrad the floor attendant had chased him down the corridor of their hotel toilet brush in hand yelling you misbehaved you bad man you left your room without giving me your key, all over the nation women were building, bullying, denouncing, censuring, so it had been in his own frail fatherless life, women inspiring and deceiving him, women beckoning him like unreachable Grails and threatening his life with desire insatiable, women ordering him to be a genius, women working him up to be Titian or ruining his career, women judging him with the great aloof gaze of Byzantine madonnas or with Sophie's furious stare, when all he wanted at this stage of his life was to cultivate a tiny plot of land like that old Georgian's and paint certain exquisite still lifes . . . as the train rumbled on through the stark dusk of the northern plain, Edmund fell into a deep sleep. He dreamt that Irina was walking slowly through the monastery town in her green jockey outfit, her heels clicking like castanets on the pavements of the silent city. She pointed her long painted fingers to north, west, all around, and at each languid wave of her arms golden domes melted into haze, fortifications crumbled, steeples toppled, with the swing of her slim hips church bells were silenced, gold crosses vanished from sight, entire kremlins evaporated into the roseate void of the Soviet evening, the town turned as still as a firmament, as inhuman as the stars . . . after several languorous waves of her lacquered nails all became solitude and emptiness again, all returned to the silence of the eternal plain, all objects wrought by man were swallowed into the brutal Soviet night.

xiii

"The most puzzling transformation has taken place in our Sophie," Claire writes Edmund early in 1964. "Imagine this: She seems to have entered a brand-new stage of rebellion against the notion of frequenting persons of any talent . . . gone are the promising painters and budding dramatists, the men courting her this year are all hopelessly conservative and very wealthy and dotty about her; does she crave shelter after all these years of pennilessness and solitude? One cannot help but be very moved and a little perplexed. . . ."

A few months later Claire sent Edmund the following newspaper clipping:

Dorothy Kilgallen reports that Sophie Ross, prize-winning *New York Post* reporter and daughter of former talent magnate Larry Ross, sprung a surprise on her friends yesterday and tied the knot with canned food tycoon Bernard B. Reilly . . . "Bee-

bee" Reilly is rumored to have bought a 30-acre
estate in Southampton just last week. . . .

"Mr. and Mrs. B. B. Reilly request the pleasure of
your company," so read the invitations that start reaching
Edmund's desk in the summer of 1964, "to a reception in
honor of Mr. Xavier P. Boyle, president of Greater
Lakes Products . . ." ". . . . to a soirée in honor of the
Uruguayan ambassador to the United Nations . . ."
Uruguay? Why Uruguay? Edmund ponders all afternoon
as he corrects papers from his Brueghel seminar. It
dawns on him the next day that Uruguay is noted for its
large importation of some carplike fish, which it is Mr.
Reilly's vocation to place in cans. In the chaste months
following Simona's final departure, no correspondence
more perplexes Edmund than the invitations to Sophie
Reilly's numerous parties in Long Island and New York,
engraved in florid script on Tiffany's heaviest stock.
Edmund even begins to read the women's page of *The
New York Times*, in which the Reillys' prodigality is
frequently scrutinized. Beebee buys a town house in one
of the most exclusive blocks of Manhattan's East Seventies, commissions Sophie's portrait from Larry Rivers
and Andy Warhol, pays unprecedented prices for a
Sheraton table and a Louis XIV armchair at Sotheby's.
Much is made of the Reillys' prodigal travels. They fly
to Glasgow for a weekend to premiere an opera; to Peru
to pick up several bolts of custom-made textiles for their
living room; to London to bid on a case lot of 1937
Mouton-Rothschild, leaving on the *Queen Elizabeth*
three days later to ensure their vintage minimum distur-
bance. Claire seems so enthralled with her Sane chapter
and her civil-rights marches, and Jeff with his teaching
and his sports, that the Howells don't get a firsthand view
of the Reillys until the fall, when a note from Jeff
capsules his impressions of the new ménage: "It's like
some African principality . . . outlandish dark servants

standing at every door just to open it for you, champagne flowing throughout the day, and our old friend wandering about in her finery, not quite as sylphlike as in the last few years, warbling, 'Beebee has the caviar arrived, where are those chandeliers? . . .' "

In April of 1964 one of Edmund's seminars in Impressionism had already been canceled because of a student rally against nuclear testing. The following month he'd lost a class in medieval Flemish to another group protesting the ban on travel to Cuba. The pickets and rallies that proliferate the following fall center about the issue of students' rights. John gets arrested with his students on the very first sit-in. Reverend Edwards is speaking in every corner of the campus about restoring credibility to the community. Throughout the autumn's demonstrations Edmund spends an increasing amount of evenings at home, reluctant to engage in student-faculty discussions in which he's bound to be branded as ultrareactionary. In his free hours he begins to write a series of articles attacking the new vogue for Pop Art and rehearses delicate dishes for himself and his cat—sorrel soup, kidneys flambéed in Armagnac—wondering when he can ever again impress his colleagues with them. Claire's letters only mirror the mayhem growing in his former paradise. "I'm cheered by the prospect of joining the San Francisco–Moscow Peace Marchers when they pass through Boston next month; I'll walk with them for several weeks before going South to register voters, have found a marvelous au pair Irish girl to take care of Victoria while I'm away; Jeff is beside himself of course: 'What will the *family* think Peb?' He's being kept quite busy thank heavens by a local field hockey association which calls itself Marvelous Mothers and Fabulous Fathers. . . ."

In November the Free Speech Movement is formed, several thousand Berkeley students immobilize a police

car for thirty-two hours in protest against the arrest of
one of their peers. "Our campus swarms with all the
accouterments of twentieth-century horror," Edmund
writes in the first of his letters to the campus paper, *The
Daily Californian*. "We live in a melee of gas masks,
clubs, guns, walkie-talkies, motorcycle jackboots, pickets, banners, bullhorns, armed astronauts adorned in
garish motel bathroom colors . . . crowds scream and
bodies interlock as the world's most privileged children
protest their oppression . . . meanwhile a fashionable
new breed of youth-adoring professors weep at their
students' plight in the midst of liturgical parades that
equal the pomp of Seville's Holy Week. . . . Let our
young idealists go South and join Martin Luther King's
magnificent movement for human equality! What do
these admirable goals have to do with the hard-earned
freedom owed some twenty thousand men and women
of our university, the freedom to teach and to be
taught? . . ."

On the night of December 2 some 950 students are
arrested after an all night sit-in in Sproul Hall. Joan Baez
entertains the crowds by singing "We Shall Overcome,"
bids them to face their struggle with love in their hearts
and leaves shortly after midnight. At 3:05 A.M. the
governor of California broadcasts a message giving the
police the order to arrest. John goes to jail again. Mario
Savio bites a policeman on the thigh while being dragged
away.

"Beleaguered teachers!" Edmund writes *The Daily
Californian*. "Have we forgotten what our authority
represents? We're elected to preserve the only sacred
values there are left in our secular society—the sanctity
of intellectual tradition, the authority of history. Have
we forgotten that the university is the only sacred
precinct where those values can be learned, that it is not
an ivory tower but an active temple? The only alternative
to our authority—and we are capitulating to it today at

Berkeley—is the breeding of a new generation of barbarians, of a people without a historical memory. . . ."

Professor Richter pens this letter in an empty classroom after running through the slides he has assembled for that morning's lecture—"After Pollock?"—in his seminar on twentieth-century art. He is the only occupant of the building. A general strike has been called to protest the previous night's arrests. The possessed youth gesticulating and shouting in the begonia-decked lawns outside his window, those once docile angels who'd taken the place of the children he'd yearned to have, are betraying him . . . as he finishes his letter a student runs through the building with a bullhorn announcing that thousands are rallying that afternoon at Sproul Hall to condemn Governor Pat Brown, the regents, the president, the chancellor, the police, the United States government. Edmund packs his book bag and drives to the supermarket. He buys four days' food for his cat and for himself, returns to his flowered cottage in the Berkeley hills, padlocks his doors for the weekend to protect himself from the possible intrusion of ruffians handing out more petitions. He opens a bottle of Cabernet Sauvignon, puts on his recording of Monteverdi's *Vespers for the Year 1609*, places his latest acquisition in sight of his desk—a fine little *sang-de-boeuf* vase, Ming Dynasty. And he sits down at the typewriter to compose his attack on the new art, Vico purring, purring at the edge of the sunny window.

"The phenomenon of Pop Art presents us with still another tightrope act in the circus of public taste. . . ."

The beloved object has returned (this is the thrust of Edmund's polemic) but in what a monstrous and debased manner! "Museums displaying fenders of wrecked automobiles, papier-mâché bas-reliefs of women's girdles, portraits of Donald Duck, enlarged comic strips, paintings produced by rolling nude ladies in pigment! Cartons of Brillo pads, carefully copied hamburgers, toothpaste tubes and six-foot-high lipsticks!" "Cannibalism of the supermarket!" "Parody, cynicism of perpetual pastiche!" "Art history moving again from tragedy to farce!"

The din of voices reaches Edmund every few minutes like waves of nausea from the protesters' rallying point twelve blocks away. Edmund plugs up his ears with wax and continues writing. With a passion that surprises him, he goes on to defend the Abstract Expressionist painting he'd attacked so vigorously ten years ago.

The president of the university, the radio announces, has canceled all classes and called the entire community to meet at Berkeley's Greek amphitheater. . . .

"Unlike the debased kitsch of current Pop, Abstract Expressionism had embodied most of the values of traditional humanist art: dynamic form, lyric power, a distilled celebration of the glory of the created world. . . ."

Mario Savio was refused the right to speak at the amphitheater and was dragged offstage in front of a cheering crowd of eighteen thousand. . . . The Free Speech Movement has received telegrams of support from Bertrand Russell and James Baldwin. . . .

After finishing the last draft of his attack on Pop Art, Edmund drives to a village on the calm side of the Sierra to avoid setting foot in downtown Berkeley. He mails his article, renews his supply of victuals and sits down at the typewriter again to write another letter to *The Daily Californian*.

"There are no more efficient prophets of totalitarianism than the virtuosos of cheap guilt presently holding toy guns to our heads and forcing us to politicize institutions whose very essence is to stand above politics. . . .

"By biting a policeman on the thigh Mario Savio (self-appointed Robespierre of our Student Soviet) has earned himself the dazzling new label of 'charismatic leader,' thus debasing a hallowed Greek word to a label for moral parvenus. . . .

"As for the Songstress of the Dispossessed arriving at Sproul Hall in her gleaming Jaguar, it assures us that Berkeley has become nothing but a massive entertainment to the world . . ."

A partial quiescence returns the following spring. Edmund is enthralled by the teaching of his new course, "Stoicism in Seventeenth-Century Painting." His articles on Pop Art have received the kind of controversial attention he's beginning to enjoy—raves from the older generation of gentlemen scholars, vociferous attacks from younger dealers and critics. Every morning over breakfast Edmund proceeds to the women's page of *The New York Times* after glancing at its art critique and book review. He reads with interest that Beebee Reilly has bought a quantity of Sèvres at auction and has built New York City's largest private wine cellar in the bowels of his town house; that Sophie has developed what *The New York Times* describes as "one of the city's most curious salons." (Sophie photographed during an interview, standing by a Ming vase of the feeblest period, something newly round about her face: "Being a hostess is an exciting, demanding, full-time vocation. . . . I've never had a sense of roots until now; don't you think modern society is intensely rootless? . . . Actually I know almost no one in New York, I never know any of the guests at our parties, it's amusing to meet *new* people all the time in your own house. . . .") In May, Edmund was invited to give a paper at an art historians' conference being held in Philadelphia the following month. He accepted with pleasure, and that very day booked a plane reservation for his first trip to New York in several years. He would satisfy his curiosity about the Reilly ménage, attend his convention and later drop in on Claire and Jeff in Nantucket. As Providence would have it, still another invitation reached him in Berkeley a few weeks before he left: "At Home to Celebrate a Birthday: Mr. and Mrs. B. B. Reilly, 125 East 77th Street, June 25th, from six on."

The walls were of oak paneling. He stepped upon Bokhara rugs. A black man in white turban opened the door when Edmund arrived at the Reillys shortly after six and ushered him into an immense dining room on the ground floor. It immediately struck Edmund that Sophie could not have engaged in a more violent revulsion against the stark Village flats, the lonely motel rooms, she'd lived in for the past decade. The dining room occupied most of the ground floor and aspired to the ornateness of the most exclusive men's clubs. The Anglophilic opulence of its Sheraton, Hepplewhite, Queen Anne and ponderous silver services summed up all that Larry Ross had aspired to in the 1950s. Nibbling on translucent caviar and radishes carved in the shapes of tulips, Edmund walked about the room with the critical eye of a seasoned fellow acquisitor. They'd managed to paint their dining room a hideous shade of blue. It was awfully hard to mix an ugly blue, but they'd quite succeeded. The Sheraton breakfront might have been elegant as a showcase for Greek pottery, but it was presently filled with a florid Sèvres that clashed conspicuously with the fluting of English woodwork. And he should tell Sophie to apply a duller wax to her Queen Anne chairs, which presently shone with an almost vulgar maroon gleam. . . .

"I'm Mrs. Reilly's chief butler, Mr. Edmund, sir. . . ." Another turbaned black man was greeting him by name and bowing. "Madam refers to you as her oldest childhood friendship; she must felicitate her birthday guests upstairs but she told me that you were commencing a long voyage and asked me to see that you were adequately refreshed as soon as possible upon your arrival." "I'll be up to see her in a moment, I'm having a marvelous time looking at your splendid house." "As you wish, sir. Madam warned me that you are of solitary disposition and might prefer to take a turn away from the maddening crowd. May I suggest that you enjoy a visit to the library on the mezzanine, to which Mr. Reilly has just added a collection of Jack Londoner. . . . You might also study our noted wine cellar, first door to the left in the hall. . . ."

Edmund opted for the wine cellar, which he had already read about in the women's page of *The New York Times*. "Ah, Sofka, what a sense of drama you've developed!" The arches and vaults of the cavernous space were most carefully copied from engravings of medieval cloister architecture and recalled a stage set for the death scene of *Romeo and Juliet*. Edmund, so admired in Berkeley for his amusing little wines, took time to admire the velvety labels of '33 Mouton Lafites and 1885 Fine Napoleons, the silver tasting cups, marble boards and other refinements of the wine collector's trade which accompanied the Reillys' rare vintages. Edmund began to walk towards the second floor with great apprehension, infinitely dreading the revelation —surely startling—which Sophie's hedonistic new incarnation would offer. Reaching the second landing, still carefully avoiding the din of crowds and any room where he might find her, Edmund continued to climb the stairs to where he assumed he would find the master bedrooms. He stood on the landing and stared at a wall ornated by two portraits of Sophie, one in a neosurreal vein (walking by a tempestuous seashore in Victorian dress, holding a parasol) and another cubistic enterprise in which her eyes descended in mournful triangles to her chin while she strummed on an eggplant-hued guitar. Ah, yes, she loved to pose, but who in heaven's name had advised these outlandish commissions? He must find out more; from the door to the left came the familiar odor of Sophie's rose toilet water; he tiptoed towards it as

reverently as an archaeologist approaches a cache un-
opened for decades. He opened the door, and was
reassured.

Only his dear Sophie could inhabit this room, it had a
wondrous sense of impermanence, it looked as if she had
just arrived or were about to leave, its floors were bare
and uncarpeted, her clothes hadn't even been put into
any closet but hung from windows in lieu of curtains.
The heaps of dusty books piled on the floor reflected the
rich fluctuations of her interests—studies of Third World
economics and guidebooks to Hawaii, histories of Renaissance paintings and exegeses of Marxist theory,
biographies of Democratic presidents and of women
physicists, how-to books on losing weight and improving
recorder performance. And all about the room were
strewn those traditional fetishes of her travels—
postcards of Renoir nudes, photographs of the Mont
Blanc, Spanish shawls—which Edmund had last seen six
years ago in Italy. It was evident that she did not permit
any member of her large domestic staff to even enter this
precinct of the house. On a narrow, barely made single
bed lay the same satchel which she and Edmund had
shared during their trip to Tuscany, the stuffed koala bear
which he remembered from Sealark and Charles Street.
And what happened on this austere little schoolgirl bed?
Not much, Edmund surmised, not much. Surprised by
the pleasure he derived from this vision, he now wandered down the stairs towards the roar of the crowds as
slowly as he could, paused a second at the landing and
pushed his way towards the bar. "Large bourbon,
straight up."

A dapper, silver-haired man with a black patch over
his eye came towards Edmund, hand outstretched. "Ah,
you're her dreamboat," B. B. Reilly said. "My wife still
refers to you with that euphoric nomenclature. You seem
to be an insuperable part of her early life." Here was a
household, Edmund reflected, whose men clearly en-

joyed using florid language. Beebee spoke a kind of night-school English which seemed to have absorbed large doses of fresh vocabulary without fully digesting them, and cloaked the faint trace of an undefinable foreign accent. "I'm terribly glad to meet you," Edmund said, raising his glass, "here's to your great happiness." "My wife has the most luminous judgment of any hostess in New York and she tells me that you're catapulted towards a meteoric career in the field of art history." "I've just been voted tenure," Edmund said as modestly as possible. "I may not get my full professorship for another two years." "I wish you success in that transcendent enterprise. Your European background must allow you to perceive reality with a detached retina." "Have you been abroad a lot also?" "I often travel for severely transactional reasons. . . ."

Blue eyes. A handsome clean-shaven gent. The eye patch and the impeccably tailored clothes gave him the elegance of a Hathaway shirt advertisement. Sophie'd always been a sucker for good looks. The relationship might be complicated. He didn't understand life. Edmund stood at the living room's entrance and resumed his study of the Reillys' decor. He startled at the sight of a half-dozen more portraits of Sophie hanging over the convoluted marble mantelpiece. Beebee's esteem of his wife seemed to have expressed itself in a need to immortalize her features in as many pictorial styles as were known to the 1960s. And what a choice of artists! What were bestowed place of honor in this room but those currently fashionable monstrosities which Professor Richter was decrying in classrooms and learned papers! Hanging a few yards away over an Empire settee were twelve multiple silk-screen portraits of Sophie by Andy Warhol. By the window, another triumph of Pop Art depicted her in a glaring kitchen, smiling at graphically detailed stacks of supermarket items . . . George Segal's white plaster cast of Sophie seated in a chair,

looking like a victim of the Pompeii earthquake . . .
Sophie by Robert Rauschenberg, her features outlined
against the frottage of a photograph of the World Series
. . . ah yes she had always adored to pose! And now she
had spent the past year posing for those very idiots whom
Edmund was attacking in several distinguished publications, and was about to savage at his forthcoming
convention!

Beebee Reilly still stood at Edmund's side, appearing
to know as few people at his party as Edmund did. The
garrulous guests filling the room seemed as purchased as
the newly hung atrocities sullying Sophie's image on the
walls; it was a gesticulating, middle-aged, ravenously
eating throng dressed with the glittering maladroitness of
the Reillys' decor; many women surmounted with hair-
dos of immense size and strange convolutions ogled each
other with inarticulate murmurs and shifted through the
room like shoals of perplexed fish. . . . "The Château
Lafitte forty-five I've uncorked for my wife's birthday is
notorious for its contumelious bouquet," Beebee was
saying. "I've devised an unusually delightful way to
exhibit our hostess's beauty tonight; I hope you will find
the vision as delicate as I do . . ."

Edmund cut the conversation short with as much
civility as he could muster, for Larry Ross was hobbling
towards him, crippled by a recent stroke, vastly fattened
and baldened. Edmund held out his arms to this old
protector. "Ah, *Kinder*, who are these dolts?" Larry
whispered as he embraced Edmund. "Is this what we sent
her to Ethel Walker's and Smith and Mara's ballet school
for? What have these people accomplished, they're not
creative, they're not famous, they're not even young
. . . and you, Edmund, the distinguished art historian,
are you going to become the Berenson of our time?
Listen, Mr. Renoir, if only you'd stayed around, had
some patience, by 1958 we could have had you at the top
already, a truly distinguished gallery, the Bergdorf

Goodman of the art world like Betty Parsons and if not Parsons at least Sam Kootz; one of his cousins was the brother of one of my big screenwriters . . . and by sixty-two we could have had a one-man show at the Whitney, the Modern, these are great times for artists. . . ."

"That's the trouble, Larry, times may be too great."

All this dying was something wasn't it, Maestro? First Mrs. Sanford and then Camilla, both gone a few years from each other, who else was there to survive? But what a brave little girl he had in his Sophie, what a saint she'd been to them, sharing every dollar she earned, free lancing night after night after her hard day's work to pay for Camilla's hospital bills, and now this Reilly was being most generous too, whoever he was. . . .

Edmund suddenly heard Sophie's pearly laugh ringing through the room; his apprehension and curiosity became untenable. He excused himself from Larry and swiftly pushed his way through the crowds, he walked towards the familiar joyous sound, he reached the middle of the room and saw, from a distance . . . Sophie seated on a Louis XV chair, which in turn was set upon a wooden platform, like a little throne. She had regained some of her adolescent weight since Edmund had last seen her, how much one couldn't tell, for she was wrapped in a voluminous robe of studded tapestry that recalled the vestment of some primitive idol and a regal diamond tiara sat atop her mop of unruly gleaming hair. Seated on a throne, wrapped in tapestries that recalled the sack of Ninevah, the fall of Tyre, there was his Sophie. . . .

"Sofka," Edmund called out severely from the middle of the room, "Sofka, what the hell?" She turned towards him and gave him her ebullient laugh, stretching out her jeweled hand with what he recognized to be profound tenderness. "Dreamboat, at last!" Edmund elbowed his way farther through the tuxedoes, the taffetas, the whispers, the rhinestones, the garrulous voices, the tubs of

rented caviar, the rented guests, remembering the sad
ravenous émigrés at the parties he and Mara had attended
to relieve their hunger and their loneliness. Upon this
moment of Edmund's return to New York his years in
Berkeley filled him with anguish and anger, productive
and blazing years, obsessed with acquisitions and honors
and exhibitions of his conquests, replete with clever
antiques, flamboyant Simonas, papers of great clever-
ness, lectures of devastating charm. For a very fleeting
moment which would only return fully many years later
—would then even change his life—Edmund was suddenly flooded with the desire to retreat to a distant place
and support himself by humble occupations, mending
nets, grinding corn, gardening for others, making sails,
anything, anything rather than the rapacity of his past
few years at Berkeley or the squalid glitter of the Reillys'
opulence . . . but this sense of gluttedness and guilt
blazed only for a few seconds. Sophie continued smiling,
he came towards her dais, renewed acquaintance with
her smell of rose and musk; the fertile odors thrust him
into a dual state of panic and desire. Sofka, fellow
sufferer on sailboats, beloved model of his brief and
brilliant painting career, the most tenderly dutiful and
giving of the two or three women who had obsessed his
life, she whom he had trusted would become a star of her
generation; had he been guilty of not clearly enough
showing his love for her, not instilling enough courage?
"What do you think you're doing," he blurted out as he
stood at the foot of her dais, "will you please get out of
that ridiculous chair? Immediately!" "Marriage," she
laughed, "just another stage of life's way . . ."

She continued laughing and the fluted sound reassured
him a little, perhaps the nomad was resting, drawing
strength for future struggles in a rented tent, this travesty
might be as brief as some of her earlier excursions, he
would make sure it would be her last! Sophie stretched
out her arms towards him, he bent forward to touch her

dear face, stumbled on the step of her dais and fell to the floor. Our lives are hidden from us, like our deaths, he thought as he lay briefly at her feet. But instead he said severely: "This is impossible, Sophie, impossible! I'll take care of you, I'll kidnap you tonight, I'll do anything to get you out of this monstrous place!"

xiv

Halfway in the middle of their stay in the Soviet Union, Edmund decides that the whole trip might be a fiasco. Don't kid yourself fellow the recovery of innocence is an idiotic enterprise. We're diving into each other like pilots on reconnaissance missions, insights fitful, sometimes savage, we're trying to turn back to some golden age which may have been more violent than we've dared to admit; the recapture of youth is as brutal as most nursery rhymes, here is a candle to light you to bed here is an ax to . . . In the last evenings of their stay in Leningrad, Edmund starts drinking with Evgeny. Sophie is out walking alone every night, allegedly documenting the attitudes of Soviet women to natural childbirth, détente, abortion; half the time Claire is out searching for Sophie or else she's trying to phone Moscow on her blasted missions. Other members of the Intourist party are equally irksome. Irina keeps chiding the Zabars for dropping out of the official tour to visit synagogues, "rubble of no historical significance." Mrs. Jones has heard that face-lifts are free and wonderful in Russia and wants to come back with her friends to have it done here. Ah yes *remont* Edmund quips by all means have one. The Rolls-Roycers have broken three ashtrays at the Dollar Store after consuming too much vodka at lunch and Ted Weicker is praising the Soviet Union for its low crime rate, where else in the West can you walk alone so safely at night?

Soviet bars close at ten o'clock. Edmund and Evgeny head for one of Leningrad's foreign currency bars, dark chromed spaces filled with the din of rock, with vapors of American whiskeys and tobaccos unavailable to Soviets. Tempted but diffident, Evgeny follows Edmund to these haunts with a stealthy air. The ruby-mouthed Soviet women in deeply cleavaged silks who accompany some of the foreigners remind Edmund of the German officers' molls who filled Parisian bars during the Nazi occupation. . . . Edmund orders a bottle of Black Label and often needles the Russian about the state of his country.

"I've evolved a new theory on this trip, Evgeny, I've realized that civilizations contact each other through their poisons. Take heed, brother, think of the way the Indians were done in by our first colonizers; it's our liquor those poor bastards wanted rather than our alphabets or medicines, just the way you crave our Marlboros and Pepsis and odious music without giving a hoot about our human rights. . . . Look at this Western decadence which you'd all sell your icons for if you had any left; your country reminds me of a fruit that's rotting before it's even had a chance to ripen. Listen, Evgeny, if I were a member of your Politburo I'd be more authoritarian in these matters, more severe . . ."

"Severe?" the Russian repeats loudly over the din of the rock, keeping his spectacled eyes on Edmund.

"Severe, severe!" Edmund cries. "The last thing I'd wish on you is to become like us. If I were one of your leaders I'd safeguard our ancient Slavic values, resurrect our glorious ethnic traditions; oh, I'm an unabashed romantic, I'd only allow balalaikas, Georgian songs, Kalmyk zithers, Cossack dances . . . in old times your craving for debased Westernness was restricted to the upper crust but now you've become one huge beggar's opera; look at how these dens are corrupting your youth with their black markets!"

Evgeny resettles his spectacles with a firm thrust of his fifth finger. "One position is that we're still suffering from the aftermath of the Great War, Gedmund; your foreign currency is immeasurably helpful to our economy."

"One position, brother, is that you're brilliant at finding excuses for every shortcoming you have. Soon the Olympics will provide your next five-year fuck-up plan, no toilet paper in Kiev, all of Leningrad in *remont*, it's the Olympics and so it'll go until 1984. My position is that your beggar's opera is based on that tragic need to ape the West which grew in the isolation of your steppes, and you hate us with that particularly bitter hatred which the imitator has for his model. . . ."

"How can you criticize us, Gedmund, when your society is so permissive that your pornography, your media violence, are on the verge of destroying you?"

"Oh don't take us as a model, Evgeny, I'd close it down, close it all down."

"Time may have come for you to start defining human obligations along with human rights, Gedmund. . . ."

"You've put your finger on the American tragedy, dear friend; our honeymoon with spineless permissiveness is over! We're yearning for restrictions, authority, tens of thousands of our kids joining half-crazed religious cults in which they're programmed like robots around the clock; you're seeing in us Narcissus in Chaos, the final wasteland of bourgeois individualism. . . ."

There were many such exchanges, habitually cordial.

"Those two fine women you travel with, Gedmund, you've known them for long?" "Thirty years." "Perhaps you were almost married once to one of them?" "Almost to both of them." "*Colossalnoe delo*," the Russian murmurs, "a colossal feat. The thin darker one, she is always trying to phone Moscow, she has relatives there?" "Relatives of friends, trifles, I wouldn't bother with it in your KGB reports." "And which one is more difficult to live with?" "Oh, don't ask me, brother, they've both become impossible, impossible, perhaps they always were. . . . Do you expect me to live with simple women, without divinities? I'll never settle for a modified rapture . . . let's drink in reckless communion, Evgeny Sergeievich!"

After a half bottle Evgeny offers sparse details of his own life. During the height of the Stalinist terror his family had stayed up until dawn hours playing cards to assuage their fears of being rounded up by the KGB, going to bed only in exhaustion . . . he'd once been much in love with a teacher of history who became too interested in Polish culture . . . he'd once written a paper on Dreiser at university, he might soon leave Intourist work and take an advanced degree . . . after such moments of candor he picks up his coat and explains that he must go home because his grandmother is waiting for him, his grandfather has a kidney disease, a cousin is arriving from Lvov. "Communists always want to go home," Edmund sighs. Evgeny gives a guarded smile, taps his knee with his *Pravda* as he reminds Edmund of the next morning's tour schedule. Their conversations often end with Evgeny saying, "Ah yes this is Wonderland Gedmund Petrovich." "Wonderland, right?"

One night on their way out of the hotel Edmund and Evgeny pass some members of their Intourist group in a corridor. One of the Rolls-Royce couples is trying to entice the Zabars to have a nightcap in their room. "One more to celebrate this gorgeous country, Zabs, clean as a whistle! No longhair kids standing in Red Square yelling hell no we won't go!" "No Gay Lib," his wife adds assertively. "You think we're crazy, Prof," the Floridian says to Edmund with his wide disheveled smile. "Here's to effete intellectual snobs," his wife raises her glass. The Zabars are trying to be pastoral, proposing Bisodol, urging an early bedtime because of the 7:00 A.M. waking scheduled for the next morning. The Rolls-Roycers' lapels are replete with insignias of Lenin exchanged with Soviet teenagers for T-shirts and gum—Lenin aged four, cherubic and blond-curled as Baby Jesus, Lenin as high schooler, Lenin as fiercely bearded leader. "We too are a Wonderland, Evgeny," Edmund says as they leave for their evening outing.

Sophie burst into the bar of the Astoria shortly after midnight.

"Soph my love, what have you been up to this time?"

"Out for a walk in the Dostoevski district, Edmund; I climbed up the stairs to Raskolnikov's room, saw the courtyard on which Sonya's window looked out . . ."

Claire came in next. "Oh thank God, she's here . . . I was so worried. I saw her walking by the Admiralty and then I lost sight of her in the dark. . . ."

Edmund stared at Claire and continued trying to understand her after thirty years. She stood above them fingering a variety of papers stuffed into her boyish raincoat, her skin the color of clean sand after a storm, looking at the bar with her haughty, abstracted glance. "I may return," she said after hugging Sophie. "I must go upstairs to finish some letters."

"Don't worry, dear heart," Sophie called out after her, "I've survived alone in the streets of more perverse cities. . . ." She downed her Scotch in one gulp, put her arm around Edmund. "Ah if you knew what extraordinary creatures these two are, Evgeny, treasures . . . unearthly . . . or perhaps too earthly. Let me explain . . ."

"Let her explain." Edmund leaned his head back on Sophie's shoulder. "We'll have one of our frequent consciousness-lowering sessions."

"Well I'll start with Claire, it's easier, more brutal. I'm a Slav too, Genia, and I'm inebriated with candor tonight! When we were young I used to see her pacifism as a kind of magnet which could absorb all evil in her own frail person . . ."

"Oh her nonviolence is of sterner ore than any knives, Genia, her silences are bombs with time fuses."

"But later on I saw a few more dangerous things in that purity of hers—it's genuine, mind you, genuine, yet what has it done but trigger us to more and more outrageous behavior!"

They drank. The rock band started playing Presley. Four Swedes sang "Auld Lang Syne" and loudly clapped while their ruby-mouthed Soviet escorts did the twist in the middle of the room, a drunken young Russian accompanying a group of Danes weaved about the bar yelling obscenities, Evgeny rapped his *Pravda* nervously against his chair.

"Have you ever had anyone like that in your life, Genia," Sophie leaned across the table towards the Russian, "someone whose purity destroys? She's moved by compassion for the world and the lives she's touched most deeply may be ruined!"

"How well you understand human nature!" the Russian shouted with feeling.

"She's ruined our lives hasn't she Eddem, but with such style!"

"Turn off the soap opera, Soph."

"Well you came here for the truth, didn't you Edmund?"

"I'm not sure anymore my love." Edmund refilled their drinks, sat between them, arms folded. "I'm beginning to think that we need illusions even more than truth if the three of us are going to live together from now on."

"Live together? Who said we were ever going to live together?"

"I say so. Right now. I thought of it just now, at this

very moment. I think we've totally fucked up going it alone, especially you and I. . . . I'm about to propose it at our next plenary session, propose some revolutionary form of triadic household."

"But you will torment each other so," the Russian lamented.

"The three of us, what madness! As usual you're terrified, you're avoiding your real needs, Edmund. . . ."

"What is he doing?" the Russian shouted over the din of the rock.

"Avoiding, avoiding! It's her alone you want, Edmund, her alone! Why not just grab her now that she's finally free?"

"You are all so Slavic!" the Russian exclaimed.

". . . I need to be more refueled than ever with illusions, Sophie, and I can't abide this hemorrhage of openness. . . ."

"The more Clara tortures you the more she loves you?" the Russian asked.

"Yes yes, what insights our friend has, she's indeed grown increasingly dependent on us over the years!"

Late at night Evgeny's pale leonine head nodded slowly, methodically, over each word. "How I enjoy your calisthenics of the soul!"

"Love is only one thing, Genia," Sophie said, "it's the willingness to die for the other. . . . I've come to your country with the only two people I've ever known for whom I'd willingly give up my life!"

"You heroic fidelity to each other moves me so," the Russian exulted. "A toast to her, to the mysterious third one!"

"Yes, yes," Sophie cried, "to her who's clarified our lives by the suffering she's brought us . . ."

They drank.

"Do let's toast some more cheerful matters, Gedmund!"

"To the noble suffering of the artist, Evgeny Sergeiev-ich!"

"To the glorious traditions of Russian and American art, Gedmund Petrovich!"

"To the glories of the Hermitage! When the deuce are you taking us there, Genia? . . ."

"Hermitage *remont* is over, Gedmund, we finally take you there tomorrow!"

"To our striving for the ideal man!"

"And for the ideal woman!"

Sophie buried her head in Edmund's shoulder.

"To your tears, Sofia Larionovna," Evgeny drank, "to Sofia's tears!"

"Yes, to her beloved tears!"

Edmund came knocking at Claire's door early that morning complaining of a furious headache; perhaps he might have come to her without that excuse—she hovered at the door's edge in a long childlike white nightgown, rubbing her eyes—the hotel window behind her opened out upon the tuliped expanse of St. Isaac's Square—as he engaged her firm, tense body for the first time that year he was reminded that this most severe of individualists would only come to him at her own pace, her own time, refusing to ever be dictated to or defined by anyone—throughout the twenty-five years of their extremely rare lovemakings he'd learned that there was no frigidity at the core of her abstinent life, that her complex, delicate flesh could be as unleashed as that of any woman he'd known—Radiant 5:00 A.M. light flooded her oval face as she stared at him with pale eyes drained of their habitual defiance or aloofness, filled with an almost sassy playfulness, as if she enjoyed the surprise he had in her unfettering—He put his lips to her face in a ritual sequence he'd begun a quarter of a century ago, first on a cheek, then on each closed eyelid; how maddening she must be to other men because of her ability to control lust, making her rare gifts of it with freedom incomparable—he'd come to think of sexual encounters as a quest for information executed in a spirit of curiosity and high playfulness; a line had been haunting him, " '*Je ne veux pas jouir, je ne veux que savoir*,' " he whispered to Claire that morning—But this knowledge was denied him, this satisfaction she held back, her Nordic eyes reflected nothing but an immensely serene affection, the self-containment of a planet—he fell asleep feeling gratitude for a life in which a rich full spectrum of friendship, passion, brotherly love had been incarnated into each of his two deepest bondings—when he woke, Claire had already left the room, he remembered with a burst of immense joy that it was the day to go to the Hermitage. "What a crazy night we had," he told the Zabars and the Weickers at breakfast, "everyone was drunk, the Swedes were singing, the Russians were weeping, or perhaps the other way around, I don't know anymore, you never know in this country."

xv

The ferry blew its amazing horn before it came into sight. Edmund stood at the Hyannis landing playing the game he'd once shared with his mother, choosing the most magnificent family scheduled to board the vessel. He settled on a Buick whose cargo included six bicycles and a great amount of fishing rods cunningly strung onto the roof, four children, three enormous and anxious Irish setters (he'd always remembered an abundance of setters on the island, as if they were a more trustable token of family bliss than poodles or terriers), a proliferation of barbecue grills, tennis rackets, picnic hampers, and two parents of some beauty impatiently waiting for the boarding to begin. The slender, green-eyed female of the pair stepped out of the car to assess the imminence of the ship's arrival to Hyannis, staring fiercely at nothing in the manner of athletic women. Her setters yapped nervously at a pug on the road, beach towels tumbled out of hampers, her flaxen-haired children were arguing among themselves, the eight-year-old pulled at his younger sister's ear, the child protested with shrill cries, the older girl—a beauty of fourteen or so, the same age at which Edmund had first met Claire—reprimanded her siblings while carefully rebraiding her long pale hair. The mother chided gently also, turning her head towards her brood with a soft laugh, whispering to her husband don't scold on the first day of vacation. As Edmund stood among the fishing instruments, the beach gear, the remonstrances, the Andover T-shirts, the vapors of copulation and nourishment, he remembered how the ferry had looked to him two decades ago; it had glided across the dark water like a blazing caterpillar, metamorphosing into a moth of bridal whiteness as it slid past the lighthouse. But when it rounded the cape this morning it changed from insect to mammal in the space of a few moments, it plowed through the oily sound with the heaviness of a wounded whale, spluttered and spit as it spun on its engines to thrust its maws towards the dock; Edmund lost the image of lightness, bridal whiteness, the ferry had become . . . something else. He had just turned thirty-five this past spring, and in a few weeks Claire would be thirty-five also. The vessel made its final docking, slid into the oily fences of its berth and expelled scores of vehicles—food trucks, early thrifty vacationers returning to the gloom of summer cities—before ingesting its new load. The magnificent family expressed its joy, their setters panted quickly, their blue Buick slid voluptuously into the ferry.

Halfway into the passage Edmund had a talk with a clergyman of extreme black and whiteness—pale eyes, silver hair, white socks, sternly black little suitcase. The priest expressed interest in the fact that Edmund hoped to soon become chairman of Berkeley's art history department and spoke movingly about the Church of il Gesù in Rome. They went on to an amusing conversation about grace; the priest was clearly a Jansenist. "It comes down upon you like rain." He fluttered his dark arms upwards, his long pale fingernails clicking above his head like castanets. The Nantucket coast finally came into sight, offering its beauty like a Puritan woman baring her breast, uncleaned pearls of pale gray houses spread against the harbor, docks filled with coquettish shops which Edmund did not remember there a decade ago. It was shortly before noon when the vessel docked. And stepping alone onto the pier amid the throng of vacationers Edmund decided to postpone his meeting with Claire and Jeff for a few hours. A handsome risk, looking up such friends after six years, he'd been wary of it for months. So he started drifting through the town, peered into Lilliputian gardens and houses that had so enchanted him decades ago, tried to recapture the island's nursery-rhyme spell, walked aimlessly down thoroughfares called Coon Street, Beaver Street, New Dollar Lane. Within a half hour he realized that he was more or less following the movements of the couple he'd studied at the Hyannis landing. They were easy to sight by the splendor of their hair, their children, their dogs. And he proceeded to linger behind them even more meticulously, lurking a block away, feeling like a thief as he watched them act their roles in this theater of family happiness.

How many children there were about, filling the streets! The infant population drenched the air with small sounds of crude and tender timbre, like the din of verbiage in high wind. On tepid threatening days not fine enough for the beach, vacationers parade through such resorts dressed in fishermen costumes of slickers and high boots. It was the Fourth of July (national birthday of a people more dedicated than any other to the cult of happiness) and Edmund wondered whether he could feel part of these happy crowds if he acquired the right props: a child to hold by the hand, a sand pail, a little striped umbrella. He followed his adopted family for another hour at proper distance, admiring the beauty of the children about him, marveling at what it would be like to have married Pebble and be vacationing like this every day of the month, answering his son's questions about birds as he biked downtown for his morning papers, wondering when the wife's period would be over, feeling solicitous about a baby's bowel movements, worrying about the ingress and egress of several earthly frames. Whatever happiness he'd had was of such a different order that he barely felt part of the humanity milling about him. He often felt the burden of his solitude; I sometimes wish we could reproduce alone he'd recently told John Mirsky, like amoebas, like Adam, sculpting part of our bodies into perfect children the way we try to shape our students. . . . Edmund remained a respectful block behind his adopted family as they stood in line at a bakery, procrastinating his view of Sealark for a while longer and wondering what life was about.

The family's mood had become exacerbated. "I'll sock you one if you don't stop yiping," the ten-year-old shouted at the freckled four-year-old. "I shall not have that language in my house, Jeremy," the beautiful mother exclaimed. "I hate islands," the eight-year-old offered. "The children are tired," Father said. "Do we have enough beach chairs, honey?" "Of course, sweetheart." "And towels?" "Yes, yes, love." They received what they'd stood in line for and six mouths gravely bit into six sugared doughnuts. Edmund suddenly felt bullied by the purchasing, staring, chewing crowd; all that was ogled and swallowed in this bureaucracy of repose looked as suspect as its lobster-infested place mats and wooden captain dolls; he'd stared and loitered with others, he'd sat in the sun licking an ice-cream cone and bought a vulgar T-shirt, at two in the afternoon he ceased following the vacationing family and walked back to the ferry landing, he hovered over the ropes by which he'd stood with Mara decades ago at the end of the worst holocaust in human history. And then he started walking towards the Sanford house, trying to recall a line of Sartre's that Mirsky had recently read him, " 'I did not know what to do with my body,' " how did it go . . . ah, there it was, " 'I did not know what to do with my body in the midst of this tragic crowd which was struggling to amuse itself.' "

* * *

Claire Sanford Howell has gutted and eviscerated her mother's house, scrubbed it of nearly every vestige of her childhood. Gone is the china striving to imitate the shapes of frogs and various forms of bird life, the painted poodles, sailboats, piglets, roses and carnations, the ducks swimming across green swatches of petit point ponds. All is now limpidly white and unadorned, reminding Edmund of Claire's own pale face when it emerges from the water after a swim. Frenzied chintzes and floral rugs have given way to monastic burlaps and raffias, Babsie's wondrous flower arrangements have been replaced by a few trailings of beach foliage and seashells arranged in geometric patterns upon denuded tables. But the most amazing change of all has occurred on the walls! Claire has turned Sealark into a veritable museum of social protest. The living room, which first undergoes Edmund's scrutiny, literally swarms with photographs of humans marching, picketing, fasting, getting arrested for the cause of peace or of equality. And all is carefully dated and labeled, with Claire's particular brand of didactic care, with fastidious concern for educating the most casual visitor into the various reform movements that have swept America in the past century.

God knows Claire's interest is not new, simply more systematic. Hanging over the mantelpiece is a portrait of the Nantucket-born suffragist and abolitionist, Lucretia Mott, whose burning Quaker gaze is familiar to Edmund from the walls of Claire's childhood room. The air of wasted constancy on the faces of the colleagues who surround her, the stubborn stance of their folded arms, the severe part in the women's flat hair, exude the rigor of purpose that now pervades the house. In 1918 twelve women in large hats clench their fists as they sail for The Hague to plead for the end of all wars, conscientious objectors are herded into a Utah jail. Some years and decades later throngs protest the indictment of Sacco and Vanzetti, Jeannette Rankin is besieged by reporters shortly after she has cast the only vote in Congress opposing its declaration of war against Japan, the civil servant Rosa Parks is dragged to jail after refusing to move out of her bus seat. Amid parades of societies opposed to the vivisection of animals and posters advertising meat-replacing substitutes, Edmund also recognizes Sir Bertrand Russell being arrested in an antinuclear sit-in in London, A. J. Muste leading a protest against atomic tests in the Algerian Sahara. As he wanders through rooms once florally serene Edmund is perplexed by this proliferation of humanity being herded through streets and thrust into paddy wagons, this melee of contorted faces shouting for many varieties of liberation. Yes, too many! That is perhaps Claire's tragic flaw. The diversity of causes dramatized on these walls— suffragism, vegetarianism, laborers' rights, animal rights, numerous varieties of pacifism—expresses an almost frivolous abundance of dissenting passions. . . .

Edmund stared out of the window at the unchanged view he'd painted two decades earlier—rowboats bobbing like petals on the glass of the harbor, yachts steered by tall blond men playing captain setting out for an afternoon sail. And when his eyes turned from this serene idleness to the images of struggle scattered about Claire's rooms he felt more at peace than he'd felt for several years. He would realize much later—Edmund always realized things awfully late—the reasons for his surge of pleasure: palpable proof that Claire was not suited for the docile felicity Plinker and Jeff had intended for her, that she resembled Edmund in some mutual complexity of destiny. . . . It was close to four o'clock. Under the arrogantly peaceful face of Bertrand Russell that surmounted the hallway table a note informed him of the Howells' afternoon schedule. He seized one of the bicycles leaning against the garden fence and pedaled to the tennis club.

Edmund could have known that if Claire ever resumed her island life he would find her on a tennis court at 4:00 P.M., and not at base line but right at that net position where she'd spent much of her adolescence, volleying the ball with that swift aggressive turn of her shoulders which he'd always thought of as her most characteristic gesture. This is precisely where he did find her, but the following was less predictable: Right there at net, Pebble was threatening to throw a fit. As coltish as ever and dressed in virginal white, she was shouting at her husband, who was about to start a match of mixed doubles two courts away: "Now for Christ's sake, Jeff, why didn't you give me that message earlier! You know perfectly well that dozens of my friends can be arrested down there at any moment . . . really!" "How many times have you forgotten to give me messages, honey," he said with a cordial smile. "Yes, about some damn hockey game or faculty meeting, not about matters of life and death, what time is it precisely, Jeff?" He was languorously swinging his racket in preparation for service. "Oh, I guess around four or thereabout." "For heaven's sake, I asked *precisely* what time is it?" she cried once more. She threw her racket to the ground and ran off the court towards the clubhouse, pleated skirt waving about her thighs like that of a teenage gymnast, leaving her own doubles matches stranded. "It's precisely two and a half after," Jeff called out after her, "just look at the club clock, Peb!" Edmund had witnessed the preceding scene from some fifty yards away, and was approaching the courts as he heard Jeff say with a smiling apology to his pretty partner, "Sorry, Rose sweetheart, Pebble's constant damn crusade in the Deep South."

Jeff bent down to tie the laces of his sneakers. He kept his head up as he kneeled, radiating his amiable serenity towards the courts. Not one of his three oldest friends, Edmund reflected, had changed so little since adolescence. There was still the beginning of an ingenuous smile on Jeff's lips, an expression of optimism so unaltered that one imagined he retained it in the privacy of his ablutions. Living with this large, sumptuously beautiful man might have been like living under some tall belfry clock which struck each hour with a resounding din to reassure us of the excellent order of mankind. Since adolescence Jeff had stared with equally affectionate protectiveness at boats in the harbor, strangers in streets, children in playpens. And this benignancy was negligible compared to the reverence he offered those persons he might have been the last of his generation to call "the fair sex." "What perfection and grace," his eyes seemed to say when he looked at a handsome woman. "You can be my redeemer, my guidance and inspiration!" "Careful crossing the street," Edmund remembered Jeff saying throughout their adolescence as Claire, Sophie, April, Babsie, ventured towards Main Street on the smallest errand. "Careful crossing the street!" he shouted again in New York City as they exited from theater or debutante dance. Yet there was a strain of nastiness in Jeff which had to do with virtue. Like Pebble he was ever ready to carry the burden of others. But unlike her crusades for voter registration in the South his were the concrete familiar others, childhood friends, blood-kin tribe. And he wished his virtue properly exhibited, his gifts of happiness meticulously accounted for. If the rescued did not collaborate with the rescuing procedures according to Jeff's own ideals of felicity he was capable of sabotaging the whole mission. . . . After he finished tying his sneaker that afternoon Jeff turned again towards his pretty partner with a radiant smile which expressed his capitulation to her charm. The smile waned into a gaze of cynical annoyance as he saw Claire slam the door of the clubhouse. He clutched his racket rather grimly and prepared for service. His afternoon match was ill-fated, for it was then that he saw Edmund and called out to Plinker, who had been sitting in a chair by the court with a small girl on his lap: "Look who's here, Plink, look who's finally come back to us!" And before clutching Jeff's shoulders Edmund saw the old man hobbling towards him too, arms outstretched, accompanied by a girl of six so strikingly resemblant to Claire as a child that Edmund could have shouted out with the pain of memory.

"So . . . have you come to stare at my happiness, rabbit love?"

Claire was kneeling in her parents' former vegetable garden, digging up clumps of weeds, chucking them haphazardly over the fence.

"People come to stare at each other's happiness in these resorts the way Sunday visitors go to see pandas in a zoo, we're full of families parading their delight like protesters carrying pickets, big signs saying PERFECT AMERICAN FAMILY, BE THE PERFECT FAMILY!"

She continued digging, not looking at him.

"I expect that's the way you expected to find me, sitting on the beach with needlepoint of ducks on a green pond, bustling children about proclaiming our bliss . . . well if you've come to stare at my felicity dear one you should get a refund on your boat fare. . . ."

"I miss Babsie's flowers," Edmund said.

She glanced up at him with a bitter, wry little smile.

"Ah you would miss her flowers, wouldn't you? . . . Well I'm not Babsie and I'm not April and there isn't enough of dear Plinker in me either, maybe I should leave you here to keep housey with Jeff. . . ."

"I'm going back to Alabama next week," she added bluntly. "There's a lot of work to be done in Alabama."

The skin of her arms and legs were like bolts of sand-colored satin. She'd changed little since the brief

visit he'd paid the Howells in England six years ago save
for the very fine lines about her eyes, which intensified
the anger of her gaze. This trace of the passing of time
struck Edmund as sharply as a change in his own body.

"A little lettuce, parsley, carrots, I'm seeding it all
before I go South again. . . . Plinker would be despon-
dent if he didn't see something growing here before
summer's end, just a few goodies to keep them quiet."

"I'm sure you're doing the right thing . . . the garden
before leaving, I mean."

"Oh, do contradict me more than that," she whispered.
"Aren't you going to dispute me as you always used to,
E. R.? Have you come back after all these years just to
agree with me?"

As she pulled up a clump of weeds and threw it over
the fence he leaned down to avoid being splattered with
the loam.

Poor rabbit hurt his paw, Vicky put it in a splint maybe?
Plinker was walking from the boat landing to the house,
holding Victoria's hand. She clutched a basket in which
a tiny animal reposed. Victoria was frail and pensive,
with light brown hair and glacial blue eyes that tortured
Edmund with remembrance. Plinker's walk was made
very slow, more majestic than ever by his gout; he could
only see at close distance and from his lawn he gave all
passersby the wave of a royal personage passing through
crowds in a limousine. That's Uncle Edmund over there,
Mummy and Daddy's oldest friend, doesn't Victoria
want to give Uncle Eddem a good-night kiss? All right
sweets, later.

"Oh I could have continued to play Elgar so beautifully
at St. Paul's commencements, Eddem, I could have gone
on sitting there year after year seeing that bright ribbon
of life go by, hearing a racist headmaster mouth his
platitudes about being better Americans let us praise

Thee Lord who's given us this wondrous day to send our children onto the road of manhood, Jeff always cried at commencement, those beautiful rich boys seemed to carry his only assurance of immortality, his only faith in the ancient order being able to forever perpetuate itself. . . ."

She had migrated to the other side of the lawn, to the abandoned cutting garden where her mother's parterres had once bloomed in such profusion. "*Achillea*," she muttered, "does best in dry exposed places, like me. *Hemerocallis*, each bloom lasts for a single day, as I do in this house. . . . You know what's wrong with me, Eddem, I've simply never wanted to be like any woman I've ever known in real life. Not like my poor loving Babsie who grew mad in the gathering of flowers or the tragically happy classmates I still meet in the streets of Boston, wheeling prams with the smell of morning sherry on their breath. . . ."

"You were always the quintessential critic."

"Ah, the critic, an old friend of yours, right? He has a nasty gift of mimicry, he's like an immense pair of spectacles through which all of the world's ills are hugely magnified, he's grown so omnivorous that he needs to be curbed . . . or better, anchored to a community of critics. My critic needs group support, that's why he's off to Alabama. . . ."

She looked up at him with that cunning which those who profess unworldliness can wield like a club of stone.

"What about Viola Liuzzo, a woman just like me looking for salvation?"

Fog rolling in from the ocean. Town wrapped in banks of misty brilliance. Thumping of the day's last tennis balls, flap of furling sails from the Yacht Club around the corner. Plinker walking up a neighbor's path in the property next door, teaching Victoria names of flowers that had long since disappeared from Sealark. Lily of the valley, plant pips two inches apart, it's that little thing every pretty bride must have. Edmund recalled Chesterton's description of Saint Thomas Aquinas approaching death: "The confessor, who had been with him in the inner chamber, ran forth in tears and whispered that his last confession had been that of a child of five."

Claire gestured to Edmund as she moved from one part of the property to another; she seemed to want him continually by her side during her tasks.

"And what about you, Eddem? You've had your Guggenheim and your associate professorship, next year you'll start getting honorary doctorates and distinguished chairs here and there, what kind of a future do you dream of for yourself?"

He cleared his throat. He joined his index fingers thoughtfully to his blond beard, Dr. Richter charming audiences from the lectern.

"Well, many things. Having power for instance. Give me two or three years to get the chairmanship of the department and I'll really clean it up, restore all kinds of outmoded disciplines. No more fashionable permissiveness, much stress on classics and iconography . . ."

She stared up at him, inscrutable.

". . . plenty of room for metaphysical speculation that'll bury the positivistic nonsense; I'll make it the best traditional school in the country. I also look forward to being sixty-six; upon retirement I'll move to Venice into a strictly inodorous palace with cooks, frescoes, tapestries . . ."

She burst out laughing with all the abandon of her youth.

"I'll look like a tenor who's too old to make love but is still redolent with charm, I'll wish for conversion each time I hear the organ, the Reverend Edwards already has great hopes for me."

She threw spadefuls of earth playfully over her shoulder and he knew that underneath what he now saw as mayhem she was as resilient as ever.

"Ah Eddem we do need you to wake us from our Puritan earnestness, as Babsie used to say. Now. What about our Soph?"

"Oh I tried hard enough to get her to come up this weekend; between the two of us we might have straightened her out a bit . . ."

"Eddem dear, I worry about her violent shifts of moods, the gloom she was in last year, the manic hedonism of this season."

"I've always thought of psychoanalysis as a science for moral parvenus," Edmund said. "Yet her fluctuations are such it might be a last resort. . . ."

"However," he added pointedly, "she retains the courage of frivolity, as I do."

The one time Edmund saw Claire and Jeff alone together they were discussing matters of the household with attempted civility.

"Beach chairs, Clairsie."

"Do you mind?"

"Not at all, I'll go on the A.M. Also, April phoned, Katrinka has no room for her and she wants to drop in on us next weekend with the children."

"How beastly."

"Now, sweets, it's the family! We'll do a clambake the day she comes, and the next afternoon we can have a nifty sail to Siasconset . . . do give it your one oh oh," he added sharply as he walked towards the boat landing.

"One oh oh," she murmured as she picked lettuce for supper, looking absentminded.

Before dinner Edmund was asked to hold Victoria on his lap. It is possible that he had never had a child on his lap before. It is possible that he had never before closely experienced the smell of a young child's flesh. The texture, the odor, of Victoria's face was terrifying in its novelty. In this flesh of palpitating innocence there was already some principle of procreation which he had never detected—perhaps never dared detect—in her mother's wiry body. He put his face close to the child's hair, closed his eyes, inhaled deeply. In the immaculacy of her hair's fragrance he recalled some moment and texture of his own childhood that had slipped into oblivion, some smell of his own body being scrubbed by Mara. The child turned her face swiftly towards him and he felt the inexplicable delicacy of her skin upon his cheek like the brush of a flower's pistil. The fleeting gossamer joy of her cheek upon his made him feel the somber weight of that splendidly groomed body of his which had never reproduced, which had seldom merged with its highest object of desire, this girl's mother. . . . And who would bring up this superb child? Women were leaving home to find a possible death in good causes, schools were dissolving under the threat of radical idiots, the daughters of women who'd gone mad from staying at home were going mad from being too much in the world. He missed intensely throughout this visit the presence of Elizabeth Sanford, that half-crazed creature of common-place conversation whose singular contribution (and he suspected it was a gift peculiar to women) had been to bring comfort to those about her. I'm becoming more conservative than ever, Edmund reflected with pleasure.

Before Victoria went to bed Claire embraced her daughter with a tense desperate tenderness and held her very tight. She sat her on her lap and brushed her hair with the silver-handled brush that had belonged to Babsie. How the child delighted in her mother's touch! She had looked distant, amused, in the men's arms all afternoon. But now she sucked her thumb, eyes closed, her head collapsed against her mother's shoulder as if it were the only place in which she could abandon herself to her childhood. After Victoria's hair was straight and gleaming Claire clutched her again and rocked her softly, eyes closed.

Looking suntanned, rested and moral, Jeff sat in his upstairs study that evening writing mail-order houses for numerous articles with which to ornate his denuded house. He ordered shell-shaped night-lights, monogrammed note pads, crème brûlée ramekins, cocktail glasses etched with herons sailing across brilliant skies. He had told Edmund as they'd biked home from the tennis club that his dream was to retire fairly early from the teaching profession and live year round in this part of New England, supporting himself "by some profitable little local commerce." Designing nautical instruments . . . strengthening the local lobster industry . . . he might import some sheep, as he had in Great Britain . . . useless to even mention such projects to Claire, she went berserk at the thought of ever living on the island . . . meanwhile he aspired to make the house as comfortable as Babsie had had it. As Edmund sat sipping Scotch with him that evening Jeff lovingly studied offerings of bowl and whisk sets, wind-chill meters, butter churners, portable weaving looms.

"See, Eddem, the trouble is that I looked forward to marriage more than to anything else in the world! I was going to be a great husband the way I was going to be a great teacher; I wanted to have four children and build a perfect little community. . . ."

"You poor bastard."

"D'you know the single most important thing we're doing in a great school like St. Paul's, Edmo? We're training good husbands, loyal men. What better service can we offer society than to train them for ideal marriages?"

Edmund was damned if he was going to shape students into ideal husbands but it wasn't the right time to differ; he was agreeing with everyone this weekend to keep the household from going to pieces. In Sealark's attic, two floors above Claire's displays of fasting pacifists and picketing monks, Jeff had installed a veritable sanctuary of military values. Walls adorned with portraits of uniformed ancestors—Admiral Howell, strikingly resembling his offspring, leans on his sword during a lull in the Spanish-American War; General Howell of the Battle of the Bulge stands in a field in Flanders, foot poised on a cannon. All about the floor of Jeff's refuge the elaborate collection of toy soldiers from all ages of mankind which Edmund had so admired in their adolescence—silver-helmeted Roman legions shoot arrows from clusters of plastic trees, medieval foot soldiers charge across moats and drawbridges, generals in crimson jackets inspect regiments; and at center stage a two-inch-high Napoleon, hand thrust into his vest, is led away by one of Wellington's blue-jacketed aides-de-camp.

"You know what the schoolboy is, Edmo? He's like a base ore that can be forged into precious metal in the crucible of a great school and then polished to shine with a dull, rich luster; that's why we need to get him as young as possible, to forge his courage and loyalty; one of the masters has a neat way of putting it, Eddem, he compares it to making a perfect martini. You need the right proportions of unswerving loyalty and individualism, the old geezer says, the loyalty of the character is the gin . . . but Edmo the way young anarchists are going today they're getting to be like a ghastly potion of ninety percent vermouth!"

"I know only too well, they're odious."

"I work my ass off to correct the balance, Eddem; I teach three history courses, coach two sports, advise the military history club, I have seminar on sixth-form responsibilities Tuesday and Wednesday night, sex education on Thursday, I take my turn in chapel once a week; teaching is a continuous act of faith . . . like

great husbands, Eddem, good teachers are paragons of
loyalty and firmness who're capable of exploding in
righteous indignation. . . ."

"I strongly believe in anger."

They sat opposite each other at the table laden with Jeff's
books of military history, finishing the bottle of whiskey
set between them.

"And what are you going to do about her?"

Jeff opened his arms with a helpless gesture that added
to the irony of his smile. He'd always been reluctant to
discuss his private life with anyone, nothing Edmund
respected more.

"I don't mind if women take over the world, old sport,
what I'm afraid of is their values . . . sensitivity to the
suffering of unknown hordes, splendid on the private
plane but what if it enters the realm of public affairs,
forces the masculine tone to pass from the nation?"

"Quite so, a reign of mediocrity, hollow phrases about
better worlds!"

"After we get through with animals' rights they'll give
us theories about plants having emotions, rocks feeling
pain, there's no end to it, Eddem, how are we ever going
to feed the planet?"

"Even though I don't have one I'm even more concerned with the survival of the family," Edmund sighed.

The bottle was depleted. Even as an adolescent Jeff had
had the most honorable manner of holding his liquor,
amiable cheeks flushing, smile widening into the evening
until he fell benignly asleep in some chair. Even now
when he more or less fell onto the sofa the gesture had a
certain choreographic splendor. "Peb and I will make up
tomorrow and she'll have a super plan for saving the
Congolese . . . where are you going?" Jeff muttered as
Edmund paced about his study. "Nowhere . . . I mean,
I might take a turn around the block a bit later." "Careful

crossing the street," Jeff whispered, and then fell into a deep sleep. Sitting at the table littered with volumes of military history Edmund felt sadness in the felling of this simple complex man. Fellows like Plinker and Jeff were becoming like snow leopards, an endangered species. Edmund had returned to the island longing to taste again of that rich dull luster Jeff spoke about, of that historic order that had nourished his fragile exiled self upon his arrival in America. And if this most stalwart of worlds was crumbling where was the refuge, could the center ever hold? Edmund raised Jeff's feet up more comfortably onto the sofa, put a pillow under his head, continued staring at him by the light of the army lamp that illuminated Jeff's toy battles. There was in Jeff a Puritan Don Giovanni which incited him to aspire to the unconquerable, to climb every Everest of the erotically accessible, even there clearly exhibited valor was of the essence. He'd probably persevered to win Claire precisely because she was so particularly unseductable, and when the process of taming her ran amok his moods might well turn vile. There lay le Puritain Moyen Sensuel, Jeff of the loyal hard-on, Jeff of the dutiful erection; in sleep his profile was almost feminine in its beauty, resembled Donatello's *David*. Edmund looked out the window and stared at the tragic set of New England innocence it had been the Sanfords' and Howells' honor to preserve, at that frozen nostalgia for a purer age shouting through the white spires of floodlit churches. When Plinker and Jeff would be called away the heroic age of America would come to an end, age of high ideals and the most elegant hypocrisies. He didn't wish to leave that fragrant face of Jeff's which even in sleep continued to shroud all pains in a benign ironic smile; he would have been happy spending the night on the same couch, coiled in whatever remained of Jeff's certitude.

He went to bed humming an old school song familiar to the Sanfords and the Howells.

"Hath he fulfilled the promise of his youth . . . and borne unscath'd through danger's stormy fields . . . Honor's white wreath and virtue's stainless shield . . ."

"Almighty Father bless our land with honorable industry sound learning and pure manners defend our liberties as Thou has in the recent world upheaval and grace our house as we have honored Thee in Thy Tabernacle in this year of our Lord 1955 . . ."

"*Sixty*-five, daddy sweetheart, it's all right, all right."

". . . bless all who teach and all who learn among the beloved teachers gathered here today that they may train young souls in pursuance of Thy will and grant that in humility of heart . . ."

"Save us from Communist vegetarian pacifists," Jeff intoned, "help us build mighty fortresses to ward them off." He was in a vile mood at that Sunday lunch; not so much from his headache, Edmund had deciphered, but from the announcement of another of Pebble's imminent departures. The day was halcyon. Victoria was running about in a little apron, helping her mother to bring dishes from the kitchen. Still dressed in her bathing suit, Claire had set the table quite formally with the little that remained of Babsie's silver. In the desolate white dining room ornated with humans agitating for redress, sunlight dappled by the sound gleamed on the same crystal and china as it had precisely twenty years ago. Plinker hovered over the table, leaning on his cane, his mouth open in the bewildered manner of the very old, his eyes traveling from Jeff to Claire to the photograph of Bertrand Russell over the breakfront.

". . . save us from the savers," Jeff continued as he set the roast on the table. "Ban the Bomb Banners, enable us to resist the resisters . . ."

"Mediums, vegetarians," Plinker muttered.

Edmund found Claire's next tactic quite extraordinary. She proceeded to propound domestic information of the grossest common sense: April's toilet-training theories were outdated, not a chance of getting her to listen to Dr. Spock, a string quartet from Boston was playing at Town Hall on Wednesday, the mushroom dish she'd fixed them today came from the *Alternative Commune Cookbook* and wasn't it heaven? Edmund feared greatly what would come next: confrontation, accusation, the pain of history.

"Edmund, you want to be a swell friend to little Victoria?" Jeff was sharpening his carving knife, flourishing it with theatrical gestures that worried Edmund. "Why don't you stick around and help me play dad? When Mommy's here she keeps the vegerino meals coming right on sched, bang bang, but when she's away saving the world it's up to us men to stave for ourselves. Join the club of the bereaved, Eddem, greater love hath no man than to share his family with his friends, the little he has of it. So here's the real grub, and is it delish; Vicky, watch Daddy carve the lovely roast. Thanks for uncorking the wine so nicely, sweet Plinker, I drink a toast to . . . our happiness. Not a chance, let's try again. To the cunning little pacifists who'll save America! Don't knock them E. R. or they'll creep up on you! *Salut! Na Zdarovie!*"

Edmund felt great anger rising. His childhood craving for china, silver, dining rooms, his lifelong love for the solace of rituals, the polonaise of etiquette . . . they were trampling on the torn garments of his youth, whatever there was left of them. He stood up and took his turn shouting.

"Must this family always be going mad in some way? Can't you pull yourselves together and lead this country again as you always have? Where's your stamina, where's everything? You can't even do a proper Sunday lunch anymore!"

Nantucket, Mass.
July 8th, 1965

. . . at some point in that meal, Soph, with that haunting view of the sound unchanged since the day the four of us first had lunch together, I found myself in an argument with Claire that went somewhat like this: Your pacifist friends wouldn't give a rat's prick about watching the world burn, right, they'd let someone else do that dirty little business? . . .

Well, you know perfectly well how she'd retort, she didn't sound that different from the way you would have in one of your earlier incarnations: You desiccated passive academic always locked in your ivory tower she cried, are you saying you believe in violence? Not at all I replied, it reeks of spontaneity. I'm just stating that there's a lot of brutality in your nonviolence Santa Clara, you're being duped by the new manufacturers of liberation, another big business that's about to boom in this country. . . .

Part Three

The perfect interlocutor, the friend, is the one who offers
me the greatest possible resonance . . . Friendship could
be defined as the space with the greatest sonority.

ROLAND BARTHES

xvi

Titian's *Shower of Danaë* depicts a naked woman reclining on a richly rumpled bed, a wreath of pale braided hair winding between her perfect breasts. Gold, rose, mauve glazes cast on her flesh the luminous grain of time-worn silks, of a camellia on its last days of bloom. One leg is bent at the knee, her head leans back on a pillow as she stares at the shower of golden coins that descends from the sky above her. Her expression is one of rapture, of abandon. Yet the painting is full of doom, russet shower bursting upon Danaë from a somber thunderous sky, Godhead manifesting itself not in a beneficent stream but in some awesome explosion. And at the right of the canvas an aging woman servant greedily holds out her arms to catch the falling gold, her sear of vice and rags hovering like another storm cloud over the maiden's sumptuous flesh.

Edmund stands before Titian's *Danaë* on a June morning in Leningrad's Hermitage Museum. Let Dr. Richter write an ideal last paper in which he'll elaborate on the ambiguous symbolism of this split radiance, gold and sperm, greed and grace, man spending his sperm on his hard-earned coins, sky god spending itself in a rain of gold. Previous instances in which an effusion of riches is a sign of grace: shower of coins blessing Hänsel and Gretel as they fall into their innocent sleep; Grimm

brothers' *Sternhaler*, wealth of gold raining down upon
the pious orphaned virgin who offers all her clothing to
the poor; the young hero of still another German folktale
soars above his city on a giant bee, dispensing golden
showers on all the marriageable girls of his province.
One could speculate on the roots of such legends in
primeval agricultural myths, in the ancient rites which
call on male gods to fructify the fields of female earth.
Teutonic legends merely Nordic variants on Zeus's rain
of gold and the mysterious events of the Immaculate
Conception, Danaë was even seen by some medieval
scholars as a prefiguration of the Virgin Mary. And so
the cloudburst of coins descending upon Titian's reclining maiden (this would be an amusingly farfetched aside
of our discourse) could be compared to the fertilizing
beams of grace that flow to Mary from the angel's palm
in paintings of the Annunciation. "Dr. Richter will give
his last lecture of the century tonight on 'The Iconography of the Shower of Gold as a Prefiguration of the
Word.' " One could stress that in earlier depictions of the
Danaë myth (Correggio's, Gentileschi's) Danaë stretches
out her own hand with considerable greed, seems as
guilty of cupidity as the elderly attendant hovering by her
side. But this is where Titian shows his psychological
cunning, transposes all avarice unto the hag who hovers
over the rapturous girl, purifies his heroine into a symbol
of amorous and celestial grace. . . . Also! Essential to
elaborate right here on the splendid Oedipal elements of
the Perseus-Danaë tale: Danaë's father, ruler of Argos,
warned by oracles that he would be destroyed by his own
grandson, imprisoning his only daughter in a brass
chamber to preserve her virginity; sky god's divine rain
piercing through the fortress wall to conceive Perseus,
the redeemer king, Perseus later performing heroic feats
to protect his mother's chastity, destroying her tyrannic
captors with the head of the Gorgon Medusa whose sight

turns men to stone, "Snakehaired creature fought and won through lurid air on strident, whirling wings . . ."

The city of Leningrad glimmers a floor below the windows of the Hermitage; sharply etched buildings washed with pale hues of confectioners' colors, familiar from the aquatints hung about Mara's bed in their tiny New York rooms; the walls of the General Staff Headquarters across Palace Square are the pale yellow of fresh butter. Edmund had looked away from Titian's *Danaë* for a moment and realized why the image had long mesmerized him: the very tale of his adolescence, fatherless Edmund and chaste much-courted Mara whose marriage led to her destruction. A curiosity about his father's identity had recurred periodically throughout his life, like bouts of very mild malarial fever. It's odd that you don't wonder more about who he was, John Mirsky had once said. Well perhaps he was another salesman of fake degrees from the University of Heidelberg, Edmund answered, like that creep my mother fell for in her blini parlor. Do you realize that you can only joke about it? John had persisted. . . . Some years ago, shortly before dying, Grisha had finally given Edmund the key to his father's identity. The first Edmund was a gifted but unsuccessful painter who had killed himself with laudanum out of fear of not making his proper mark upon the world. It was as dreary and simple as that. He had never even been a writer. The epiphany had explained Mara's long-suffering silences, her awesome nurturing of her son's gifts, her determination to bring him early fame so as to enjoy its fruits during her own short life. The revelation had strengthened Edmund's disdain for any form of suicide, existential, too chic, bad literature! Genius wasted, talent spent. His father had just been . . . a shower of sperm, a man spending himself in a shower of golden talent. . . .

Edmund goes on to pace about the ornate gilt-ceilinged galleries of the Hermitage. Earlier that morn-

ing Intourist Tour No. 137 had been guided through
chambers surfeited with marble surfaces and precious
stones, through doors flanked by caryatids and columns
of jasper, malachite, lapis lazuli. " 'Everything in St.
Petersburg is colossal, innumerable,' " Edmund had read
to Claire over breakfast from a nineteenth-century traveler's diary. " '. . . the costliness and glare of the
courtiers' apparel, and a profusion of precious stones,
create a splendour of which the magnificence of other
courts can only give us a faint idea . . . many of the
nobility are almost covered with diamonds yet the same
nobles sleep on the floors of their palaces to avoid the
vermin of their beds, have a great part of their estates
pledged to pawn shops. . . .' "

Impatient to reach the galleries of European painting,
Edmund had walked restlessly that morning through
rooms of pink marble where Moorish fountains cascade
into alabaster basins, had stood before a twenty-seven-
yard-wide map of Russia whose cities and rivers are
indicated by rubies and emeralds. The Rolls-Roycers
exult over the quantity of gems, the Zabars ask Edmund
studious   questions   about   French   influences   on
nineteenth-century Russian art, the Weickers photograph
every portrait of royalty in sight. The Americans are
particularly elated by Fabergé's eight-foot-high sapphire-
studded gold clock in the form of a peacock which makes
a total revolution of its wings upon the striking of each
hour. " 'Once outside nature I shall never take/My bodily
form from any natural thing,' " Sophie whispers to
Edmund as she stands in front of the blazing bird.
" 'Once *out of* nature,' " Edmund rebuts, she's still
getting it wrong after thirty years; "give me the next
lines, sweetness. . . ." " '. . . but such a form as Grecian goldsmiths make/Of hammered gold and gold
enameling . . .' " He kisses her forehead and wanders
on. The Hermitage contains 1050 rooms 1170 staircases
and fourteen miles of floors and galleries, Evgeny calls

out; Dr. Richter is advised to strictly follow the order of the guided tour. Edmund goes to stand before a Memling which he suspects is false, searches for Claire. Standing by a window he sees the gold needle of St. Paul's Cathedral rising ethereal towards a mother-of-pearl sky, Claire passes him by with her abstracted gaze, flat brown hair hanging straight as a schoolgirl's; at times he wishes he could drink her, ingest her so as to know her from the inside of himself. Shreds of their early life return as he comes back to stand before Titian's *Danaë*, Claire at the Sealark piano playing *Für Elise*, sunlight pouring into the room from a gull-filled sky while Sophie trims his hair with Babsie's gardening shears, Jeff radiant with heroism brings him hot broth every hour, it's the day after Edmund's almost drowned and the household has gathered about him and caters to his every whim; in the next room Plinker growls out orders to his Wall Street firm over the phone . . . another point to make about the image of Danaë! Ambivalence of money, gold's demonic attributes never enough stressed, outward sign of inner grace as well of lowliest corruption. The foulness of riches, Midas choking on his fortune, finding death in it. Luther had gone further than anyone else in associating wealth with excrement and Satan, "Money is the word of Satan," "*Simia Dei*, ape of God." Gold equals grace also equals defecation. The prophet of Protestantism receives his first illumination in the privy of his monastery at Wittenberg, later envisions the Apocalypse, the Second Coming, as a rain of gold that turns to fecal filth. Ambivalence of the most potent symbols, shower of gold that is both sinful offal and symbol of God's love!

"Gentlemen and ladies," Irina calls out, "we are now entering the great rooms of Hermitage's Dutch paintings, collection begun by Catherine the Great with help of French philosopher Diderot. . . ."

Much greater stress on grace in Rembrandt's version of *The Shower of Danaë*. The iconography of coinage disappears, Rembrandt dematerializes gold into pure light, transmutes the shower into a blaze of radiance which streams in from the upper left of the canvas. The northern Danaë does not lie in the erotic pastoral loggia of Venetian nudes but on the alcoved bed of a proper Dutch interior; contrast her modesty, her Puritan reticence to the brazen hedonism of her Venetian counterpart . . . the torso of Rembrandt's figure is half raised on a folded arm, she greets the effusion of light not with the voluptuous abandon of Titian's maiden but with the serene, surprised gesture of an Annunciation scene. The cloudburst of radiance pouring down upon her seems to bring happiness to all; the aging servant at Danaë's side is devoid of the greed of her own Venetian counterpart, stares at the split radiance with the obedient awe of a worshiper at Mass. Light! No ambivalence there, an element of redemption wherever you turn, Australian shaman gaining his magic powers by swallowing rock crystals, Augustine, the light Grace pours into our inner eye. . . .

In the early seventies, trying to ease Claire through her convent phase, Edmund had used the term secular Pelagianism to stress that her current search for grace could be delusory, that she could find whatever she wished to call salvation by returning to the palpable political suffering of others. Which she'd eventually done beyond the call of duty; such was the nature of the errand they'd debated a few nights ago and a myriad of her other dedications. In that austere period of her sisterhood he'd told her that grace could lurk on many levels, in the hard decision, the clear memory of a mother, behind every closed door of the courage to be. He had confided to Claire that if he were ever to paint again (this desire was then just nascent) he would have to find many new sources of fortitude—a new wellspring of trust in himself, a new fund of trust in others, a disdainful indifference to most criticism, a vastly purified life lived far beyond the pale of that public scrutiny which he had come to think of as demonic. To paint again would require some upwards mobility of trust, rebecoming as unwary as a small child, shed of all fear of foolishness, trusting all, believing in love and loveliness, believing in the spilt radiance of belief.

Edmund begins to walk out of the Hermitage after having mustered the courage to tell his two loves, two Muses, about a curious decision: On this particularly light-flooded morning he will tell them that he's about to radically change his life again. Sophie will have a fit, he can already hear her, at your level of success, achievement . . . Edmund smiles at the travelers assembled with him in the Rembrandt gallery and feels a happiness he hasn't known for decades.

"What's so new and exciting, E.R.?" Sophie whispers as she comes towards him.

"He's manic, marvelous this morning"—Claire taps his elbow with her notebook—"pouring forth pure sunshine."

"Our own dear tyrant, what's come over him?"

"Are you suddenly happy, Edmund love?"

"Happy? He'd need a Nobel."

"A superb new insight to share with your classes next term?"

"Oh, I'm not giving any more classes. *Finito*, I'm quitting, I'm leaving Berkeley."

"When," Claire says excitedly, "precisely when did you make that perfectly extraordinary decision?"

"Quite some time ago, it's precisely what I came here to talk to you about."

"You're totally out of your mind" (he could have said it for Sophie, journalists are so predictable), "when anyone's at the top of their . . ."

He doesn't hear the end of her sentence. He's spun around and is walking swiftly towards the museum's exit. He's placated Evgeny with declarations of urgent bodily needs. He walks through a gallery hung with quattrocento masters he's dissected for decades of classroom lectures: note the drapery language, the bleak featureless landscape which emphasizes the monumental isolation of the figures. He pauses once with reverence before a Fra Angelico depicting the Virgin and Child flanked by Saint Dominic and Saint Thomas. The sun is God's sun and light stems only from the saints; for Fra Angelico there is no nature independent from God's hierarchy. Self-absorption of Angelico's figures, incorruptibility of their inwardness, saints as well as artists know that loneliness is the central condition of their vocation; how clearly this is stated in their fiercely lowered eyes, the isolation of their gestures . . .

He resumes his swift walk towards the Neva, passes through the palace's barbaric expanses of marble, jasper, malachite, walks by a bronze life mask of Peter the Great —eyes dilated as those of a Gorgon, brutal face set upon a monstrously thick neck—standing amid the vulgar gilt of caryatids. The artists with whom we've communed this morning have achieved most of the goals of heroism and religion, they've forced us to remain perpetually in their presence, they've conquered death; in these rooms the suffering of history is temporarily eased, time the destroyer is imprisoned and held at bay. . . . All of art is one gigantic guerrilla expedition against the chaos of experience and the silence of death. . . . "Orpheus dismembered will continue to sing, his head floating down our rivers . . ." The artist works on the faith that he contains in himself the source of his eternity, still engages in that communion with the immortal which is said to have passed away with the waning of the gods. . . .

That was one way of putting it, E.R., not very

satisfactory, too much of the old Romantic tripe. Divinity of the creator, artist as sacred vessel—bane of our existence! Debased Faustianism, elitist ooze, Kraut metaphysics doled out in seedy art schools . . .

Try again, Richter.

I want to be more of what I could have been.

Edmund walks to the embankment of the Neva and stares at the swiftness of the river's flow. He climbs down a flight of stairs, stands a foot above its eddies. The Neva swirls in tortuous currents from some icy lake many miles east of the city, flowing senselessly to lose itself in the glacial waters of the Gulf of Finland. Edmund opens his trousers and relieves himself. The little arch of gold vaults triumphant over the stone embankment, descends into the innards of Russia's most brutal river. Edmund spends himself graciously into the pool of his unknown forefathers, he sheds years of pain as he flows into their victories, their passions, their unknown sins. He watches his arabesque for a felicity of time and when it subdues he feels great loss, great regret, that such moments of joy can not last for an eternity. His bliss flies above him in a dazzling troika, a flock of swans echo his delight on the black water, the Sphinx of Russia laughs all about him with bared fangs, all noise ceases on the Neva; the corrupt world waits for its absolution, tail lowered, like a guilty dog, all sleeps for a while—humans, palaces, canals—and then bells begin to ring again over the city's golden fleece.

Edmund turns back towards the green-and-gold immensity of the Winter Palace, stares at the great bronze statues that stand atop the ice-green roof. Their arms are raised in various gestures of command, pleading, exhortation. Edmund is still for a few moments until he sees his friends flowing through the portals of the Hermitage. Flanked by the chattering Zabars and the photographing Weickers, Sophie and Claire walk slowly onto the quay of the Neva, their arms about each other's waists.

"Freedom, *svoboda*!" he says as he hastens towards them.

"Dear God" (he also knew something similar would come out of Sophie), "what a country he's chosen to find that in."

xvii

He heard Spanish being spoken, toilets flushing, dogs
barking somewhere next door. Sophie was wearing a
turban. A large parrot hovered over Edmund, staring out
of a mean yellow eye. This was New York? A man sat
by the window, smiling, peeling carrots. Sophie had
lined up seven large canvases against the wall by the
fireplace, they were her paintings, damn it; here he was
impotent before his life's passion and she was dabbling
away with excruciating freedom, even with a measure of
talent. . . . It was 1969. What was life about? He
already had a headache. Edmund leaned back against the
pillow on Sophie's bed and inhaled his joint. Sophie
seemed to have divorced and remarried and was wearing
a turban. He also saw organic cookbooks, amaryllis
plants in various stages of phallic splendor, effusions of
batik, a tyranny of mirrors, pillows and tatami mats
strewn about the floor. All was precisely as it should be.
Claire was serving a two-week term for civil disobedience in some D.C. jail and Sophie was shacked up
with a bodyfreak Off-Broadway star who was peeling
carrots of bright cadmium orange. Two months ago
she'd notified him that her radio program, *Tell It Like It
Is*, was being syndicated to thirty-seven stations and that
she'd started going to the Art Students League at nights.
America was going mad. This generation thought it

could master, domesticate everything. The mirrors lining Sophie's living room reflected myriad areas of the parrot's plumage, shimmering panels of cobalt, alizarin, chrome yellow. It was 1969. Why was he lying on batik sheets?

The room thrummed with that same brand of feminist rhetoric he'd heard on Sophie's program all the way to Berkeley. "Someday I also want to write a novel which expresses sexual experience from an intensely female point of view," she was saying. "Mailer and Henry Miller piss me off; I mean how do they know what it's like for a woman to have her first orgasm or suck a man's cock?"

"If you can't talk like a lady at least talk like a gentleman," Edmund muttered.

The actor wore a gold chain with a small squat Buddha around his neck. He had dark glasses and long wavy brown hair and a Chagall-blue jacket with gold braid on it, like the prince's in *Swan Lake*. The actor was quite famous. Edmund had seen pictures of him in a half-dozen publications in the past year alone. He'd seen him in *The Village Voice* doing a *Cherry Orchard* in modern dress, playing the schoolteacher in SDS costume. He'd read about his performance of a sleep tableau in which he lay naked for twelve hours in an environment of red silk. Sophie finally had an artist of her own again! And in the corner of the room stood her new easel, surrounded by dozens of fresh lustrous canvases. She smiled at Edmund radiantly, hair more Titian-sumptuous than ever. Her breasts hung splendid and braless under a T-shirt which said Liberate the Presidio Seven, her hips were swathed in a lamentation of African cotton. She stretched her arm up rhythmically, as if practicing one of her old dance exercises; dark soft hair stood like a small forest in the snowfield of her underarms, her ancient floral odor wafted towards him with the precision of new lilacs. Come away with me he wanted to say, erotic sister,

beloved companion of my happiest days, come away!
Shared studios of our youth, plaster casts, the paisley
shawls we'd draped under vases of fresh roses . . . She
stretched her arm still higher; her perfume pulsated
towards him along with the torturing smell of his
abandoned oil paints.

"Well what do you think about my paintings?"

"They're interesting." He inhaled, deeply this time.
"Watch your edges."

He was a donkey, flying through the room, braying.
The actor's shoulders had grown a tender hue of crimson
as carrots mounted in his bowl. Today, today! the parrot
screamed. Edmund finished his joint and leaned back on
the bed, peacefully looking at Sophie's canvases. All
was spherical, orbed, drawn with remarkable precision
and executed in excruciatingly fleshly hues, sometimes
dimpled with what seemed to be a proliferation of
nipples. Abundance of genital shapes, dark chasms
surrounded by delicate labial convolutions, crimson
clefts, violet orifices, botanical curiosities honeycombed
with the fluting and thrumming of biological tissue. . . .

"You're sure painting with your ovaries on your
sleeve. Powerful sense of design. Are you two planning
marriage?" Edmund feigned a yawn.

"Institutionalize the rape and bondage of women?"

"Legal whoredom!"

"So. No nuptial benediction," Edmund murmured,
relieved.

Edmund squinted at the paintings and at the titles labeled
on the edge of their frames. *Rosa Luxemburg, Let It All
Hang Out, Homage to Eleanor of Aquitaine*. Cathedrals
of convoluted tissue, femaleness offered as some primeval covenant. Serrated, revolutionary labia bulging with
assertive tendrils (*George Sand*). Shy pearly labia nestled in collars of elaborately drawn lace (*Homage to*

Emily Dickinson). Fleshly labia palpitating around assertive central slits (*Charlotte Corday*).

She said: "You're threatened, aren't you?"

"Uhh . . . why?"

"Let's be existential, Edmund, one of the reasons
you're so threatened by my imagery is that women have
an infinite capacity for orgasm."

"Uhuhhh."

"Uhh, uhuhhh, a new academic tic of yours. Not only
can we have eighteen orgasms in a row, honeybun, we
can also fake them."

"Really. Good luck, my precious darling. Just watch
your edges. That saturated yellow at the extreme right of
the canvas . . ."

"Always talking about form, Eddem, is that your only
karma? What did you think I was going to paint, fields of
daisies?"

"Today! Today!" the parrot screamed.

"The problem of avoiding emotional strain can only be
cured by the praxis of nutrition," the actor was saying. "I
see in you the fatigue, the banal metaphysical fatigue of
a man still striving to find himself . . . it can be allayed
by daily intakes of lecithin in normative doses, and
you'd better check on your glycogens . . ."

They had sat down to dinner.

". . . glycogens are the existential component of our
biological spectrum, they tune, they vivify, they turn the
body of despair into the hope of the future. . . . The
American diet elevates innocent stupidity to a form of
suicide, pure Thanatos at six P.M. across the fifty-two
states. . . ."

"You could only have found him in California," Edmund
muttered to Sophie when his host went to the kitchen for
the next course. "I've come East to escape that monstrous state and see the two loves of my life; one's in the

pokey and the other's telling it like it is with a Sausalitan carrot freak. So rising media star Sophie Ross is preaching the gospel of self-revelation, playing high priestess to our new nudism of the soul. . . ."

"You're so pathetically closeted!"

"Closeted, Soph! My closet is my haven, my most precious refuge, my repressions are truly collector's items! You've become infected with the cult of openness, sweetheart, that diet of absolute candor you feed me on your program and off it is ruining the culture as fast as anything else. . . ."

The first phase of grass always made him talk very quickly, he packed his words in as fast as he could in apprehension of the torpor that followed.

"Civilization, dear Sofia Larionovna, depends on ceremony, which is the veiling of the truth . . . listen, honeybun, since we have a minute alone I'll tell you a little story. I had a lover last year who tortured me with her passion for unadulterated candor—a fetishist of the authentic . . . she insisted on disclosing every detail of her life and I've never been as miserable, Soph, never. . . . Whether she picked up a hi-fi repairman or shared a bacchanal with a triad of stoned sociologists she described her encounters with the sordid detail of a botanist's journal. . . . I threatened to leave her; since she didn't have the imagination to lie I begged her to deceive me, that's how tedious these unsolicited accounts became. . . . I insulted her, I told her that I didn't ask of a lover to be faithful but simply to remain interesting—all to no avail; for a year I lived *folie à deux* with this voluptuary of the sincere. . . ."

"You never did give women enough space," Sophie said.

Garlic course after garlic course was arriving. There had been a gazpacho as thick as ketchup, stuffed peppers in which whole cloves of garlic lay enthroned like pearls.

In between his trips to the kitchen the actor noted that Pliny had listed garlic as the finest recipe for longevity, that Eleanor Roosevelt's doctor prescribed three cloves a day to retain memory. Sophie and her man hold up their bowls with both hands and make a small bow of the head to each other at the beginning of each course. Edmund asks which ashram they've picked that up in but by that time everyone's having trouble hearing each other. Miles Davis is on full blast. There's been much wine. The grass is catching up with Edmund. "Listen to those drums!" the actor says to Sophie. She raises her eyes to the ceiling with a knowing smile. "It must be like this every night," Edmund says; "is it like this every night?" His voice floats faint and piping above him, he's as detached from his voice as the melodic line of the trumpet is aloof from the saxophone's, the harmonic strains of tomato and pepper each draw their slow separate strings across his tongue, other voices float polyphonically above his head. "I'm driving down to the Sunday demo in D.C. for Clairsie's birthday," Sophie says; "a bunch of us from Women's Strike for Peace are going to stand under her jail window and sing happy birthday; that kid has her shit more pulled together than anyone I know. . . ." "Garlic doesn't admit the possibility of overdose, it's been proven that Bulgarian garlic eaters don't get cancer. . . ."

"Gene is thinking of doing a modern-dress Hamlet which he'll intersperse with recollected fragments of his own analysis, and then he might do an Othello for The Living Theatre in which . . ."

"We must discipline our ego to keep our ideas to ourselves," Edmund hears himself saying. "Whoever is ready to say anything is ready to sell anything he says. . . ."

They nod their heads to the music, throwing specks of garlic to the parrot.

Oh they haven't heard Professor Richter's sermonette

on the decline of the West, have they? This is the peak
rush hour of the Western gods, and is the traffic ever
heavy going out of town! Yes he's used to being labeled
reactionary, he's even been attacked on his own Vi-
conian grounds . . . Vico—the seventeenth-century
Neapolitan philosopher, after whom his cat is
named. . . .

They all laugh loudly for a minute, spilling wine.

Vico prophesied that we've got to return to an age of
barbarians before we can resurrect our gods; well that's
where he breaks with Vico, resurrection isn't as sure as
Vico thought.

Vico, Vico the parrot calls out.

What did they think?

He realized that he'd spoken in Russian for the last few
minutes and that Sophie was holding a monologue.
Crack them open she was saying about the celebrities she
interviewed on her radio program, lob to their backhand,
make them reveal themselves when they're off guard
. . . the jazz was so fabulous that she was thinking of
becoming a jazz trombonist next . . . they all laughed,
spilling a lot of wine on the floor. The actor was serving
something called consciousness three pudding. Carobs,
dates, nuts, cinnamon sang polyphonically upon Edmund's tongue. "I'm like, like . . . man, laid back, I'm
really together," Edmund tried. But his tongue slowed
down, clogged on its nourishment, seemed to take an
infinity of time to simply cross his mouth, ground for
sound but could only emit single words that flashed with
great solitude somewhere above his head. "E.R., remember that poem we used to say as kids?" Sophie
slurred tenderly, " 'Once out of glory I shall never
take . . .' " " 'Once out of *nature*,' " Edmund slurred
back. " '. . . my bodily form from any worldly . . .' "
" 'no, *natural* thing . . .' " A wave of dates rose in his
throat and he suddenly desired to be totally alone, he

only wanted to enter a small dark room and enjoy his state of profound idiocy by himself, he wanted to climb into his night-night and cover himself up and hug his solitude, his urge for solitude was as overpowering and demanding as the call of an imminent bowel movement. His hosts were still dipping wooden African spoons into consciousness three, shaking their heads to the music as he rose to leave. For some agonizing minutes they stood at the door embracing him and promising eternal affection, pledging to take him to a Sufi farm in New Jersey the next time he came East, planning to travel with him to Nepal, to Algeria, to Greece as soon as the colonels would leave, at the next demo they'd all three share a room together in D.C. . . .

Edmund went back to the Westbury Hotel and started assembling every lamp he could find in his suite. Then he surrounded his bed with them. He was consumed with fear that someone, anyone, might come in and disturb his private, precious imbecility, the lamps would be his sentinels, his guard of honor, he found lamps mounted on ceramic statuettes of red-shirted polo players, ardent Italian lovers. He had to address a convention of art historians the following morning and he'd taken two rooms in the kind of hotel that his mother and he had aspired to decades ago and he was only beginning to afford, the kind with pearly doorknobs, careful imitations of Louis XV chairs. He went to bed and floated in his new luxury, enjoying his haze of idiocy, relishing the calm of a room which had admitted no novelty or change in over thirty years, there were footsteps in the corridor, people threatened . . . he got up once more before falling asleep and assembled the lamps more tightly around his bed, lamps mounted on simpering eighteenth-century shepherdesses, winged Hermeses . . . he fell asleep. He had a dream about his mother:

They climb the stairs of a great warehouse, they enter

an immense room totally walled and ceilinged with feathers of hundreds of varieties of wild birds, goose and guinea hen, peacock and snipe, feathers thickly laid on, not an inch of space between three-inch-thick layers of plumage, russet pearl shimmer of turtledove, emerald brilliance of the rings about pheasants' necks. Amid this splendor walk four or five enormous creatures of upright carriage, covered head to toe in plumage, some dun as owls and others of resplendent parrot hues; they speak a language unlike any he's ever heard, a soft cooing and gurgling, a tender chortling as kind as the flow of water over polished stone; they point to diverse areas of the wall or ceiling. Mara gurgles and trills back to them in their own tongue, the most resplendent and desirable feathers lie on the ceiling so Mara grabs his hand and they fly through the width and height of the room, smoothing their palms over the wings of many a silken bird, hovering at length to caress the gleaming plumages, they swoop from swansdown to shimmering egrets to bronzed guinea hen. . . .

Edmund woke up brutally at the sound of his alarm clock, bright morning sunlight New York 1969, he'd flown across the United States for the purpose of giving a paper on Tintoretto that morning and seeing his two great loves, his two remaining Muses, who were nowhere to be seen as he remembered them.

xviii

The visitors' gallery in the chapel of St. Agatha's Abbey was set at the left of the apse. When Edmund wanted to attend an Office during his visits to Claire he came in well before the appointed time, loving the mystery of the space at its most tenebrous, before any candles were lit. Shortly after she'd entered the monastery he'd gone to hear None, the Office preceding the nuns' afternoon work period. A thin white curtain had remained drawn across the wooden choir screen of the chapel, fluttering in the summer breeze like a moth's wing. And from behind it there emerged the frailest, most ethereal chant imaginable, the nuns singing the Alleluia of midday on a single spectral note, perhaps high E . . . the timbre of their voices was supplicating and expressed a certain helplessness . . . the single tone of their litany floated wraithlike above the sounds of nature proliferating outside the small chapel, blackbird proffering its liquid trill, guard dog barking . . . The pale incantation lasted for ten minutes, the candle was blown out, the room was once more dark, a band of women in dusty gray work robes and muddy boots streamed out of the chapel and went out again towards their fields, their sheds, their kitchens, to continue their task of survival. . . . Claire had told him that her favorite Office was the Matins sung between the hours of 4:00 to 6:00 A.M., which was exclusively dedicated to the singing of the Psalms. Once in a rare moment of insomnia Edmund rose at four to hear Matins and was preplexed by the thought that throughout the world tens of thousands of his contemporaries were still dedicating over five hours a day to chanting sacred litanies—Matins, Lauds, Mass, Sexts, None, Vespers, Compline—"simply singing in celebration of the ground of being," that was the way Pebble had put it . . . perhaps if he let himself go and thought of sacred life as simple celebration, thought of the Lord as a great Will diverting Himself in the garden of His creation, the meaning of her present life might become clearer to him . . . the world and time could be the dance of the Lord in emptiness, and the silence of the spheres the music of a wedding feast . . . there is a painting of Zurbarán's which reminded him of Claire when he stared at her standing at the back of the chapel, one of three lay sisters coiffed in a simple veil, her beauty more impassive, more imperturbable than ever, the perfect oval of her face, the slightly arrogant mouth . . . it was in this state of stubborn self-determination that she had realized her fullest and most complete womanhood . . . on another occasion some sly beckoning of her eyes led him to go up to the altar at communion time with the handful of worshipers from the nearby village who came to daily Mass . . . he walked up to the altar and closed his eyes, remembering the icy ting of the Communion spoon on his lip in the Orthodox church, in the Eucharists he'd shared with his mother . . . now the wafer lay tasteless and fragile on his tongue as a single snowflake; he felt nothing and went back to his pew.

In the tempest of opinions and regrets that followed Claire's exit from the secular world (*"Folie mystique!"* exclaimed Cousin April, who had left her second husband and taken a string of courses at the Alliance

Française), the central trait of Claire's character was curiously overlooked. Except for Edmund, no one took into account her excessive will to autonomy, her lifelong struggle to liberate herself totally from the privileged world she'd been born into. History's made it clear, Edmund would say, that most persons striving for sainthood or the monastic life are endowed with a perfectly remarkable will to power; why else do they so frequently pray for humility? Yet even Edmund admitted that the timing of this decision was extremely singular. Throughout the 1960s thousands of men and women had been leaving the traditional religious life to work for precisely the same secular causes that had been obsessing Claire. Nuns who'd been forbidden to read anything beyond the collection of saints' lives on their convent bookshelves were telling their students that picketing was a form of praying and attending weekend seminars on revolution. Benedictines who had written on the contemplative life for arcane theological journals were protesting the Vietnam War with acts of civil disobedience and singing hymns over piles of burning draft files. It is in February of 1971, at the height of this rebellion against all traditional premises of salvation, six months or so after her father's death, that Claire went to live as a lay sister at the Abbey of St. Agatha, a community of cloistered Anglican nuns in eastern Minnesota.

For several preceding years she has engaged in a ritual that has already caused much consternation to her family: Claire Sanford Howell, progeny of all that's most decorous in American society, has been repeatedly dragged away by policemen in antiwar demonstrations. There is a core of austerity in her that adapts with an assentment almost perverse to the rigors of prison life. By 1970 she's been arrested twelve, fourteen times. She comes into a cell, takes off her shoes and sits cross-legged on the prison floor. The night's visions sway about her in a haze of absolution as she observes the cold animal rage of women's eyes clutching the bars of their cells, the pistols slung on the hips of jail matrons patrolling the corridors, the graffiti on cell walls saying ARISE AND SHINE YE SISTERS OF THE WORLD. In the late sixties Claire had engaged in civil disobedience with a nun who convinced her that "in witness to the poor" they should refuse bail and choose instead the alternate penance of five days' imprisonment. She henceforth refused bail at all her arrests and deepened that sacrifice with a water fast. (Edmund gently scolded her, in a note from Berkeley, for "indulging in that greed for personal salvation which might be the most obnoxious greed there is.")

With questionable precision, psychologists have tended to divide humanity into the healthy souls who are content to be born just once and those problematic "twice-born" spirits driven to search for redeeming conversion. One of the intricacies of Claire Sanford's character is that she doesn't belong clearly to either category. There is little issue of conversion or "rebirth" in her decision to leave the secular world. She's never entertained, for instance, the fashionable Anglican custom of turning to Roman Catholicism. To the contrary (as she enjoys stressing in her letters) she's being more faithful than ever to "the rock bottom of our own tradition." Her decision seems to be forged in that iron of the soul which drives most reformers and revolutionaries to return to earlier levels of purity and rigor. In the months preceding her departure for the convent, for instance, Claire spent much time reading medieval history, concentrating in particular on the great abbesses of the early Middle Ages. This obsession had also been instigated by one of the many priests and nuns she worked with in the antiwar movement—a Franciscan who lectured spiritedly, during an all-night vigil at the Pentagon, on "Women's Autonomy in the Religious Orders." And if Claire ever came close to a state of trance it might have consisted of some historical meditation on these paragons of female independence. Women of such forceful presence that they became fabled for stilling storms and taming wild beasts, founders and administrators of great separatist enclaves, females so powerful that they didn't allow bishops into their monastic settlements! Saint Melania, converter of Byzantine emperors, Saints Thecla and Lioba, girls of noble birth who left their families to escape unwanted marriages and ended their lives as contemplatives in mountain retreats where they healed and taught the hundreds who came to them. Women saying no to the dictates of family, leaving marriages that enslaved them to the cycle of childbearing, pioneering enclaves of peace and learning in the chaos of barbaric forests, defying the patriarchal order, creating the truest semblance of equality offered women in the West. What transcendence, what a release from the tyranny of nature, Claire would write in one of her letters to Sophie! What a splendid improvement on our pathetic new concepts of women's liberation!

"I never did like the Reformation," she wrote in her P.S. "What an erosion of our autonomy, what a blow to women's right to truly determine their destinies!"

On a clear morning in 1971 she'd pack a small bag of personal effects and leave her home in Concord with a long letter to Jeff (two impeccable carbon copies had already been mailed to Edmund and Sophie) announcing her decision to go and live, for an indeterminate amount of time, at the Abbey of St. Agatha in Four Rivers, Minnesota.

There were two separate letters for her twelve-year-old daughter Victoria: one to be opened before her departure, another one a year hence.

She didn't claim to have heard any voices, sensed Presences, experienced transports. Her departure for

Minnesota seemed as calm and measured as the little notes she'd written to herself since childhood, those neatly labeled exhortations towards self-perfection scattered among the pages of her Book of Common Prayer and her cages of recuperating animals.

The first visit Edmund made to St. Agatha's occurred some three months after Claire's departure, and was preceded by several communications concerning the behavior expected of him at the abbey guesthouse, where relatives and friends of the nuns were allowed to come for limited four-day stays:

"Be advised that the abbey lodge is open to visitors for only a few hours of the afternoon, and for good or for worse that's where we'll have to meet. I asked the mother superior for visit permission a few weeks ago and it's been granted. . . ."

"Your essay on Van Der Weyden's Deposition sounds like an ideal project to work on here, and if I told you not to bring your darn typewriter I'd feel as if I were ordering Kenneth Clark not to write. So yes do bring it, but only use it in your room with the doors closed so as not to distract other guests who seek the meditative silence we promise them. . . ."

The abbey was set in heavily wooded Minnesota terrain, several hours from the nearest large town. And the guesthouse where Edmund came to stay for his visits with Claire was situated at the bottom of a steep hill a half mile or so from the abbey proper. The rustic dirt road wound upwards through several stands of pines, then through sloping fields edged by laurels and apple trees. The abbey church loomed before the visitor at a sudden turn of the road when one least expected it, its small gilded cross outlined darkly against the setting sun. Edmund had arrived on a halcyon evening in late May for his first visit, feeling great need to look at the landscape which Claire was confined to seeing day after day. In an expanse of valley within the monastic enclosure he glimpsed well-tilled fields of corn and wheat, thriving vegetable gardens and fruit orchards, pastures dotted with Hereford cows. A frail, high strain of women's voices emerged from the chapel, they must have been singing Compline, the last office of the day. Mallows, day lilies, buttercups, blazed in the small field at his side. On a summer evening like this twenty-two years ago he had kissed Claire for the first time and felt her resistance, that mineral resistance to the expected which was the core of her being. A beaver shuttled swiftly, silently across a nearby pond, carrying formidable amounts of twigs towards his dwelling, his canine face emerging sleek and intelligent above the umbrous water. He dove repeatedly to prepare the terrain of his habitation, floated several large balls of mud across the pond to heap them upon his dam, his paws often scrubbing his face as if to sanctify it for a new bout of work. It appeared to be the first sunny evening after a stretch of rain, the air was filled with the fervid buzzing, gathering, soaring of spring insects. Edmund picked a few wild flowers to take to his stark room in the guesthouse. Before walking downhill he stared once more at the serene enclosure in which Claire had chosen to continue her struggle for self-perfection. In this tiny community as closed and self-sufficient as the beavers' pond nearby, what a challenge it was to curb one's drives of greed, envy, pride!

Before going to sleep he started a letter to Sophie, who the year before had begun a vigorous new career as television correspondent. She was presently on a long-term assignment in Jerusalem, where she was living with a journalist named Amos. O Protean contemporary women, he began as he sat down to write, free to metamorphose until the end of their days . . . (he always strived for a dramatic opening when writing to

Sophie.) Polymorphic creatures tackling vows of chastity at forty, struggling with doctorates in sociobiology at fifty-six, dropping their first acid at sixty-two like Mrs. Tillich. . . .

"O brave new world," he continued his letter, "that is seeing the Odysseizing of women, the Penelopizing of men."

"It was in November or so of 1970, Eddem . . . I was standing with some nuns and priests in a small room in a black section of Boston; we were having a Eucharist in preparation for an action on the nearby draft board. . . . The room we stood in faced a black tenement, a backyard full of boards, rags, trash, debris, buildings that looked as if they'd been struck by a series of bombings . . . it all had a quality of occupied territory, as if the people in that building were captives living under some foreign rule. Only one room in the tenement looked lived in, and at its window sat a woman hugely swollen with some disease who fanned herself with a newspaper and held a wasted, screaming child on her lap. . . . The Epistle reading that day had been from Corinthians Two: 'I've been in danger in the towns, in danger in the open country, in danger at sea, in danger from so-called brothers . . .' And as I began to think about these lines everything in my field of vision suddenly took on a curious and intense existence of its own. That is . . . everything suddenly appeared to have an immense interior *space*, to own an individual life as precious as the whole universe. To save that woman and child, to go out to them and not only feed them and get them work but particularly to give them the courage to live on seemed as important and quite as difficult as stopping any war. . . . Eddem, this wasn't a vision I insist, it was something simpler. . . ."

She had moved towards him an hour ago across the parlor of the abbey lodge with a merry, rolling gait. And he was both startled and perplexed to see that she'd never looked so well. Her cheeks had gained a startling new ruddiness. She had even plumped out a little bit. ("Hi, cookie," he'd said when they'd embraced. What does one say? He hadn't known precisely what to say. "You're looking so marvelous! What a marvelous place!") Her erect posture, her crisp walk, had something newly determined about it. Dressed in a surprisingly contemporary long gown of brown serge, a lay sister's simple white veil floating about her head, there was his Pebble walking towards him with a radiant smile. . . .

"I do want to stress the difference, Edmund; in that moment in which I seemed to make my choice there was none of that sense of unity or merging mystics report, none of that business of All Things Are One . . . no, the absolute opposite, everything stood out with a fierce and glowing individuality. And E.R. you know how much guilt I've been burdened with for years, guilt for the very fact of surviving and being *blessed* with much; perhaps that's why I didn't even feel worthy of the happiness I could have had with you . . . well, in the surrendering I experienced that day, the guilt was . . . as if melted, melted. Burden of condemnation gone, darkness lifted."

"But, Pebble . . . allow me an indiscretion. You had no vision? You don't call that a vision?"

"No, it was rather . . . an abandonment and a return. At that moment in the bleak room I stood in, the stillness was marvelous, and I felt both . . . both deeply anguished by our *helplessness*, and supremely happy because I was *accepting* that helplessness. There was very little theology you know in this moment of mine. Simply a willingness to capitulate. An increased sense of Chris being the center of course but . . . that's too private to talk about. A passion of acquiescence."

There was a bright new caroling quality to her voice she spoke with the oddly emphatic phrasing he remem bered from her adolescence.

"You are peaceful," he whispered.

"I looked around at the men and women praying with me that morning and was filled with fear for . . . oh, this is hard to explain, Eddem."

"Don't always go so fast, Peb. We've plenty of time, you know."

"Well not so much, only until Vespers. . . . Looking at them I was filled with emotion not so much for what they were at that precise moment, more for where they'd *come* from. Here they were preparing another of their amazing acts of protest, more courageous and self-giving than anything that's been done in the Movement . . . I'd always sensed that it was the meditation and witness they'd lived for centuries that had enabled them to undertake these actions, and suddenly I had a great fear that their contemplative force was waning, shedding its power like a battery, that the world's ordinariness was contaminating them too much. . . ."

There was a silence. He found it hard to talk to her because he'd very quickly sensed that she was still celebrating her isolation, that she was apprehensive about talking about her child and that this must be saved for the last; he'd sensed a lot. He cleared his throat as he tended to do in the middle of a college lecture, looked out of the window. Claire flung back the flat brown hair that hung under her veil, a defiant gesture unchanged since childhood.

"Oh you're still puzzling," she cried out, "you're still wondering, confused about me, aren't you . . . all right, his is it, Eddem. The reality of my need for the sacred suddenly became greater than my need for any proof of s existence. And so I needed to bear witness to it, kay?"

This was delivered with such force that he was ompelled to look deep into her eyes for the first time nce the beginning of that visit. The pale eyes had anged greatly, he couldn't tell how at first. Lost their anger, he decided now. On the wall of the abbey lodge behind her chair were affixed the same stark little directives that confronted him daily in the guesthouse: WE WELCOME YOU TO THE ABBEY AND ASSURE YOU OF OUR PRAYERS . . . SHORTS ARE NOT PERMITTED ON THE GROUNDS OF THE MONASTERY . . . ST. AGATHA'S SERVES THOSE SEEKING MEDITATIVE SILENCE.

"I knew that I had to take a radical new direction in life, and this in the space of barely a few minutes, Eddem. . . ."

"Like in Somerset Maugham," he suggested. She waved her hand impatiently, stood up and paced the room.

"Hardly as colorful. You're probably trying to define my experience, darn it, everyone out there is always trying to define everything. No, I simply had a sense of urgent crisis about this being my last chance, my last possible chance of acquiring peace and strength. The universe remained as meaningless as before and even more hopelessly charged with suffering, yet more charged also with some sacred fullness . . . above all it occurred to me that all could be right if I stopped trying to do it all by myself, if I finally ceased to resist and subjected my will to a greater one. . . ."

"Ouf, that was hard," she whispered, "that decision to surrender."

"You of all people."

"Oh it *was* a struggle."

At night during his many visits to St. Agatha's, Edmund read from the pious biographies that studded the guesthouse's bookshelves. He always brought his own work with him but was curiously unable to proceed with it, as if Claire had not yet clarified some aspect of her presence here which he must still persevere to decipher. During those study hours in the evening he kept coming across curious relics of the pietistic 1930s and 1940s, account

of W. H. Auden's conversion, biographies of St.
Thérèse de Lisieux by Clare Boothe Luce. ("Precious-
ness of every hidden soul in the economy of the universe
. . . law of conservation of charity as the center of the
contemplative life. . . .") He would bring Claire tidbits
of his reading during their afternoon visits, as if to
reassure her that he was taking a small step into her
world.

"I read the most marvelous story about Elizabeth of
Hungary last night."

"Tell."

"This sainted queen had for confessor a tyrant, which I
would define as a man without imagination. He was
perceptive enough, however, to discern that the penances
imposed upon Elizabeth in the confessional brought her
into a state of joyful exultation. . . . So he searched and
searched his mind every Friday afternoon for penances
which might bring her a proper dose of pain. He finally
came up with a real zinger, he forbade her to help the
sick and the poor. But this is where she parted with him
and with the system of obedience she'd adhered to all
her life, she went right on helping the sick and the
poor. . . ."

Claire leaned forward intently towards him; she observed him during those visits with a depth of concern
she'd never given him before. "I think you should travel
more, dear one, go to Europe; I feel you're in a rut after
fifteen years of Berkeley."

"You've turned psychic in your seclusion. But let me
finish with Elizabeth. Another order of nature takes over
. . . a snowstorm screens her as she makes her nightly
trip to the sick and the poor so that her disobedience may
not be observed.

"The story may exemplify," he added pointedly,
"tyrants' excessive zeal against all forms of satisfaction."

* * *

There were many days when she'd meet him in the abbey lodge after having come straight in from working in the fields, hair tousled, dust in her face, nails still dark with mud, eyes more serene than ever. Her peevishness, her old resentment towards her family's garden . . . Edmund constantly saw many young, clear-skinned women walking about the monastery compound in sneakers and farmers' boots, their long gray garbs cinched with thick workmen's belts of heavy leather. Some had come from their beehives, others from their vineyards or cornfields Claire said, they carded their own wool, wove their own cloth. She often pointed out some nun's name as they said good-bye at the abbey lodge door, that's Sister Patrick, there's Sister Stephen, Sister Jerome. "I find them infinitely seductive," he once wrote Sophie, "like everything that's veiled."

"Sophie's gone through another metamorphosis," Claire announced one day.

"Dear Lord, not in a kibbutz."

"Oh it's for the best Eddem, just listen . . ."

Whenever she had a new letter from Sophie she'd welcome him in the abbey lodge with a joyous wave and immediately begin to read it aloud, quite admitting to her craving for news.

"Let's say I'll just talk about the eyes of these people who've lived through three wars in ten years" [Sophie wrote]. "Like most men in this garrison state Amos's green eyes have a very controlled anxiety, they're the eyes of a man who's had to be both a soldier and a monk, whose body has been struck or grazed by shellfire many times since the War of Independence, and they're still not as disturbing or disturbed as the eyes of those who live in the northern kibbutzim under a constant

barrage of fire. . . . Last week for instance Amos
and I drove north to document some articles on the
Lebanese border and I'm still obsessed by the
resigned, beaten-down gaze of the twenty-five-
year-olds to whom a machine gun has become a
fifth limb. . . ."

Claire paced the room while reading, interrupting to
open the window with a brusque gesture.

"I can't forget that moment last week when we
walked into the dining room of a settlement two
miles from the Northern border and Amos tapped
the shoulder of a young man sitting alone at the
table, he slowly turned his head towards us and
there was so little expressed pleasure, so little
recognition in that gaze that I assumed he was
barely acquainted with Amos . . . the young Israeli
just continued to silently eat his soup, staring at us
with those exhausted aloof eyes, yet a moment later
I learned that he was one of Amos's most ardent
fans, the one who constantly writes and phones to
invite Amos to this kibbutz. . . . When Amos
started to question him about the rocket attacks of
last week his friend's eyes lost some of their
weariness, grew almost angry as he barked back,
How do you expect me to remember last week's
shelling from the one before, or from the year
before that?

"Well how else can I put it Claire darling, there's
little talk about anything but the possibility of
survival in this new Sparta, one only lives for
whatever work and love one has, all's very austere
and meaningful . . . at first I was confused and
overwhelmed by this state of siege but recently it's
led me to totally reorder and redistill my existence,
face up to the brevity of life, focus on a single
task. . . . "

* * *

"What a miracle, Eddem," Claire exclaimed, "and what a serious writer she's getting to be!"

"If she survives it she'll finally start having the glory she's always dreamed of."

"No, no, totally different from the passive man-given success she'd wanted as a kid, this glory will be her own!"

It struck Edmund as interesting that Claire's seclusion led her to observe others more attentively than ever.

"Tell me this," he began another day (her costume, the room, sometimes imposed an uncomfortable formality upon him).

"Are you planning . . ." (the question was irrelevant at that precise moment but his need to ask it was immense, a fear as ancient as his love swept through him) "are you planning to take vows?"

"Oh, no great need! I'm not good enough for that! As long as I can lead their life a bit, participate in their witness. They're the rock. I'm just . . ." She searched for the image.

"I'm just a barnacle."

The humility of the reply affected him. He turned towards the window, stared at the amber pond where he often sat in the evening watching the family of beavers at their work.

She would sometimes break off their talks, at the appointed time before evening Vespers, with a terse, pithy phrase: "Sin is just a messing up of your priorities."

That child, that daughter of hers! Once or twice a year, whenever his work brought him to New England, Edmund made a point of taking Victoria out to tea. She was as pensive as ever but had grown sturdier, was not as fragile of body as Claire had been. Her large eyes were as cold blue pale as her mother's. The ephemeral touch of her adolescent cheek upon his when they met, the nascent rebelliousness of her talk, thrust him into a panic of affection and remembrance. There are people who don't care about discussing matters such as good and evil, Victoria'd once said, and they truly bore me to death. Like who for instance darling? My aunts and cousins of course, all they do is win tennis tournaments and give themselves airs going out to look for persons of the opposite sex, which is so gross. You might belong to a new generation of mystical celibates, Edmund said, a grand solution to the population problem. You know perfectly well that many people get along without all that nonsense, Uncle Edmund; my generation is strictly into friendship, anyway. . . . Uncle Eddem, do you still believe in romantic love? she'd asked him warily from behind her curtain of light brown hair. Oh I've pretended not to darling he'd said fiercely, you see I've had rather little of it.

The funny thing, he often thought when he came to the convent, is that Claire's never been so available to me. The monastery enclosure guarded, imprisoned her for his sight like the net posed over an insect. During the days he spent at St. Agatha's he experienced the delight of the lepidopterist who triumphs after years of searching for an arcane species and can stare tranquilly at his prize for hours, admiring in loving closeness every detail of mandibles and rainbow scales. Yet he knew that his love was bound to be all the more arduous because its object seemed to grow more perfect under his close scrutiny. She reversed that habitual process of human passion which wanes with the melting of distance and of dream; in her new peace and candor she was becoming, to his sorrow, increasingly marvelous. Is there something peculiar about the persons who love only once in their lifetime, he also worried, are the once-in-loves as singular as the twice-born? Is it a glandular condition, could it be dictated by early deprivation of the mother's presence (Freud, Leonardo's lovelessness), is there only one human Muse for each artist's life? Are such persons more prone to depression, happiness, sodomy, nationalism, pyromania, anorexia, are they better or worse athletes? He imagined people in his part of California forming consciousness-raising groups for the once-in-loves, associations as garrulously introspective as those for the drug-deprived, the homosexual, the adopted.

"It also happened to me in a jail cell, Peb . . . a locale which you barely associate with my decorous right-wing behavior. But I'm more radical than you think I am, my love. If I hadn't become much of an activist it's because I'm much more of a cynic than you are; the antiwar movement had always reminded me of doctors putting Band-Aids on a cancer that needs radical surgery; I've come to think that the whole culture has to be rebuilt from the basement up, priorities revolutionized, massive humanistic socialism established if such a thing exists. . . . Anyhow, I was hanging around a demonstration trying to keep my dear Slavic friend John Mirsky from getting busted for the tenth time and they rounded up the whole lot of us and I got dragged away at last, thinking mightily about you, to the strains of one of those detestable hymns that have their proper place in church. . . . I'd been finding little meaning in anything that year, a medal at the College Art Association for my book on Caravaggio, honorary degrees from Brown and Vanderbilt, letters of corroboration or protest with flattering frequency from the readers of my articles . . . I could accept honor after little honor and feel numb, indifferent, blah; I'd turned down visiting professorships at Harvard and Chicago because the only reason I'd have moved would have been to be nearer you or Soph but you were both so nomadic there was no hope of ever catching you anyway; I could see no alternative to continued steeping in the poisoned juices of Academe . . . until the day I sit in a jail cell staring at a graffito that says what do we want freedom what do we get bologna sandwiches. A tall blond page boy out of Botticelli walks in and lies down on the bunk opposite mine and starts berating me for not signing some damn faculty petition that had been passed around the previous week . . . he'd started in art history and had switched to pol sci because it was more 'relevant' quote unquote and I dug into him for that . . . the memory is dim now because I was so extraordinarily taken with Toby's presence. Oh I'd had several decorative persons in my life in the past decade as you know, average fare for a department chairman, pert grade-grabbing sophomores wanting to squeeze me dry of every inspired thought on Degas, divorcée potters with a proclivity for interminable foreplay . . . it had been pleasant, it had been lonely in turn. And suddenly here is a Botticelli facing me in a cell, holding a copy of Regis Debray in hand. . . ."

"And you had Pater?"

"Close, Peb, close. Ruskin. An idiotic ideological argument ensued, what's appropriate reading in these times of crisis and so forth, Toby was clearly baiting me; you're sitting back and letting society rot Professor while mouthing inanities about the stones of Venice. He lay on his bunk orating, orating as from a soapbox, and suddenly leaned down to seize the book from my hand. As that pale rather beautiful hand traveled towards me I put my mouth to it and bit him, as satisfying as planting my teeth into a peach in a moment of hunger on a hot day . . . thinking as I did, what barbarians these times have made of us. There was the taste of blood on my tongue, and in his eyes an air of startlement that verged on amusement, pleasure even. Those eyes were a curiously dark brown, like water at night, so dark that you couldn't distinguish the iris from the pupil, which would make his periods of drug ingestion maddeningly difficult to deal with in the next months we were to spend together . . . a time devoted of course to reforming his character in my perennial Pygmalion fashion. Oh how readily he turned from the rigors of his Trotskyite student cell to the sybaritic pleasures of my little Pouilly-Fuissés while retaining the luxury of his Marxist rhetoric! You must know the I Want Everything generation as well as I do, they want the revolution and the palazzo; you'll do well in Italy, Toby, I told him the week he left, you'll get taken to cell meetings in chauffeured Alfa Romeos, Rolls-Royce radicals of the world unite. . . . Of course there were the sweet good moments too that would flood me with regrets for months after we quit, so much that was malleable, splendid about him; much occasional sweetness, and that long slender body wandering naked about my house with the insouciance which it's been the genius and the depravity of this generation to cultivate; the moments when I stared at his face below mine, as into the mirror of my own lost youth. . . ."

"But we're babies, Edmund! You keep talking as if we're so ancient! I feel I'm at the very beginning of the best life I'll ever have!"

"That may be an agreeable asset of being one of the twice-born, my dear; as for myself I feel decidedly ready for reincarnation . . . well, bless me sister if I have sinned, just a recent installment from the epic of my tragic flaws."

"I've told you before, E.R., I think you need a change," she whispered.

How soothing, after all these years, to have her advise him! In 1973 Edmund would accept a visiting professorship to a New England college, having carefully determined that Minnesota was equidistant from California and Massachusetts.

* * *

"How is she?" Claire had whispered towards afternoon's end during the very first visit he'd made to St. Agatha's. Her face had tightened with pain. A vast expanse of her new armor (faith, serene obedience) was shed in that moment.

"Victoria's unbelievable," he said. "Demonically independent, like you." He was trying to pace his visits to alternate with Victoria's, who came every three months or so. He always tried to add a new fillip of information. "She's doing particularly superb work in Latin this term."

Claire's eyes widened with interest, amusement. "Latin! Right up the old family tree . . . Jeff's been good enough to write often, and she writes all the time . . . are you absolutely sure that she's very well?"

"Oh you know how impeccable Jeff is." "Impeccable. Otherwise I couldn't possibly be here." "Don't rationalize," Edmund said severely.

Her eyes cast down, undecipherable.

"She's beginning to look at boarding schools," Edmund continued. "She's drawn to Milton, and lately to St. Paul's, of course . . . you might have heard that they're taking in girls beginning next year, going co-ed."

Her eyes fluttered briefly in merriment. "Oh I wonder how Plinker would have felt about that desecration."

"Are you absolutely sure she's very well?" she'd ask at the end of each visit. He'd reassure her, she'd smile and let him go with one of her funny little koans.

"As for myself, I desire nothing in particular, which means I'm *really* well."

Four Rivers, Minnesota
February 1972

Well, dear Jeff, after having tried radical dissent she's trying radical obedience, which can come to more or less of the same thing. Her "crackerjack plan for salvation," as you call it, does seem to be a tough, old-fashioned way out of modern quandaries, but I beg you to honor her decision (if only in the spirit of history) as one of the more imaginative alternatives a liberated woman can find in our time. . . .

You keep falling into the dangerous trap of labeling it "self-abnegation." In our present tornado of carnal propaganda we seem to forget that celibacy is not necessarily a form of self-denial, that it's equally served throughout history to enlarge our secular powers and achieve the full potency of our selfhood, that it's been as much practiced by the tribesman readying himself for the big hunt or the warrior preparing for an important battle as by the shaman, priest or hermit. . . . Her "love affair with God," as you *so* cutely phrase it, is by far the most radical act of independence she could engage in. You forget how devilishly *consistent* she is, dear fellow; only the devil is more consistent than she is. . . .

Jeff! In the recent past when Edmund stood in an airport on the way to one of his conferences he had seen Jeff waiting for a plane, waiting for a woman. . . . Jeff kept his hands in his pockets as he smilingly waited, as if nervously fingering handfuls of loose change . . . the trousers of his perennial Brooks Brothers tweeds were cut on the short side, in the manner of the 1940s, and underneath their cuffs there stretched an area of immaculate athletic sock. . . . Faint gray now streaked that excellent head of short-clipped hair and gave him an added air of venerability. . . . Jeff the ever-ready groom, Jeff the king of honorable sensuality stood there expectant, smiling, fair, and over the years Edmund came to associate Jeff's particular cut of Brooks Brothers trousers with the loneliness of early middle age, the

peculiar restlessness of its flesh, the incandescent fur-
tiveness of Puritan adultery. . . . On the first instance
the woman who appeared looked strikingly like Cousin
April. Her hair was sleeked into a smooth glossy
pageboy, as in the 1944 graduation pictures taken for the
Miss Hewitt's yearbook. Her fair athlete's face was both
lined and warmed by frequent sun and her pink lips
opened in a photogenic smile as she clutched Jeff's arm.
Edmund imagined that in his school-bound life at St.
Paul's, Jeff could only have met these women at commencements, faculty-parent teas, parents' weekends,
soccer matches . . . Edmund never greeted Jeff on these
occasions, knowing the extent of his friend's moral
delicacy, his stated probity . . . he'd usually duck into
some restaurant to buy cigarettes, find a phone booth, do
anything to respect the zeal of Jeff's search for happiness. . . . These women, this charm-braceleted chorus
line of Jeff's middle-age felicity, sometimes carried
beach bags embroidered with sailboats and pussycats, or
stepped off the plane from a sunny Southern provenance
still wearing short golf skirts, brief socks with
pom-poms. . . . What better reassurance could Jeff have
of the ancient order than these slender Junior Leaguers
with faint crow's lines and gleaming eyes whose braces
barely seemed to have come off their teeth? . . .
Edmund enjoyed visualizing people's domestic interiors
and he imagined them at home, admitting Jeff to their
bower while their husbands were on business trips, their
children away at camp or boarding school . . . there
might be a curved oval dressing table with starched white
organdy ruffles like the ones that April and Katrinka had
had in the forties . . . some childhood fetish—a white
and woolly stuffed dog on a floral bedcover . . . the
fetish would lie on the floor of the pink and flounced
divorcing woman's bedroom as she tossed in bed crying
with joy at Jeff's hungry, competent lovemaking. . . .
Once in New York a colleague had enticed Edmund to

have a drink after a lecture and he'd actually seen Jeff with Katrinka at the Waldorf Skylight Room; his palm was placed on the small of her athletic back as he steered her towards the dance floor with the same rolling, confident sailor's gait with which he'd moved through Larue's, the Stork Club decades ago. . . . Katrinka had recapped her teeth, remarried twice, lost some of her overbite . . . in the last years (so Edmund had gleaned from Sophie, who always knew everything) Jeff had confined himself to shuttling back and forth between these two companions of his youth, April and Katrinka, Katrinka and April . . . a year after Claire had left for Minnesota he saw Jeff and April at the corner of Fifth Avenue and Sixty-second Street, outside the Knicker-bocker Club, at the exact same spot where he'd seen them in the late 1940s when he accompanied Claire and Sophie to some coming-out party . . . April was tanned and fitter than ever and had a barrette in her hair and wore a mink instead of a panda and was saying in her clearest Locust Valley lockjaw, "What a nifty idea, dearie, we'll fly to . . ." The cuffs of Jeff's Brooks Brothers suit rode frugally high over his ankles and they were buying a little bag of roasted chestnuts from the street vendor, precisely as they had when he'd glimpsed them on the same street corner a quarter of a century ago.

"Who won Wimbledon this year?" Claire once asked during one of Edmund's visits to the monastery. "I think it was Kodes and Billie Jean," he answered. And then continued: "Nixon should be prosecuted; if only Ber-trand Russell were still around to start a proper tribunal for war crimes, there should be another Nuremberg. . . ." He remembered that he was using the same phrases she'd used five years ago. She was fingering a daisy and looking absentminded.

"I've realized here that any politics not grounded in

spiritual substance will dissipate into failure," she said, "will even breed its own violence. . . ."

"Dear one!" Edmund leaned forward, flecked a speck of dust from the sleeve of her stark serge gown. "Didn't you know that everything begins with mysticism and ends in politics to begin all over again in mysticism?"

He had little idea of how traditional her beliefs were, whether the nuns questioned her concerning their catholicity; she preferred not to discuss such "dogmatic" things. The few definitions she made had a limpid, brutal simplicity.

"How do you pray?" he once asked. "I mean, this has always struck me as the most difficult. How do you name Him, or It or whatever?"

"No matter. You have to name yourself first. Then it just comes."

"And what . . . what if that fails?"

"Oh dear, you worry too much!" she laughed. "No matter! If you don't find it in prayer you might find it in your own true work."

On one of his last visits to Claire, Edmund stopped at the pond neighboring the abbey on his way back from Compline and watched the beaver at his work . . . the animal was shuttling back and forth across the water with large branches in his mouth, depositing them upon his dam. . . . Each time he waddled onto shore and hovered near Edmund for a few seconds, as brown and lustrous as the water that was his home, before diving back for further tasks. The intricate steering mechanism of his forelegs, whirring about like propellers . . . The animal rose before Edmund one last time at the edge of the pond, monumental in the mystery of his work, his compulsion . . . and then as the mist rose over the darkening orange dusk he dove into the water again for its daily recreation. He swam about in large slow circles now, not fetching or carrying anymore, moving about in pure play, no purpose, all pleasure . . . once or twice he lashed his tail out upon the water with a flat broad motion, exploding the darkening pond into high white sprays and spumes . . . then dove under and came out again and swam again long into the night in wide meditative circles, having become his own contemplation, his own survival.

gone by at Amnesty without some communication from her. . . ." Claire walks slightly ahead of Sophie in the flower-budded park, head bent, hands locked behind her back, with that isolation of purpose they remember since her childhood.

"Back home we have a joke," Edmund whispers to Evgeny as the Intourist group moves slowly towards the mausoleum. "One day Lenin's body is gone from the vault and the guards find a note on the pillow. It says 'Returned to Zurich to start everything over again.' " The Russian's boreal inscrutable gaze, perhaps hiding amusement. Edmund focuses his camera on the domes of St. Basil's. The Spassky Tower merrily chimes the eleventh hour. The soldiers guarding the mausoleum door change again in frozen ritual, two new men goose-step alongside the sepia wall, stride up to each of their colleagues at the door, present bayonets, spin on their heels, take their place at the entrance of the tomb. As the visitors' line moves still closer to the mausoleum the green of the guards' epaulets becomes even more raw and brilliant, a green out of nature, Edmund whispers to Sophie, the rawest chemical viridian; they're close enough now to hear the soldiers' boots swish against the wool of their greatcoats as they goose-step back along the battlements of the Kremlin wall.

The evening before Edmund, Claire and Sophie had taken the subway again to visit with still other friends of Baklanov's. Their hosts had laden their kitchen table with an abundance of miraculously found food, filled it with whatever shreds of cheese and cookies they'd found in their cupboard, a relative appears with a bottle of wine, another with a can of mussels, more friends come bringing bread, the table soon fills with food miracu-lously gathered. I had a Russian mother, Edmund tells the hosts, there was this tradition for us also that not an inch of the tablecloth could show when we had visitors, we lived in great poverty but those may have been the happiest days of my life. "Truly he's had trouble having faith in anything since," Claire remarks. Edmund looks up at her, frowning.

"There are two paths to liberty," the daughter of the house says. She is short and powerful, a sociologist whose permit to teach has been revoked. "The path outside, in the open, in society, and the inner freedom which we struggle to retain when we're deprived of our public freedom."

"We live in a state of domesticated desperation but we retain an inner freedom which no despots can destroy," her mother adds, turning to Claire. "The human spirit must struggle so hard here that it might become fuller than yours."

"What nonsense, my dearest!" one of her sons exclaims. "There's nothing uplifting about our suffering; we console ourselves by searching for redeeming features when there's nothing to it but animal fear and pain."

"Whether there are listening devices in our homes is beside the point," the daughter of the house continues. "The fact is that our fingers constantly point to the ceiling and we're afraid of ever opening our mouths."

"It's up to us to help you out of your suffering," Sophie whispers at some point. "We wish to share it with you."

"Of course you do," the daughter of the house says gently. "You Americans have an admirable way of wanting that which is uniquely our own and unshareable."

Claire would tell Edmund, on their way back to the hotel, that these were the people who would take her see Baklanov's mother.

They had noticed a curious detail about the dwelling they visited in Moscow: The entrance door to each apartment was padded on the outside with a thick substance of quilted leather, like the padding of walls in insane asylums. Sophie had seen this as a symbol: The interiors behind these doors, she said, were havens of sanity and goodness from which the mad official Soviet world was isolated as in an immense security cell.

"Her son and husband died in World War Two," Edmund is still translating to Sophie from the old Ukrainian at his side, "she's a retired teacher, she says it's the last time she'll ever see Vladimir Ilich. . . ." As it approaches the bronze door of the Lenin mausoleum the visitors' line quickens, begins to be swallowed more swiftly into the tiered structure of rose granite. And before they know it the tourists stand directly next to two stern young guards at the tomb's entrance, who hold their faces high and their eyes skywards as if to evade all human gaze; all becomes increasingly glacial as they approach the door, even the soldiers' flesh seems made of some substance new yet unorganic—marzipan, the plastic of new toys. One walks through high bronze doors, two more guards stand at the head of the stairs bayonets thrust forward, fingers covering their lips to impose silence, then there's nothing but the shuffling of feet down a long black porphyry stairway, a mighty whirring of air-conditioning machines, the moment is very brief and frozen, one is herded swiftly through a small luminous room, the serpent of humanity circles silently around a brightly lit glass coffin, inside it lies a very small bearded man in a black suit, his face very pale, his delicate hands clutching a book; Sophie would remember the suit as being made of velvet but this would be denied by Claire and Edmund; before they know it they're climbing up another staircase through the sanitized darkness, herded by lapidary soldiers holding fingers vertically across young faces of peach hue.

They reenter into blinding sunlight and move through

the avenue of fir trees at the back of the Lenin mausoleum, filing past dozens of obscure generals and presidents of councils memorialized in busts of stone.

"Incredible, I can't believe it, death taken as archaically as that, trying to preserve his spirit by keeping his body intact, pure Pharaonism at the heart of the world's most technocratic state . . ." Claire's voice is high, excited, and they know she'd launched into a soliloquy. ". . . pure Pharaonism, the leader's spirit continuing to guide the people as long as his body can avoid corruption. . . ."

"We have joke too," Evgeny says, coming up to them beside the modest bust of Stalin set among other effigies of forgotten leaders. "Under capitalism man exploits man, under Communism it is the opposite."

"And you know Edmund this all reminds me of you," Claire continues with her way of not listening, "reminds me of what you've been for these past twenty years dear heart. . . ."

Sophie was already gone and Claire had turned away from Edmund that morning with a quick step, striding towards the subway. Edmund had gone back to his hotel room and gone to sleep. In the past year he'd vastly increased his capacity to sleep away his moments of annoyance or confusion. "I demand an explanation of that perfectly outlandish statement!" he'd first shouted at Claire as she'd begun to cross Red Square. But she'd just blown him a kiss and continued walking, calling out, "I'll see you tonight. . . . Let's have a drink after dinner."

She was faithful to the appointment.

"A group of glorified undertakers tiptoeing through the morgues of history in search of more corpses to embalm . . . that's what you said art historians were, right?"

They were sitting in the foreign currency bar on the

ground floor of their hotel. He kept staring at two Soviet women across the room with Cupid's-bow mouths and deeply cleavaged blouses of blue silk who reminded him again of Paris in his childhood, wartime, the German occupation.

"Are you really strong enough to change your life again, Edmund? You've wanted to freeze, arrest the past, history's been your cop-out, your second mother, your only Muse . . ."

"All the other Muses were out of town."

"But now that you've decided to paint again the Muse will only return if you have faith, and true faith can only exist with a considerable measure of doubt, and you've never accepted the necessity of doubt. . . ."

A rock band thrummed in the room and he lightly cupped his hands over his ears to hear her better.

"To have faith in God, in love, in art, is to have faith in something that is infinite. And therefore faith must be uncertain because its infinite object is being received by a finite being. . . ."

Her eyes blinked twice, slowly. These were tough issues. She'd never let him get away with anything.

"The element of uncertainty in faith can't be removed. It must be accepted. The courage of uncertainty is what you need, you haven't taken a risk in your life, you've always wanted to be dead sure of your fame, your eventual glory, your immortality. . . ."

She slowly rubbed her powerful hands against each other, as she had in their conversations at St. Agatha's.

"Anyone who's dead sure is dead, Edmund. Where there's daring and courage there's the possibility of failure, the risk must be taken.

"Otherwise you'll only paint sentimental little sea-scapes or fashionable empty abstractions," she added with her old bluntness.

Their conversation was brief. They hugged each other

good night and went into the desolate maze of their hotel corridors, both searching for their own rooms.

During the last two days of their stay in Moscow they walked out every night to stare at the amazing sight at the center of Red Square: Guards in unearthly green standing at bronze door. Blinding cones of light pouring down from the Kremlin's sienna battlements. Tiered temple of frozen rose denying the finality of death.

One night as they stood in front of the mausoleum watching the changing of the guards the militiamen stationed in front of the Kremlin walls started shouting orders, chasing all pedestrians off the center of Red Square, Claire grabbed Sophie's arm, scores of citizens dispersed like docile cattle, a moment later a limousine swept like black lightning into the space habitually forbidden to all motor vehicles, it was immense and gleaming, its windows curtained. A gate suddenly opened in the bloodred battlements, the vehicle sped swiftly across the stone lake of Red Square and dove into the darkness of the Kremlin's might.

XX

Claire appeared at Edmund's door on the Williams campus one winter night holding all of her worldly possessions wrapped in a square of burlap, having left the convent the day after Jeffrey Howell's death. She had first flown directly to Boston to be with Victoria and came to Edmund four days later in the middle of a heavy blizzard. She would succumb the following day to a severe bronchitis complicated by pleurisy. She was dressed in one of the nun's habits she'd worn for three years, some inches hurriedly chopped off with a pair of kitchen shears, wearing nothing over it but a thin sweater which Victoria had forced upon her that morning. She hadn't phoned him because she "refused to disturb his difficult schedule," the bus stop was three miles from his house but she was "used to a great deal of walking." Shivering in front of the fire as Edmund heaped blankets on her, Claire had sat with her chin resting on her knees, staring at the fire. Her shoulder blades were fiercely outlined under the folds of her altered serge dress, there was a bluish, cavernous cast of exhaustion or undernourishment under her eyes. The anguish of losing one we've not loved well can be more painful than the death of a great love.

For the following weeks she knew only the outline of Edmund's face hovering continually over hers in the blur of her fever, heard only the hoarse, grating voice of Edmund's aging cat, the soft thud of his cheek rubbing against her bed. She woke in and out of her haze of fever to see him sitting in an armchair by the bed correcting students' papers or moving about her as soft-footedly as his cat. He hovered above her one last time late at night as he came in to bring her a mug of hot milk and adjust her bedcovers. She always pulled the quilt on the wrong way, he chided, short side down, she was determined to get chilled again, didn't know the first thing about home comforts. Every night he hovered over her in his frayed blue robe as she was falling asleep; he adjusted her quilt and lifted it high with a wide impatient gesture; it fluttered over her like a canopy, a benediction before coming down with a gentle fall to which she grew so accustomed that on the evenings when he worked late and she'd already fallen asleep before his last visit she woke at dawn with a sense of loss.

A man in early middle age whose thick mane of sandy hair faintly showed the gray beginning to lace it; tanned, stubborn-chinned face; those deepened lines between nose and finely chiseled mouth which increased her own sense of time's passing. From her captive point, immobilized at the center of his world, Claire began to observe Edmund gyrating about her. He had the domestic obsessions of an only son who's survived the love of a penurious, possessive single mother, he saved leftovers for soups and frugal stews, loved all childhood smells and tastes, believed in ancient remedies for every bodily ill—inhalations of tincture of benzoin, hot porridge in the morning. "Another cup of broth Peb dear, please lambkin, I want you running marathons in a fortnight. . . ."

Jeff Howell had died while searching for his own stability, conversion of life. The plane he was traveling on crashed in a snowstorm in the woods of New

Hampshire. As Edmund reconstructed it, he had boarded it to rejoin the estranged wife of one of his colleagues at St. Paul's, a loving blonde who rode a great deal and much admired him, and for whom he'd even begun to think of the possibility of divorcing Claire. Jeff had remained fairly happy to his last days. After Edmund had begun his visiting professorship at Williams College the preceding fall he had met Jeff for lunch several times in the vicinity of Boston, halfway between their two schools. Jeff had spoken glowingly about Victoria's performance at boarding school, summer life on the island, his yearly voyages abroad. The last one was to the Galápagos, the scale of its birds was amazing, there were many stunning mating habits to observe in the animal population. . . . Victoria had a summer job tending the flower stands on the island's Main Street, the purple gladioli Edmund always looked for were more glorious than ever. . . . They'd often had huge beach expeditions with April's and Katrinka's tribes, scores of them ranging from the ages of five to sixty going out to the clam beds near the lighthouse and bringing the clams home and everyone giving a hand in making a fine linguini sauce and watching the ferry come in against the sunset . . . shall I ever want that happiness again? Edmund wondered as he joined Jeff in a second martini.

A heavy snow had fallen upon Massachusetts the month of Claire's return and remained undisturbed by thaw, their landscape was stilled for weeks in the brilliance of a deep New England winter. As Claire regained her health Edmund was struck by her reluctance to make contact with the splendor of the world outside his rooms. When her fever had ended she'd spent hours by the fire, reading, mending his clothes, writing daily letters to Victoria. As she grew still stronger she began to glide wraithlike across the floors of his apartment, working quietly, talking little. Every domestic duty—the dusting of his books, the kneading of a bread dough

—seemed to be savored with meticulous fervor, with the calm of a litany.

She had a way of keeping her eyes averted from the window during such tasks, avoiding all view of the outdoors.

"You can't imagine the glory of the landscape, Peb, let me bundle you up and drive you out for just ten minutes, we could go to the village and surprise Victoria with a lot of books when she comes home this weekend. . . ." (Ah, that word to use with her at last, "home.") "Do you mind going without me dear heart?" "As you wish."

He often ran his fingers through her thin brown hair.

As Edmund came home from campus and saw Claire profiled in his window, drawing a sewing needle with swift high strokes, he sometimes recalled his youthful visions of future happiness. Claire and Edmund continuing to live on the island six months of the year, Edmund painting eight hours a day in a large skylit studio facing out to sea. . . . Two children at the most; after a few years they'd move to a large city most of the year for the sake of good schooling . . . half of a brownstone in the East Twenties, two golden children growing, a guest room upstairs where their godmother, nomadic Aunt Sophie, could come to stay in between her reporting trips. . . . "All juvenile, corny, not as interesting as it's turned out to be." They were in a three-room flat on the edge of the Williams campus, on the top floor of a shabbily genteel Victorian house which they shared with the chairman of sociology. Edmund was teaching seminars to wealthy students who didn't know the difference between Bacon and Bakunin and participating in discussions of interminable tedium on whether to add a course in Carolingian architecture to the next year's curriculum. Claire was a frail, haggard woman with traces of admirable beauty remaining in her face and roughened field worker's hands of almost masculine power. Had the failure of her lifelong urge for self-determination, always aborted by men, by Jeff, partly broken her will to recover? Throughout her convalescence she took brief naps throughout the day in odd places of his apartment, on a blanket by the fire, curled up at the side of his desk, with the abandon of an enfeebled animal.

Their first domesticity.

His boots scraping on the doorsill as he came in from the snow, bringing the logs for the evening fire. He came in with more wood than he could carry and threw it on the hearth with a wide brusque gesture, shattering splinters onto the rug. She brushed them off, chiding gently. "Why always so rough, you'll burn the house down. . . ." "I'm really very brutal." He had a habit of squatting on his heels in front of the fire for a good while to make sure that it didn't flare up too high.

On cold nights she forced him to take a long hot bath before going to bed to help his arthritic knee.

Vico was now almost nineteen, a Siamese cat with eyes of lapis lazuli unclouded by age who hunted for heat throughout the winter. His voice had become an almost soundless call, a hoarse grating yawn accompanied by an immense opening of jaws which Edmund compared to those of the beasts in Assyrian bas-reliefs. When he settled on his blanket in a corner of Claire's room he lowered himself ever so slowly, first one arthritic limb then another, holding his breath as if to suppress a groan. He wreathed himself lamely about Claire's leg as she rose every morning, purred his gruff note of thanks as she bent down to caress his head. "I'll go berserk when it's the end of him," Edmund said. "I'll get you one you may love almost as much." "Oh never, he's the only one who's taken the time to know me well."

He slept on a folding cot in his study, had given Claire his bedroom at the beginning of her illness. He had frequent nightmares and she came into his room when he cried out in his sleep. During these visitations he burst out in short, subhuman cries, his body trembled with a long tremor like that of an animal dreaming. She loved to see his body hulking under its lair of covers, a dark blue, breathing mountain. Soon I must help him, she kept telling herself, eventually I must rescue him, fearing that these phrases were akin to Saint Augustine's O Save Me God But Not Quite Yet.

Some years ago when she'd left for St. Agatha's she'd often meditated upon those Irish pilgrims of the Dark Ages who'd set out on sea journeys with no particular destination in mind, aiming solely to abandon themselves to Providence. They'd floated as randomly as possible into the Atlantic, entrusting themselves to the hazards of storms in hope of being led by His Will to a solitary place where they could find a new level of grace. During her stay at the convent she'd maintained this same sense of submission to Providence, of random journeying. And she was filled with both anguish and a singular new peace during those winter months of her return as she lay sheltered in Edmund's care. Well now she might have to chart a course again. Well yes she might, with his help.

She saw all about her the carnage of her battle for self-perfection—the lonely success of Sophie's middle age, her child's uncertain future. Jeff.

O Great Spirit, she'd often whispered during her illness, give me the humility to finally understand others as well as they've loved me.

"Love in middle age!" Edmund wrote in one of his frequent letters to his friend John Mirsky in Berkeley. "A process of hulling, husking, denuding, fleecing, decorticating our early dreams, a stripping away of illusions so radical that we create a new dialectic of the passions, a romance of the real."

Claire and Edmund often talked about how life had to be lived in the years that followed the forty-five-year mark: A massive process of centering, focusing, zeroing in. She: Confine yourself to small but intense acts of compassion, use the little stuff rather than the big stuff, Saint Thérèse de Lisieux said.

He: How to find a way to survive on those fringes of society which are the only proper place for an artist and yet survive.

He muttered often about the dark times ahead, the imminent rebarbarization of the West. "It's later in history than I thought, Peb; what a Pollyanna I was a decade ago, the university as a temple of the intellect, my foot . . . temple's in ruins, heap of rubbish accommodating gigantic festivals of the ego; those pals of yours at St. Agatha's may have the right idea, sever most ties to the marketplace, set up your own islets of salvation. . . ."

Claire finally observed (this was all discovery, discovery!) the full anxieties of his forty-fourth year.

"Dad may have been saintly," Victoria said, "I'll miss him till the day I die. But to be absolutely frank I approve of Mamma's life more."

The hair was a shock of light brown silk, like her father's. The pale blue eyes had the guarded irony of Claire's.

"What do you mean by saintly, sweetheart?"

"Well they're the ones who think human nature is very perfectible, who have utterly peaceful characters and love people with great ease. Mamma isn't saintly, she's trying to be a saint, which is a very different matter. . . ."

"And what do you mean by that?"

"She's one of those people who probably carry more evil in them than most others and have a low opinion of human nature and are the great workers for change . . . that's what makes her so difficult and interesting really."

She had recently turned fifteen. Her life's singular events—her mother's absence, her father's death—had occurred when she was just old enough to grapple with them. She had a way of masking her brooding moods with a clever, disturbingly precocious conversation.

"Mamma sees so much evil in the universe that she has to work much much harder at being perfect. It's a path I understand well because I too believe myself to be profoundly evil."

She bent her head, nodding tragically. It was two months after her mother's return. They were walking in the Williamstown woods picking early wood violets as a bouquet for Claire—another attempt to induce her out of doors. On the earlier weekends she'd come home from school Victoria had stayed at her mother's bedside staring at her with intense curiosity in between long bouts of reading aloud—they'd spent March on Teilhard.

Victoria bent down to pick a fern. "You see that's the fascinating thing, Eddem. Goodness is much more of a mystery than evil. In Bible class at school they only talk about the mystery of evil. Well the irony is that it's *goodness* which is much more of a mystery."

Edmund paused in his flower gathering. Was this precociousness in matters spiritual an inherited trait? Would one be able to breed generations of theologians and mystics by proper selection?

"What I'm most grateful to Mamma for is that she taught me to take utterly nothing for granted," Victoria said during another walk. "Daddy took all that society offered him with open hands, without ever saying the no no no that's essential to a genuine life; he was much easier to live with. . . ."

"And what are you going to be like?"

"I wish to be difficult too, Uncle Eddem. I trust a few people implicitly like you and Mamma and Aunt Soph about idiotic matters of everyday survival, but about absolute concerns—what's the good life and so forth for me—oh, no no, only I can tell what's best."

There was a silence. Pity the young men growing up in 1974, Edmund thought.

"I mean, what else is feminism about? The true feminists of the future have to go in my mother's direction and have total control over themselves, refuse to be brainwashed by the propaganda machine of the sexual-industrial complex. . . . Eddem, can you pray?"

"I wish I could. But I'd better just concentrate on taking care of you and Mom. It's the duty of men of action to take care of you contemplatives when you fall into the ditch."

That put Victoria in a state of considerable merriment. As she was able to indulge her passionate affection for her mother this grave child began to laugh more often, with abandon.

"So you think of yourself as a man of action! The dissenters in convents might be much more active in the world than you are because they're truly radical critics of it."

Occasionally her mother's former arrogance announced itself.

"Imagine anyone accusing contemplatives of not being useful! Those placid yes-men in the regular world have the usefulness of suckers."

"But don't worry, Eddem," she added, "*you*'re a born educator."

"Alas."

"Edmund," Claire often said, "I wish you'd paint again."

"You sound like Sophie used to. . . . I'm not boring enough to be an artist these days, darling, I believe in old-fashioned things like giving pleasure. Have you seen what's being exhibited today, Peb? The aesthetics of tedium, ladders and rods of steel set at ninety-degree angles to each other, a hundred and forty-eight little black dots set out on white canvas, films showing one idiot eating a doughnut for ten hours, oh, *ils vont trop loin, tu sais*! How I miss those tornadoes of self-indulgent paint I yiped about too impetuously two decades ago, the primal energy of Pollock; today it's the new Puritanism denying us pleasure in any form, as if Jonathan Edwards had been recalled by séance to rule the art world. . . . The shocking became so boring that the only next step was to make the boring shocking. Collective boredom as the newest species of terrorism, of psychological hijacking. . . ."

"But you're too afraid of not being instantly loved!"

He drew a little bit for the first time in two decades. He began by drawing Claire's hands, her feet. Her blunt-nailed hands were rougher, more powerful after her arduous years away. Her feet were unchanged, the bare delicacy of Botticelli's *Primavera*. He drew Victoria reading, his cat Vico drinking the noon sun on window-sills. At first the pencil was like some clumsy rock in his hand, recalcitrant, unyielding, he recalled with pain and longing the days when it had been like the nimblest and swiftest of his limbs. Over the weeks it softened like a piece of clay warmed by pummeling. He still muttered as he drew, as he had in his twenties.

"There's nothing more presumptuous than emptiness Claire darling. Contemporary art has succeeded in finally killing off the Muse. The rude French began it all, of course, with the vogue of insulting and boring the audience, Duchamp, Dada . . . we're living in a solipsistic Museless world whose vestigial religion is the cult of Nothing, at whose shrine the proper liturgical response is a yawn . . . nothing to do but create enclaves where we can thumb our nose at fashion and resurrect, shelter, nourish, surrender to our Muse. . . ."

If she'd ever marry him (this was once said in a playful bantering tone) he'd have such a powerful live-in

Muse and paint with such ferocity that he might even refuse to go out of the house, be just the kind of recluse she'd become in the past months.

Perhaps, she replied in that cryptic little manner she'd acquired at St. Agatha's, an artist is simply a person who's invented an artist.

They'd learned from brief, desperate letters the previous year that Sophie's Israeli husband, Amos, had died from shrapnel wounds suffered during an assignment on the Lebanese border and that she was returning to the United States. Then after some months of silence she had written them to start watching the MBC ten o'clock news. And one day Sophie's radiant smile began to appear almost daily, her hair abundantly teased, her face painted with the most lustrous art. And Claire sat in front of the set as if that beloved face were rebuilding her bridge to the world outside of Edmund's rooms.

These were the years when former Vietnam activists were rechanneling their energies into the issue of human rights. Sophie began to forward to Claire the literature she received from Amnesty International. And while still convalescing Claire pored over dossiers relating to imprisoned Soviet dissidents, Brazilian priests.

When Edmund missed the seven o'clock news because of a task at college she complained about the frivolity of Sophie's assignments. "I wish they'd give her more important news, Eddem; they had the impertinence to assign her a birthday party for aging lions at the Bronx Zoo, a woman of her brilliance!" "She'll fight her way out of that very quickly," Edmund predicted.

A few months later Sophie was promoted to the position of anchorperson for the weekend nights and they never wanted to miss that. "More violence tonight," Sophie would begin the program with her lustrous violet smile, "the Near East crisis is growing to a head, police readies for confrontation as looting grows in Newark's slum areas and a Brooklyn church is ransacked by three masked men. . . ." When will she ever find time now to come and see us? Claire and Edmund complained. Wouldn't it be lovely if the three of us could have a vacation together? Claire said. One of these days soon we must take a long trip together Edmund agreed.

One day while sitting by the fire Claire knew she must unburden herself of an emotion which had grown to immense proportions since her return. Can I dare tell him, she wondered, shall I ever dare. She feared that if she didn't have the courage to offer him her new knowledge the essence of tragedy might work itself out between them also—tragedy, the process of learning things too late.

For weeks the words were ready to rise in her but the ancient, ancient reticence kept holding them back—she was quieter than ever, staring a great deal at the fire, the aging cat Vico stalwart on her lap— Certain things are harder than ever to say in this time of ours, she finally said one night, our world has increasingly shunned sentiment in favor of irony. . . .

This makes the writing of novels and the expression of great loves most difficult, he agreed, not to speak of painting decent paintings.

Then her words came out with startling simplicity as he sat on his heels watching the nascent fire in his supple, primeval farmer's squat. "I've meant and meant to tell you," she said, "that I love you so much I'd gladly die for you. Anytime." She'd quickly returned to her reading. He'd shot her a swift, almost suspicious look, the glance of a primitive tribesman startling at the sound of a foreign tongue.

"I'm sorry," she said.

"Don't be." He rose and walked to the window.

And now it lay behind her, a flat, calm object, her proffered life.

* * *

One day in late April when Victoria was home for the weekend they finally got Claire out of doors. They'd teased and teased her, saying she wasn't good enough yet to deserve being a hermit, and on a fine warm Saturday she'd finally stepped out the door, blinking at the sun, her arms linked through both of theirs. Edmund knew how bold that simple step could be. He knew that the greatest gift he'd ever received—the passivity of her winter's bondage—was coming to an end.

They finally took possession of each other (Claire and Edmund) during a great spring rainstorm when the wind so buffeted the windows that they'd sat by the fire making believe they were at sea on a Europe-bound schooner, hearing the surf pounding against the porthole of their cabin. . . . Later that evening as he engaged her fragile body and assuaged his life's fiercest appetite, knowing for the first time her potential for joy, he cast away a burden which he had borne most of his years. And this act of possession thrust him into a new age as distinct from his past life as his adolescence had been from his childhood, serving as a rite of passage as well as of fulfillment.

Under his touch every moment of her body miraculously grew to pleasure like a grain of sand swelling into an acre of the earth.

Yet he knew that no search for joy could ever guide her life. And that the certainty of her love, for a time, would continue to depend on the extent of his proffered freedom.

Whereas she sensed that if he had his will he might take her to an enclave quite as distant and arcane as the one she'd just returned from, as deeply secluded as his long, solitary love; that the exile he'd impose upon her might be even more irrevocable than the one she'd once chosen in total freedom of the will.

And so when he let her go after having strengthened her into renewing her freedom, feeling as if he were letting go some bright shining bird that might be his soul, it was only in a spirit of very distant hope.

xxi

Vico old friend you're my talisman you're my life force
how's this for an image Pussums you're like that Golden
Gate Bridge right over there, you're the chain on which
the beads of my life are strung . . . so hang on
sweetheart the only thing I'm going to do this winter is
see you live to the age of twenty, I've set myself that
goal the way I used to say I'll finish my thesis by the time
I'm twenty-six, by thirty-five I'll be chairman of the
department, our agenda isn't tainted by the impossible
little brother there's a handful of you who've even made
it to twenty-two, twenty-three, it's sheer continuance we
want, the older we get the less words matter, sometimes I
even want to forget to read and write, I only want to
growl with you and babble and whisper like the aspen
leaves in August and do some modest magic again,
describe the tongue of a hummingbird a night of love the
mirages over hot asphalt explain youth and old age . . .
Edmund is spending many hours this winter sitting still
with the cat on his lap. For two decades the Siamese has
hunted the sun's heat in the window of Edmund's
apartments in Berkeley or Williamstown, vigilant whiskers taut against the sky, blue-gray flanks as still and
solid as mountains in the distance, the most constant
landscape of Edmund's life; but this winter it's safer and
more consoling to hug the cat close flesh to flesh. So for

many hours the two sit together in front of the window or the television watching life go by, Vico in Edmund's lap, deadly petals of the paws furled inwards, occasionally raising his steady blinking eyes towards his friend's face; staring at those wells of speckled gold and azure Edmund often tries to assess the meaning of this winter as if he were observing it from the cat's depths, he's never been very good at seeing things from anyone else's point of view, he studies the blue cisterns filled with a knowledge unanswerable to any man and tries to measure in them the hours of his life. You've seen me in a lot of incarnations haven't you old friend, young Werther copping out of art because it might ruffle his damn little ego, Professor Richter grooving on his Pygmalion act, then the demons swept over us didn't they, something hit us, something snapped, yet we're not that badly off Vico, look at those pretty girls going down the street with their book bags what are they going to do but study sociobiology, buy five-piece bedroom sets, betray their husbands, love Beethoven, bang dishes in the kitchen, go into orthodentistry at forty-six, remember nothing about their childhoods but a little pond they fell into at the age of five and a patient, mysterious animal like you . . . Vico's silken tail waves like a metronome, he greets the touch of his master's hand with a hoarse brief call of thanks. And after a few hours of sitting this way before the window or the television they go back to bed and go to sleep.

Upon leaving Claire and returning to Berkeley the preceding spring Edmund had decided to change his life. He wasn't yet sure how he wanted to change it. So he'd walked to the grocery store, bought a stock of canned goods for himself and the cat and taken to his bed. Upon waking in the morning they have their breakfast, watch television for a while and then move to the window to enjoy the late-morning sun. They sit facing south, Venetian blinds tilted down so as to get full sunlight yet

not be seen from the street. And when the cat has
warmed his flesh, signaled well-being with faint
rhythmic roars, Edmund carries him to the pillow that's
lain for twenty years at the foot of his bed, he gets in
between the sheets and sleeps again until the afternoon.
Upon waking he reaches for a book on his night table to
take a few notes on his current project, "The Wane of the
Muse in European Art." The two bachelors then repeat
their gestures of the morning. They go to the sun at
Edmund's western window, stare towards a view which
had once struck Edmund as the world's most sublime,
ethereal bridge spanning the blue bay like a bracelet of
bright bone, magnolias and centennial firs burning in the
glow of a faithful sun. They watch students and teachers
pause at the street corner, biologists carry bags of Finast
potatoes, sociologists wheel prams; splendid young
1970s women often strike poses of great languor by the
mimosa tree outside their window; waiting for the traffic
light to change they take out little mirrors to study pearly
teeth and restiffen lashes, they're buffed and spruced like
poodles just out of parlors aren't they Vico and look at
how politely they're talking smiling to each other again,
the young have regained some of their manners that's
one thing you can say about them, they've dallied back
to their fraternities to attend to soufflé recipes and the
perfecting of their orgasms, listen Vico sweetheart one
must honor the extraordinary variety of tactics humanity
devises to survive despair, others might have increased
their proclivity to liquor or to Mexico but we've chosen
to sit, to dream, to sleep, I assure you I'm utterly sane
old Pussums, I've never felt more composed emptier
more calm, I feel little, I desire nothing, I suffer not at
all, this afternoon I'll write a sentence about the modern
artist's sensuous union with nothingness or his celebration of absence, all rage has left me, I feel generous,
vast, drained, like those folk who change into their
cleanest clothes and rearrange furniture before turning

the light out one last time I want everything about me as orderly and still as I am, I'm in tune with the times for once, bravo, Faustian man is dying; there's little to rescue and even less to invent so live in the wind young folk, lots of sambas, smiles, sailing races, wine-tasting fests, breathing exercises, lots of compliments to the ladies and please let's call them ladies again. . . .

Towards evening the cat gently paws at his master's sleeve, clambers down from Edmund's lap, moves slowly towards the kitchen with the stiff, dignified gait of his great age. They eat. They prepare for bed. And before going to sleep they watch Sophie give the ten o'clock news. There she comes Vico, our switchboard to reality, pretty scary being watched by ten million people every day, look at our beauty with the Titian hair. . . . "More violence tonight as thousands of citizens rally for protest in strike-ridden Uruguay," she says with her marvelous smile, "back home John Wayne goes into surgery . . . a birthday party is held for Siamese twins who were separated five years ago . . . Wall Street averages show industrials up one point two . . ." Edmund's head begins to nod again when Sophie's voice goes off the air. He stares satedly at the art objects that fill his room, the *sang-de-boeuf* vase by his bed, the Tang scroll on the wall opposite him, a pre-Columbian statue acquired in the early sixties stands on the desk, prize of his collection, eight inches high and monumentally inscrutable. ". . . Now for a station break . . . Wannamee Village/Florida's most beautiful old age community . . . Year round tennis courts heated swimming pools a rich and rewarding social life . . ." Edmund returns to his exile of sleep.

At summer's end Toby, the most beloved and rebellious student of Edmund's 1960s, phoned to say that he had married and had just returned to live in Berkeley, could he bring his wife for tea? Edmund said he'd be enchanted and closed his eyes and tried to imagine an ideal woman for Toby; he thought of the Meissen cups standing on his mantelpiece and these gave him the image of what he hoped her to be: fragile, orderly, floral, a woman of Mozartian translucence, a voluptuary of the domestic whose linen closets would be neatly stored and labeled, filled with sachets and pale blue ribbons. He fancied Toby and his young wife constantly shopping together for crass little delicacies to fill their nest with, comparing eggcups and the swell of wine goblets, ah yes such a woman could confine Toby as severely as a cup's function is confined by its form and glaze; he saw her as the principle of order that would tame this figment of the sixties' wildness, this imagined couple were a symbol of the exhaustion of the West, our growing lassitude must be accepted with the most serene acquiescence, Toby of the long matted hair and Ché Guevara buttons who'd stood in torn sandals at Sather Gate shouting about the creation of new worlds is coming home with a little beauty who's rechanneled his ardor into the choosing of place mats and tea services and better quality of air. . . .

Toby's wife came and was precisely the way he'd hoped she'd be. She was dressed in hues of off-white as delicate as the barks of birches and was equally fragile of line. Her pale hair was neatly rolled into a bun all around her head, she said Professor Richter I soon want to study the middle period of Fragonard, she drank from her teacup as if it were a magnolia leaf and asked if she could bring the baby for a visit. A few weeks later, at the beginning of term, Edmund disconnected his phone and ceased to answer doorbells, responding solely to the communications which his friends Luke Edwards or John Mirsky slipped under his door. He presumed that Toby and his family had moved into a neighboring block, for several times a week as Edmund sat behind the Venetian blinds with Vico they wheeled the baby down the street;

they'd glance up at Edmund's window, squinting and frowning with curiosity. And Edmund would watch them until they became specks on the bright Berkeley street, would watch Toby's long now languid body ambling in the sun as he wheeled home the little luxuries of his new world, would stare at the pale hair through which he'd loved to run his hands when it fell to below the shoulders, now cut to a helmet of tight curls like those of the Apollo Belvedere.

"In Ethiopia we have evidence of thousands of executions of political dissidents and systematic use of torture —" (so a letter of Claire's reads) "three thousand persons alleged to be sympathetic to the opposition shot just last month—many of the victims ranged in age between eight and twenty—bodies publicly exposed in Addis Ababa every night—we know of instances of children denouncing parents to break out of their captors' hands—methods of torture include the tying of heavy weights to male genital organs, insertions of red-hot iron bars into the vaginas of nine-year-old-girls, etc. . . ."

She must sit up night after night in the bleak little Boston flat she'd taken after they'd parted and she'd found work with a human rights group, photographs of dissidents strung above her desk, attempting to continue that course of self-denial which had marked her life . . . at times Edmund addresses an envelope, writes Dear Peb on the top of a piece of paper and keeps it on his desk for several days out of fear that one adverb might upset the tenuous half-promises they'd reached in the spring. When he allows his pen to touch paper again he writes something like this: "I'm increasingly grateful for my new sabbatical and the essay on the Muse is going quite well—reversal of attitudes towards the artist's melancholic temperament particularly fascinating to trace in the early Renaissance, the medievals had equated melancholia with sloth and condemned it as one of the seven capital sins—but the Humanists resurrected Aristotle's view that melancholia is the Muse's inseparable companion, a noble trait gracing all men gifted in the arts—"

There are times when Edmund sinks even more deeply into his languor and fails to get dressed, remains in pajamas for days, catnaps all over the chairs of his undusted room rather than make the effort of walking to his bed; his friend John thinks this is all sublime, sublime. "Your ego is . . . utterly diminished in your inaction, yes? The Will abolished! A passivity . . . almost mystical in nature!" (Volcanic splutters, barely intelligible groans of admiration.) "Ah I've got it, I've got it dear one, the saint as slob, or perhaps the slob as saint. . . ."

John's sexuality has abated with his increasing flesh and his Slavophilia now centers on twentieth-century Russian poetry. He comes to lie on Edmund's couch to groan out his disillusionment with love, with the Soviet Union, with the academic life, "To sell our thoughts like farmers at market, phooey, how vulgar! Our terrorists of overactivism, our Stakhanovites of awakedness, I yawn at the very thought of their vigilance. . . ."

"What's the use of striving anymore, John, when the laboratory of the twentieth century is closed, everything's been seen to death, look at the pluralistic decadence of our art world, social realism Postimpressionism Abstract Expressionism photo-realism Minimalism floating in a broth of torpor like alphabet noodles swirling in a baby's bowl. . . ."

"Listen to Mayakovski's prophecy, Edmund, 'There's less and less love, less and less daring, and time is crashing into my forehead . . .' "

"Good Day America, this is Sophie Ross at MBC with a special report from our fiftieth state where the sun is blazing at a gorgeous eighty-seven degrees and the beach forecast is for safe gently swelling surf, we're here to bring you a scoop on

the biggest new industry in Hawaii. . . ." [Sophie
on Waikiki, orchid lei around her neck, stray lock
of hair seductively blowing in the wind.] "Now
what would you guess is the biggest cash crop in our
seven-island wonderland, fellow Americans,
pineapple, sugar, citrus fruit? Guess again. . . .
You've given up? It's marijuana . . ."

Edmund watches carefully for the scheduling of Sophie's special reports; he keeps the cat on his lap
throughout most of the day and they're watching increasing amounts of television; the stillness of his body at
those moments seems to heighten Vico's comfort; towards Christmas the animal began to drag himself very
slowly about the house, there's a great shuffling of
covers, a few stoic groans as he gets up on his rheumatic
hind legs and limps forwards to perform his ritual
greeting, rubbing the rough stubble of his whiskers
against his master's cheek.

"Marijuana is now a billion-dollar cottage industry fostered by rebellious Hawaiian labor unions
who're just plain bucking federal authorities; the tall
green weed is even grown on terraces and condo-
miniums throughout the fiftieth state and in some
buildings five out of seven residents are grass
farmers. . . . Here we are in the Honolulu office of
State Senator Neil Abercrombie, who's been urging
his legislature to decriminalize the cash crop. . . .
Neil, what reflections do you have on this lucrative
new trade?" "Uh, it's Hawaii cowboy style, Sophie,
part of the frontier ethic of doing your thing; it's
being sold at every street corner, we haven't even
got enough room in our jails for our offend-
ers . . ."

Cradled in Edmund's arms before the set Vico resorts to his old jokes, pretends to sleep and suddenly flips over on his back to paw the air at imagined birds, feigns vigilance towards a buzzing fly, expresses contentment by that slow blinking of the eyes which Edmund sees as his way of smiling.

". . . Back at MBC studio this morning we also have Dr. Murray Kempner of Columbia University, author of the recently published book *Keep Off the Grass*, and his views might conflict sharply with those of Senator Abercrombie." [Sophie back in New York, in chaste white cashmere.] "Marijuana's a grave danger to all human organs, Sophie, particularly the reproductive, a disaster to our future generation of offspring; we have conclusive evidence that the sperm of men who're light to medium smokers doesn't develop properly and that the surviving offspring of female monkeys fed marijuana during pregnancy are hypotrophic and hyperactive. . . ."

"Are you still lying around week after week, Edmund, going through an acute phase of male climacteric?" Edmund's torpor seems to concern Sophie and she returns his phone calls punctiliously. The fluctuations of her moods from manic cheer to depression increasingly alarm Edmund; she often blurts out her reprimands in a flat, Valium-drugged monotone. "I diagnose it as acute anomie . . . early senility and advanced agoraphobia complicated by a total collapse of the will. . . ." Or else, in one of her more exultant moods: "Treasure! What's new and exciting in the life of sloth?" "I just phoned to tell you that you're my pipeline to reality." "Are you really all right, darling?" "Yes yes." "You didn't see my special on Jeremy Thayer, that prof who experimented with psilocybin in the sixties, highly controversial, watch for it, we're rebroadcasting, you know I'm always there when you need me." "Yes yes, you're always somewhere, honey, I hope you're getting enough sleep." "I love you and everything."

The last time Edmund has seen Sophie he'd behaved miserably. Claire was still in her convent, Sophie had recently returned from Israel, she'd flown to see him in Detroit where he was attending an art historians' convention. Edmund had found this event depressing. Three thousand men and women were there with stick-on labels saying Amherst, Wayne State, University of Florida, they swarmed through the halls of a large hotel in search of teaching positions, they were writing more and more about less and less, they catnapped in corridors waiting for interviews, these hordes of academics encamped with their dissertations on "The Iconography of the Harp in Sixteenth-Century Bas-Reliefs" and "Aztec Symbols of Parturition" looked like the hostages of a plane hijacking bivouacked at some Near Eastern airport. Edmund had fled the convention right after giving a paper on Caravaggio, driving to the airport hours ahead of time to wait for Sophie in a bar. There was something noble about her newly chiseled face which reminded him of a grave young matron in a Roman frieze, which both confused and seduced him. Her Israeli husband had died that spring, three weeks after their marriage. He saw new little lines at the corners of her eyes during dinner and kept turning to a mirror to scrutinize his own face while she talked. A pregnancy at forty-three, always risky at that age, yet she'd thought of keeping the baby but soon after Amos's death she'd decided on an abortion. . . . Edmund disliked listening to such things, he'd talked about Caravaggio. "Can you imagine any man more radically different from the cautious academic I've become than this ruffian revolutionary genius, Soph, this first of the bohemians who lived like a bandit in the slums of Trastevere, this *artiste maudit* whose biography is chiefly derived from the police records of his time . . . You've suddenly become a woman," he interrupted himself, "and I've remained a messed-up kid." She listened as carefully as ever with her newly tragic, guarded gaze, looking at him at three-quarters, as if posing for camera. He needed to bathe in that rich intimate presence of hers which after almost thirty years had gained something of the marvelously incestuous; it was a time when one impulse of Sophie's might have settled all, might have brought him that constant and predictable happiness which he'd been denying himself, but she was guarded, steeped in her recent sorrows. . . .

He'd felt all this very early in the evening and had become extremely drunk. He'd driven her about the unfamiliar city in a rented car, insisting on one last drink, and they'd ended up in a homosexual nightclub where a pale young male in rhinestone-studded G-string gyrated on top of the bar amid a crowd of braying men. Edmund had played the pinball machine, drinking whiskey with beer chasers. He'd leaned over the machine like a jockey, shouting at the silver ball that sped through its maze of electric-blue machine gunners and motorcycle racers, he jerked the handle sloppily and the ball kept ricocheting off the walls, dribbling slowly into its nearest exit; Sophie stood by him sipping on a glass of wine, looking absent; he remembered later shouting imprecations at his own arid virility, at the silver missile that never reached the delicate ovarian channels between the rich round globes. In their hotel room he was too drunk to make love and fell asleep for a few hours. Dawn light flooded her body as he woke next to her and he was dazzled by the familiar milky splendor of her skin, the youth of a body steeped lifelong in pleasure—he'd not had a woman for some months and returning to her was like returning to one's childhood home after a long absence, imbibing the mystery of history and desire in the smell of a centennial lilac bush—he was grateful again for her subtle hands, her courtesan's suppleness —they lay breathing in each other's arms as they had ten or twenty years ago in Florence, Nantucket, New York — " 'Three hundred men between your thighs,' " he whispered, " 'embracing all love turned false, again, again . . .' "—her familiar "Where's that from?" —"Catullus . . . a page or two before he says, 'Friendship is here, my heart/Richer than love or passion' "—he realized with guilt that he would wish to have her like this until the end of his days, occasional, unbinding, more refreshing and torrid than any bodily substance he knew—in the past she used to say "three years," "ten months," naming the passage of time since their last lovemaking with an accuracy he often hated—but this morning she simply stared at him with those great golden eyes, stared at him with a new desperation he was terrified of plumbing—"What sumptuousness you are," he said, "you are my Orient, oh no more metamorphoses Soph, just give me more of what you are today, I'll never have enough of what you've become. . . ." He fell into a brief sleep thinking of all the men who must have known her in the past decade, creatures not worthy of touching one inch of her glorious skin, scrupulously fashionable men with water beds, sleek lofts in SoHo, exotic new therapies, triple alimonies, odious new theories of expanding their consciousness, they jogged, they fasted, they consulted nutritional healers, they sat on executive boards of Esalen, they worried about children who'd joined Fascist cults, they tried Tibetan meditation, they believed in open marriage, late twentieth-century monsters, virtuosos of the psychobabble of the self, America, America . . . When he woke again Sophie had already left the room, the city.

* * *

Such things happen suddenly. A day came when Vico couldn't raise himself off the bed without Edmund's help. Edmund woke later than usual and wondered why the animal had failed to bring his morning greeting. He raised his head towards the cat and met his gaze. The animal's silken bluish flanks were stretched out behind him with great rigor, he stared back unflinchingly through those azure eyes that had become increasingly speckled with gold in the past year, like the turning of leaves after great frosts. How easily the cat breathed when he cradled against Edmund's breast and they lay very still in bed! Edmund now took all his notes that way; on the days Sophie didn't do the *Good Day America* show he tried to catch the five-minute roundup she occasionally gave at noon by keeping the set on throughout the morning.

"We've got a gorgeous ten-thousand-dollar kitchen work center complete with radar range for you lady if you spin the machine right . . . why, you're crying, oh don't cry lady just spin it again sweetheart, come on let's go after that ten-thousand-dollar spin. . . . SHE'S GOT IT! SHE'S A WINNER! A WINNER! There are some more prizes coming this morning on *The Price Is Right*, folks, the winner of the next game will receive a free two-week stay at the Corfu Hilton so stay tuned for our station break . . ."

—get your early copy of the spectacular up-and-coming best-seller *Too Young to Die*! Stories of thirty-two superstars who died in the prime of life —Marilyn Monroe, Bobby Darin, Freddie Prinze, Billie Holiday, Jack Cassidy, Sal Mineo, Judy Garland, Elvis Presley. . . . What did them in, what was the nature of their anxiety? Get your

mail-order copy today special prepublication price
twelve ninety-five—

The noon mail arrives inviting Dr. Richter to offer this
or that lecture, partake in symposiums and seminars;
Edmund amuses himself by rolling up each letter and
aiming it into the wastebasket across the room; if it lands
right the last third of our life will be okay Vico, if it
misses it'll be a mess, hey, look who's out this morning,
Dick Stoddard from Classics, another honest suntanned
scholar another alcoholic of the single object, "Augustan
View of Providence as Reflected in First-Century Num-
ismatics" was his thesis I believe, admirable citizen,
what nobler task than to turn the new frat brothers into
coin freaks, and there's Mrs. Toby her tummy out like
Cranach's Venus again what do you think of that Vico,
she's off to envy neighbors and birds, talk on the phone
for hours, wipe away dust, curse the government, love
Rachmaninoff, moan at the touch of a beloved, grouse
about the rain, remember nothing about her childhood
but a mysterious pair of eyes like yours. . . .

"Religion doesn't cash itself in like science or art
history, fellow," the Reverend Luke Edwards says during one of his visits to Edmund's room. "I do think this
more than deserves your passionate attention, you don't
seem to accept the *is* of God's presence because you're
so hung up on the *must be* of proof. . . ."

"Are you offering me mystery, Edwards? Now mystery *is* something I've great need of in my life." Edmund
shuffles languidly across his room, the cat cradled
against his chest, dusting his possessions.

The reverend leaps up from his chair in the hope of
another conversation. "Yes yes, that's where it's at,
fellow, part of the magic of Christianity is that nothing
is ever totally understood, got to recycle that, Edmund. . . ."

Dr. Edwards has drawn closer still to God since becoming university chaplain and his culinary skills have become so noted that Dione Lucus occasionally phones him for a recipe. He's credited for returning to the Christian fold many students who'd been seduced by Oriental cults, and he looks upon Edmund's reclusion as a covert, unacknowledged thirst for Deity.

"I believe you do have faith, Edmund, but you have it at a very low temperature . . . got to unpack this, Edmund, the grand strategy of the world religions has been to diagnose the flaw in ourselves and point to some deliverer who'll overcome it in the future . . . don't you sense such a flaw in this outstandingly slothful new phase of your life?"

"The future seems too ethereal to merit primary concern."

"But neither are you dealing with the present, fellow; it's this refusal which the Church has always condemned as sloth, one of the seven deadly sins, you know the Bosch. . . ."

"There's nothing less real than the present, Reverend. Today's news wraps tomorrow's fish."

Edmund sits at the window, staring at the bay hung like a surplice from a cloudless sky. Laughing co-eds walk by, hair scrubbed into curtains of silk. The wife of a biochemist researching crystals does a headstand in the neighboring backyard, suntanned legs twirling like mandibles on an emerald lawn.

"In a truly imaginative metaphysic, Edmund, man can become all things by suspending understanding, the existential cash comes with an abandonment to mystery, Edmund, not with proof. . . ."

"This notion has met with less than universal acceptance."

The chaplain comes close to losing his patience. "Well, do phone if there's anything you need . . . 0800, year of Charlemagne's coronation. . . ."

Have a nice day Edmund calls politely as the door slams, best wishes to the department. Sleep is a very busy condition Reverend, more active you can't get, God sends us songs in the night . . . shall we capitulate to his demands for emotions gaseous and overflowing Vico, got to unpack this Pussums, the self is what hurts, the solution to the identity problem is get lost, is there life after birth as the Buddhists put it, some things are not quite true but are too good to be wrong, has our turn come at last, what do you think little brother, or is it forever too late, the exile is long, cunning we're running out of . . .

Edmund wakes up at night to see that the cat is properly covered, tightens the blanket about his flanks as we would a child's. Sophie is away for most of February. In March, Vico turns twenty.

"I'm thinking of calling my essay 'The Demon of Noontide,' " Edmund writes Claire, "a term Chaplain Edwards tells me was used by the Church to describe that aridity of the soul which plagues monks in the midday hours of contemplation."

One day as they sat looking at the street the cat seemed to try struggling off Edmund's lap and he understood that Vico wished to lie on the windowsill again. He placed him on a pillow in his ancient position, turned towards the sunny street, but the animal continued struggling, asked for a different angle of vision, opened his jaw in a noiseless call to say all was not right yet. Edmund turned him the other way, his head towards the room. And Vico finally lay still and stared back in peace, his new golden eyes blinking with gratitude. It was as if he'd chosen Edmund's room as the last sight he wished to fill himself with. His pain was swallowed in the determination to be stoic—so Edmund saw it—his eyes were a sacred cistern of knowledge even unavailable to him.

In the last days Vico's eyes would remain closed for long moments of time, he opened his eyes in a new way, not upon the call of a voice or the din of conversation which John brought with him but as though to simply look at the room for a moment before closing his eyes again; to remember the room better or simply to see that it was still there.

He died on a day in late March when John was reciting Mayakovski: " 'The poet's word is your resurrection, your immortality citizen bureaucrat . . .' " Edmund had looked towards the window. There was a clenched finality about the way the animal's eyes were closed. He'd covered the animal with its little blanket, not able to carry him to the backyard. It was John who had to do it for him. They carried him there some hours later, they buried Vico in the backyard under the mimosa tree. The nightmares Edmund had that night were not so much dreams as distorted visions induced by malefic spirits. Every art object in his room writhed and pulsated with a Satanic agitation, the cabbage plant in his Tang drawing swelled like a corpse in water to monstrous size, leaves dismembered, tendrils floating about the room like scum on pallid lakes, the Meissen cups shattered into dust, dissolved into a fine colorless powder that choked him like a smog; at early dawn the delicate little pre-Columbian statue he kept on his mantel began to advance across the room, her white lunar body increasing to human size as she came nearer; in her original state her arms had been crossed over her breasts a few inches above the primitive triangle that indicated her sex but now the right hand raised itself off the pure narrow chest, arm broken at the elbow in an archaic angle of sacrificial gesture, the idol loomed close above him, lunar, absent-mouthed, machete raised over his bed . . . he woke crying out, turned the light on, stared at the tiny statue calmly standing on the mantel, the empty pillow at his feet, saw about him the room of a fastidious scholar noted as a connoisseur of the admirable, a gatekeeper of the exquisite; he went back to sleep still haunted by the statue, its association with rituals that preceded the existence of recorded time, rites of atonement testifying to our dread of all that is feral, he reflected on the primal terrors which have led us to domesticate animals such as Vico since the beginning of speech, creatures providing a link to the lowest most implacable forces in the chain of being, beasts which could bring an illusion of safety to the natural jungle of our minds, the solitude of our forests.

He phoned Sophie the next morning. He'd thought of announcing a grave illness and then decided against it. He simply phoned to ask her whether she could come to Berkeley in the next few days. She was in one of her elated moods, she'd just returned from Alaska where she was doing a special on the pipeline, she was compassionate and loving, she sobbed briefly when she heard about Vico; when Edmund's voice failed him she asked him whether she wasn't being supportive enough. But she simply couldn't find time to see him that month, she was off to Jerusalem again the following weekend to interview Begin, then to Geneva to interview some Iranian dissenters Claire had told her about. . . . "Try hard to fit me in, sweetheart," Edmund said, "I'll ring you at three tomorrow." "Don't phone me until after five, at three I have a cardinal."

She called back five minutes later. "Edmund love, if you truly need me you know perfectly well I'll drop it all, I'll leave everything for you at any time, all we've got is each other, I've been more depressed in the past years than at any other time in my life. . . ."

"Damn it, Soph, speak up sooner, I never know what's on your mind anymore."

She paused. "I've learned to repress, to hide, the way you always told me to, Eddem."

"You know I'd give up my life for you anytime, don't you?"

"Maybe I'll take the next plane."

"No no no, you've got all that . . . Soph, I may need you even more in a few weeks."

"Promise?"

"Absolutely sweetheart."

"Really sure?"

"I'll do all right."

"You know I love you and everything."

He wrote to Claire, telling of the cat's death and then continued: "It's clearly Dürer's great engraving *Melancholia I* which offers the first modern concept of artistic inspiration—the cult of melancholy (and later alas of boredom, of the void) now begins to absorb the ancient Muse—"

Every four or five years over the past three decades Claire had sent him an utterly memorable letter.

I feel that notwithstanding much public concern (Soph, Edwards) over your present phase of silence, stillness, you've spent one of the most fruitful and healing winters of your life. What they call your passivity, indolence, etc., may be nothing more than a stripping of yourself greatly needed to return you to essentials. It's as if you've worn a series of masks for twenty years, darling, masks of the hardened cynic, the bureaucrat of academia which have nothing to do with the creature inside. The danger with any mask is that it may force one's true features to emulate it, it's urgent that we remove masks before it's too late, before our features have hardened into them irreparably . . . you've been a translation of yourself, Edmund dear, and I look forward to reading a more real you very soon. . . .

There's a conference on the abolition of the death penalty she has to go to in early May, then she must see Victoria through her exams, wouldn't it be splendid if she could talk him and Soph into getting together for a few days sometime later in the spring . . . just think, twenty-five years since that's happened, she'd consult Soph as to dates, etc.

On interview programs which follow Sophie's occasional appearance on *Good Day America* severe gray-haired women with doctorates in sexology advise teenagers to pet to orgasm rather than go all the way; doctors of the male sex angrily protest that petting will never be a substitute for genuine penetration; fifteen-year-old girls speak movingly of what it's like to come out of the closet as a Lesbian. On the soap operas that lie like a lonely plain between the morning shows and Sophie's evening news Americans still seem to have many dreams and aspirations, some Americans confess deep love for each other in candlelit restaurants upon the occasion of a thirtieth wedding anniversary and others worry about their daughters going out with porn photographers; an amazing amount of the soaps revolve about the sagas of adulterous doctors. There's one particular show, *General Hospital*, which mesmerizes Edmund because of its fastidiously elemental passions. The first time he watches it Monica is about to give birth with great danger to her life in a country house isolated by a violent snowstorm—her doctor-husband (Eric) is trying to get through to her by ambulance in the company of a colleague (Alan) whom Eric suspects is the real father of the child about to be born—one of the three women helping to deliver the baby in the snow-stranded house is Alan's barren wife (Leslie) who is also a doctor—During Monica's arduous unsedated labor Dr. Leslie hears Monica scream out the name of the baby's real father,

Alan, Alan, I'm giving you the son you always wanted
—both doctors, cuckold and adulterer, arrive to the
young mother's bedside, the baby is safe but Monica's
life will remain in danger for some time, stay tuned for
the station break—

—Buy the *Star* for Jeane Dixon's special column!
Jeane Dixon predicts again! Marriage for Princess Caro-
line of Monaco, trouble ahead for the pope, Teddy and
Joan on the splits . . .

"I believe you might be heading towards a nervous
disorder," John says softly one morning. John tries to
distract Edmund by giving him a refresher course in the
Russian language. He brings his tape recorder and a set
of cassettes he'd made twenty years ago with the help of
a voluptuous specialist in Lermontov. "This is Professor
John Mirsky and this is my friend, Tamara. Good
morning comrades! *Zdrastvouitie tovarishtchi!* Repeat
with us . . ."

Whenever Edmund sees Sophie's face on the screen
she infuses him with a small yearning for the outdoors,
he gets out of his pajamas, dusts his possessions, goes
out to buy some food. He savors every second of his
excursions because the effort of deciding to go out is very
great, he stands a long while at each traffic light, he looks
carefully from side to side like a child just taught to cross
the street alone.

On warm evenings other exiles to California drink
wine on their verandas. The bay lights up in the distance
like a surplice of velvet studded with a thousand little
stones. He likes best those days when Sophie has an
extensive interview with a personality deemed controversial. What cool, what aplomb, his Sophie is indomitable,
she can handle anyone! He finally catches the interview
with Jeremy Thayer she'd aired the previous fall.

"Good Day America, this is Sophie Ross at MBC
greeting you on Wednesday April second; we have

a very special guest with us this morning who's come to celebrate his sixtieth birthday with us, Dr. Jeremy Thayer. . . . Good morning, Dr. Thayer! Dr. Thayer, you've had a long varied career which began with a distinguished teaching position in the University of Michigan's biology department, you went on to be the guru of the turn-on, drop-out generation after your pioneering research with psilocybin, commonly known as psi. . . . As you look back on your long career, Dr. Thayer, how do you think you affected the generation that's just coming of age today?"

"Sophie, I probably encouraged, abetted, stimulated, prompted, aided, incited, inspired, persuaded more people to grow than any other human being in history."

"It's said that you yourself have taken some six hundred psi trips since you began to research the drug, is that correct, Dr. Thayer?"

"That's right, Sophie, I think I'm one of the smartest people in the country today. . . . I'm writing three or four books a year, I'm challenging the Judeo-Christian ethic, I'm helping people all around the world to get rid of their guilt. . . ."

"Now, Dr. Thayer, I want to show you a photograph. Here's a photograph of a handsome twenty-two-year-old college student, Nick Nordlinger, who jumped off a windowsill to his death after experiencing the drug which you were preaching to America . . . Now behave yourself, Dr. Thayer, you're going to stay right in this studio, you're not going to get up and walk out, behave yourself, you're sixty years old today, Dr. Thayer. . . . Do we hear a phone ringing . . . yes, we hear a phone ringing, it's the phone call we were waiting for from Phil Nordlinger. Phil Nordlinger, what part did psilocybin have in your son's death? Dr. Thayer, please . . ."

"That's ghoulish, I won't let that killer Nordlinger answer such a ghoulish question. . . . Nordlinger made fun of millions of kids, he even got to the White House and cooperated with the death machine which hundreds of thousands of young Americans protested with the help of my drug. . . ."

"That aging hippie . . ."

"You got to the White House, didn't you, Mr. Nordlinger, it's Phil Nordlinger himself who killed his son. . . ."

"Gentlemen, we must pause now for a station break. . . ."

—*Too Young to Die*—Biographies of thirty-two entertainment superstars who died in the prime of life . . . George Gershwin, Rudolph Valentino, Carole Lombard, Cass Elliot, Mike Todd, Hank Williams, Buddy Holly and others . . . walk with them from their humble beginnings to their tragic ends, enjoy reading about their ups, their downs, their traumas . . . call toll free for this luxury volume at half price—

"Tell us this, Phil Nordlinger, did you feel responsible for your son Nicholas jumping out of the window?"

"The first thing I say to parents who've lost their children, Sophie, is stop whipping yourself, get rid of your guilt . . ."

"It's Phil Nordlinger himself who killed his son, you got to the White House, didn't you, Phil, I've had enough of this. . . ."

"Please stay seated, Dr. Thayer! You're sixty years old today, Jeremy Thayer! Yes of course, do as you wish, Dr. Thayer, good-bye, Dr. Thayer

. . . to round up the show . . . oh I hear the tears in your voice, Phil Nordlinger . . . there were no health centers, no early-detection centers yet, were there? . . . I hear the tears in your voice, are we ever going to beat the drug problem, Phil?"

"People want to be happy, Sophie, so they'll keep on taking drugs, even aspirin can be a dangerous drug, Sophie. . . ."

"Phil, thanks a lot for being on the show, you're a real pro, Phil, thanks a lot . . . that's all for today, ladies and gentlemen . . . what would *you* do if your kid were smart and well-behaved and belonged to the Ku Klux Klan and couldn't graduate? Tune in tomorrow for Sophie Ross at MBC. . . ."

—Oh Delite/Dynamite/Diet Rite/

"Monica, we're not going to lose you . . ." "Please, Alan, if it looks like I'm not going to make it you tell me, okay? . . ." "You're the center of my existence, Monica, if you don't want to live for my sake then try to live for the sake of our son. . . ."

—We created Enfin, elegant, sensual, so French, the fragrance of the year—

"Alan, your wife told me that you talked things out, did you tell her that you love me?" "Yes I did, Monica, it was rough. . . ." "I was afraid it was all over between us. . . ." "How could it be . . . are you going to cop out on us or are you going to hang in?" "I love you, Alan, it's wonderful to say that. . . ." "I love you too, Monica. . . ."

Edmund saw Toby and his wife go by his window again every few weeks, she was coming to the end of term, swollen-bellied in the splendor of the April sunshine.

He saw other men and women wheeling children and

groceries who were writing theses on the dynamics of Borromini's ceilings, on the development of early Slavic polyphony.

He wanted to paint again.

It was a day in April when he hadn't been able to reach Sophie for three weeks; she hadn't answered his messages so it was evident that she was out of the country. On the jacaranda tree outside his window a cuckoo was counting the hours of his life; he asked several questions about himself which he couldn't answer alone. He didn't want to alarm Sophie and Claire. He wanted in fact to disalarm them. He wished to sound utterly composed, quite healed, almost formal. He took out some pen and paper and this is what he wrote.

Berkeley, California
April 14th, 1975

Sophie, dearest nomad,

I'm aware of the variety of places you might be in as I pen this missive. Woody Allen's arms, Giscard d'Estaing's dining room, documenting the reforestation of Wall Street from the top floor of the World Trade Center—You may wonder why I'm suddenly writing after weeks of trying to track you down by phone at every Hilton I could think of between Caracas and Amman—It's in hopes of seducing you with the following proposal—Why don't you, Pebble and I take a trip abroad sometime soon to celebrate three decades of that lifesaving course referred to as our deep and lasting friendship?

After all, Sofka, here we are turning forty-five, a threat to be confronted head-on; there's no period that requires more *choice*; I'm beginning to think there's nothing much more to genius than an enormous talent for *choosing*. . . .

To hell with restraint, with theory, he decided in midletter.

> What I wish to recreate between us, Sofka, is that ethereal summit of candor which only friendship can offer and which is more drastically needed than ever in mid-age, that desperate time when we must cease to be cannibals of our own hearts, must take the risk of total truth-telling in order to make the last third or fourth of our existence bearable, must recenter our lives upon the only human bond in which the tyrannical cycle of self-deceit is broken . . . at our age there's little else to live for, I'm asking for the brutality of mirrors and the fearlessness of angels at this proposed meeting; oh, I'm asking for a lot and I refuse to take any less than a radical stripping of each to each . . . think about it.
> Forever, Edm.

Sophie's secretary phoned to say that Ms. Ross had just returned from Bucharest with a severe bronchitis and was writing back to Dr. Richter that very day.

> New York City
> April 21st
> Darling, funny that in focusing on the problems of our shared age you center on the issue of truth whereas I've been zeroing in on the problem of facing death, of saying okay you bastard I'm grateful for every scrap of time you throw me but it's time I confront you head-on, dare to stare straight down your jaw, let's not fool ourselves Eddem the fear is central to me; since Amos's own death I've been unable to fight my way into any of the courage I need to survive without totally drugging myself with work; I haven't taken a day off in

four years and I'm terrified of what would happen if
I do, so I need to give a little thought to the prospect
of your truth-in (what a flip-flop you've made on
that one by the way).

Love always   Soph

The letter alarmed Edmund, but was followed two
days later by another one:

E.R., I've decided it's a great idea, I'm lonely as
hell and need some radical doses of sister/
brotherhood! Do you realize it'll be the first time in
a quarter of a century the three of us will be together
for more than a day? I'm already dreaming of all the
places we could meet in: Kenya (to catch the
wildlife there before it totally disappears), southern
Morocco (stupendous architecture, greatest hash
around) or what about Scandinavia, Iran? Listen,
I'm game for anywhere as long as we can be
together!

Miss you miss you   Soph

Boston
April 28th

Dear heart,
    How superb that we've agreed to do it. However
Sophie angel there are several countries on your list
that I've grave misgivings about; I know you
journalists are supposed to be objective but Iran has
one of the most repressive regimes in existence, as
for Kenya I wouldn't think of touching it until they
ban all shooting of wildlife . . . let's think some
more.

Loving you always   Peb

Berkeley
May 1st

Sofka/A brief P.S. to add that Peb also vetoes Morocco for obvious political reasons, has been on Gelusil all weekend just thinking about it. As for myself I boycott Scandinavia; nothing to look at except the boobs of all those odiously liberated blondes and at my age I'd rather get my hard-ons from Tintoretto. So let's give it more study, my sweet.

Je t'embrasse   E.

Roma
May 10th

Shit man between Peb's pacifist ecology and your macho aesthetics are we ever going to decide on a place here we are in an age of limitless jet travel and we can't find one city to meet in is this supposed to be a parable on modern freedom or something? Just a jet-lagged gripe between assignments.

S.

Berkeley
May 12th

Chère Bedouine,
How would you feel about the Soviet Union? Peb may veto that too damn it on the other hand she might decide she can do some good there, let me know—

E.

New York City
May 16th

Dearest both/

The Soviet Union really puts me off you can only go there with Intourist and that's totally run by KGB goons who OD you on propaganda and spy on every step you take. . . .

S.

Boston
May 18th

Dear heart—I think Eddem's plan for the Soviet Union is magnificent—Nevsky Prospect, the Hermitage, Tolstoi's childhood home! And if we hurry we could get there in time for the white nights.

Peb

New York City
May 22nd

Peb, Edmo/Just back from Tijuana and want to say that the USSR suddenly strikes me as perfect; weather is reported very variable there in June so pack plenty of sweaters and don't forget solid folding stools for the museums.

Love you love you can't wait
S.

xxii

Sophie stood on a parapet above the Moscow River, her
hair flaming like a monstrance in the light of a streetlamp. She raised a leg in arabesque, stretched a hand
over the water. Edmund ran towards her on the embankment, not daring to call her in fear of startling her into a
fall. The colonnaded palaces of Tolstoi's time flowed
past him in a ribbon of lemon light, he saw her turn on
one leg very slowly, as if practicing her childhood
dances, extend another arm towards the livid river. He
reached the parapet and crouched a few yards from her
feet. The muddy wash of the Moskva lay twenty feet
below them, he looked up and saw her pale cheeks,
closed eyes, the dazed face on top of the wavering body.
The current was extremely swift. He feared startling her
and didn't know whether to leap up and seize her by the
waist. He crouched there for a moment, wishing he could
die for her. Her hair flared again in the light of a car that
cruised down the embankment. Edmund shouted for
help, waving at the car; he saw the beginning of her fall,
she fell towards the water sideways, with considerable
indecision, as if she'd continued trying to grip the
parapet but had lost her balance after a brusque movement. Then he heard a low thud upon the water,
darkness. He climbed up to dive in after her, strangers'

arms held him back, shouting at him in his mother's tongue. A few minutes later there were sirens, more cars.

After Sophie lay safe in a hospital bed he sat by her side in a room the hue of dusty sun-parched mint leaves. A smell of archaic herbal medications recalled moments when Mara had bent over his own childhood illnesses —valerian, belladonna. Many photographs hung on the walls on either side of the narrow windows; he held her limp hand and stared at the pictures. Ice-grizzled skiers saluted the Soviet flag in some northern outpost, smiling Tatar women in mountain landscape chiseled at frames of cloisonné metal, Buddhist temples rose by the side of Lake Baikal. Claire was away that day visiting Baklanov's mother. Edmund had told the Soviet police that Sophie was an expert swimmer but had not realized the dangerous swiftness of the river's flow. Every hour impassive women doctors came into the room to check Sophie's pulse. Edmund waited for the stirring of her hand in his, stared at the pictures of the brutally vast land. Volcanoes in Irkutsk, a soccer game at the Minsk tractor plant, poetry-loving physicists hold a reading of Mayakovski in Siberia, "The poet's word is your resurrection, your immortality, citizen bureaucrat." Sophie's face had been scrubbed of makeup and she had a white cotton bonnet on her head, resembling the child who'd plunged into Nantucket waters beside him. Towards noon her arm began to twitch, her eyelids flickered. Edmund rose to sit at the head of her bed, stroked her forehead.

"Why why why?" he whispered. "You and your sacrifices, Sofka. . . ."

"Do I look old?"

"Don't talk yet . . . when will you start living for yourself, Soph, when will you cease having enough goodness and craziness for all three of us?"

"I can *so* talk . . ." He leaned his head close to hers, listening for the slurred, sedated words.

"In fifteen years we'll all be sixty, Eddem." Her head nodded in sleep every few minutes but there was an indomitable will to speak.

"This isn't the way I want an end, Eddem, I don't want one of these solitary northern ends, I want a Mediterranean thing, I want . . ."

He paced the room when she dozed off, returned to stroke her head as she found words more clearly.

". . . I once heard Amos describe his grandmother's death, she lay in bed with dozens of offspring and relatives about her and in the last hours each of them held on to some part of her body, all those warm hands clutching you, we three have had lonely lives."

"And where would we be without each other, Sofka? Sofka, will you please explain why?" She waved her hand impatiently.

"There was always in you and me a terrible slowness, Edmund; we're the kind who resist understanding, Claire seized her knowledge early and used it as a tool to control everything and everyone about her. . . ."

Edmund rose and stood by the window, trying not to listen to her too closely. For the past three weeks he'd been able to shed both solitude and restraint; bombarded by the presence of his two women he'd felt the rational fabric of two decades dissolve, the sum of his life lay about him every day in a rich jumble of pieces whose growing multitude alarmed him; it was like staring at several trunkfuls of archaeological shards being dumped into a pool of muddy water at his feet. This is precisely the information I came here for he thought upon waking every morning but I don't dare dive for it yet. . . . The city lay before him with cartographic clarity. In this bastion of atheism there isn't a place from which you can't see a church Claire had said. Nursery-hued, often flaking, mostly closed, churches heaving through desolate cement like islets of candied Orient, like flowers thrusting through carpets of decaying leaves. The hospital looked down upon the oldest settlement in Moscow, that Arbat whose serpentine streets still bore the Oriental stamp of its Tatar builders. The great fire of 1812 had spared a few islets of European grace; colonnaded palaces on which Tolstoi had modeled the Rostovs' mansion flared like single daffodils in the cement iceberg of the modern city. . . . "Prepare yourself for a nation that seems to have been singled out for suffering," John Mirsky had bellowed out as he saw him off on his trip, "for a people that looks on its suffering as its vessel of redemption. . . ."

"Just think!"

Sophie woke from a brief sleep, coughed lightly as she spoke.

"Eddem, just think how little Peb ever *desired*, and yet everyone every detail of everything was completely taken over by this mist-wreathed nun of ours, while you and I were always desiring but never having. . . ."

Almost drowned twelve hours ago, she lay there dumping more shards into his well.

"I'll tell you what I want said at my funeral if someday I really pull it off right, Eddem, I want it said she embodied something of humanity's search for total freedom, her honesty was exquisite."

He sat on her bed, kissed her forehead.

"But you and I may have confused freedom with license, Soph; I'm finally seeing that license has to do with the liberty to pursue goals and aims, whereas freedom . . ."

"Oh, do tell!"

". . . is something else. I don't know yet."

"Well, let me know when we're seventy, okay? All I know, Eddem, is that it's hard when people who've been fighting beside you for a long time splinter off and you must find someone else to fight on with; that's hard at our age, when there may be so little time left. . . ."

She dozed off again. Edmund continued staring at the drab terror of Moscow. His numbness of the early morning was disappearing. He felt ineptness rather than anger or guilt. Throughout the trip the women had been subtle and variable, instruments so finely tuned that trying to fathom them he'd felt like a thick-fingered plumber tinkering with one of the capricious delicate fountains of the Hermitage. The best metaphors he'd found for the mysterious chemistry of great friendships had to do with processes of distillation, information. I go to my friend steeped in the turbid dirty water of my self-ignorance and he/she will give me back to myself crystal-clear as spring; I've dived into the muddy depths of my passions without success and my friend will by some alchemy refine it, guide me towards the shards; without a friend I remain morbid, undecipherable, a garbage heap unto myself. For three decades Sophie and he had excelled at brutally distilling each other but Claire had always abstained from criticizing Sophie, had protected her like a lioness from his attacks; her candor of the past few days may have been too sudden . . . the previous evening after returning from their visit to Baklanov's friends the three of them had talked late into the night. Claire kept broaching the idea of their eventually living together; this is our last chance to kidnap you from your hideous life, Soph, to brainwash you of that idiotic industry which is working you to death, we need you to set our lives in order. Sophie had pretended to be amused, oh you alcoholics of purity you're mad if you think I'm going to hang out in some frugal little community of salvation; when will you realize that I'm not really one of you, that I want every gaudy little American bauble ever dangled before me, penthouses and awards from the Newswomen's Club of America and lunch at the Four Seasons, the whole bag, what do you think the Ross education was about? Leave me be with the only illusions I have left she'd cried out the night before in the bar of the hotel.

She woke again, her voice returned to normal.

"You don't even need me as a critic anymore."

"What on earth do you mean, silly girl?"

"Nietzsche's phrase about the ideal friend being the beautiful enemy, the most vigilant critic . . . you're both so well now that you don't even need me as that!"

At dusk a doctor said that Edmund could take Sophie back to the hotel the following morning.

"You and I have been followers, Eddem; we've always been determined by the measure of someone else and she never was."

But in the past few days Edmund had felt that some nefarious imbalance of three decades had been broken, that he was standing splunk at center, in immense control. So he rebutted:

"I've ceased to follow anyone, Soph, and you can cease too."

He may have spoken too sharply. Her voice rose with an anxiety which he didn't want to hear.

"The kind of thing I've just been through today comes after a crisis and not during, Eddem, when we've ceased fighting not during the fight, when there's nothing more to be done. . . . I had to live with the two of you for this long fortnight for the first time since we were twenty to fully know . . ."

"For Christ's sake, you could have kept me so many times, Soph, how many times! That winter we met in Detroit . . ."

"Shut up, Edmund, I want you to be happy with her! Be happy with her, can't you give me what I ask of you for once?"

"You've lived with your body, Sophie, and this is a tale of passion, isn't it . . . which has little to do with the flesh."

"For once!" she shouted. "For once give me what I want!"

He would always remember the triumphant timbre of that voice, the hair tangled with sweat lying like a pool of brandy on the hospital pillow. Then she cried a great deal. She was brought some broth, a pill. He would remain by her bed until morning.

"It worked in part," she said as she fell asleep for the night. "It may have worked a little bit, your big Slavic truth-in."

On the day before flying home Edmund, Claire and Sophie took a cab to a small monastery they wished to visit in the outskirts of Moscow. They sat on the grass on a June Sunday in the park attending the main church. Sophie was still a little weak, she kept her head on Claire's lap, never letting her eyes off her face. The alleys were filled with women who dozed in the morning sun as they waited for service to begin, they lay on benches with paper bags that held their day's nourishment, radishes, hunks of bread.

"Little's been known about Volodya Baklanov for six months, save that he's increasingly weakened by his fasts," Claire began; "his mother has been living like one of those hunted creatures of the thirties, kept alive by a few friends who're staking their own freedom to take care of her. No phone, threats to intensify reprisals against her son if she continues sending messages to the West . . . to lessen the risk of being observed she'd decided not to transmit any more messages but somehow she's come to trust me. So yesterday when I rang her doorbell there was no problem, her friends had received the message that I was coming. . . ."

Claire closed her eyes for a second and as she opened them again Edmund saw them as weary and skeptical as those of the aged women dozing on the benches. The church they sat by was the most beautiful he'd seen in the past weeks, a paschal whirl of titanium white surmounted by domes of gold-speckled cerulean. On a small colonnaded porch of the monastery a young monk in a brown robe stood very erect, hair tied back in a long braid, staring at the fields ahead.

"Immediately to the left of the door was a dark room that looked like . . . like a kind of shrine. Several people seemed to be sitting around someone, I couldn't see well at first; I went into the room and Madame Baklanova lay there propped up on pillows surrounded by little offerings her friends had brought, bits of Western medicines and magazines, candy, old clothing. Her face is as sallow as that of some relic yet her eyes are very blue, very kind and lustrous and not even angry; she has a gastric ailment which requires very special medication and she obviously doesn't dare go to any hospital for it . . . she'd received a message from her son just two weeks ago and the news is as bad as we'd expected; he's fasting again and this time seems determined to fast until death or freedom . . . she didn't complain, she only stated, stated the facts. And then she gave me her radiant smile and we talked about the icon over her head, she said that her kind of Christianity isn't based on atonement or sacrifice because they've already taken place, when she prays she already tries to find the joyful communion with God she'll have after death, she compares it to the trusting joyful games children play with their fathers. . . . She also said this, we mustn't let our suffering *ghettoize* us, she used that word, we must always remember those who suffer even more than we do. . . ."

"But it's impossible to leave them this way," Sophie whispered. "What's to be done?"

She still lay on the grass, her head on Claire's lap. Claire gave a small laugh, almost cynical.

"What's to be done? We can only work gram by gram, one drop of saving at a time. All the information on

Baklanov's condition is right on me; I took notes and threw them away after coding them; I've also a petition to the West signed by several Russian scientists who're staking their freedom again asking for Baklanov's release. . . ."

The benches had emptied. A drone of voices was flowing from the church. Claire, Edmund and Sophie walked towards it. They entered a dark space seething with women moving about and prostrating themselves before many icons, a file of bearded priests in pink taffeta robes wound slowly around the iconostasis, gold and precious stones flamed from their domed hats and massive crosses, from the cupola above a Christ gazed down impassively, right hand raised in warning or in judgment. On a table in back of the church worshipers had heaped offerings to the monastery, farm produce, bunches of apples and hunks of bread; there was no focus and no center to the celebration, only a seething crowd of women in a state of anarchic fervor who bowed and sank to the floor and moved about and constantly crossed themselves, who muttered snatches of prayers or sang a phrase of litany before stopping to kiss the icon of some saint and move across the church to another one; in midroom the central image of the Virgin was gravely wiped by an attendant between the salutations of its visitors; Claire leaned against a wall, supporting Sophie's head on her shoulder, eyes fixed on the image of Christ above her head. In the scant dusk of candles the pink-robed priests continued to wave censers about the blazing screen; this fragrant heavy cloud of muttering and chanting and prostrated flesh, of poverty and abundance, of a spirituality as dense and anarchic as the lichen of the ocean floor, recalled to Edmund the Sundays of his childhood, Mara kneeling on a stone floor in Manhattan praying silently for beloved dead whom she refused to share; he walked to midchurch towards the icon of the Virgin, approached the bent melancholy face leaned towards her chiseled tranquil eyes, brows furrowed by hieratic lines of suffering, chaste mouth turned downwards in hopeful sorrow, gold leaf blazed about her columnar neck like God's holy fire; he put his lips to hers and in a gesture as alien and familiar as the genuflections of his childhood he crossed himself three times, in the Slavonic manner. Sophie's eyes remained closed, Claire watched him with interest. He'd never forget how easy it was, for a moment, to believe.

"Your intelligent traveler books his trips to the Iron Curtain well ahead of time," Arthur Zabar said as Intourist Tour No. 137 Destination Tbilisi-Kiev-Leningrad-Moscow boarded a bus for its farewell banquet. "He'll be careful to plan much further ahead than for any capitalist country."

"Arthur studies the travel pages of the *Sunday Times* the way others read the financial or theater section," Ethel Zabar explained.

"We're already booked for Czechoslovakia this fall and next spring we're scheduled for Hungary," Mr. Zabar added.

"New York is going to seem so dull after this trip," Mrs. Weicker remarked to Mrs. Jones, "don't you get bored in America?"

"Brazil is next on our schedule unless some smart lefties get the upper hand," Mrs. Jones said. "There are several Rolls-Royce dealers in that handsome country; we'll get a dandy reception but I doubt if you can beat the Soviets for sheer *joie de vivre*."

"These Iron Curtain countries seem so hospitable and warm," Mr. Jones said, "and we just loved the food."

The Rolls-Royce dealers were thrilled with their purchases. Mr. Jones alone had bought three stuffed panda bears for his grandchildren, four fur hats, several Ukrainian flowered shawls, many painted wooden dolls and a twelve-piece set of imitation Popov china, three of which he'd broken at the Dollar Store after consuming his luncheon vodka.

"Pay attention, please, to beauty of sunset on ancient walls of our Arbat," Evgeny spoke into his little microphone, "built by Tatar hordes who occupied Moscow in twelfth century."

As they drove by the Bolshoi Theatre, Sophie was photographing a flock of ravens settling on the head of the statue of Karl Marx. Edmund was murmuring to Claire the winged, aerial names of the Kremlin churches: Annunciation, Assumption, Archangel.

"We have thirty-two other theaters in Moscow with permanent companies and large repertoires," Evgeny said, "thirteen concert halls, two circuses and one hundred and nineteen cinemas. Our Soviet people are passionates of art."

"It is raining!" Irina exclaimed. "Rain is a very good sign, it is sign that city is sad to see you leave and that you will all come back soon again."

" 'Good night, Irene, Good night, Irene,' " the Americans sang, " 'we'll see you in our dreeeeeeams.' "

"Let's buy the girls electric samovars at the Dollar Store right at the airport," one of the Rolls-Royce dealers said to Mr. Jones. "Hey, great idea," Mr. Jones agreed.

"I hope you're feeling better, Miss Ross!" Mrs. Zabar said. "We certainly look forward to your special on the Soviet Union on *Good Day America!*"

"Have you ever seen little children so well taken care of, beautifully dressed and nicely mannered?" Mrs. Weicker exclaimed. "Look at those little people over there in the smart blue suits and red ties."

"They are members of our Young Communist League Mrs. Weicker, and we have even younger term of honor we call our babies Oktiabristi at the age of two or three a soon as they can recognize portrait of Lenin."

"How too dear!"

"Such an effusive, warmhearted people," Mr. Weicker remarked.

"Never known such dolers out of claptrap as these Soviet guides," Mr. Zabar said as they stepped off the bus.

"Both repellent and curiously moving, like much in this country," Claire commented.

A floor show accompanied the abundant farewell banquet held at a restaurant specializing in Central Asian cuisine. Muscular sword-dancers in Cossack costumes were particularly applauded, a mournful redhead in sequined gauze sang "Volga, Volga, Beloved Mother," a Siberian rock band played "When the Saints Go Marching In" on electric guitars. Evgeny was immensely enjoying his last talk with Intourist Tour No. 137. "All through our long history Russian people have enjoyed arguing about what is love, what is death, what is God." "I have admiration for your great Dreiser but I also confess passion for John Updike."

After much vodka the Americans fell upon the ample, brutàl Soviet fare of pickles and potatoes, lard and cucumbers, grilled mutton and smoked fish. There were many toasts.

"To our struggle for the future of Democracy!" Arthur Zabar exclaimed.

"To Muscovy, this remarkable handiwork of nature . . ."

"To our shared goal of mutual trust . . ."

"It is with a joy tinged with sadness that we look for the last time in the eyes of our American friends . . ."

"To our women!" Edmund drank.

"To our artists and poets," Evgeny shouted towards Edmund, "magicians of our tribes!"

After dinner Edmund, Sophie and Claire receive permission to walk home alone through Red Square. Sophie walks in the center, her friends' arms around her waist. All seems ice and flower in Moscow's durable lacquer night. They watch for the last time the spectacle at the heart of Soviet power: tiered shrine of frozen rose denying the finality of death. Marzipan-cheeked boy soldiers guarding the temple's entrance. Single red star of the Spassky Tower blazing over all like a threat of eternity.

"*Les passagers d'Air France en provenance de Berlin sont priés de se rendre au guichet des controles . . .*" "*Passagieri Alitalia en partenze para New Delhi sono pregati embarcare immediatamente . . .*" "Is this the flight to Istanbul?" "No this is Air Congo 673 to Beirut. . . ."

The Moscow airport was mayhem. They'd decided to stop in Paris on the way home to see the Matisse show. Claire and Edmund had tried to talk Sophie into taking an extra week's vacation, flying home with them and going on to Nantucket. Edmund had to find himself a solid warm house there for the winter. That's where he'd determined to spend the following year, they needed Sophie's advice, her sense of life's comforts. But Sophie was adamant about going right back to work, she'd fly to Paris with them for a day and go on to Monte Carlo where she must do a special on the film festival.

On the bus that drove them to the airport Edmund had started writing postcards to Berkeley which he planned to mail from Paris. For his friend John he'd chosen photographs of the poets' statues which dot the squares of Moscow: Curly-headed Pushkin, hand inside vest, brooding against a backdrop of new lilacs; Mayakovski striding with clenched fists, trousers waving in sculpted wind.

"In the monolithic despair of certain Russian lives there's not even room for love," he wrote, "only for a certain kind of fierce, passionately self-sacrificial friendship; there's no way they could conceive of the *self* here the way we do, for with enough communal suffering th self breaks down, becomes an untenable entity of speech, a myth . . . one leaves Moscow saying I want to wake up from the nightmare of their history. And yet I'll miss this country as much as I dread it because of the massive spirituality which continues to thrive in its people like random flowers thrusting through cement; they haven't begun to be tainted, for instance, by that tragic disease of the West in which sexuality has replaced man's fate. . . . Was it Dostoevski who said that Russia exists only for the purpose of teaching the world a lesson?"

". . . Claire, by the way, may have played a modest role in the eventual release of Baklanov . . . ah yes that may be my Claire's vocation, to greet the resurrected. . . ."

"From July on, dear John, you can reach me care of General Delivery, Nantucket, Mass. Things are falling into place. You're welcome to share my solitude up island anytime you want. . . ."

Just before customs they walked one last time through the desolation, the stained and brutal bleakness of Soviet public rooms, past dour distrustful guards and surly-eyed women hovering over arrays of gaudy wooden dolls.

"We'll see you very soon again, Gedmund Petrovich! When will you return to us, Clara Pavlovna?"

"Ah, you lie so sweetly I could kiss you, Genia! It may be years before we're allowed the luxury of a reunion."

They hugged in parting at the airport. The Russian put into his embrace a heat which he'd refused to put into words.

"To your wonderful eyes, Sofia Larionovna . . . to your splendid gaze, Clara Pavlovna!"

"We'll see you in a thaw or two, Evgeny Sergeievch."

* * *

There was a delectable sleekness, efficiency, comfort, about the Air France craft which their bodies had not experienced for the past several weeks. Perfume flowed in fragrant washrooms. The seats were cloudlike. *"Ce soir nous avons les papillottes de veau Vacheron, une escalope bien fine avec une pointe de moutarde et d'echalotte . . ."*

All was succulent, fresh, sumptuously spruced and perfectly functioning, Edmund commented, and seemed a wasteland of the spirit.

Sophie went to the back of the plane to interview the Air France steward about his impressions of the Soviet Union. Claire took Edmund's hand. "I need you," she said. "We're about to have the best years of our lives."

He had not time to express his startlement at her gesture. For as their engines began to whir there was great commotion on the runway a few hundred yards away from their Air France craft. A cageful of snakes about to be boarded onto an Aeroflot plane (Sophie surmised they were destined for some zoo in a distant northern province) tumbled out of the truck from which it was being loaded. The cage's latch broke upon falling, several dozen beasts writhed swiftly unto the ground, the running brook of terror spread with extraordinary speed around the Soviet plane. Carfuls of Soviet soldiers rushed out of the hangars, sirens blowing; they attempted to stake in the animals with makeshift fences but the cloaked power of the dust evaded the barriers, continued to slither in all directions of the runway. There was much shouting, much commotion. The Air France craft lifted up on angel wings before any of its passengers could learn how the problem was solved. Edmund looked out at forever, across the land of his mother's birth.

xxiii

The island air is both dark and brilliant. The lengthening
shadows of autumn haunt him. In late afternoon Edmund
sits in the November sun reading Vasari, Kierkegaard.
During weeks when he or Claire have been ill they don't
leave each other's side. Wrapped in blankets on their
terrace they sniff at the last essence of afternoon light,
argue gently about the call of birds. Listen to the
redwing. Not at all it's an oriole. I don't need to even
look at it love, it's a male redwing. Claire has taken up
the piano again, goes to Quaker Meeting. They often
wake early and walk in certain moors to watch geese rise
on heavy wings, assembling into the tumultuous v of a
flight south. We're still young she'd said one day, this is
a spring, in some sort of way we've always wanted each
other. It must have been July for the wild roses were in
full bloom on the lion-hued dunes, the beach on which he
used to draw her when she was eighteen was steeped in
the slow fermentation of the rain. He'd stared with love
immeasurable at the slender high-waisted body that had
always reminded him of some archaic clay idol, she'd
bent down to glean a seashell and he'd admired the high
young breasts which wrinkled now about the nipples
with the savageness of time, the fragile skin of underarms grown even paler with their age. They'd decided to
repurchase Claire's old family house from its present

owners, at first it seemed as simple as that. Claire is
thoroughly attentive to Edmund, she is often tired. She
takes much care of her kitchen, she tends the herb corner
of the garden she once detested, she works hard at
making Edmund's life as pretty and safe as possible. At
times her fierceness seems broken. At times he worries
that she's lost that part of her he used to love the most.
My exile may finally be over he often says. Every few
weeks in July he walks to the ferry landing to watch the
ship disgorge its burden of summer happiness, its plenitude of cribs, collies, rackets, playpens, golf bags,
picnic hampers. The tribes seem smaller, the one-child
family predominates, the father is often absent or else he
is alone, coping with the hurried fastidiousness of the
divorced. There are fewer families and more solitude,
there are many single men, single women, or else men
with men, women with women. Edmund watches it all
like a native now, with a trace of resentment; they're
invading my paradise. He walks back from the ferry with
his groceries through files of coquettish clapboard houses
celebrating the chaste peace of our country's youth, amid
the din of many voices celebrating summer. He looks
forward to October when the days grow brief and the
shadows long, when the haven of his adolescence seems
his alone as it sinks into the solitude of its winter. When
they first moved back to the island Claire and Edmund
shucked scallops in winter to help earn the down pay-
ment on Sealark; they stood deep-booted in freezing
warehouses plunging their hands in buckets of hot water
as they struggled with the tough grimy mollusks' shells.
We survive with little news and no gossip Edmund writes
John, we're admirably estranged from reification hy-
potheses, polemical desiderata, metalanguage and alien-
ating hierarchies of values. I'm living in my first
permanent embrace with a woman and a soil. With much
emotion and painful slowness I paint lemons, peaches
roses from my garden, luminous tankards of water

Muse equals Great Mother equals infinite faith and patience. I'm like a paraplegic relearning to use his limbs, like a rider mounting a fierce Arabian left wild in pasture for many years. I'm not saying this seclusion is the best for me, it may be deathly, I am a plodding patient man, slow to come to understanding. We miss our dear Sophie, to whom nature is a one-night stand, and who keeps threatening that we'll soon feel nostalgia for nervousness. . . .

In the first years Edmund is often melancholy. He works in a shed behind Plinker's old vegetable garden, refusing to show his paintings to anyone but Claire. He is certain of her love but is terrified of his own uncertainty, of the risks he is posing to himself. Am I finally saving myself from the black velvet of universal emptiness, from the night and murk of nonbeing? He lays his grounds with ancient craft so they will survive for centuries, once again slowly heating rabbit's skin glue in double boilers, slowly stirring in chalk to make the gesso with which he primes his canvases. On his more melancholy days Claire brings him lunch in the studio, suggests a stroll in a moor where she's walked many times that month but which always soothes him. What does he really think of as she watches him shuffle up the path under the lowering winter sky, bringing in wood for the evening fire? The continuing threat of failure and nonbeing? The futility of all art in our time? The particular futility of his own? Edmund's somberness is as opaque to Claire as her new docility is mysterious to him. He knows that something precious has left her life and he knows that she'll never admit it. In his youth he'd thought that upon marrying Claire he might finally decipher her with total clarity, read her as closely as the palm of his own hand. But one day during her convent years she'd told him that such knowledge could never exist on earth. She'd quoted Saint Augustine, We too, dear ones, will someday see each other's hearts but later, for now we yet bear the darkness of our flesh. So only when the thugs of eternity come after us, Edmund had said. She'd preferred such words as Later, Afterwards. At times he is resigned; opaqueness, mystery nourish the greatest loves; must be accepted, even hallowed. The more you love the less you understand. The game of reality and appearance done away with, a mystic impulse, my ignorance becomes knowledge, I know best that which I do not know.

All art is a joke anyhow he says as he opens a bottle of wine for supper; it's all an illusion anyway, there's little to work for but the peace of life.

Just look at those poppies.

Nothing like them is there, three years and they've never stopped budding.

Next spring we must try some anemones.

They didn't leave the island more than twice in the first few years.

Plinker's tall body often haunts Edmund by the gate of his vegetable garden, stooped and yellow-faced, rake in hand. The garden is now mine, Edmund's. I've come to claim it for you. I've come back to give your daughter precisely the happiness you wanted for her. I most love this spot of earth in early winter when I can admire the persistence, the tenacity of things, the parsley persevering under its hoar of frost, the obstinate succulence of turnips wrenched from the ground with heavy spades. The world outside seems ridden with trivia and impatience. I admire doggedness, upagainstness, permanence, slowness, any patience as long as mine. As he works his garden Edmund often remembers a decaying Italian villa in which he'd once stared at a row of sculptured torsos overgrown with mosses and lichens, suspended in metamorphosis between animal and vegetal nature, and that's the way he feels on many days, increasingly rooted and blurred into his first and last terrain. Sometimes I'm afraid of rusticating, of becoming totally overgrown by the tenacity of the soil I've chosen. The refuge might be dangerous but I am leading a most beautiful life. I may have chosen life over art again. I have chosen a kind of quality of quality.

Six of one and half a dozen of another.

When Claire walks back from the country store every night at dusk she stares at a stand of pines that looms with particular starkness at the last bend on their dirt road, pines bristling and opaque against the peach of winter dusk. He is the shape and doom of my life. He's the vessel into which I've chosen to pour myself in order . . . to survive? No. In order to simply pour myself. He's like the medium with which through which the artist struggles to find his meaning. He has become my only meaning. He is as inevitable as the fact that these pines will loom over the dormant meadow until the day they're cut down. I am drained of much indignation. As a child I'd felt anger at the great feast days of the Church because I'd thought they'd bring some miraculous transformations of the cosmos which never came, well they never came. No more need to stress my separateness, to strip my rooms of all but the bare essentials. Surplus is our common fate.

She goes to Boston for a week a month to continue her work in human rights.

They believe in the family. Victoria comes up frequently from Harvard, where she plans to take a degree in theology to become a minister of the Episcopal Church. Our pursuit of freedom has become excessive, Victoria says, we've sacrificed communal duty to an excessive preoccupation with individual liberty, classical libertarianism isn't working, we're stuck again, never forget what Mom learned at St. Agatha's, hell is oneself, not others. . . . oh God not again Claire whispers, I couldn't go through it anymore. Edmund teases that Victoria will become the first woman bishop.

Back home Claire often sits in the library compiling documents about the torture of dissidents in Peru, Afghanistan, Iran. Above her desk there hangs a photograph of Baklanov and his mother, both restored to health since finding asylum in the West, standing at the entrance of a German university where Baklanov now teaches. Lying in their bedroom Edmund hears the scribbling of her pen on paper, as patiently persistent as a litany. He continues to find her quieter, more mysterious than ever.

Claire loves to look at Edmund's body as he stands naked to the waist in their garden, a body as finely tuned as it was at twenty-five, helmet of gray-streaked dark blond hair curling about the muscled neck, firm torso of a man who's been relatively frugal with the joys of the body. One night as she knelt beside him tending her rosemary plants she thought she saw the stand of pines advancing towards her, an umbrous army of verdure, resignation, permanence, she knew again the depth and enshacklement of her new happiness.

He seldom talks about art anymore except to say: Complicity in the evils of the age is the artist's greatest sin. The artist must address himself to a clear but distant viewer, an angelic viewer whom he cannot merely seduce or entertain. In this most tempting of decades he's the one who must impose the greatest rigor, the most severity on himself to survive.

There are days when he makes himself a bowl of Cream of Wheat and goes to bed at 6:00 P.M. too depressed to read or talk. And it takes all the force of her love not to be angered by what she calls the artist's vice of melancholy; on such days she refuses to have his anguish affect her, he becomes like a swollen limb of her own body bordering on gangrene, she refuses this infection, she does not lance his pain with questions because she's learned that there are archaeologies of the unsaid we make silent pacts to not disturb. On such days he resents her chosen distance as she sits in the library writing more letters about strangers suffering in distant places. From her desk at the window she occasionally stares out at the tragic stage set of her island's innocence, at a frozen nostalgia yelling heavenwards through sparse white spires of New England churches, at the primordial ocean water in which her brother drowned plying the rudder of a sailboat in her tribe's deathly urge to compete, she stares at this town she began to detest as a child but which Edmund had insisted on recalling her to, as another husband had before him. This is how they want to get infected by my so-called purity, my pedantry of virtue.

At some point during such evenings Claire manages to talk about the birds she's seen that afternoon or to praise Edmund's last painting, to bring more herbal tea into the lair of his seclusion, to be precisely what he's wanted her to be for now thirty-five years; and through her shrewd bringing of new joy, her carefully choreographed resurrection of his faith, he recovers with remarkable agility. He sits at the breakfast table the next morning smiling again, deep blue eyes the hue of lupines on a sunny day, saying that soon he might be ready to show his paintings to someone else than her.

She is new to the art of helping those she knows and loves, not even rusty but new. Her vocabulary is limited. The laboratory of the twentieth century is closed she repeats after Edmund, the cult of constant innovation has passed. There's little or nothing to invent anymore she writes Sophie, all is permitted now, he can paint any way he wishes and be loved again; soon he'll regain the glory he abandoned in his youth, you'll see!

* * *

After a few years they worry that their island sanctuary is being despoiled. Community theaters, pottery and watercolor and yoga and ballet classes, various other forms of the 1980s' striving for self-improvement proliferate in the vicinity of the old Town Hall. Young men with scraggly beards weep in coffee shops after their consciousness-raising sessions alongside angry girls in frayed jeans and granny glasses. Coteries of art lovers move to the island in alarming numbers and give fawning parties for exurbanite novelists who celebrate the occasion by insulting everyone at hand. Glamorous divorcées from D.C. who've slept with everyone in public office are remodeling lobster shacks on the old wharf in odious hues of primrose yellow. Trust-fund hippies in scalloping gear winter on the island to play fisherman, and say "I'm going to America" when they take the ferry to the mainland. Falseness seems to pursue us everywhere Edmund complains to Sophie during one of her weekend visits. We face a historical quandary she replies; our cities are increasingly difficult, more and more of you purists retire to the vacuum of the countryside, where you claim to enjoy nature and complain that you do not rub enough against other humans to create meaningful art.

Claire and Edmund now pick up TV magazines that come free with purchases of groceries over ten dollars, they study them for the scheduling of all of Sophie's special reports, they read interviews in other publications that describe her solitary but excessively busy life, her "monastic dedication" to her "phenomenal career," her arduous backpacking vacations to the wilds of Ceylon or Nepal, the macrobiotic diets she engages in to ensure the perpetual freshness of her skin. "The alarm rings at 4:15 in Ms. Ross's Sutton Place penthouse but the star newscaster is already awake, hair freshly washed for one of her special reports on the *Good Day America* show, sitting under the dryer with the early-bird copy of *The New York Times*. . . ." In 1980 Sophie realizes one of her many dreams, she becomes the first woman to be anchorperson of a presidential party convention.

—"It's now clear that Senator Kennedy will stay out of sight until the end of President Carter's speech . . . will stay out of sight until the faithful gather for that family picture on the podium which might provide next week's magazine covers. . . . You don't need to be an expert on body language to expect a rather frigid meeting up there; even if they end up raising their arms together it'll be a pretty empty gesture at this point, like the sound of one hand clapping. . . . Let's switch now to NBC correspondent Jim Pettit who's covering the Kennedy headquarters for us at the Waldorf-Astoria. . . ."

—"That's not exactly a small compact fuel-efficient car the senator's getting into, Sophie . . . but there he is getting into it . . . Ted . . . Joan . . . the three children . . . the limousine is pulling out of the Waldorf-Astoria . . . we can hear the sirens that'll accompany the senator through darkened Manhattan towards his rendezvous with destiny at Madison Square Garden. . . . Back to Sophie Ross now at Central Control."

—"Thank you, Jim. . . . While we're waiting for the vice-presidential nominee to begin his speech we'll have a few words with Governor Babbit of Utah, who's kind enough to visit with us at Control Headquarters. . . . Governor Babbit, Jimmy Carter has a long grueling campaign ahead of him this fall, a rough uphill fight, how would you define the principles for which his Democratic party platform stands?"

—"We've always been the party of ideals, Sophie, we're the party that's always looked to the future. . . . Ideals are like stars . . . you reach for them but you can't touch them with your hands . . . you follow their light the way those fearless seafaring men followed the stars that guided them to their destinies on dark desert waters. . . ."

—"Governor Babbit, don't you think a lot of people are going to leave this convention hall feeling it was a smoke-filled room with a lot of rhetorical smoke screening in it? . . ."

—"The party's more united than you think, Sophie . . . it's united against a common enemy, against big money and deceitful propaganda, the American people aren't going to believe the lies that go into that propaganda. . . ."

—"Thank you so much, Governor. . . . We're quickly approaching the acceptance speech of the vice-presidential nominee, Vice President Walter F. Mondale. . . ."

—"We Want Fritz / We Want Fritz / We Want Fritz /"

—"Thank you . . ."

—"We Want Fritz / We Want Fritz/"

—"Thank you thank you . . ."

Every day Sophie keeps in shape by swimming a hundred lengths of the Olympic-sized pool at New York University, where she received an honorary doctorate last fall. She keeps her personal life extremely private. It is possible that she doesn't even have one, that she works as hard as she does in order not to miss having one. Sophie is one of the two or three American women most in demand as commencement speakers in our nation's colleges. She has taken up needlepoint to calm her nerves. Her birthday and Christmas presents to her close friends and to her goddaughter Victoria remain extravagant. She has recently reread all of Balzac and Trollope. She is now able to sleep five or six hours a night at a stretch. She loves to come up to the island on weekends because few people watch the news there; she can relax and take off her babushka and dark glasses. The days she shares with them on the island are among the happiest of the Richters' year. Several million Americans are said to be affected by Sophie's opinions. She often jokes with Claire and Edmund that she has a recurring nightmare in which she dreams of being precisely the opposite of what she is, there are many children depending on her in this dream and she must cook for fourteen every day and is constantly running out of food and everyone is perpetually shouting at her asking her to feed them more, feed them faster. . . .

Edmund Richter's first exhibition of paintings in twenty-five years was held in New York to considerable critical acclaim. It was written that Richter's work embodied our current return to humanistic values in many of the arts, that it was the work of a man who believed in communicating his emotion about the beauty of the created world.

Critics praised "the muted, radiant surfaces of his lyrical still lifes," "the angelic chastity of his humble objects." Once again they compared him to Chardin: "Richter captures the poetry of domestic existence." They expounded on his rigor of form, on his avoidance of the nostalgia prevailing in much of the realism presently returning to Western art.

It was noted and admired that he was extraordinarily slow to produce. "Behind the tranquil splendor of his canvases one detects agonizing and laborious hours, a pugilistic struggle with the medium throughout which the artist must retreat, correct, must stand for hours in an agony of hesitation."

Eager art dealers, plump and spectacled, come to the island to offer Edmund more exhibitions. They sit in the studio by the sound over wine and Greek olives, greedily eyeing the half-dozen paintings he's finished that year.

He explains that he's always believed in an art of equilibrium and celebration and has quite simply waited his turn, that the greatest happiness is the longest in coming.

Interviewers describe him as "a man of tranquil contentments who believes that sanity is the most profound moral option of our time."

It is noted that over his easel there hangs a comment of Chardin's made to Diderot shortly before the painter's death: "*De la douceur, messieurs! Avant tout de la douceur!*"

"So what's next?" Edmund writes John Mirsky. "I'm acquiring a reputation that'll give me ulcers again, a dealer I can't trust, art collectors who want me as the main course on their dinner party menu, reviewers who'll soon shoot me down once more, jealous colleagues who'll wish I'd OD'd on shooting up, punk-rock groupies in Nazi uniforms with paper clips on their eyelids at my vernissages . . . the jackal viewer is ever ready to hound the Muse to death. Next year they'll accuse me of slamming the door on the twentieth century and of not dealing with questions raised by post-Lacanian structuralism . . . oh, I can't get rid of my distrustful nature, Ivan Maximovich, and I've always been dead right."

More dealers come, smiling, eyeing. Hyenas in syrup, Edmund says. Edmund and Claire rent a small weekend cottage up island, no phone, an hour from town. There they take walks in the gorse-covered heaths where he'd long sought her as a child, through gentle violet undulations scattered with bayberry and shadblow, glossed with the gleam of golden aster and sweet arrowroot. This must be the love of oldest age, she thinks, to worry each time he comes in ten minutes late when he's taken a afternoon walk alone; to feel amputated each time he walks a half hour by himself.

The contemporary artist, Edmund tells some magazine, runs the risk of destruction because the world still believes there's a trace of the divine in him. And society has nothing else godly to consume.

"Don't be so old-fashioned, gentlemen critics, do us a favor and dedivinize us, cease torturing us by seeing us as the elect! We're simply makers of documents, more meticulous craftsmen than most."

"I resent it deeply," he tells Claire one morning over breakfast, "when many persons have access to my state of mind."

Sometimes he fears he's been too infected by her purity.

They continue to be happy, as far as one understands the meaning of that word. They save their money to see Victoria through graduate school, enjoy a few trips abroad. If history permits it they will often return to Russia. This is their dream, to return to the country where they resolved some of the difficult alchemy of middle age.

They also talk of leaving the island to live still farther away, to a place still more distant and pristine. They're not sure where to move to. It's hard to decide these days.

Every evening at ten o'clock Sophie's face glows towards them from under the liquid midnight of the stars. "Give me twenty-eight minutes," she says, "and I'll give you the world."

ABOUT THE AUTHOR

Francine du Plessix Gray is the distinguished author of *Lovers and Tyrants*, *Divine Disobedience* and *Hawaii: The Sugar-Coated Fortress*. Her work has appeared in *The New Yorker*, *The New York Times Magazine*, *The New York Review of Books* and other publications.

From Playboy Paperbacks, novels guaranteed to entertain, delight and captivate you

____	16567	REQUIEM FOR A DREAM Hubert Selby	$2.25
____	21061	RITES OF PASSAGE William Golding	$2.95
____	16846	ROUGH STRIFE Lynne Sharon Schwartz	$2.75
____	16982	SATIN AND STARS Joanne Kaye	$2.50
____	16830	STEPPING Nancy Thayer	$2.95
____	21074	TENDER OFFER Alexandra Marshall	$2.95
____	16787	THAT VANDERBILT WOMAN Philip van Rensselaer	$2.75
____	16934	TIME OF DESECRATION Alberto Moravia	$3.50
____	21014	THE TIME OF INDIFFERENCE Alberto Moravia	$3.50
____	21095	TO LOVE AGAIN Joanne Kaye	$2.50
____	21001	TWO ADOLESCENTS Alberto Moravia	$2.95
____	21108	TWO PLUS TWO Alan Cochran	$2.95
____	16945	TWO WOMEN Alberto Moravia	$3.50
____	21073	WAY OF THE DRAGON Jillian Austen	$3.50
____	21100	THE WOMAN OF ROME Alberto Moravia	$3.50
____	21079	WORLD WITHOUT END Francine du Plessix Gray	$3.50

582-7